"Kaye Michelle's novel, Return of the Heroine, taught me how to connect with my spirit guide, and to channel that wisdom into my everyday life. Whether it was the warmth of her tone, her skillful handling of dramatic events, or the sheer passion of her characters' commitment -- or a combination of all -- this book left me forever changed."

Stuart Horwitz, author of Blueprint Your
Bestseller: Organize and Revise any Manuscript
with the Book Architecture Method.

"Perhaps the most moving story I've ever read. Kaye Michelle has made Joan of Arc come to life in more ways than one in this surprising novel--at once both modern and deeply historical. I found Joan's life an inspiration and felt more connected to my own spiritual guides as I read about Joan's. Joan of Arc even showed up in my meditation!"

Lisa Tener, Creator of the Award
Winning Bring Your Book to Life Program,
Book Writing Coach, Author

"Although the story of Joan of Arc is familiar, Kaye Michelle tells it in a way that brings an intuitive understanding and clarity to the spiritual relationship between Joan and her divine guidance, the voice of Archangel Michael. I loved the worlds the author created and was sad to leave when I finished the book. There is such wisdom and inspiration for all of us in these pages."

Pamela McIntyre, PhD, former Chair of the
Theatre Department, Wheaton College, Norton MA.

T0375165

RETURN
OF THE HEROINE

A Novel
By
KAYE MICHELLE

RETURN
OF THE HEROINE

KAYE MICHELLE

BALBOA.
PRESS
A DIVISION OF HAY HOUSE

ISBN: 978-1-4525-6279-7 (sc)
ISBN: 978-1-4525-6280-3 (e)
ISBN: 978-1-4525-6281-0 (hc)
Library of Congress Control Number: 2012921123

Balboa Press books may be ordered through booksellers or by contacting:
Balboa Press
A Division of Hay House
1663 Liberty Drive
Bloomington, IN 47403
www.balboapress.com
1-(877) 407-4847

Cover design by Matthew Howley. Author photo by Gabrielle Mottern.

Printed in the United States of America

Balboa Press rev. date: 11/20/2012

For all women.

"It's not the life that matters, it's the courage that you bring to it."
Yogi Bhajan

PROLOGUE

Jane skipped down the first few stairs of West Point's Administration Building when she felt the back of her neck tighten. Something was out of place. Though it was a warmish March day, cold seeped out of the walls and slid icy fingers down her spine. She forced herself to focus on the hem of her gray slacks.

Suddenly Jane's vision shifted. Her slacks morphed into a natural-fiber cloth, heavy linen. Soft-soled leather boots covered slightly smaller feet. The feel of cold stone through the thin leather sent a paralyzing chill through her legs, and the fine blond hairs on her arms stood alert. Right before her eyes the square stairwell transformed into antiquated rounded castle walls. She put a hand on her chest and let out an audible gasp.

She heard shuffling footfalls echoing in her head while her heart beat out a more rapid rhythm with each downward step. She grabbed hold of the handrail to steady herself; she was in two locations at once, a palimpsest of sorts. Impressions of a time long gone bled through into this time: split, in mind and spirit.

Some unseen hand tethered her to a dark, fearful scene. Death hovered quietly by her side, waiting. Her chest constricted as she gasped for air. The scent of burning wood stung her nostrils.

Somehow she had parted the delicate fabric of time. French voices swam in her head. Movement was all around her, hands pulled at her. Tired, hungry, and discouraged, she wanted to slump down, give up. Far off noises of a gathered crowd made her ears ring. Jane could hear Jehanne crying out, *Oh, dearest God, help me!*

ROUEN, FRANCE

MONDAY, MAY 20, 1431

My tattered silk cape, an extravagant gift from my king at a time when I held his favor, offered little protection against the biting cold. Tiny snowflakes swirled on the wind, seeming like they would never land, cloaking the town in a white shroud, and blew into the carriage in drifts. Each lacy flake, fragile, yet when massed with others of its kind could halt armies and kill without reservation.

I witnessed this snowfall from the deceptive protection of a covered carriage as it transported me to an English prison on French soil. I was at the mercy of an element more powerful and frightening—human fear.

By the time we rumbled across the drawbridge and pulled into the inner courtyard of Bouvreuil, the Earl of Warwick's castle, in Rouen, a layer of snow covered the roads, roofs, and the top of every exposed surface, including the heads and shoulders of the men who rode as guards beside my carriage.

The bishop's dry droning voice interrupted my memories of my last days breathing fresh air and pulled me reluctantly from the padded seat of the cold carriage back to the hard wood chair in the courtroom. Through the lattice mullioned windows behind the bishop, I watched a tree sway greenery back and forth. It was the middle of May, usually a time for hope and new opportunities.

I should have run back then. I would have made it to safety under the cover of the falling snow. For the hundredth time memories of the last few moments of relative freedom rolled around in my mind and served as an escape from the misery of the present moment. Experiencing a little cold and hunger then would have been preferable to the events of the subsequent five months in this prison.

"Jehanne d'Arc." Bishop Cauchon's voice boomed and echoed off the vaulted ceiling. "I command you to swear oath and relate the truth of all subjects asked of you."

Heat rushed to my face. Frustration simmered through my veins. I let my gaze rake around the castle's main chamber. Priests, monks, and learned clergy from the University of Paris, fifty or so of them, sat on platforms placed in a U-formation. Most were draped in the scarlet robes of the church, while a few wore humble brown garments of the monks. This wall of clergy appeared as daunting to me as the entire English army. Quill-armed scribes held their feathers aloft waiting to record my words.

I wondered if the bishop would allow my every word to be recorded, or if he, out of fear, had instructed the scribes to strike those truths opposing those of the superstitious and power-hungry clergy. It was more likely that they rewrote each word so that I would appear to be confessing to the church's manufactured claims, heresy being their main argument. I stood in the middle of the U-shaped sea of red, shackled at my wrists and ankles, guards to my left, right, and behind, and fully understood the enormity of this injustice. I attempted to keep emotion from my voice and answered, "I repeat, as far as my revelations are concerned, I will tell you nothing."

The bishop's voice rose with unchecked fury. "Swear to tell the truth."

"Watch what you, who claim to be my earthly judge, undertake, for you assume a terrible responsibility on yourself. You presume too far. I have taken the oath daily. That is enough," I bellowed and slammed my chained fist onto my thigh.

Bishop Cauchon won the politically prestigious task, appointed by the English and Burgundians, those Frenchmen loyal to the English, of giving me a full trial. My trial was overseen by the University of Paris, whose loyalty lay with the King of England, while its members tripped over each other to be recognized and given political and financial rewards. Bishop Cauchon himself would benefit by being given the honor of the highest bishopric and lands befitting his new office.

Cauchon's face turned as crimson as his robe, and he began to shake with fury. Several other priests and judges hurled threats at me. They could not comprehend that I was a woman claiming to communicate directly with God's agents, the angels. Their myopic view of the world held no room for a young woman capable of leading men into battle. And there was certainly no room in their limited minds for a young peasant woman, dressing as a man, to succeed at reviving the fading embers of hope within the hearts and minds of the people of France. Before I was captured, people would rush from their homes and line the streets to see me ride by on horseback. I must humbly say that it was their country and God they honored, not me. I hope God's record books will indicate that I acted only from my faith in the desires of my divine counsel and never did I act for personal gain. In fact, I did not feel at all comfortable with the pomp and parades. I would much rather remain in the shadows and lead a quiet farm life like my family did, but God had other plans for me, which I honored as best as I could.

Gesturing with his short arms in fur-trimmed sleeves, the bishop stormed, "You will suffer instant condemnation if you refuse to take the oath."

"All the clergy in France could not condemn me," I shouted back at him proudly; I would not be bullied or tormented by a priest. "I completed a mission authorized by God. My wish is to return to Him. I am finished here."

Bishop Beaupre, older and more austere than chubby, yellow-jowled Cauchon, interjected in an attempt to break up the battle between us. "When was your last meal?"

"Midday yesterday," I answered flatly. I was not sure why this sudden concern about my diet. They only wanted to keep me alive so that they could make a public spectacle of me and burn me in the market.

Bishop Beaupre cleared his throat, glanced at Cauchon, who nodded assent to him, and asked, "Do you think you are in a state of grace?"

The entire castle hall went quiet. Scribes held their quills at the ready.

I had not even a counselor assigned to assist me in this farcical trial. I realized that only a situation as absurd as this would be created by God for some reason beyond my simple understanding, so I honestly answered, "It is God's affair whether or not I am in a state of grace. With all humility, it is my wish to be in God's grace . . . always. For I would be most unhappy if I were not." God's opinion of me was a serious matter. Nothing mattered more.

A great uproar broke out within the hall. A number of priests smiled at me, surprised, while others gesticulated vehemently and argued among themselves.

"She's a witch," one of the priests cried.

Archangel Michael, one of my three guardian angels, whispered in my ear, as he did frequently, offering counsel and instruction when I needed it. His presence, more important to me than bread and water, always offered an insight to the situation at hand. *Dearest Jehanne, the question was a scholarly trap. According to church doctrine, no one could be certain of being in God's grace. If you answered yes, then you would have convicted yourself of heresy. If you answered no, then you would have confessed to your own guilt. Well said.*

When the noise within the hall quieted, I added calmly, "Were my intentions not of a pure heart, I don't believe my heavenly voices would come to me." I paused, feeling emotion rise within me, then continued, "I wish that everyone could hear them—the voices—as well as I do myself." I added, "I have greater fear of failing my voices, in saying something that displeases them, than I have of you."

Appearing flustered, Bishop Beaupre adjourned court suddenly. My guards escorted me, wordlessly, through the castle's darkened hallways, my chains clanking arrhythmically up each step, back to my cold tower cell. Silent tears rolled down my now-sunken cheeks. I realized I would never be able to play their game. For weeks and months, I withstood their mind-spinning questioning in an attempt to stay ahead of them without betraying my heavenly voices or my own flesh. I would not force myself to go against that for which I stood.

The injustices placed upon me over the last months were finally taking their toll; the great chamber of my heart began to close. I gave everything for my God, my king, my country, and my love. It was all lost to me now, and I had nothing left but the scant skin on my bones.

I would allow the shadow of death to stand beside me and pet my hand. I would allow my grip on the rope of humanity to slip. It became clear I would die at the hands of the English and French traitors.

Later that day, as the sun began to leave the sky and pale purple shadows crept along the curved tower walls, I watched my head guard, John Grey—they always had two or three in the room with me—grow increasingly agitated. I found his constant agitation more irritating than my itchy mattress. I much preferred the disinterested neglect of the other two guards, William Talbot and John Berwoit.

"So, Jehanne, are you really the virgin they say you are? I believe you are a camp whore—spreading your legs to all your captains. Right? That's why . . . you won. Your men won the battles for you. You must be a demon in the hay . . . uh?" He tried to provoke me, his face red with intensity.

5

I dared not answer him lest he become more vexed.

"No men at all. Is it true?" He leaned over me, his grimy face twisted in a sneer. He shook the chains at my wrists, bating me to respond to him, breath as malodorous as his disposition. "You're lying. You bitch. You don't know what you're missing. Maybe that's it . . . you don't know the pleasure from the man's prowess." He stood upright and untied his woolen hose.

God, please protect me, I thought and directed this prayer to my angels. Panic slithered through me as I dug my heels into the meager mattress of my prison bed. I managed to go all this time, two years in the constant presence of men-at-arms, with my virginity intact. I forced myself to focus on my heavenly voices.

Saint Catherine crooned in my ear, *All will be fine.*

John Berwoit, shorter and stockier than lanky John Grey, stepped into the room. "What's going on?" His slate-colored, lazy eye rested on me briefly before he turned to his fellow guard.

"I'm showing *la Pucelle*, our maid, what she's missing," Grey jeered as he lowered his hose and grabbed hold of his engorged penis, goading me, his eyes bulging. "Look at this. Look!"

I glanced over at the sausage-like appendage he held between his hands. I'd never seen a man's organ up close. Startled, I turned away, my heart thudding. He moved to within inches of my face. Shaking it, he growled, "You must want this. Jehanne, how can you resist?"

"Do you see, monsieur, how much God loves you?" I replied despite the fact that I was backed up against the stone wall.

His sweaty forehead crinkled in confusion. "Come on . . ."

I took a quick breath and glared at him with all the courage I could muster. "You must know God loves you—because if I had my sword in hand I would cut that thing off. Just one flick of my wrist, in a flash, your manhood and brains would be lying limp on that filthy floor."

Berwoit doubled over laughing. Grey's appendage drooped.

Humiliated, Grey turned away, pulled up his hose, violently tied the laces, and pulled his tunic down in a huff.

I turned my face to the wall in order to conceal a victorious smirk and bid my heart to slow down.

"Someday, Jehanne, you will pay for this. Someday . . ." He strode the short distance to the old stool near the deep, narrow window of our tower room, and clearing his throat, he leaned into the opening and spat. Wiping his mouth with his sleeve he sat down hard and glared at me shooting invisible daggers from brown bloodshot eyes.

"John," I said and lifted my chained hands, shaking them at him, "I pay already."

The others continued to laugh, but neither John nor I felt this was a laughing matter. My virginity was the backbone of my mission to help France.

Dearest Archangel Michael, why is it I find myself in this horrid situation? What did I do wrong?

Archangel Michael's deep voice resonated clearly in my head. *Dearest child, you are so brave. You have done nothing wrong. Just as you were born to lift the siege of Orléans and deliver the crown of France to the dauphin, you were born for this.*

Why would I choose to be thrown in prison unjustly and betrayed by those I sacrificed my life to help? My heart still ached at the reluctance of my king, Charles of France, to buy me back from the English. He'd had several opportunities but chose not to blemish his tenuous reign with my controversial presence in his court.

As always the presence of my angels helped to dissipate my sadness and fear. Since just before my thirteenth birthday, I had enjoyed the visits and guidance of my three angels. Each continually offered love and encouragement in their own unique way. In the presence of Archangel Michael my heart felt more resilient and my mind became as sharp as a carving knife. Saint Catherine offered tenderness and wisdom while Saint Margaret buoyed my heart and gave me courage.

Archangel Michael continued in a soothing resonant tone, *Jehanne, you are a magnificent brave soul who has come to assist in the growth of humanity. You have come to illustrate two things. First, by example, you have chosen to lead a life inspired by God, without an intermediary. Your life as a spiritual warrior will inspire many far into the future to follow the divine voice within. Second, your life as a prisoner will, by contrast, illuminate those out-of-balance seats within the royalty and hierarchy of the church.*

But, why did I not just go into a convent? It would have been much simpler—for me. I pushed myself to sitting, ignoring the dizzy feeling in my head and wiggled my feet to bring back lost circulation to my bound ankles.

Yes, it would have been more simple for you, but far less meaningful for the world. You are creating history in this very moment. Every minute you spend in chains will be met with years of inspiration, not only for the people of France, but the entire world. You have come to show and create a desire for spirituality. This desire will ripple outward, empowering people to connect to their own divine purpose without the need of an intermediary. Those men in positions of power will fight this change for a long time, but, in the end, freedom of faith will prevail.

The injustice of your experience at the hands of the church and royalty will open the eyes and crack open the hearts of thousands.

Saint Michael, I fear you are not correct. Will the people of the future know of my love for my country, my desire to serve my king and my God humbly? Will my reputation be tarnished by these so-called men of God? Are they writing my words or are they building a case against my sanity and my honor? I wish I could tell my own story and show I am no different than any other man or woman. Please protect me from any harsher treatment and help me to find the courage to get through today. I stretched my shackled wrists over my head to lessen the ache in my shoulders.

You are always protected. Even if something feels harmful, your soul is ever whole, ever radiant, ever unblemished. You will be free soon. In fact, this whole journey will be complete in eleven days. Focus on your breathing. Feel your heartbeat and you will know we are with you. This is your secret weapon to move through this part of your mission.

Remember, Jehanne, how it all began. Remember your faith. Remember it all. Send your memories out into the future, project your mind so that young women and men of the future can, if they choose, pick up your inspiring courage and unflagging faith and know the truth about you.

Remember . . . remember . . . You have eleven days.

Archangel Michael's voice echoed in my head as I lay there contemplating his words. I could hear the rumbling of a thunderstorm's approach. He said eleven days. Did he mean I would be set free, sent to a nunnery, or martyred? Strangely, in that moment, I did not care. Sleep overtook me until a clap of thunder rattled my tower. As I listened to the showers drenching the land outside, I contemplated where to begin with my memories. The thought that my angels would help my story find its way into the hearts of a few in the future helped me garner strength.

Lightening struck. Flashes of light danced on the walls of my room and a warm energy encircled me. I let myself slip back in time and released my memories into the belly of the storm.

Everything felt soft and warm. Back in time, I could see my home and my family in Domrémy, northeast, many miles away. We lived in the part of France, the province of Lorraine, that remained loyal to the French crown. Random memories floated through my mind: my papa's strong shoulders, my maman's raw working hands, the smell of our sheep, our family garden in the spring. It all moved, shifted, and came into focus, and then shifted again.

The pain of prison disappeared as I slipped deeper into the past. I was back at home, and it was early summer in 1427, when I was just fifteen years old.

Sidestepping the small puddles dotting the dirt path, I skipped the short distance to the back door of the barn, which, oddly, sat ajar. It was not typical for the door to be opened—Papa's strict orders. I cautiously pushed the roughened wood door open wide enough for me to slip through. It took a moment for my eyes to adjust to the dim interior of the barn. The sweet smell of last season's hay, combined with animal droppings, tickled my nose in an oddly reassuring way. Rustling from the far corner drew my attention. I slid my feet two steps closer to see what made the sound. Grunting sounds accompanied a low, moaning warble.

Mon Dieu! I flinched.

There he stood, my brother Pierre, with his back to me, his hose unlaced and hanging around the top edge of his knee-high boots. The crease of his bare buttocks became visible beneath his tunic each time he thrust his hips forward. A female hand reached up and cupped the back of his head and pulled it down toward a face I could not see. Pale chubby legs wrapped tightly around his waist. Her booted feet bobbed up and down in rhythm to his thrusts. With her other arm she frantically grabbed at his clothing in intense passion. Such desire I had never seen.

Mon Dieu! I thought again, shocked at what I saw, but at the same time I felt caught in their spell of love, surprised by the feeling of warmth in my own nether region. It was like someone lit a match. Forcing myself to move, I stepped back, banged into the door, righted myself, and emerged wobbly into the morning sunlight. I began to run back down the path, this time stepping in the puddles and splashing mud up onto the side of the barn. I scrambled away from the embarrassing scene as fast as I could to the first place I could think of—church. However, when I arrived on the doorstep of St. Remy I found the doors locked.

Where can I go? I thought, looking up at the short steeple, then down at the stone steps. I rested my hands on my knees to catch my breath.

"Bonjour, Jeannette!" Two village women with their arms filled with fabric, dull shades of surge linen, called to me using my childhood name.

"Bonjour, Madame Estellin, Madame Joinville," I replied a little too curtly, for they glanced at each other.

The mysterious feeling still burned between my legs. I needed to move. I ran through the fields of barley and short sunflowers, past the cattle and the Fairies' Tree, all the way to the little chapel in the Bermont oak forest at the edge of my family's land. The muscles in my legs cramped with exertion, my lungs burned.

Old rusty hinges groaned as I shoved the aged chapel door open so hard it slammed back into the wall. I rushed up to the simple altar and dropped to my knees on the dusty floor. Clasping my hands together, I lifted them to my chin and closed my eyes to see about the strange feelings. Relief. Everything felt normal.

"My dearest God and saints," I prayed fervently, gazing at the plain crucifix hanging on the wall. My voice sounded heavy in the closed space. "I promise to be always true to you. I swear my chastity to you as long as it pleases you. I give my heart, my soul, and my body to you, God." The longing I felt pulsed through my entire body.

"Please transform any earthly lust I may have into devotion to you, my God in Heaven. I know no man will be able to satisfy the desire in my breast, so I will settle for nothing less." My own yearning surprised me. "Please make me a servant of your peace, let me sow hope where there is despair . . ."

Sensations inside me, and formless pulsing in the air around me, alerted me to the now frequent presence of my angels. My body began to tingle. A bluish light hovered over the altar.

Archangel Michael began speaking to me inside my head. For nearly two years I had heard the voices of my angels. At first I felt alarmed and feared for my sanity, until I realized they only gave encouragement and always surrounded me with feelings of love.

Dearest daughter of God, we have heard your most devoted pleas of service. There is a task of great importance to your country. You have the choice to embark on a journey to provide relief to a town, which will be held under siege by the English and Burgundians. You also have the opportunity to help reinstate the crown's presence in France. This will require great courage. If you agree, prepare yourself for this journey in a little over a year's time. Know all of your guardian angels love you. Though only Archangel Michael spoke I could feel the presence of the others around me.

"This mission sounds impossible for a peasant girl such as myself. I have no knowledge of the ways of war or courtly manners," I answered out loud.

Trust. Dear child, trust. We will all be by your side guiding you all the way, step by step.

Pushing myself to standing, I bowed my head with humility at the thought of this task given by God. A picture of a victorious battle scene flashed behind my eyes, and the joy at completing such a task filled me with a sense of purpose. "I have the courage needed. I'm sure I do," I said wholeheartedly. "I choose the mission put before me."

We are glad to hear of your enthusiasm. When you dare to commit with your whole heart, to your deepest desires, your heart grows to accommodate the task at hand, no matter how daunting. You know you are on the right path when you feel joy at the prospect of continuing on, even in the face of challenges. We are quite confident in your courage, dearest one. For now, return home. If you find it helps you to stay focused, you may confess to your pastor to keep your intentions clear. Eat well and be ever helpful of those around you. Know that when you help others, you serve yourself and God in Heaven.

"I am most grateful of your confidence in me."

The flash of lights intensified, revealing a magnificent angel holding a shield, and a sword hung at his hip. *I am Archangel Michael, and you will hear from me again.* He smiled and disappeared.

Joy enlivened my flesh as I turned and skipped out of the chapel. Judging by the sunlight blinking through the tall oaks, it was midday. Birds twittered nearby, and a gentle breeze washed over me, brushing my skirts around my legs. I broke into a run upon entering the fields and headed for home where I would need to catch up on chores.

Days went by before I could look my brother in the eye without blushing and remembering the sensual scene in the barn. As far as I knew, he had no idea I had witnessed their loving. One evening after dinner when Papa and the boys went into the village, Maman pulled me aside. Wiping her reddened hands on her skirt she said, "Sit down, Jeannette." Concern wrinkled her ruddy round face. "There is something I must tell you."

"What is it, Maman?" I sank down on the bench at the table, a little worried by the firm set of her mouth.

"Jeannette, have you noticed your father's strange mood lately?"

"Maybe . . ."

"He told your brothers he often dreams you will run off with a band of soldiers. He gave strict instructions to your brothers to drown you if it comes to pass." She searched my face for a reaction.

"That is ridiculous, Maman. Why would I do a thing like that?" I tried to disguise my astonishment in my father's accurate premonitions of my future. This confirmed my notion that it would not be wise to tell them of my visions. My mission held more importance than their feelings.

Exactly 545 Years Later

May 20, 1976

May 20 began as an ordinary day. Bill and Mary Archer took the scenic drive, Vermont Highway 7, through green rolling fields. Brilliant sunlight blinked through the small spring leaves of oaks and maples lining the highway. They drove from Burlington, Vermont, where Bill's parents lived, south toward their new home in Rhode Island with the windows open.

The only worrisome aspect to the lovely morning was the fact that their tiny daughter, Jane, held snuggly in Mary's lap, had kept them up most of the previous night with a bad spring cold. She was just over eleven months old.

Mary stuck her head out of the window in an attempt to clear the niggling worry knotting her insides. Soft, coffee-colored curls whipped around her head. She let the mountain air assault her face and settle her nerves.

It still surprised her—the force of her love for her daughter. She would do anything to protect her. Mary mused how Jane was the eldest daughter of the eldest daughter, back four more generations to Mary's great-great-great grandmother. Little Jane made six generations of eldest women giving birth to first-born females. She wondered if that meant Jane had some kind of fabled or mystical strength, as it seemed to be the stuff legends were made of.

Jane squirmed in her lap as she opened her eyes from a short nap. She smiled her usual cherubic two-toothed smile. Mary smoothed back the fine light hair off her baby's forehead. "Oh, Bill, she feels warm again."

"We'll take her to the doctor when we get home to Rhode Island, OK?"

Jane knit her tiny brows together, wrinkled her nose, and began to cough. Her face turned a brighter shade of pink. She struggled to get off Mary's lap and pushed her chubby legs into her mother's abdomen in protest. She wanted down so she could crawl and explore on her own. "D . . . d . . . d . . .," she whined. The effort brought on a fresh wave of coughing.

"Oh, sweetie," Mary soothed. She brought the child up to her shoulder and began to pat her on the back. The coughing subsided and her little body relaxed. She snuggled into her mother's neck and drifted asleep. Her child's nuzzles reminded Mary of the first few months after her birth and the quiet moments spent nursing in the soft blue light of predawn. It seemed magical then.

Bill let his left hand ride the waves of air out the window as he cruised down the two-lane road. Weathered split-rail fences ran alongside the car on both sides. He glanced sideways at his girls and smiled. When he looked back through the windshield he spotted a mammoth cloud hovering over a mountain in the distance.

"Looks like a storm's coming," he said, pointing to thick dark clouds as they crossed in front of the sun. He ran a hand over two days of dark stubble on his chin. They passed a sign for Emerald Lake State Park on the right. "We'll have to check that park out some time. Though, I don't think Janey is well enough to stop today, do you?"

"No. Can you drive faster? I'm feeling a little worried, Bill."

A stiff breeze buffeted the car from the west causing Mary to crank up her window halfway. Jane whimpered and wiggled. Her coughing sounded like a puppy barking.

Mary tried bouncing her on her knees.

The first raindrops slapped against the windshield even though the sun streamed over the tops of the approaching clouds in iridescent rays onto the rolling farmland on their left. The corona of a rainbow appeared briefly.

"Beautiful isn't it?" Bill said.

Lightening zagged in the distance. The storm front resembled a huge puffy skyscraper.

"Wow, those clouds are enormous and moving fast," Bill exclaimed. "I think they're called cumulonimbus."

"Bill, I don't care what they're called. Can you please keep your eyes on the road?"

Rain fell with more insistence, big fat drops. They rolled up their windows but not before Mary's shoulder became soaked.

Mary tried to give Jane some juice, but she pushed the bottle away with her teeny fist and continued to cough. Her pretty petite face was contorted and red with pain.

"We have to do something, Bill!"

"What do you have in mind?" he said intensely. "I can hardly see out the windshield, and the wipers are on high." Waves of water rolled off the side of the windshield. Thunder crashed. It grew so dark the few cars passing them in the other direction had their lights on.

"Look for a place to stop," Mary said, blinking away tears.

Bill gripped the steering wheel with both hands, craning his neck to see through the deluge. They passed a cemetery on the left. Bill looked ahead for refuge from the weather.

Trees waved back and forth with the gusting wind. "There. Up ahead. Is that a farmhouse?" He had to yell to be heard over the rain drumming on the roof of the car.

Jane's cries began to sound like choking as she gasped for breath. Mary patted her nervously on the back. "Shh . . . shh. It's OK, Janey," she whispered but wondered how effective her efforts would be as her own body became stiff with fear.

16

She began to pray as Bill maneuvered the car almost blindly into the gravel drive of the farmhouse.

"Wait here," he shouted as he sprang from the car and sprinted, hunched over, to the front porch. There were moments when the rain swallowed him completely and he disappeared from view. The house looked dark. Mary thought if someone were home she would see a light on inside. The charcoal sky hovered so low it seemed to touch the roof of the house. In between lightning strikes Mary noticed an older barn to the right. Its door banged open and closed with the force of the tempest.

Jane's ribcage heaved between Mary's hands as she fought for air. Thunder shook the car.

Without waiting for Bill to return, Mary clasped Jane to her chest, put her other hand on the door handle, and took a deep breath. Like she was diving under water, she flung open the door, wrapped both her arms around Jane, and ran the one hundred yards as fast as she could toward the banging door. Rain drenched them both by the time Mary made it to the safety of the barn. Inside two horses were neighing and straining against their tethers.

Mary made a quick assessment of her surroundings then chose a spot that afforded the most light near the open door, so she could see her baby and remain a safe distance away from the frantic horses. She sat on a bale of hay and gingerly released her child into her lap.

Jane's face appeared ashen. Her open mouth moved in an effort to get air just like a goldfish.

"Oh, God, please help my Janey," she cried. "Pleeeassse!"

Where was Bill? She put one hand on her child's chest and prayed. She prayed and pleaded with every deity she could think off. She tried to recall all of the saints and gods from her world religions classes back at Simmons College. "Please help my baby. Please help my Janey."

While she was praying Bill ran through the door. In the time it took him to walk from the door to where his girls sat, Jane had closed her eyes. Her body lay motionless. Mary looked at her husband, her own eyes wide with disbelief. They gazed back at their child—the love of both their lives. She appeared peaceful. Sweet.

Jane's stillness rippled outward.

Both Mary and Bill held their breath. Thunder murmured from far away and continued to roll closer. The horses grew silent. The only sounds in the barn were that of rushing water. It was like the heavens had opened and a waterfall cascaded all around the barn.

They waited for her to move.

Time stopped in Mary's mind and began to reel backward. She remembered playing with Jane and her squealing with delight at the antics of Bill's parents' cat. She remembered when Jane stood for the first time, crawled for the first time. She recalled Jane's robust cries after she was born and how filled with life she seemed. How could it be over?

Bill stood frozen to the ground, rooted, unable to think. Surely this was not happening. He thought of all his dreams for his daughter and how her birth had brought him and Mary even closer. In a strange way Jane completed them and brought them a joy he never dreamed of.

Mary opened her mouth to let out a wail but before she could utter a sound, a deafening clap of thunder tore at the sky over the barn. It felt as though the roof of the barn ripped open. The ground shook. Blinding lightning charged and illuminated the air all around them. The horses reared and bellowed and pulled at their restraints. They pounded the earth with their hooves.

Mary felt electricity surge around her daughter's body and pass into her own heart, making it flutter, before it spread outward through her limbs. She swooned momentarily from the sheer force of it.

Movement under her hands drew her gaze downward just as Jane's gold-speckled eyes flew open. For a moment the look in those familiar golden eyes appeared wise, ancient, knowing. Jane took a gasping breath in, sputtered it back out, then radiated her usual smile at her mother.

ROUEN, FRANCE

TUESDAY, MAY 21, 1431

"Get up," Grey demanded and kicked me in the thigh. He thought I was asleep. It was his favorite game, to wake me when I slept or torture me in some fashion. I wondered what they had in store for me today. I rolled my eyes up toward the timbered ceiling and sent the same prayer I had muttered hourly since the Burgundians captured me a year ago. Oh, God, give me strength to get through this day; may I be one day closer to the freedom I so desire. If prayers were thread I could have woven enough fabric to stretch from my cell in Rouen to my hometown, nearly three hundred miles away.

My guards John Grey and William Talbot dragged me down the spiral stairs, through the castle, and down into the castle's dungeon, a rank, fetid chamber where several priest-judges lined the curved wall. Though Talbot's breath stank from too much drink, he held on to me more gently and caught me with firm calloused hands whenever I'd trip. Grey appeared the weakest of my three guards and frequently sought approval by treating me cruelly.

In the dungeon, the master torturer, an older man with a scarred face and mangled hands, brandished torture implements in an effort to get me to change my story and admit my nonexistent guilt. He sneered at me through rotten teeth.

"If you tore me limb from limb and threatened me with death, I would not change my story," I said for the hundredth time. In truth, death began to seem a welcome option for me. I listened to their whispered voices echo off the weeping stone. They spoke about me as if I wasn't there.

"She isn't like—we've never seen a woman as strong—"

"She a witch and should be punished as such."

"We need to be careful with this one—save her for the public, I say. This is the best lesson for the French patriots. We need to instill fear, to keep something like this from ever happening again."

"Le'me prepare the faggots and the platform in the town square."

Dominican friar Martin Ladvenu flashed me a concerned look and spoke, "No, not yet. We need to get the votes from all the priests from the University of Paris. She has won the hearts of some of our most loyal priests and learned clergy—they are growing fearful. They fret—thinking she is the real thing, you know—and worry harm will come to them if they vote against her. Let's wait."

Bishop Beaupre rubbed his mottled beard with an aged hand. "I agree. Though, Cauchon will not be pleased no harm came to her. Torture was his idea. The man is possessed with hatred and would just as soon burn her in her tower cell." He grew thoughtful then announced, "Dismissed!"

Relief flooded through me. My empty belly had been tied in knots. After my guards led me back to my cell, I lay listless on my bed and requested succor from heaven. Just as I began to experience some relief from the incessant waves of anxiety, an assemblage of six red-robed priests followed by the ever-roiling Bishop Cauchon entered my cell and gathered around my cot.

From the start of the New Year until early spring, the bishop called to order numerous public trial sessions held in the great hall, and just as many private sessions held in my prison cell. They condensed all of the proceedings down to "The Twelve Articles of Accusation."

The bishop's acne-faced cleric opened the parchment containing The Twelve Articles of Accusation and read them out loud.

"First—One Jehanne d'Arc pretends to communicate with saints in Heaven beginning at thirteen years of age; she states they instructed her to wear male attire; she claims salvation and refuses to submit herself to the church.

Second—She admits to convincing the king to believe in her through a sign, as well as placing a crown upon his head with an angel by her side.

Third—She affirms her companionship with Saint Michael and other saints.

Fourth—She declares certain things will occur by revelation obtained from these saints.

Fifth—She admits that it is the will of God for her to maintain wearing men's clothing, therefore, she committed a sin by receiving the sacrament of Holy Communion in that garb, which she says she would sooner die than quit wearing."

In order to quell the rage within me I focused on the dusty beams on the ceiling and prayed for strength.

The cleric droned on with self-importance and spitting disdain. "Sixth—She admits to writing letters signed with the names of Jesus and Mary with the sign of the cross. She also admits threatening death to those who would not obey her. And claims that divine will was the reason for all she accomplished.

Seventh—She gives a false account of her journey to Vaucouleurs and Chinon.

Eighth—She also gives an untrue account of her attempt to kill herself at Beaurevoir, rather than fall into the hands of the English.

Ninth—She offers false statements of her assurance of salvation, provided she remains a maid, and never committing any sin.

Tenth—She pretends that Saints Catherine and Margaret speak to her in French, and not English, as they do not belong to the latter side.

Eleventh—She admits to the adoration of her saints, disobedience to her parents, and making the statement, 'If the evil one were to appear in the likeness of Saint Michael I would know it was not the saint.'

Twelfth—She refuses to submit and comply with the Church Militant, and the 'Unam sanctam ecclesiam catholicam,' and, all things pertaining to sacred doctrines and ecclesiastical sanctions."

At the conclusion of the reading, the bishop's cleric flashed a pompous scowl in my direction and wrinkled his nose as if I were a filthy rat in the gutter. His narrow view of the world could not conceive of the likes of me.

"I deny it all," I said without looking at any of them.

Each article was an outright lie or a gross distortion of my words and deeds. They left me alone with my contentious guards, who gossiped in the corner like a bevy of milkmaids. Taking advantage of their lack of attention, I began to release a torrent of frustration at my angels in Heaven. I kicked my shackled feet in a tantrum.

Saint Michael, why aren't you all protecting me from this? I'm not working for you anymore. Do you hear me? I feel duped by everyone involved, from my king and priests to you, my dearest friends in heaven. You have sacrificed me for your cause. Well, I no longer want to play at this dangerous game. What have you to say to me now?

I dug my fingernails into my palms. If I were free I would need a long ride, through fields and over all the rushing rivers of France, to quell this distress.

You are caught in your fearful thoughts. See if you can expand your mind. It's your mind, dear one, which squeezes your heart.

Pardonnez-moi? You only desire I acquiesce to your wishes.

Dearest child of God, your mind is squeezing your heart closed.

My mind? You mean my thoughts? You mean my accurate assessments of this ridiculous situation.

Unflummoxed by my dark mood, Michael continued to murmur, *Your mind is the cause of your pain.*

Ha! My thoughts are causing me pain? You, my dear friends, are sorely mistaken—my guards cause me pain. These priests . . . and Bishop Cauchon . . . you! I am hurt. My heart hurts with the pain of these men. My chest feels squeezed, giant hands crushing my love for others. God, himself, uses me as a pawn.

Remember, men have doubted you before, called you names, and you could not be swayed or daunted in your path. The only difference between then and now is your doubt of yourself, and your fear and judgment of them.

How can I not fear them? They hold me captive. I cannot sleep. Tortured by my guards day and night. They are winning. I pulled at my iron tethers and felt the sting of the raw flesh at my ankles. Michael's resonate voice began to penetrate into the hardened angry places within me, despite my determined resistance.

Jehanne, you must now become a warrior of your mind. You must slay every thought that causes you pain. Stay vigilant, sweet one, in the province of your mind, with your mind's sword you must the thoughts of doubt, and fear, and judgment. I'm not sure if I understand. Don't all thoughts come from truth? I still wanted to make him wrong, to blame someone for this catastrophe.

Absolutely not. What man does not understand, and will not for centuries, is that God is in each and every man and woman. The minds of men squeeze their hearts shut, and when their hearts are squeezed shut, they leave no room for the presence of God. Man becomes like a house with no windows. No light penetrates. The ability to see solutions becomes obscured. It becomes challenging to see the beauty and radiance of life. Shadows become the focus, distorting the truth.

Yes, I can see that. Will you help me? This does not mean I'm letting you off the hook for sacrificing me.

Close your eyes. Follow the flow of your breath and notice the flow of your thoughts.

My body relaxed. My pounding head quieted.

My chest began to rise and fall. What if they burn me as a witch? My guard threatens me and taunts me with my greatest fear—rape.

Notice your body immediately tightens responding to your thoughts. Now, Jehanne, see if you can find a thought that makes you feel safe. Find your inner warrior. What does she say?

She says I am an infinite being, and they cannot destroy what I have done already.

Does this thought feel better?

Yes. Some. The voices of my guards faded to a steady drone in the back of my head, and some of the tension in my limbs eased.

Good. All is well. Practice this technique with every painful thought, and you will be free within the province of your mind. No one can lock you out of your peace or chain you to suffering unless you let them. Rest now, dear one. You are loved.

I felt washed in a fountain of renewal. Scenes of the future flashed onto the screen of my mind. I understood there would be others to take up where I left off. I watched as the citizens of France in the future burst into the king's castle and captured him and the queen. I watched a great metal blade as it sliced through the monarchy and initiated a government of the people. Further into the future, I saw women wearing the same clothing as men. I witnessed women ruling, giving orders to men and women. Female soldiers in a new land march and lead men. I could hear requests for heavenly assistance and strength. Encouraged, I sent prayers far into the future and felt the love of those who studied my deeds. My life felt meaningful and my suffering worth the numerous benefits that would abound as a result.

I hoped they remember me, and my deeds, with kindness. I hoped the people of the future know that I always acted with love and I followed the guidance of my angels in heaven faithfully.

Memories again washed over me, and I let them spill into the future to travel to the hearts of women and men. I was no longer chained and captive. Instead, I was riding. It was night and snow pelted my face. My horse's rhythmic breathing became mine. I could feel each hoof meet the frozen earth, every muscle of his flank as he rode for me. I gave into him and allowed my body to move with his so he would not have to exert more effort than necessary.

The memory faded. My mind floated in the comforting blackness of the night sky and then found another memory on which to land.

It was just before my public life began, when six men, loyal and willing to take a chance on me, escorted me through dangerous territory to see the would-be king, the dauphin, where I would offer my help and heavenly inspiration in service to the plight of my country, France. We had set up camp for the night and lit a fire to cook our dinner. Our intimate gathering included the only two men thus far who believed in my vision, Jean de Metz and Bertrand de Poulengy and their servants, Colet de Vienne, the young royal courier, and Richard the archer who provided protection and nourishment. Richard's excellent skills with a bow kept us well fed.

"The properties of fire resemble the properties of inspiration," I whispered to the men. "An ember sits smoldering, and depending upon the wind, it will either go out or burst into flame. Our hearts are like the ember waiting for direction from the wind. Have you ever seen fields after a wild fire?" Dancing flames reflected on the illuminated faces and tired eyes of my guardians.

Wind whistled through the leafless trees standing all around us. I could not decide whether the trees felt foreboding or protective that night. The far-off snorting of a wild boar told me the time was ripe to act with a warrior's heart. With a shaking hand I poured red liquid from a wine flask into a cup and took a long drink. It warmed my belly and helped me relax. My very life rested upon the success of this journey. As a young woman of seventeen years, I gambled everything on the guidance I received from three angelic voices and their promptings to embark on this mission for my country.

Tearing a piece of stale bread from my side pouch, I dipped it in the wine to soften it and ate. I took a deep breath of cold, smoky air and continued, "Fire burns away the brambles, the waste from years past and voilà, a beautiful profusion of life blooms more vibrant than before. This, messieurs, is my task. We must fan the fading embers within the breasts of each man and woman of France. Do you understand?" Despite the heat of the flames, I shivered.

"Oui." Their grave responses hung in the frigid darkness. We spoke quietly, so as not to bring unwanted attention to our small group, always wary of pillagers, and huddled closer around the crackling fire while a pheasant that Richard the archer had deftly killed with his ash bow sizzled.

A familiar warmth from the center of my chest alerted me to the presence of my angels. Turning my attention inward away from the men and fire, I listened to the sweet voice of Saint Catherine.

Dearest daughter, you have succeeded in inspiring the hearts of these men. Their desire to help you will provide them with the most powerful tool of war, passion. Continue on with your journey knowing that your angels in Heaven are with you. We will provide you with signs of inspiration along the way. Tomorrow, you should plan on leaving early, before daybreak, to avoid marauders and pillagers. Know we love you.

The voice of Saint Catherine faded, leaving me warmed and calmer. Merci, I said to her in my mind. Her presence lifted the nagging worry born of travel through enemy Burgundian territory.

"Jehanne, how do you propose we fan the flames of hope for the people of France?" Bertrand de Poulengy asked as he cut hunks of meat off the blackened spit with chubby, wind-burned fingers. Poulengy was my first friend and believer of my visions. His jovial optimism continued to give me hope during the weeks I spent waiting in the walled city of Vaucouleurs for approval for this journey from his captain, Robert de Baudricourt.

Robert de Baudricourt, who opted to stay behind in Vaucouleurs, realized that it would take an act of God to get the present king-to-be, the dauphin, Charles, to travel through aggressive Burgundian territory to be crowned King of France in the Cathedral of Reims. Nearly seven years had passed since the death of Charles's father, the former king. This left France without a clear leader. She was a rudderless ship, bobbing in hostile seas. Division, greed, and fear threatened to tear France apart. The long war with England wore the wallets and nerves thin of all her people. Many royals in the north and west began to side with the English, like rats escaping from a sinking ship.

"We must infuse France with the new energy she needs," Jean de Metz interjected, prodding the fire with a large stick. His brown eyes sparkled under a prominent brow, making him appear as though he was contemplating the problems of the world. He held a higher rank than Poulengy. "It is time to get our reluctant dauphin, Charles, to Reims and install the crown upon his head once and for all."

"Jehanne, perhaps your only task is to light a fire under the arse of our king and chase him all the way to Reims." Poulengy's round face reddened with a guttural laugh.

"Ouais!" the men's roused voices and laughter echoed off the trees nearby.

"SHHH," I scolded. "We should get some sleep. My voices from Heaven suggest we wake early and travel just before dawn to avoid pillaging mercenaries." My gaze swept over the men. "Agreed? Who has watch at that time?"

"Agreed," Poulengy answered. "I will be on watch then. Rest easy, Jehanne."

Rolling onto my back I gazed up at the cavernous sky through the bare branches of the trees. Clouds slid across the crescent moon, causing the shadows of the tree trunks to move and shift as though the trees were rearranging themselves. Maman had warned of evil spirits wandering the forests at night. To me, evil spirits were only the fragments of suffering left behind by the daily tragedies of man. Evil spirits did not frighten me; it was the ignorance of man that scared me out of my calfskin boots. The shadows lurking at the back of a man's heart proved to be more terrifying than any darkened wood.

War offered evidence of this shadow. France had engaged in war with the English for over seventy years, and hundreds of thousands of men sacrificed their bodies and souls for the sake of boundary lines and royal feuds. My heart ached at this loss. My body trembled with the premonition of coming war. I saw myself astride a great armored warhorse, charging into a fray, banner flapping, and men bellowing "Pour la France!" behind me.

I blinked to clear the vision and wondered how I would find the courage for such a ride. Snoring from the men sleeping nearby startled me from my reverie.

I slept fitfully among the men those first few nights. To insure my safety and my chastity, I wore my doublet closed and hose bound all night long. Not one of them attempted to touch me; their respect for me seemed to grow each day we spent together. I wondered how long could I hold onto my chastity in this male world?

562 Years Later

June 1993, Narragansett, Rhode Island

As Jane Archer jogged across the sand, her light brown ponytail swinging from side to side, she wondered how she would fare being away from the ocean. She loved the seashore, especially at low tide, and often came to the beach just to watch storms roll in. The expansive horizon, the curves where ocean met land, the heady, sometimes pungent, scent of salty air, and the exhilaration she felt from watching the waves build, curl in upon themselves, and crash, all gave her a sense of awe.

The ocean was in her blood, and became her breath when she let it. As she ran barefooted, her breathing synchronized with her stride. Step. Step. Step. Inhale. Step. Step. Step. Exhale.

It was June 11, the day before her eighteenth birthday, and Jane had come to the shore to quell doubts. She hoped the pounding of the steady surf and the spaciousness of the sky would dissolve her concerns over her future.

She was not disappointed. With each step on the firm sand, she felt her worries dissipate. By the time she returned home for dinner her confidence had returned.

"Tell me why you want to go to a place that calls its freshmen 'plebes,' *and* you have to get up at five a.m., *and* you get no weekends off *all summer long*? Like . . . I don't get it," said Elizabeth, Jane's little sister, her mouth full of ravioli. At fifteen she stood two robust inches taller than Jane.

Just like that, Elizabeth's words retriggered her fear. The fear she managed to overcome only hours before. In less than three weeks she would report for Basic Training at West Point, the United States Military Academy.

For as long as Jane could remember she wanted to attend West Point. She just knew her future lay there. Though, lately, little doubts slipped into her mind, stirred things up, and unsettled her resolve.

Mary cast a curious glance at her eldest daughter, "Janey, are you having doubts? It would be completely normal, especially in your case." She paused and caught the eyes of her husband. His square jaw set firm, his way of biting his tongue. The two of them had spent countless hours talking about the prospect of their daughter entering the military. While West Point offered a full scholarship and top academics, they, as parents, had hoped Jane would attend an Ivy League school. It was their love and support for their daughter's decision that tempered their tongues. However, seeing the opening provided, Mary could not resist offering, "You have other choices. We can afford to send you to Brown. They'd be happy to have you."

"You guys don't get it. I WANT to do this. I WANT to do something important with my life. Life isn't just about driving the latest BMW or picking out the right fabric for designer window treatments, or getting manicures every other week." Jane clutched her fork with frustration and glared at her mother; color rose in both their cheeks.

Mary's love for her daughter overpowered the blow to her ego. "You're just nervous, honey. I know you didn't mean that. You know your father and I support your decision whatever that may be. It's OK to change your mind," she said with a sigh; her cheekbones became more accentuated over a forced smile. She watched her daughter stab at the ravioli on her plate.

"It's just that going to a regular college doesn't feel right. I can't explain it." She was defending her outburst and trying to convince herself at the same time.

How could she explain she was not all that sure? Suddenly, wanting to save the world did not seem as enticing as it did before. If she went to West Point she would report in less than three weeks in order to complete six weeks of basic training before the start of fall classes. Certainly the easier option involved staying home and attending Brown University with her boyfriend, a summer full of days at the beach, working an easy job, driving around listening to music too loud—all the stuff teenagers were supposed to do.

"Ladies!" Bill Archer said in an attempt to break up the tension. "This is supposed to be your birthday dinner, Jane, since you are going out with friends tomorrow. Let's just enjoy it . . . shall we?" Always the diplomat, he raised his glass of water toward the center of the table and added, "A toast to all my girls!"

The next morning Jane jumped out of bed, ran to her window, and swept aside the sheer drapery to check if the weather was on her side. "Yes!" she exclaimed and performed a little jig with her arms over her head. The morning sun shone in an endless sapphire sky.

It was Saturday, June 12, her eighteenth birthday. Jane danced from the window to her bureau and leaned over its cluttered surface to assess her reflection in the mirror. With the exception of one tiny blemish on her chin, her face appeared clear. She shrugged the miniscule mark off, thinking the sun would take care of it by the time she met her boyfriend, Nick, for lunch.

She and her friends had made big plans. First, they would take pleasure in a long day at the beach with lunch at Crazy Burger Cafe, then dinner at their favorite fish shack, and lastly, a bonfire show at WaterFire in Providence. She also hoped for some romantic time with her boyfriend, Nick, that day.

She perched on the edge of her bed and slipped on a pair of shorts—cut-off denims—and her favorite tank: this past season's track top, green with her lucky number eleven in white on the back, the one she wore when she won the Rhode Island State Championship for the mile.

Striding over to her desk, she picked up a red marker and put an X through the twelve on the calendar her mother gave her for Christmas. It depicted powerful females throughout history. June featured Artemis with her mighty bow floating in a starry sky. The image gave her a shiver. Ignoring the sensation, she counted the days. Only seventeen remained until she reported to West Point on June 29.

Nostalgia washed over her. She studied her bulletin board and brushed her fingers over the track ribbons. Each item held memories. There were four varsity letters for that year alone—cross-country, soccer, winter track and spring track—along with photos of friends.

She would miss her family, she thought reclining on her bed fiddling with the gold honor tassel from her high school graduation ceremony.

"Only good things ahead," she said out loud. It was the saying her father used whenever she felt daunted before any challenge. It worked every time. But the thought, Am I doing the right thing? still niggled at her. A small voice in her head said, *absolutely*. But, she was not so sure.

She grabbed her backpack, running shoes, and the usual beach paraphernalia, skipped down the staircase, and headed to the kitchen.

"Happy birthday to you, happy birthday to you . . .," her mother sang as she lit a stout candle, set it in the middle of a platter of chocolate chip pancakes and placed it in front of Jane. "Happy birthday, pumpkin!" She smiled her charming smile as Jane called it, revealing laugh lines at the corners of her eyes, and leaned over to give her daughter a hug.

Jane hugged her mom tight and whispered into her shoulder, "Sorry, Mom . . . for last night."

"Nothing to be sorry for, honey." She stroked Jane's long hair. "You girls are my accomplishment. I like to think of the ripple effect of raising two kind and conscientious human beings."

"That's right, Janey." Her father strolled into the kitchen and dropped a thick pile of law books onto the table. "Your mother and I take parenting very seriously. Happy birthday," he said and gave Jane a kiss on the cheek, his beard stubble rough on her face.

"Big case, Dad?" Elizabeth asked her mouth full of pancakes.

"Com'on, Bill. No books at breakfast," Mary scolded.

"Another rape case. Trust me, you don't want to know." Bill ran a hand through messy dark hair. He worked as senior counsel in the district attorney's office in Providence and had seen it all. He tried to keep his work and family separate. "That reminds me . . . Jane, you know our rule about keeping the drinking down when you are in mixed company. I've seen too many nice girls get hurt and the asshole—excuse my French—the perp claims she was drunk and the case crumbles. Promise?"

"Promise. Gotta run." She grabbed a pancake off the platter with one hand and the keys to her dad's old BMW from the Life is Good hook with the other and sailed out the door.

Jane drove around Kingston, picked up four of her girlfriends, and headed east to the beach. She glanced in the rearview mirror at the faces of her friends and imagined how different her life would be in three weeks. She and her friends called themselves the "Power Girls," differentiating themselves from the popular girls. They were members of the National Honor Society and played sports well. They would more likely be found shooting hoops with guy friends, or congregating in the back of the library, than hanging out in the mall. They were not cheerleaders but frequented most varsity sports games hollering encouragements. Their only makeup: mascara and pale lip gloss.

She drove down Ocean Road, all of them singing to Madonna's "Rain" on the radio as Jane searched for the perfect spot to park. *"Raain. Raain. Feel it on my fingertips . . . Here comes the sun,"* they sang loudly, without concern for key. She found a space in the Scarborough Beach lot and pulled in. White car doors flung open and the girls spilled out, carrying on three conversations at once.

Perfect. Low tide.

"You guys set up. I'm going to get my barefoot run in. I'll be back in a few," Jane said and handed her friend, Ashley, the car keys.

When Jane returned from her run, she stripped down to her bikini and gamboled into the water to cool off. She extended her legs out straight, letting her toes stick out of the water, and floated on the undulations until her limbs became numb with the icy cold water. She felt invigorated. By the time she toweled off and reclined on a beach chair, her body tingled with life.

She and her friends sat in comfortable silence, reading, lounging, and soaking in the bone-warming sun of pre-summer.

When Nick Bitterman and a carload of his buddies rolled onto the beach, the quiet lounging turned into a party. They came with balls and Frisbees and a kinetic excitement. After two heated games of beach volleyball, they descended on Crazy Burger like a swarm where they sang "Happy Birthday" to Jane.

This is the best day ever, Jane thought as she dug the remaining french fry into ketchup.

After lunch, back at the beach, Jane let Nick rub sunscreen onto her already pink back. "Ow," she said, but relished the feel of his hands on her skin. Flopping his fit, six-foot frame, down onto the blanket next to her he folded his hands behind his head in pure male repose and squinted into the light. "Hey," he said.

She leaned up on one elbow and imagined tracing the grooves his abs formed with her fingertips. "Hey," she said and leaned over to kiss him. He smelled of sun and onions.

"I have something for you," he said and reached over his head for his discarded jeans and dug into a pocket. His bicep flexed, like a small mountain. Her favorite part on his body was the muscle connecting his shoulder with his upper arm.

She traced this one with her finger, making him jump, and asked, "What's this muscle called again?"

"The deltoid muscle," he said.

"Oh, right." She loved the way it swelled and curved, like a sexy comma.

"Happy birthday!" He handed her a small wrapped package.

She unlooped the pink ribbon, hung it around her neck, and ripped off the paper, revealing a tiny blue velvet box. Inside it was a silver heart pendant. She kissed him again, this time longer. Kissing felt like diving under water where the world is hushed and all of one's senses are heightened at the same time. She could feel the waves within each of them building and swirling together.

"Get a room, you guys," Ashley yelled from the other side of Nick and lobbed a hand full of sand their way. "God . . ."

"Have you thought about tonight?" he whispered, blushing and smirking at the same time.

Jane didn't answer and instead yelled, "Let's go in!" She jumped up and ran toward the water.

Nick followed, grabbed her playfully, and launched them both into the waves. They came up panting and laughing, their eyes wide with the chill. She put her arms around his neck and wrapped her legs around his waist partly to stay warm and mostly because she enjoyed the feel of his arms around her. She hooked her feet behind his back as he carried her through the breaking waves to the place were the water just swelled and sank. They floated, silent for a few minutes.

"You didn't answer me," he said, pretending to pout.

"You know I want to." She nibbled on his wet neck. "Let's see what happens after WaterFire tonight," she said, hoping this would appease him.

———

Later, Jane followed two other cars north on the highway toward Providence while Nick, in the front passenger seat, held the fast forward button down on the car's cassette player. Their destination was WaterFire, a show on the three rivers in Providence. He hit play then held it down again, looking for the right song. Releasing the button he said, "Jane, listen. This is for you."

Sade's creamy voice spilled out of the high quality speakers, "This is no ordinary love, no ordinary love . . ."

"Nick, man, don't tell me you are a romantic?" The deep voice of Nick's friend and teammate, Rob, came from the backseat where he sat with his arm around Ashley.

"Just look at my woman, Rob. I have to bring my 'A' game so she doesn't leave me for any of those Army dudes at West Point."

They parked up on the hill near Rhode Island School of Design and walked in a pack toward the confluence of the three rivers and Waterplace Basin. Hundreds of people gathered and stood along the bridges and around the central basin, part of the Woonasquatucket River, as the sun sank lower. The sky blushed, creating a dome of oranges and reds far above the small city.

Nick led them to stone steps that descended to the water's edge. "This is where the fire-starters come down."

They sat, Jane on the outside, and waited for the show to begin. Music, dreamy and melodic with violins, drifted from large speakers around the basin. Jane sat holding Nick's hand, fingers intertwined. She felt her skin releasing all of the sun it collected from the day into the now cool evening as she rested her head on his broad shoulder.

She felt happy.

When just a hint of pink remained in the darkening sky, the music changed. Deep cellos and a rumble of drums quieted the crowd in anticipation. Jane turned and looked up behind her as a parade of black hooded figures holding flaming torches aloft began to walk right by her down the stairs toward the water's edge. She squeezed Nick's hand.

As drums pounded, members of the procession climbed aboard several large black rowboats. Gliding in dark water they slipped into a circular formation around the rim of the basin. Dozens of torches' flames reflected in the inky water, one figure from each craft ceremoniously lit each brazier. Bonfires leapt, danced, and floated in the dark space. Smoke drifted upward, like wispy spirits, and the air filled with the scent of burning wood.

Heat warmed Jane's face as she stared into the fires, mesmerized. Figures formed and danced within the flames. Scenes, as if history unfolded before her eyes, blinked, flashed, and consumed by the controlled infernos, invoked a multitude of feelings—anger, fear, sadness. Her pulse quickened.

The six hooded figures that had remained standing at the water's edge, turned down their hoods and removed their long capes. They were dressed in medieval garb, five men and one woman with short hair. They drew swords and began to act out a battle.

Adrenaline pumped through Jane. Goosebumps covered her arms. She felt a slipping sideways sensation as the air rippled around her. It appeared as if the woman was going to be killed by the men, and this distressed Jane. The crowd began to cheer for the woman as she rallied and with great mock aplomb defeated the men in a few swift moves. The six medieval characters lifted their swords in the air then bowed to the crowd and began to climb back up the stairs taking their exit. The woman put her hand briefly on Jane's shoulder and without saying a word continued up the steps.

"Wow, that was cool!" Nick exclaimed. "That'll be you, defeating all those men at West Point."

Jane felt bereft of speech. Goosebumps bubbled her flesh. Her mind flitted this way and that, trying to find order out of the experience. The only thing of which she felt certain, and it did not make sense to her, was that Nick would not get what he was hoping for that night. She would step onto the campus at West Point a virgin.

ROUEN CASTLE

WEDNESDAY, MAY 22, 1431

Movement and a slight pressure on my chest startled me awake. There, staring at me, was a corpulent rat. His little black eyes reflected dim morning light and his nose was only inches from my chin. "Argh!" I shouted. The rat appeared as frightened and surprised as I. When I reflexively flinched to brush him off my body, the unyielding metal from my wrist shackles cut into my tender skin.

John Grey's laughter echoed off the walls. "That creature is your breakfast," he said, his voice thick and choppy from too much drink.

"Grey," I squealed. "You'd be good to watch your behavior. I warn you. You shall find yourself taunted by guards in God's prison." I winced from the stinging pain in my wrists. "Mark my words, you will have far worse to fear than little rodents." It was going to be a long day.

Day after day my guards and I stared at the walls waiting. For five months we breathed the same putrid air, shivered with the cold, and now that it was spring, watched each other sweat on warmer days. The metallic smell of all of our sweat made breathing unbearable. I welcomed the reprieve windy days afforded from our collective stench. I can remember leaving on only a few occasions the first few months, limping on weakened, numb legs down the stairs, restricted by chains. Now, they hardly allowed me any movement. If they did not make a determination about my future soon, I would shrink to nothing. My muscles grew weaker and thinner daily.

On this clear and bright spring morning, they dragged me into the room nearest my cell. There, a young monk name Pierre Maurice, with not a whisker, freshly graduated from his studies in theology, read the final report from the University of Paris. I was not sure which details had changed since yesterday.

The hopeful place within me still believed somehow a miracle could change the current course of events. Miracles happened. I watched them happen during our battles. Time and time again, I watched men rise to the occasion and allow the grace of the divine to move them in ways never thought possible. My mind grabbed onto the possibility, but my heart held back. My heart was tired of being disappointed. Rescue seemed unlikely, and the possibility of the University of Paris releasing me felt more remote each day. I reasoned the best scenario, the highest outcome, would be my imprisonment in a convent, guarded by nuns. The thought that I may never be free to walk through a poppy field in spring or enjoy scents brought on by fresh outdoor breezes saddened me. I longed to meander through the oak forest back home to the sounds of chirping squirrels and the hawks' cries as they soared overhead. My mouth watered with the thought of eating one of my mother's hearty root vegetable stews. I wished I could dig my hands into the rich soil again and feel the oily wool bodies of our sheep. I wanted to go home.

Holding the parchment aloft, the young priest read in a righteous, steady voice, "By unanimous consensus, it has been determined that we, members of the Church, must see to it that the undeserved and scandalous undermining of the people of Britain and France, provoked by Jehanne la Pucelle, should cease." He paused, glanced at me with a look of disdain, completely unaware he was slamming the great door of my life shut, and continued, "The following charges have been rendered, and you denied them yesterday. We will reiterate your charges and suggest you consider your fate if you insist on denial." He shot a contemptuous look at me, cleared his skinny throat and continued to read from the scroll. "Her visions were malicious fabrications, and her revelations from evil spirits. Her belief in the voices of her angels and saints bespeaks an error in faith. Her words revealed her to be superstitious, presumptuous, and proud. Her clothing imitated the traditions of idolaters. Her letters to which she added a cross, to indicate that instructions ought not to be followed, were blasphemous and void."

Hmm, I thought. I had no idea that signing a cross rendered an agreement void. Perhaps I could sign the condemnation and abjure by signing the cross. This would give me freedom and not violate my loyalty to my voices in Heaven.

"Her departure from home was a form of disobedience to her parents. Her leap from the Beaurevoir tower is hereby deemed suicidal and against the Church, and her belief God has forgiven her, presumptuous. Her belief that she has not sinned, and her assumption of eternal life, considered rash. Her belief that God and her saints favored France was blasphemy and a sin against the commandment— love one's neighbor—the English. Her statements that her visions were of God and her vow of virginity show that she took illegal oaths and was idolatrous. She holds no understanding of the authority of the Church since she believes she will be judged by God alone."

When the young cleric finished by folding the scroll, Bishop Cauchon flashed me a piercing look, and in his usual condescending tone, rippling with exasperation, spoke, "Jehanne, it is now time to think carefully about this reckoning. Punishments will be inflicted upon you if you don't amend your words and submit to the Church." He took a breath and warned, "If you fail, your soul will be damned to eternal agony and your earthly body will be cruelly destroyed."

I declared, "As I have spoken throughout this trial, I abide by my words and actions." My head began to spin and my legs ached from standing so long in one place. My legs, and my spirit, were weakened. I could give them what they want and be done with it. Probably live the rest of my days in a convent prison. Not such a bad end. Then I remembered all the lies the young priest read. These deeds will be proclaimed all over France and England. All of my work, all of the sacrifice would be for naught. The love and friendships lost. My guilt would discredit King Charles of France, and, worst of all, the people of France, with their tenuous new faith in their country, would lose hope. No! I cannot give in. As much as it pains me, body and soul, I will not slander myself.

"Do you not, then," Bishop Cauchon beseeched, "think that you are bound to the Church Militant, or to anyone but God?"

"If I saw the kindling prepared, the fire lit . . . even if I were consumed by fire, I would not claim otherwise. Until my death, I hold to my words thus far."

The bishop fumed. "Adjourned!" He spat with palpable vehemence.

I began to shake. I shook like I had trudged miles in the deepest snow. Cold seeped into my blood and took hold. Could that be it? Did I just authorize my own death? I felt the warmth drain out of my face and grabbed Grey's arm to steady myself. He opened his mouth to, no doubt, make some demoralizing comment, but took one look at me and put his arm around my waist and lead me the short distance to my cell. He did not say a word. He did not need to; his face said it all. I had seen that look before, so many times, from the king to my captains and men-at-arms. It was the look when mistrust and disdain turned into respect. Warm tears dripped from my cheeks onto his sleeve.

"I am being too stubborn," I said out loud to myself.

"No," he whispered. "They are the ones who lie."

I lay down on the hard bed and closed my eyes. Instantly my cell and guards slipped away and my angels swooped in to comfort me. Their feelings of love washed over my soiled body.

Before delving into the past I decided to attempt to view into the future to see if indeed my memories would be received and understood. My angels assured me that my message would be received.

41

Relieved, I slipped backward into my own past and recalled the day I met my king for the first time.

We arrived in Chinon on Sunday, March 6, 1429. The imposing, fortified city loomed above the countryside and vineyards with its tall, thick walls and dominating towers. One of the king's squires escorted our small party across the Vienne River, up a steep incline, across the drawbridge, and into the castle keep just as the sun slipped below the horizon, leaving a mass of brilliant vermillion and golden yellow behind. The air turned cool. Torches illuminated the cobbled drive in celebratory fashion, a welcome sign. Heat from my horse gave me comfort and helped me to settle down while an intense amount of love from my angels made me tremble—a mix of nerves and excitement.

Michael's voice warmed my heart. *Dearest daughter of God, remember you were made for this moment and the moments to follow. You cannot fail. Listen to our guidance, and the way will be prepared for you. Be ever watchful of those who may not endorse you completely. There is much love for you. Be bold, confident, and above all, enjoy this moment.*

After dismounting, I adjusted the hood of my gray woolen cloak and surveyed my attire: men's hose and doublet. This is perfect, I thought. The dauphin would see me as someone serious about her business.

For years I dreamed of meeting the dauphin, Charles of Ponthieu, who will be crowned King Charles VII of France if I succeed. My heart beat excitedly in my chest, and my hands shook in anticipation. My men and I were guided through the castle to the doors of the great hall. Before the carved chamber door stood a courtly gentleman with the muscular build of a man who clearly partook in the maintenance of his lands. By the looks of his ruddy skin and shoulders as broad as an archer's, he was no mere royal, content to sit indoors and rule from afar.

"Mademoiselle, rumor travels fast." He extended his leg in a respectful bow. "We have been anticipating your arrival. From the looks of you, you had a safe journey. Many royal lords, ladies, and common folk have come to welcome you. If you are who they say you are, we are indeed lucky to be loyal to France and God. I am Louis de Bourbon, Count of Vendôme, at your service."

I curtsied slightly as Catherine de Royer, my friend from Vaucouleurs, had taught me, with as much grace as I could muster. I wanted this count on my side. "Bonjour, thank you for your kindness, I am Jehanne d'Arc. I am here to see the dauphin."

A large, gray stone fireplace warmed the huge room, and the golden glow of torches brightly lit the grand chamber. Women dressed in kirtles made of brilliantly dyed fabrics, their heads covered in coordinating finery, huddled gossiping while the men, with straight spines of the wealthy, debated court business. Conversations ceased when I entered. The dauphin was not visible at first. The back of my neck tingled under the scrutinizing gaze of so many skeptical eyes. The ladies showed obvious disapproval at my choice of men's clothing. Forcing myself to ignore their stinging judgment, my eyes searched the crowded room for the man who had the power to change the course of history: mine and my country's.

They are testing you, Jehanne. The dauphin is dressed plainly as a court member and hides among them. Listen to us and we will guide you to him.

"I take it you are Jehanne d'Arc, the one whom they call la Pucelle, the Maid." One of the royals said and led me by the elbow to another lord sitting on a carved mahogany chair. "Sire, may I present to you Jehanne d'Arc, la Pucelle." He looked at me. "Mademoiselle, the dauphin." I curtsied again, raised my eyes, and said, "Sire, while it is a great pleasure to make your acquaintance, you are not the dauphin."

A low, rolling murmur broke out in the hall. Looking around the room, past the ornately woven tapestries on the wall, past whispering courtiers, I noticed a group of three noblemen off to one side.

There, Jehanne, the man in the green tunic is your dauphin, offered Saint Margaret.

Merci, I thought and walked toward the trio, my heart beating fast in my chest. He stood in the center. Taking a breath, steadying myself, I looked directly at him. He was slender and, upon first glance, did not appear to have the strength of character befitting a king. His pale face and thin frame told me he did not get enough fresh air. "You, sire, are the dauphin." I dropped to one knee in front of him and bowed my head. Gasps and fervent whispers rippled through the room as men and women flocked to our corner.

"Rise, dear girl," he said. In his eyes I saw bewilderment and the flickering of hope.

"My noble Dauphin, God sent me to bring aid to you and to the kingdom. God bless you."

"I am not the dauphin, Jehanne." Pointing to one of the other lords he said, "There he is."

"By God's name, honorable prince, it is you and no other," I blurted. "My gentle Dauphin, I am Jehanne the Maid. I am sent by the King in Heaven who commands that I aid you to be crowned in the city of Reims as King of France."

"How can you be so sure?" The king asked, looking at his subjects for approval.

"I say to you on behalf of the Lord that you are the true heir of France and a king's son." I shot my eyes toward the heavens. "And He has sent me to you to lead you to Reims, so that you can receive your coronation and blessing. That is, if you wish it."

He smiled at me and glanced at his courtiers. "You have passed our first test. How is it you knew it was I?"

"Sire, if you permit, it will be my pleasure to tell you in private."

"That's impossible," an unhappy-looking man to his right growled at me. Georges de La Trémoille, Charles's chamberlain, obviously thought *he* was king. His long nose sat on a face seeming too narrow for his rotund body. He appeared to me a vulture who had recently feasted on an entire army of poor peasants. I shuddered under the heat of his gaze.

"La Trémoille, not to worry; I shall be safe with God's messenger for a few moments. Surely you can last that long without me," Charles chided and excused himself while bidding me to follow him into a small chamber adjacent the hall. Once inside he motioned for me to sit opposite him in a beautifully upholstered chair. The azure-blue velvet fabric felt oddly luxurious after eleven days in a saddle. "Do you need food?" he asked nervously.

"No, sire." I leaned forward to speak intimately with him. "No doubt you have heard much about me. I am here now to speak my own words of conviction to your cause. God wants you to be king."

"How can you be so sure?" He fumbled with the large jeweled rings on his hands.

Tell him he can cancel his plans to flee to Scotland if the siege of Orléans is not lifted in six months, Saint Margaret crooned.

"My voices tell me you have a plan to flee France for Scotland if the siege of Orléans does not lift within six months."

"How could you know of this plan?" he cried, fearful of conspiracy. "Who told you?"

"Sire, I can assure you, your secret is safe with me. My only messenger is the King in Heaven. He knows of your plans and advises you cancel them. You will not need to flee. I will lift the siege of Orléans by early summer and see that your are crowned at the holy Cathedral of Reims by midsummer." My cheeks burned with the intensity of the moment. The presence of numerous angels filled the room. "Close your eyes."

"You are a bold girl. Why should I?"

"Would you like to feel the presence of God's angels so you know I speak the truth?"

He closed his eyes most of the way.

"Now breathe. Relax. Feel the presence of a host of angels all around you. Go ahead, sire; it's all right. Relax."

His shoulders dropped and his breath became even and deep. Color flushed his softening face.

"Can you feel that?" I asked.

He nodded, a look of bliss blessing his gentle face, which before appeared dispirited and discouraged. Tears streamed down his cheeks and dropped onto his tunic. "I have been waiting for seven years, not knowing, wondering my fate. I watched my crazy father and four brothers die. My own mother threatens to claim I am illegitimate. I have been a prisoner of my own fear." He opened his eyes and gave me a look of gratitude. "I feel a sense of relief. Surely, Jehanne, it will take a miracle to lift France out of the sad state she is in."

I leaned back in my chair in relief. He already spoke to me as an advisor and confessor. "God has sent reinforcements; he will lead me and your armies to victory. You will be crowned king in Reims."

"The kingdom has very little money remaining to invest in battle." He became flustered; his eyes darted around the room.

"As for finances, your royal lords will eagerly contribute to the cause of France. The tide has turned, noble Dauphin. But, you should know, I shall last but only one year, maybe more; we must do good work in that year. Three things are laid upon me, to drive out the English from Orléans, to bring you to be crowned and anointed at Reims, and to drive the English out of France."

"You will have to be interviewed by learned men and priests to insure your legitimacy. See if you can win the approval of Georges de La Trémoille, my chamberlain. He is cantankerous and skeptical of any who wish to deal with me."

"As you wish, sire. I bid you not take much time with this questioning as the people of Orléans suffer each day we delay." I stood in response to his movement.

He assigned me a page named Louis de Coutes, and to my relief he escorted me directly to my lodgings in the tower of Coudray. The room's white limestone walls curved with the line of the tower. Its furnishings felt sparse after the opulence of the royal chambers, but to me it was heaven. Louis stoked the fireplace with a firm hand. He stood only three inches above me, but moved with confidence and ease. "There, you should be all set for the evening. I will be right outside your door if you need anything." He beamed, his young cheeks flushed pink with the heat of the fire.

A large four-poster bed held a thick coverlet of embroidered lace, and a creamy cotton nightdress had been laid out for me. A small mahogany wash table and writing desk gave me a sense of welcome.

I slept fitfully, my mind swimming with ideas and events to come. I awoke early with excitement despite a number of confusing dreams in which unfamiliar voices seemed to call at me from beyond, warning me, "Be careful, Jehanne!" I shook off the feeling of foreboding and dressed quickly, pausing only long enough to gaze out the small window. The Vienne River sparkled below, a blue ribbon cutting through the parched ochre fields of late winter. The expansive vista stretched for miles in all directions. Pulling myself from the view, I opened the door and found Louis sitting on the floor dozing. I tapped him gently on the shoulder. "Louis?"

He startled and rubbed his face. "Bonjour, Jehanne, did you sleep well?"

"I did, Louis, merci."

"I would like to show you something you may find interesting." He led me to a small room in the same tower one floor below. Pointing to the wall he said, "Look here . . . at the carvings in the stone." He paused, making sure I could see. "These were made by the Knights Templar who were imprisoned here over one hundred yeas ago."

"Oui, go on." The air smelled dry and stale. Rough symbols were carved into the stone. One depicted a crucifixion, another, a heart with a cross in the center, then a wheel with eight spokes. That must be Saint Catherine's wheel. Next to it, an angel with a staff: Archangel Michael.

Archangel Michael's voice thrummed in my head. *Jehanne, the Templars understood the importance of faith in the unseen. They were part, like Saint Catherine and Saint Margaret, of the chain of men and women infused with spirit and charged with inspiring others by deeds and courage.*

"Merci, Louis, this is most interesting. Why were the Templars here?"

He cleared his throat and stepped back from the confined space. "According to legend, on Friday, October 13, 1307, King Philip IV of France demanded all of the Knights Templar captured in order to avoid paying his debts to them. He accused them of heresy and pressured the pope to arrest all Templar Knights throughout Europe, and then he seized all their holdings. In 1308 sixty high Templar Knights were brought to this tower. It is said the Grand Master Jacques de Molay and Hugues de Pairaud were among those held here."

A wave of anxiety sent my pulse racing. Choking, I scrambled out into the main stairway.

"Jehanne?" Louise asked. "Are you all right?"

"Oui," I lied. "S'il vous plait, continue."

He leaned against the limestone wall and continued the tale. "The Knights pled guilty, thinking the pope would free them, but such was not the case. Later they recanted their confessions and were burned at the stake as relapsed heretics on an island in the Seine River near Par— Mademoiselle, are you all right?"

The walls tilted. I lost my footing and landed on the stair. A feeling of déjà vu flooded over me, and again the sense of warning, which haunted my dreams of the past evening, made me feel queasy.

"Désolé, Louis, I'm fine," I managed at last, hoping I didn't appear weak or of delicate constitution. "That story seemed to have unsettled me somewhat, but I'm fine now."

"Come with me, we will get you something to eat." He continued to tell a steady stream of stories while we wound our way through the maze of hallways back into the main castle. "Louis, can you show me to the king's chamber?" I asked after I swallowed the last crumbs of goat cheese and bread. I felt better— apparently I was hungrier than I thought; food, always my last consideration.

Two guards stood outside the king's chamber door. "Bonjour, mademoiselle, what business do you have with Charles?"

"Bonjour." I squared my shoulders. "My business with the dauphin is God's business and not yours. Let me pass."

"Charles will be out soon. You must wait," the taller one replied, a grin splitting his pockmarked face. He glanced at his compatriot. "Can you believe this? A girl who acts like a man?" They laughed.

I steamed and clenched my fists by my sides. When they did not budge, I lurched forward toward the door. "Do you know who I am?" I yelled, indignant.

Jehanne, remain calm. All is well. Saint Catherine broke through the firestorm in my mind.

"You are keeping me from doing God's work!" I cried and lunged again, only to find the bulk of their bodies blocking the door. I was just about to shove them when the door flung open. Charles's meek face registered confusion at the sight of me, red faced, in confrontation with his guards.

"She is permitted access to me at any time," he declared. "Leave her be."

Today he wore clothing more befitting a king. His tunic, made out of deep green damask with gold stitching, had greatly puffed sleeves over an embroidered silk blouse. His face gleamed as brightly as the sun. The fact that he took more pride in his dress and held himself more regally today was a good sign. My voices told me to help him to believe he was indeed a king.

"Come," he said, walking briskly down the long stone passageway. "I want you to meet someone." After making several turns we found ourselves in a smaller drawing room decorated entirely in red. Tapestries, floor coverings, and elegant draperies were all dyed to match—a deep crimson. It was like being inside a man's heart.

"Who's that?" I asked intensely, noticing a tall thin man standing near the blazing hearth. God, what is wrong with me today? The Templar's story shook me up. I need to speak with more reverence to the man who would be king.

"Jehanne the Maid, this is Jean, Duke of Alençon, my good friend, godfather to my son, and one of my bravest captains." He clapped d'Alençon on both shoulders. "Good to see you are still with us, my friend."

"Are you ready to fight for this man to see him crowned king?" I blurted, taking a step toward him.

"I am." He smiled graciously. "You have much fire, mademoiselle." He took my hand and bowed deeply.

I liked him instantly. Compassion lit his sparkling blue eyes set under a strong forehead and dark brows. There seemed to be depth to him. A feeling of connection, or of meeting him before, swept over me. I smiled and found myself relaxing for the first time in several days.

"I trust the good duke here. You can trust him too. He has been most loyal to me, and like you, Jehanne, seems to hold God's favor. He spent five years imprisoned in Crotoy by the English and has only just returned to us intact. His father died in the Battle of Agincourt."

"Speaking of battles," d'Alençon said and gestured for me to sit down next to him on the divan. "How are your skills at lance and sword?" He spoke to me as an equal; behavior I seldom encountered.

"Milord, I'm afraid I have not much experience in the ways of war. But, I can assure you I am a quick study." His dark wavy hair curled up at the base of his neck, around his ears, and spilled over his lace collar. Though his face appeared gaunt, his pale skin stretched over sharp cheekbones; no doubt the result of a long imprisonment. I thought him handsome.

"Milady, I would be most honored to instruct you." He cleared his throat and tossed a look at Charles, who sat across from us in an ornately decorated scarlet chair. "That is, if you permit, sire?"

"That would be most wise if we will be making war on the English." Charles looked distracted. "Jehanne, you might want to take the duke up on his offer now, because later you will be meeting with several of my advisors and church officials."

After bidding the dauphin adieu, we gathered a few weapons from the armory and d'Alençon led me to an open courtyard ringed with gardens that must be beautiful in their season. We crossed over the gravel path stepped around a boxwood hedge and settled in a diamond shaped grassy area. Picking two weapons from the pile, he handed me a short lance. My brother Jacques taught me a few maneuvers with a similar weapon after my fourteenth birthday. I liked the weight of the staff. The handle, worn smooth, felt good in my hand. He demonstrated a few defensive moves, thrusting and slicing, and I mimicked his movements perfectly.

"You, my dear, are a natural," he commented in between breaths. "You have a surprising ease with your body and limbs. This weapon is primarily used while on horseback, but it is imperative to learn to wield it proficiently on the ground as well."

"Ha!" I jabbed, then twirled the weapon between both hands, and spun around to strike at him again. "I have been working the land, shearing sheep, spinning wool, and many other physically demanding chores since I was a little girl. My body is happiest when it is being of use in some way. I despise being idle," I said, breathless from exertion.

The rhythm of my breath, and the tapping of the lances as they connected, pulsed in my head, helping me to focus. "Ha!" he responded. His movements became more serious and less playful. This pleased me. It meant he considered me a more formidable opponent instead of a mere girl playing.

"Very good." He dropped his weapon, appearing winded, most likely a result of a long incarceration. "Let's see how you handle the broadsword." He picked up two swords with leather-wrapped grips and handed me one. It measured the length of my arm and weighed more than the lance. This weapon sat uneasily in my hand.

After we both broke into a sweat he stopped and smiled at me. "C'est bon. Enough!" he yelled, tossing his sword easily into the pile of weapons. "That's it for today." He dropped to the ground, and a smile lit his face. I sat down next to him to catch my breath and leaned my arms on my knees. "An actual battlefield is a place of chaotic terror with men and weapons coming at you from all sides, each man fighting for his life with all he can muster. It's loud and dirty—blood and body parts all over the ground." He looked at me. "You are very good, but you are still a woman." He paused. "We will make sure to keep you on your horse. There, you will have an advantage."

"Sire, I assure you I will indeed hold my own in battle," I retorted indignantly. "I can be quite fierce myself and I have the protection of the King in Heaven."

"That is good." He grinned. "Even so, I would like to give you the gift of a battle trained destrier. He is one of my best warhorses, trained to trample anything, as strong as an ox and stands at twenty-two hands. He responds to leg commands, so you have the use of your hands in battle."

"Merci beaucoup. I would be most honored to ride him into Orléans in the name of our king." I studied this man who seemed old beyond his years. Perhaps it was from time spent in an English prison.

"We should get you back inside. There are many who wish to speak with you," he said, touching my shoulder gently. "Be on your guard; not everyone has Charles's best interest at heart. There are many who only care about their own skins and will stop at nothing to promote their own agendas. You may count on me as an ally."

Jehanne, you can trust him. He speaks the truth. He will be by your side for much of your journey.

"Sire, your concern is appreciated." I smiled warmly at him as we passed under the archway and back into the shadows of the castle. "Have no fear for my well-being. I possess the wisest counsel of all—my guides in Heaven. Nevertheless, I accept your offer of friendship."

"Jehanne, there you are!" Louis greeted us, breathing hard. "I have been looking for you—everyone's looking for you. Charles's advisors wish to have a word with the legendary maid, to see for themselves the rumors are true."

"Talk, talk, talk! If they would only send me into battle once and for all, our victories would prove everything."

We hastened to yet another drawing room, this one pale blues and creamy yellows. Several men I recognized from last evening—Georges de La Trémoille among others, three churchmen, distinguishable by their robes, and a few nobles—scattered throughout the room. I felt impatient and frustrated.

Angels, why don't they just believe me and send me into battle?

My dear, you must be patient. Play along for the time being. You will be riding into Orléans before you know it. We are with you. Be strong.

"Here she is." Charles stood and escorted me to a blue stuffed brocade chair near the center of the room. "Our newest hope— Jehanne la Pucelle, the Maid, who will deliver France back to her people." He cleared his thin throat and looked around the room. "These learned men have some questions for you before we discuss any war strategies."

"Dear girl, I am Georges de La Trémoille, Charles's chamberlain." He puffed with self- importance. "How can you be sure it's the voice of God you hear?"

"Milord, how do you discern the voice of an enemy from the voice of an ally?" I planted my feet firmly on the carpet and a couple of the nobles chuckled. "My voices have only helped me and no harm has come to me. The voices I hear are Saint Michael, Saint Catherine, and Saint Margaret."

"So, one day you heard some voices and decided to come seek the king's favor?" the bishop of Castres asked. His frown began at his eyes and traveled all the way to his chin.

"Non, Monseigneur, they have been talking to me for four years and bid me to wait until the time was right. At first, I doubted that a simple peasant girl such as myself could make a difference. My voices assured me that the people of France needed to be inspired to deeper faith in God and their country. It is my greatest pleasure to serve the King of Heaven and my country."

"Do you think you alone will lead an army to victory? What skills have you?" I recognized Louis, the Count of Vendôme, who smiled as broadly as his wide shoulders.

"Sire, it is God who will lead each man to victory. As far as skills, I am an excellent rider and adept at lance and broadsword." I wiped my sweaty hands on my hose. "God will take care of the rest."

Smoke from the grand fireplace began to waft into the room. "The weather must be changing," Charles offered. "Perhaps we can continue this questioning another time—"

"Charles, the University of Paris would like to conduct formal questioning," the bishop of Castres said, cutting Charles off. "She needs to be examined physically as well to confirm her maiden status. We begin in two days at the Palais de Justice in Poitiers. Until then, messieurs," he decreed, rising out of his chair. He hardly looked at me, his dislike for this whole business written on his pruned face.

"There will be a banquet this evening in celebration of our new hope," Charles declared. "You are all welcome with your ladies, of course. Jehanne, Louis will take you to my wife's chamber for clothing. I instructed her to find gowns for you to wear. Men's clothing, while appropriate on the battlefield, is not appropriate for a lady at a royal banquet."

"Sire, that is not necessary."

"Oh, but, Jehanne, it most certainly is." He left the room with a flourish, followed by La Trémoille, who whispered in his ear.

As Louis and I left the room a woman approached us. "Jehanne, I am Marie d'Anjou, Charles's wife," she sang warmly. Her petite frame vibrated with excitement. "My husband told me so much about you. You have given him hope. We seldom see his spirits as high as they are today."

"Bonjour, madame, I am honored to make your acquaintance."

She took my arm and led Louis and me through a series of smaller passageways. She walked with short quick steps as her hard-soled shoes echoed tat-tat-tat along the passageway. "I am taking you to my seamstress's quarters, one of the driest rooms of the castle. Fabrics need to be stored in the dark, especially the silks, and of course we need to keep the gold and silver thread safe from thieves." We journeyed through a labyrinth of narrow passageways down into the belly of the castle.

Entering the subterranean room felt like entering a beautiful ocean filled with multihued fabrics that flowed from rods along the windowless walls. Gowns in various states of finish hung on headless forms. This was why the king was out of money for the army. It was all there—a fortune in fabric.

Such lavish gifts were foreign to me. "Merci," I managed to squeak out. "They are beautiful, but truly unnecessary."

"Nonsense, the king requires his courtiers to look the part. You should wear the green velvet this evening—the king's favorite color."

She piled the gowns with matching elaborate headpieces and shoes into Louis's arms and led us back through the maze of hallways to her quarters. "You will allow my chambermaid to bathe you, fix your hair, and dress you, oui?"

"I hardly know what to say. Oui, madame, merci," I stammered and looked to Louis for help, but he only smirked at me. "I am not used to such treatment."

I must confess how I loved the warm bath with scented oils and the lavish sponge massage by the young chambermaid. She spent a long time brushing my hair before she braided it and twisted it up around my ears in the style of the day. Her fine light hair and fair skin reminded me of my sister. As I stepped into the cotton chemise and pants I felt a wave of nostalgia for home. I forced the emotion aside as the maid slipped the green velvet under dress over my head and tied the laces snugly in the back. I slid my arms into the long sleeves of the velvet kirtle fastened with satin buttons just under my breasts. Gold braided cording traveled along the edges of the kirtle, from the high collar all the way to the floor. After she powdered my face, she attached the matching velvet headpiece with hairpins and draped the thin, green, beaded scarf down my back.

She walked me over to the mirror. "What do you think of yourself? You look lovely, mademoiselle."

"Mon Dieu," I gasped, hardly recognizing myself. "What would my mother think? The shoes are not comfortable." I much preferred the soft soles of my suede boots.

"You'll get used to them." She leaned in close and added, "They all do, even though they will ruin the shape of your foot if you wear them too small. These women," she confided, "want to appear as petite as possible so they wear everything too small and too tight if you ask me. But, it's not my place . . ."

The main chamber basked in a golden light while tables were set lavishly around the perimeter of the room. Every table sparkled with crystal glasses and silver plates. Huge platters of food including several meat, fish, and bird dishes, each with a colorful spicy sauce, were carried in together and placed on the splendidly decorated tables alongside baskets of bread. Arrangements of fruit, boards with cheeses, and elegant presentations of sweet pastries filled the hall with a cacophony of smells and aromas.

Red wine bubbled and flowed from a fountain. I heard stories of feasts such as this, but to actually attend one felt overwhelming. This time of year French peasants spent their days sucking on stale bread and counting the days until spring. How odd that the mere luck of birth and location would determine a person's life. I sat between the dauphin and the Duke of Alençon incredulous that the banquet was held in my honor. The room vibrated with the talk, gossip, and laughter of the royal courtiers and advisors, all dressed in brilliantly hued costumes. I hoped all of this was not premature and felt suddenly out of place.

Metz and Poulengy sat across the room making faces and silly gestures. In playful retort I puffed up my cheeks and bulged my eyes.

"What do you think of all of this extravagance, Jehanne?" D'Alençon leaned over and spoke in my left ear. "You look very beautiful. . . . Hard to believe earlier today you were jousting with me."

"Sire, you saw the real me earlier. All this pomp and abundance is strange; right now there are people starving all over France."

"That is true, mon ami, but for now you deserve this little celebration. If what you say comes to pass, we will be dreaming of this night when we lie in the fields under the starry skies planning battle strategies for the next day to the music of our growling bellies. Come on, enjoy this feast; many of the spices come from far away."

Jehanne, we wish for you to enjoy the celebration. My saints said together.

"Only because you ask, d'Alençon." I was hungry after nearly a fortnight on the road, and since we arrived in Chinon, my nerves had kept me from consuming too much. Once I managed the long slit sleeves of my gown, I ate everything on my plate. The food, wine, and company put me at ease. Though we only met that morning, I knew in my heart Jean and I would be good friends. Since I had gone so long without a confidante and friend, I knew instantly when one came across my path. Knowing he had a wife helped me to feel more comfortable; there would be no romantic temptations.

The court musicians moved me to tears when they performed a song my papa played on his mandolin when I was a little girl. Could it be I left home only two months ago? It felt like two years. Life, though challenging at home, flowed organically with the seasons. I always knew what was expected of me. This life—so different.

"Jehanne, are you all right?" my new friend asked, concern darkening his eyes.

"D'Alençon, I am an innocent here; I don't belong." I swept my arm, indicating court life, and turned my head toward him so no one could see my tears. "What will happen to me in Poitiers?"

D'Alençon took my hand under the table and said, "Ever since I spent time in an English prison my sense of events has become very sharp. I get an instant feeling about things." The touch of his solid hand in mine sent warmth straight into my heart. "I believe you are exactly who you say you are and more. Your humility keeps you from seeing your own grace and glory. Jehanne, you will win them over in Poitiers and then you will indeed inspire our army to victory." He searched my face for a response. "I promise to help as long as you wish it."

I squeezed his hand, too moved for words, nodded, and smiled while the tears streamed down my cheeks. Luckily, many of those around us were too absorbed in their own dramas to notice our emotional exchange.

562 Years Later

June 1993

Jane found it surprisingly difficult to sit in the hairdresser's chair. She gripped the armrests and watched the stylist's reflection in the large mirror as she braided Jane's long hair and then reached for the sharp scissors. Jane tensed while each cutting edge was wiped dry and winced as the shiny blades sliced easily through her hair. She had worn it long ever since she was a little girl.

"Here you go, Jane," the hairdresser said and handed her a fourteen-inch length of braided hair. A clear rubber band at the top and bottom, held Jane's light brown locks. The braid reminded her of the story of Samson. Did he not get weaker from the severing of his hair?

As she tenderly stroked the braid in her hands she realized all things familiar seemed to be mutating away. The feelings reminded her of a snake shedding its old skin, and she wondered if the snake's new skin felt raw or hypersensitive like hers. Though, underneath the superficial worry, a sense of purpose enlivened her body. She felt as if she stood at the edge of her destiny, a vast canvas yet to be painted.

She studied her new reflection in the decorative salon mirror. Familiar copper eyes stared out of a stranger's head. Her new coiffure turned under slightly just at her ears with a stylish layered wedge in the back. She wished she had her mother's movie star bone structure. Just dab some soot on my chin and cheeks and I could pass for a Dickens character with this bobbed haircut, Jane thought.

"Oh, Jane, you look très chic!" her mother exclaimed and ran a gentle hand over Jane's hair.

"Thanks, Mom. I look like a little English boy."

"You're being too hard on yourself. You are as beautiful as ever."

"I don't think my hair matters much as we'll wear hats all the time." She thought Nick would hate her new hairstyle. Though it did not matter what he thought as she had broken up with him the week before. While she waited for her mother to pay the hairstylist, Jane remembered the last time she spent time with Nick.

He had orchestrated a date in the small barn on his parent's property—their favorite make-out place. The memory of their passion made her blood warm. Jane blushed right there in the salon. He had given her one red rose, set up a little picnic on the floor of the barn, and even lit a candle. It all ended suddenly when he ardently forced himself upon her. She had said no and needed to shove him hard in order to stop his maneuvers. As he lay there panting she blurted out, "I can't believe you almost did that to me. We are over!"

She drove home that night shaking. He had called several times since, but Jane could not bring herself to call him back.

Sadness still held her heart and enticed her to pray for the swift passing of the next two days until she reported to West Point. Memories of his deep voice and the way his muscular arms felt around her waist snuck into her mind at the oddest times.

After two nearly sleepless nights, a three and a half hour drive westward through Connecticut, and bear hugs from her family at Army's Michie Stadium, she entered the world she had imagined for so long: West Point—where brave leaders were made.

It was R-Day, registration day; the day the new cadets, all eleven hundred of them, arrived, hopes as high as the late June sun, to begin their lives at West Point. Collectively they would be called the class of 1997.

Later that morning, Jane stood in Arvin Gymnasium, a four-hundred-thousand-square-foot athletic complex, in her newly issued black gym shorts and white T-shirt and fiddled with the tag that hung from her waistband, which delineated all of the tasks and stations she would visit that day. Jane felt excitement as she pondered the list. There was so much to learn and she felt thrilled.

"Welcome to 'Beast Barracks,' New Cadets," a menacing cadet announced to the nervous crowd. He was all squares—angular head, shoulders. "You may have been the president of your high school class, captain of the football team, queen of the prom, or any number of things." He paced back and forth, clearly enjoying his moment of power. "You are now NOTHING. You are plebes in the United States Army. You will approach and address each cadet in the red sash with the following statement: "New Cadet X reports to the cadet in the red sash as ordered," he bellowed.

He looked at the new cadets like something he scraped off his shoe. "You will go through a series of physical fitness exams. You will learn how to march and salute and many other things you must memorize before the day is over." He paused and glowered at them, cleared his thick throat and continued, "There are only four phrases you are allowed to utter in public anywhere on campus. They are: 'Yes, sir or ma'am.' 'No, sir or ma'am.' 'No excuse, sir or ma'am.' And 'Sir or ma'am, I do not understand.' I never want to hear you utter the last one. That one is reserved for emergencies only and is highly frowned upon."

"New cadets! Line up over here!" bellowed another upperclassman with a red sash whose muscles bulged out from under his white short-sleeved dress shirt.

Jane, now New Cadet Archer, felt an expanded sense of purpose as she marched—no more sauntering, strolling, or lollygagging— around campus in her gym outfit, black ankle socks, and black leather shoes. Her grandmother would call the shoes sensible, she thought, as she stood in yet another line in the sun-drenched quad in the middle of campus that comprised of a collection of granite buildings, set on the west bank of the Hudson River. It was a place that invoked feelings of fairytale majesty and castle-like awe. Even the dazzling summer sun seemed to cast its spell on the grass of the central plain, the main parade field, making it appear greener than any other grass.

Standing in line and inching forward this time to learn how to salute, she swiveled her head around to take in and survey her new fascinating surroundings.

"New Cadet . . . no moving! That includes your head."

Not daunted in the least, she continued her survey by only moving her eyes. Out of the corner of her left eye an arched tunnel running through one building was partially blocked by a suspended, spiked gate that looked like a prop from a movie set in medieval times. Note to self, thought Jane, we will not be going that way. Out of the corner of her right eye she could see how the imposing stone six-story dorms, called barracks, met at angles and formed the large quad in which so much activity was taking place. Sun reflected off the tiny mica specks in the granite adding a magical allure to the setting. Hundreds of new cadets stood in differing lines dressed exactly like Jane waiting for some kind of scolding.

Jane heard "Step up to my line!" belted out over and over again all around her. Each cadet in the red sash spoke the same commands with his chin held high, shoulders back, spine straight, in perfect military posture.

In one such line she watched as new cadets were instructed how to turn right and left with a nifty pivot move. Four of her new classmates attempted the move. They took two steps, pivoted and bumped into one another. One unfortunate soul mixed up his right from his left, and as a result Jane could almost see the freshly cut hairs on his head flattening down with the verbal haranguing he received from the cadet in the red sash.

Once she completed each station in the quad she was escorted to her barracks. She lugged her OD-green sack filled with fatigues, dress clothes, and other paraphernalia, into her new room and dropped it onto the spotless floor. Two other girls stood chatting animatedly over their piles of clothing.

"Hi. I'm Jane Archer."

"Hi. I'm Tara Fiorello," the shorter one said and smiled broadly.

"Sophia Michaels," the taller one said extending a hand.

Sophia stood at least four inches taller than Tara who appeared to be similar in height to Jane. Tara and Sophia each had their own unique beauty. Tara's skin was olive and judging by her dark almond-shaped eyes, Jane guessed she was either Italian, Spanish, or both. Sophia was as white as they come with round blue eyes and looked more like a model than a soldier. Jane felt plain by comparison. Together, they agreed to let Sophia have the single bed, while Jane and Tara would take the set of bunk beds.

"We need to get all of this stuff," Sophia said indicating their large duffle bags, "organized into drawers and hung according to this diagram." She shook the paper in her hand. "And, we need to report back outside in twenty minutes for lunch."

Tara chuckled. "My mother would be laughing her head off. It would often take me an entire day to clean my room at home."

Sophia and Jane giggled and nodded.

"We better get moving then," Jane said.

Lunch in the mess hall won the "I can't believe it" award for the day. It took every ounce of her strength to hold her mouth closed when she passed under the lintel of the gigantic double doors of the mess hall. Washington Hall housed six colossal wings all with vaulted, dark-beamed ceilings and leaded glass windows. It was like stepping back in time to the castle of the wealthiest of kings. Each wing hosted sixty or so tables all lined up perfectly, each linen-topped table laden with a cornucopia of food. However, there was a price for this culinary decadence—rules, lots of them. Eating became an exercise in control, an art every cadet aspired to master. Jane wondered how she was going to consume the recommended four thousand calories per day.

It only took her a few minutes to get the hang of eating while sitting up ramrod straight with her body a fist's distance from the back of the chair and a fist's distance from the table. She focused her eyes on the center of the table as instructed—learning the art of peripheral vision—and managed to devour a burger, fries, a helping of lasagna, and a slice of Martha Washington sheet cake in less than twenty minutes. She realized that even her eyeballs would be stronger after a few weeks at West Point.

———

The next couple of weeks raced by with a flurry of activity: marching, eating, running, physical fitness exams, more running, memorizing army facts, more eating, room inspections, one-minute showers, and five a.m. wake-up calls. By the third week, training entailed obstacle courses and the army's more intense version of team-building activities in the forest, designed to stretch, pull, and tug the new cadet into a fit and tidy soldier.

Three weeks into basic training, summer heat penetrated into the forest with little breeze. Jane lugged her thirty-pound backpack with her M-16 rifle slung over her right shoulder. Sweat ran down her forearms, dripped off her elbows, and dropped onto the dirt path. Sun flickered through the tall oak, maple, and pine trees, and the scent of pine floated on rare hot breezes.

Kaye Michelle

"Left . . . left . . . left, right, left," they chanted, marching in rows two by two, their voices echoing through the forest.

"Whoa, whoa, whoa, used to date a beauty queen," the collective voices of the plebes cut through the silence of the woodland. "Now I date my M-16 . . . whoa, whoa, whoa." At the words, Jane shot a smirk sideways at Tara, who marched beside her. Tara laughed out loud in the middle of the chant causing her squad leader, cow/junior, Mark Sullivan, to jog up beside them. He gave them a playful scowl, wrinkling his lightly freckled forehead. His good nature helped his squad progress through the challenges of the last few weeks. Many of the other squad leaders scowled and hollered all the time.

"Took away my faded jeans, now I'm wearing Army greens," Tara and Jane sang pretending to be serious. Sullivan nodded at them, gave them a wink, and dropped behind. The ground vibrated and rumbled with unified footsteps, and the air rang with the voices of eleven hundred fledgling soldiers.

Jane loved chanting while they marched; the cadence of the music added energy to her movements, and the sounds of their voices gave the feeling of cohesion to the small army. It took them a couple of hours to reach their destination, another physical-challenge course.

"Archer, you're up," Sullivan said. He stood close behind her on the small platform anchored to a large oak tree. They were thirty feet off the ground.

Jane swayed, feeling the subtle effects of vertigo tricking her eyes. She blinked to bring the board into focus. It was nailed to a large log connecting her platform with another, twenty feet away. It may as well be a mile, Jane thought. She hated heights.

Several feet below her hung a safety net but it appeared to have the strength of her great-grandmother's hair net. Beneath the flimsy ropes stood her squad mates. "Come on, Archer! Whoop! Whoop!" they chanted.

She wiped sweat from under her eyes and put her hands on her hips as she assessed the situation. Come on, Jane, one step at a time, and it will be over in a snap, she coached herself. She much preferred

64

some of the other obstacle course challenges, and would even take low crawling in mud over anything to do with heights.

"Archer, this isn't like you. Where's our fierce soldier girl?" Sullivan asked. His voice gave her the courage to go for it.

She took a breath, lifted her chest, and brought her back molars together with determination. She felt lucky to have a squad leader like Sullivan and loved to make him proud. So far Beast Barracks, Cadet Basic Training, had felt easy. She enjoyed the order, the physical demands. She loved being part of a big team, moving and marching as one unit. Up until this moment she seemed to sail through all of it.

Jane lifted her arms like a tightrope walker at the circus and began to walk. Carefully, she put one foot in front of the other on the beam. They said it was a two by six board, but it could not have been six inches. Five maybe. Or, even four and three quarters. The ground floated far below her.

She counted to keep her mind from derailing her. Three. Four. Five. Six. She wobbled then caught herself by pinwheeling her arms. She took another breath and marveled at the sensation of suspension; she could be a squirrel scampering across a branch. A crow called nearby, and the brilliant summer sun cast kaleidoscopic geometric patterns in the air around her.

Seven. Eight. OK, halfway. A breeze picked up, swaying the branches of the surrounding trees. Light and dark shadows moved across the log and put it in motion.

She fell.

Everything slowed. She had to fight to determine which way was up, like she was tossed by an ocean wave. Down. Down. It seemed to take a long time before she landed on the net. But she only rested there for a second. She bounced and felt the weightlessness and disorientation of being airborne once again.

Then it all went black and a feeling of softness surrounded her. She floated and felt held in the arms of the comforting dark universe.

"*Jane . . .*," a female voice whispered to her from the darkness. A hint of a form came into view then faded away. The voice called again, "*Jane . . .*"

"Archer! Archer! Are you with us?" Sullivan's southern accent commanded from far away. At first, Jane wanted to block out Sullivan's voice and focus upon the sweet beckoning, but pressure on her chest pulled her back to her body lying on the forest floor.

Jane lay on her back looking up into the filtered sunlight through the canopy of the trees and into the concerned faces of her squad buddies Tara Fiorello, Alex Raphael, and Patrick Ash.

"Give her some space," Patrick said and shoved Alex aside. At six foot two inches, Alex stood several inches taller and weighed a good thirty pounds more than Patrick. It was Alex's good nature that prevented him from resisting.

Jane attempted to talk but could not catch her breath. Pain ripped through her back, and it felt as though giant hands squeezed the thin bones of her rib cage. She gasped and stiffened in alarm. Breath would not come. She bolted upright and pounded her hands on the ground.

"You're OK. You're OK." Sullivan tried to sound confident but Jane could hear concern around the edges of his words. This frightened her. He gave her a smack on the back. "You had the wind knocked out of you, that's all."

The restriction released all at once and allowed her to take a burning breath. Tears threatened but she blinked them back. She felt completely dazed and disoriented. "Oh, shit" was all she could say.

"Here, try to stand," Patrick said and grabbed one of her outstretched arms. His round face flushed with sincere concern and his dark almond eyes, his inheritance from his Vietnamese mother, twinkled over high cheekbones. Jane caught herself staring at Patrick until tall, lanky Alex grabbed her other arm and together they hoisted Jane up to her feet. Tara hovered around them like a nervous mother, her dark eyes filled with worry.

"You were magnificent. Flying through the air. You bounced off the net and landed . . ." Alex couldn't even finish he was laughing so hard. He laughed until Tara punched him in the shoulder.

"Jeez, Raphael!" Tara said. "Shut up. . . . Give her a break."

"That's enough, New Cadets," Sullivan bellowed and stepped between them. He turned to Jane. "Archer, get some water." Casting dark eyes around the group of eleven he asked, "Who's next? Raphael, I believe you're on deck. Get up there."

"Sir. Yes, sir," Alex snapped. As he climbed up the ladder, he waited until Sullivan turned his back and then flipped up his middle finger at Tara. She did not flinch in the slightest, and instead gave him a cool stare-down.

For Jane, it felt good to feel the dirt of the forest floor under her feet. She took a deep pine-scented breath and pulled her canteen out of her pack. Shake it off, Archer, Jane said to herself and spent the rest of that afternoon focused on supporting and cheering on her squad mates.

That evening Jane lay on her narrow army bed with a cool washcloth over her forehead and allowed herself time to review and sort out what happened earlier that day. Falling had felt surreal. She willed herself not to think of the voice in the dark and reasoned that she may have hit her head on the way down. Either she suffered from a mild contusion or the cumulative stresses of basic training were getting to her.

A wave of exhaustion hit her. She imagined her life back in Rhode Island, and how if she were home she would be helping her mother with the preparations for the annual family reunion. Tears threatened and she allowed them to flow. This would be the first summer she missed the reunion and all of her cousins, aunts, and uncles at the shore. Jane's tearful release triggered a similar signal to her tired body. Muscles taut for weeks from physical effort began to let go and rest upon sore bones. Turning onto her side, she curled her knees up to her chest and fell into a turbulent sleep.

Just as Jane predicted, over the course of her plebe year, her first year at West Point, she transmuted into a higher functioning version of herself. She became honed and polished. Her dreams and aspirations became more pragmatic, practical. Her sharpened mind and physical strength gave her a deep, unshakable confidence. In a quiet hopeful way she wondered what the future held.

ROUEN, FRANCE

THURSDAY, MAY 23, 1431

Lying flat on my cot, while all three of my guards picked at their disgusting teeth, I realized that fear spreads faster than disease. It lands silently on doubt, rooting there. It spreads rapidly, choking out all hope and faith. Our greatest enemy is not the plague. The most insidious adversary of our time is fear. The contagious aspect of fear, like disease and pestilence, escapes no one, regardless of rank, status, or religious standing.

These "men of God" claimed to be purveyors of grace, in God's favor. However my experience of them was unbridled fear. The desire for power, in an attempt to hide the fear or the perverse thrill of instilling fear into others, seemed to be one of the fruits of the Holy Catholic Church. I am shocked, cut to the bone. This wound, I feel more deeply than the flesh wounds of battle.

I realized that I must fortify myself continually against this "fear of God." What have we created? How is it that the most beautiful and faith-filled men do not rise to inspire, but instead are held down, ridiculed. It is not God these men of cloth worship. They worship power over the hearts and lives of men and women, feeding them a false sense of safety. I have more respect for the foul-mouthed warrior, willing to lay down his life for God and country, than these pampered weaklings who fearfully hold God's shield in front of their hearts. They have no idea what it means to serve God, to act in God's name. The lowly peasant, offering his last loaf of bread to the ill neighbor, is closer to God's breast than the fur-cloaked pompous bishop, afraid of his own shadow, trusting no one.

Oh what I would do, what I could do, if I were not in this stinking prison. I have seen what many have not. My faith in those ruling our nations has been crushed, dashed like a lost ship in a storm upon the rocks of an inhospitable shore. I would much sooner negotiate the unsteady waves of the life of a simple village peasant than attempt to live with integrity among the wealthy royals. While Mother Nature can be harsh, she is not vindictive, scheming, or self-concerned. If life is to be a struggle for all of us, I much prefer the struggle of nature to the struggle of power. Conceit hides behind every beautifully woven tapestry hanging in ornate cavernous rooms. Intrigue, they eat for breakfast, lying, for midday meal, and they quenched their thirst with the blood of their brothers. Fear sits in the mortar, oppression in each stone of these magnificent castles, built upon the suffering of men.

"God, don't you see these boastful bigots?" I whispered to the dark wooden beams of the ceiling. "Why do you not strike them down? I don't understand!" Again tears dropped from the outer corners of my eyes onto my rigid bed.

God, this causes me grief I cannot begin to express. My chest feels like it's splitting apart with the falsity of your representatives. I am disheartened, disillusioned, and beaten. I cannot play this game they want me to play, and neither do I want to. They appear foolish, all those men against little me. I walk into the chamber where they sit smug and fat-faced, and their fear assaults me in waves, nearly knocking me over. What a charade.

My heart is beginning to feel hate for the bishop and this terrifies me, God! Fear snuck into my open doubting places and found a home. Fear took hold within my breast because I let it in through the door of hate and judgment. "I judge these men in defense of you, my God in Heaven," I whispered, gritted my teeth, and craned my neck to see a patch of sky through the narrow window. "Oh, angels, please talk to me," I said into the cool morning air.

My dearest child, please do not worry about your heart for it will always be pure.

With the sound of Archangel Michael's etheric voice my body relaxed.

It is merely the part of you building a defense inside that feels the hatred. Stay strong, dear child, for you are creating change by sitting in this prison. Have faith in men that they will understand your example. It may not happen as you wish, or as quickly as you wish, but rest assured this trial will be known. Their falsities, their ignorance, and their fear will be understood by more people than you can imagine. Continue to keep us close and rest in the comfort of the infinite love you hold within your own body.

John Grey, who had fallen into a restless sleep, shifted his position, snorted and swatted a fly away from his nose.

Your suffering will be an inspiration to those who hear of you, your unwavering faith, and your willingness to trust your heart and your creator even six hundred years from now. Women then will be treated more fairly by men.

Allow yourself to feel the light with your physical heart. Let it expand and fill you. This is your surest defense against fear and manipulation for power. Let the light radiate into the hearts of those in the future and allow your memories and wisdom to travel with the light. Your suffering will be over soon. Continue to trust the plan. Not only Saint Catherine and Saint Margaret, but I and all the angels, are with you always. Your soul is safe, child. I hold it myself. No sword or word, nor any amount of fear or betrayal, can harm you. In reality you are undying and unborn, limitless, boundless. You are an angel sent to earth to bring about a change. Men do not change willingly. Take heart, dearest one. We are always with you.

"Thank You!" I mouthed to the heavens and allowed myself to drift off to sleep where I remembered my journey and the hopeful beginnings of my mission with Jean d'Alençon. I allowed myself to slip and tumble back through time to the days that felt filled with dreams of the future. It was Friday, March 11, 1429, Jean d'Alençon accompanied Louis and me on the thirty-mile journey south to Poitiers, with the dauphin's entourage, through small towns and villages where people gathered to cheer us on.

Upon my friend's advice I used the ride as an opportunity to practice using my legs instead of the reins to control my new horse. My mistakes were humorous. We laughed often. In an attempt to get my horse to move forward, I squeezed with my knees instead of my lower legs and my horse moved backward. Laughter, a welcome break from the serious business of trying to convince idle men of my faith in God.

We arrived in the late afternoon just as a steady rain began to fall. Louis led me to a house within the town belonging to Parliamentary Advocate-General Jean Rabuteau. As usual, I felt ill at ease at first. His wife, a loquacious chubby woman with milky white skin, welcomed me with open arms and eagerly showed me around her home. "We are so very happy to have you stay with us. Indeed it is an honor. Please let me know what I can do for you to make your stay more comfortable. Are you hungry? Would you like some food?" She talked and bustled around in equal measure. I wondered why this woman was not thinner with the amount of extraordinary energy she put into conversation and hosting.

The next morning, with Louis and d'Alençon by my side, I attended church at St. Peter's Cathedral with its sweeping white stone arches. The cathedral was the inspiration and vision of Eleanor of Aquitaine's a few hundred years before, which added to the allure and contributed to the grandeur and majesty of the building. If she could create something like this, I could certainly stand firm in front of my inquisitors. We kneeled up near the front in the almost empty church. Dearest angels and saints in Heaven, please I bid you, come to me now. Imbue me with strength and wisdom. I called upon

Archangel Gabriel, the newest addition to my angelic retinue, and specifically asked for help with my words and requested additional insights into the matters at hand. I prayed in earnest. A white mist of love and peace descended upon me and swirled around my body and those of Louis and d'Alençon.

"Ahh," gasped d'Alençon. He looked at me, his blue eyes swimming with emotion. "I can feel them. They are here, aren't they?"

I nodded.

Thank you, dearest angels, for sending me this loyal friend who understands me and holds the capacity for the understanding of spirit, I prayed.

He indeed will be a loyal friend and brother in arms for you. Dearest daughter, you have done well. Allow your body to relax and let us fill you with our presence, inspiration, and love.

After several minutes, Louis began snoring next to me. He must have been exhausted to fall asleep on his knees. I tapped d'Alençon on the arm and whispered, "We need to go."

For my first examination, Yolande, the Duchess of Anjou, queen of Sicily and Charles's mother-in-law, gathered a number of educated women to examine me and validate my claim of maidenhood. We had met for the first time at the banquet, and again, I was struck by her beauty for which she was well known.

It felt embarrassing and uncomfortable to be naked in a room filled with women bearing witness to this important examination, but I also knew I was in good hands with Yolande. She stood regally next to two stern looking women, my examiners. If they ruled against me, my entire campaign would be null, as my premise rested upon the fact that I was the virgin maid from Lorraine, like the legend. The legend predicted a maid from the Lorraine region of France would end the one-hundred-years war between Britain and France.

"Have you ever let a man touch you or kiss you with desire?" the buxom one asked, none too kindly.

"Never!" I blushed, remembering the scene in the barn with my brother. They laid me out on the hard floor on a piece of white silk and began exploring my body with their cold hands. Each of their faces serious, their mouths set with the importance of their task, their air and demeanor cool.

"She is intact!" the woman declared. Chatter swept around the room. "Shhh! We are not complete yet!"

"I concur," the second stern woman announced. "She is intact and a virgin. You may get up and dress, Jehanne."

Spectators, buzzing with conversation, spilled out onto the street like bees leaving a hive.

Later that morning at the appointed hour, I entered the great hall, Palais de Justice, on the arm of the dauphin. Parliament and many esteemed and learned theologians, experts in church doctrine and political advisors, assembled, waiting for us in the cavernous building. Above us loomed a vast wooden-beamed ceiling supported by white limestone walls with graceful arches embossed along the length of the space now packed with spectators, royals, and common folk. Eleanor of Aquitaine inspired the creation of this magnificent hall as well as St. Peter's Cathedral. I hoped, since these proceedings were taking place in a building inspired by a woman, it would bode well for me.

I searched the crowd for my friend Jean d'Alençon and found him standing opposite me against the far wall. He caught my eye and smiled. The opening talks of propriety and "usual this" and "customary that" were lost on me. My mind did not grasp a single word until they were directed at me. The archbishop of Reims, Renault of Chartres, introduced some of the priests, judges, and lawyers, and it seemed he took a very long time. Some of the names included the bishop of Castres, Master Pierre of Versailles, the king's confessor Gérard Machet, Simon Bonnet, bishop of Senlis, and the bishops of Maguelonne and of Poitiers. One of the lesser priests was a jovial looking Dominican friar named Seguin.

"Jehanne la Pucelle, d'Arc, can you tell us how you came to be here and why you came to the king?" the bishop inquired, rolling each word out of his mouth with a flourish.

"Oui, Monseigneur, I came at the bidding of the King of Heaven. My saints first came to me when in my family's garden about four years ago. They told me God had great pity for the people of France. The love from the voices often made me weep for joy. For some time, my counsel advised me to go to Vaucouleurs to seek the support of a captain who would help me gain an audience with the dauphin. Now I hope you good men will grant me permission to travel to Orléans to lift the siege for God and France."

Friar Seguin asked kindly with a thick accent from the south, "My dear, why do you call the king the 'dauphin' and not the 'king'?"

"He won't be called king until he is crowned and anointed at Reims," I answered as plainly as I could. Some of these questions seemed superfluous to me.

Friar Seguin smiled and looked at his fellow judges, some of whom quickly jotted notes. More questions were asked, and I answered as I had so many times before. The bishop adjourned the examination around noontime. He decreed that we would meet at the same time the next day for more questioning. I stood to leave, wondering just how many days these proceedings would take, when many of the spectators descended upon me to ask questions and blocked my exit from the hall. Panic rose, constricting my throat. Archangel Michael can you help free me from this mob? Suddenly a small commotion erupted on the outside of the crowd.

"Pardon, pardon." The voice of d'Alençon broke though the din of the crushing crowd.

"D'Alençon, I am here." I raised my hand up in the air so he could find me. The crowd continued to push, taking my breath away.

"Dear people, s'il vous plait, allow the lady some space; clear away!" he implored, trying to forge a path to me. The crowd began to peel reluctantly aside. When he got to me he put one arm around my waist and pushed the remaining spectators away. "Come." He dragged me by the arm to the back of the building where his horse stood waiting. "Hop up, quickly before they find you."

I did as he commanded, and he mounted in the saddle behind me while I grabbed onto the long red mane of the horse to steady myself. Since he used the stirrups, I had to squeeze the horse with my legs to stay on. Reaching around me he grabbed the reins and with a "Ha!" we were off galloping through the busy streets. He veered to the right off the main thoroughfare and headed toward the outskirts of town.

"Merci, mon ami!" I yelled into the wind, relieved to be outside in the fresh air, away from the crowds and judging faces.

"My pleasure!" he yelled back into my hair. "You were great in there!" He took his left hand off the reins and encircled my waist with his arm and held me tight.

I leaned back into him still holding onto the horse's mane. It surprised me how much I enjoyed this closeness as we settled into a steady gallop. I could feel the muscles of his thighs contracting against my backside as he maneuvered the horse. We headed over a small bridge into the countryside, past blanched fields, silent sprawling vineyards, and distant farmhouses. Our breath coordinated with the landing footfalls of the horse in a heady rhythm. We moved as one, into the forest, a beautiful, silent, pine-barren forest. The horse's hooves landed more quietly on the carpet of pine needles. I leaned my head back onto d'Alençon's chest, and he rested his cheek against my head. Time seemed to slow down as my heart expanded with the heat in my body.

What's happening to me? We rode not talking, not wanting to break the spell encircling us. Nothing existed but our breath, our bodies, and the steady cadence of the horse. The sun slid in and out of the clouds as the trees floated by. Is this what love feels like? I felt intoxicated. He squeezed me tighter, and I pressed my body back into his. He released his other hand from the reins and hugged me deliciously to him as he kissed my hair. This . . . can't be . . . right.

My entire body seemed to be on fire, a wonderful consuming yearning. I could hardly stand it and wanted more at the same time. I wanted to melt into him. Is this love?

"Chérie," he crooned into my ear.

Trees whizzed by, and it seemed the entire world fell away. Strange feelings mesmerized me. This must be love, I mused. My body pulsed with a new aliveness.

How can I love him? I can't possibly. I remembered my vow to God and my mission. Guilt arrested the bliss. I felt torn between *this* love and my love and commitment to my mission. How could I jeopardize the tenuous relationship I built with the dauphin? God, don't do this to me.

"Stop d'Alençon! Stop the horse please!" I cried, tears blurring the trees. A sob welled up inside of me.

"What's wrong, Jehanne? I thought . . ."

I jumped off the horse. "Non! God, why are you doing this to me now?" I screamed out loud and ran into the forest a few yards, then dropped to my knees with sobs that shook my entire being. My heart felt like it was tearing from my chest.

"Chérie, don't cry." He dropped to his knees in front of me and placed his hands on my shoulders. "It's all right."

"Non, it's not all right," I choked out between sobs. "We can't fall in love, not now, not here. Why would God play this cruel joke?" I looked at him, marveling at his handsome face. "Have I not been faithful and devout? Have I not given up everything to do this work?" I shook my fists in the air. "Why?"

"I don't know." He hugged me close and stroked my hair. "Shh, shh, all will be well," he crooned in my ear. "Call on them now. Ask them what we must do."

"Non. Non. Non." Anger took over where the grief had been.

"Go ahead," he urged. "Ask them for help. Here sit down."

"Perhaps you're right, " Reluctantly, I took a breath and sighed. "Angels, we need your help. Will you please explain to us what is happening?" Instantly I felt their presence. Fresh tears began to flow.

D'Alençon took my hand. "I can feel them," he whispered.

Dearest daughter, we hear your cries and fully understand your distress. This is part of the plan. You see, the love your friend is inspiring in you, is needed for the success of your mission.

I don't understand. I'm supposed to be a virgin.

He, darling girl, is showing you how much love you have inside of you. The love you feel from him is your love being reflected back. His feelings for you help you unlock the love so you may become a beacon of inspiration for the people of France. Jehanne, your beacon will shine so brightly people far into the future will see your light.

What does this mean? We can't possibly have a man/woman relationship.

No, you will not have a physical relationship. This, dearest one, is the hard part and will take much strength from both of you. Your love will grow and you will allow it to open your hearts to the people. Look at your ring, the one your father gave you.

My ring?

Yes, notice the markings Jhesus-Maria. This is not the Virgin Mary but Mary Magdalene. Mary played the role d'Alençon is playing for you. She helped Jesus mirror the tremendous love back out to the people so that he could be a beacon. It is the balance of the male/female energy that creates a lasting effect on the earth. The Templar who made the ring understood this principle.

I don't know if I can do this.

Allow the love and joy to flow. Do not block it. If you expend it through physical contact it will dissipate. It will get easier as you relax into the process. It's truly simple: Let the love flow through you, and back and forth between the two of you, without physical contact. It is your choice as always, Jehanne. We are here for you with much love.

The voices left but the feeling of well-being remained. I squeezed his hand. "Are you ready to hear what they had to say?" I turned to face him. "You look radiant!" I exclaimed. His face shone, luminescent.

"Oui, I now understand how you had so much courage to come by yourself at your age into the world of men." He pressed his full lips into a contemplating line. "While I did not hear their words, ideas and pictures came into my mind. Let me try to articulate what I discerned?"

"Oui, I'm listening."

"I have the sense the feelings between us will help your mission—that my love for you can never be physical, but it will fuel your work. I'm to love you and be there for you but without making love to you."

"That's right." I shifted my weight on the pine needles and took both his hands in mine. "Do you think we can do this?" We sat in silence for a moment, and then I said, "We have no choice, do we? The alternative is to succumb to our feelings and risk scandal. You are married, and the fate of many rests in my being a virgin. The people of Orléans are suffering as we speak. We are their last hope." Again, tears spilled onto my cheeks. "We have no choice but to do it this way. I don't know if I could go forward without you by my side."

"It is an honor to be part of this holy plan. In a way, God prepared me for this by placing me in an English prison for five years. I was your age when captured, only seventeen. There were no women."

"My fair duke, we should depart. The dauphin expects us at dinner this evening, oui?" I stood and brushed the pine needles from my hose.

"Chérie, I want you to understand something before we go." He pulled me to him and with his deep voice he murmured in my ear, "I have never felt this love for any other. I will honor what God wishes, though it will not be easy. I only wish for one kiss, which will seal my heart to yours."

"We mustn't. I cannot kiss you."

His face fell and he hung his head. "Regretfully, I understand. Still, I swear to love no other but you," he vowed.

"As do I," I agreed, grateful for my strong mind. If it were up to my body I would crumble and fall into his arms and allow him to kiss me.

We mounted the horse in the same manner as before. I leaned back into his chest and tried to control my feelings. We let the horse walk out of the pine forest wanting to savor this fleeting moment of contact. Early spring sun peaked through the branches, creating geometric patterns of light and shadows on the ground. Chirping echoed through the canopy of the immense trees, whose trunks appeared orange with the afternoon sun. They felt like sentries guarding this precious time for us.

"We need to be sure that you are guarded all the time now. I didn't like what happened to you earlier today when the mob nearly crushed you." His chest vibrated with his words. "I will speak to the king about this and volunteer for the position."

"I agree, though I will miss my freedom and moments of solitude. I will be grateful for your presence regardless."

We arrived back in Poitiers just as the church bells tolled the afternoon hour. "I would like to attend afternoon Mass at St. Peter's."

"Do you understand the mass? Isn't it in Latin?" he asked.

"No, I don't understand. But I've heard the words often enough to gain comfort from them. It's mostly the feeling I get when my counsel comes to me in church—it's stronger and I find the beauty of this church inspiring."

"Have you read the Bible?" he asked in a whisper.

"No, I neither read nor write," I replied, feeling slightly ashamed of my ignorance.

He hesitated a moment and looked at me, his blue eyes wide. "Then your faith is truly a gift from the heavens."

We hung to the back of the church this time to avoid the people.

Rest easy, Jehanne, we are with you and your duke. Be conscious of your movements and attentions to him to keep your reputation clean. All is well. We will guide you every step of the way. All you have to do is ask.

On March 22, the judges sat as they had every day for ten days prior, lined up in two rows in the shape of a horseshoe. Bishop Castres stood to ask the first question.

If they repeat the same questions again today I am going to walk out of here and ride to Orléans all by myself, I vowed silently.

"Jehanne, you have been given gifts of horses and rich clothing. Is this why you came to Chinon; to trick the king into giving you riches?"

"Monseigneur, if I came only for clothing and trinkets would you see me dressed thusly, as a man, every day of these proceedings? When Marie d'Anjou first offered me rich women's dresses, I refused."

I turned as I spoke to be sure they all could hear me. "I will cut my hair as a man's to prove to you how serious I am of my mission." I grabbed hold of one of my braids. "Give me a knife, and I will do it in front of you now, if it will end this questioning."

The hall erupted with boisterous chatter and laughter.

"That's enough!" The bishop boomed with a hint of a smile. "That will not be necessary."

"Mademoiselle d'Arc, in what language do your saints address you?" asked Friar Seguin with a Limoges accent so thick I could barely discern the question.

"French. I hear them more clearly than I hear you." The words fell out of my mouth before I could catch them.

Many in the crowd giggled and others gasped. The Friar's irritated face silenced the hall. He continued, his ruddy face set with determination, "Do you believe in God?"

"I believe my faith is greater than yours." Again the bold words spilled out of my mouth.

"I, for one, cannot believe in this sacred mission of yours unless you show us all a sign; without such a sign I can hardly allow the king to place any men in peril merely on the strength of your words." His face grew red and his body shook.

"I have come on orders from the King of Heaven to raise the siege of Orléans and lead the dauphin to Reims to be crowned. By God's name, I did not come all this way to give signs. Dispatch me to Orléans, and I will show you a sign of victory. My saints told me that it is God's will to save the people of France from the calamity that is upon them."

Giome Amery stood up and responded rather passionately, "Then there is no need for soldiers. Let God deliver them."

"In God's name the soldiers will fight, and they will be granted a victory," I exclaimed loudly with frustration. I was ill content with this repeated questioning and I disliked being held back from accomplishing that for which I was sent.

A great uproar broke out in the hall; the crowd erupted and cheered, "Send her to Orléans."

The bishop had to stand and yell to be heard. "We are adjourned. You will have our answer today."

I breathed a sigh of relief. D'Alençon, who sat behind me every day since the first, grabbed my arm and pulled me through the crowd yelling in my ear, "Surely they will crush you with love after today. We need to get you out of here." Jean de Metz seized hold of my other arm, and together they pushed the throng aside like ploughmen on the first day of spring. We ran to our horses tethered and waiting at the water trough for our quick escape. Leaping up and onto our horses, we galloped out of town, our capes billowing behind before anyone could follow.

"Whahoo!" Metz whooped as we crossed the bridge on the outskirts of town. We dismounted in an overgrown gully between farms. "I am glad to be on your side, Jehanne. I pity the English Earl of Suffolk when you get near him."

"I was afraid I pushed them too hard." I did not feel as celebratory as Metz, and from the looks of him neither did d'Alençon. "I grew tired of the examination. They only questioned me to show off their own knowledge and assert their own position in the king's court."

"Everyone knows that is true," d'Alençon offered. "You were audacious and strong. It's up to them now."

As we mounted up to return to town my angels gave me the news. *Your mission to Orléans has been approved, Jehanne. It is a wonderful job you have done. Congratulations! Be prepared for the onslaught of townsfolk when you return.*

I chose not to convey this message to my friends, so I would have the few moments of riding to digest the news. They would hear soon enough. Joy and the tremendous weight of responsibility hit me at the same time. My stomach flipped. Trepidation rippled my flesh. What if I heard my angels incorrectly? No. I would not slip into a lack of faith in my angels. They had been right about everything so far. I took a breath and kicked my horse's flanks.

As we approached the town the faint sound of church bells rang out over the fields, and judging by the angle of the sun, it was not time for any service. The bells from St. Peter's and Notre Dame rang in celebration. I looked at d'Alençon and smiled. The town erupted with jubilation. People packed the streets ringing cowbells, singing France's national song. When they saw us, many ran alongside our horses touching our legs, cheering and blowing kisses.

Two knights on horseback caught up with us, requesting to speak with me. D'Alençon stopped them and questioned them first. "Jehanne, these men are from Orléans and wish to talk with you."

My heart leaped. Finally, I felt of some use. "Bonjour, I am Jehanne la Pucelle." I positioned my horse between the two men.

"Bonjour, mademoiselle," the younger one spoke. He looked thin and tired and his short hair stuck up from riding. "I am Villars and this is Jamet de Tilloy, we are knights of Dunois, the Bastard of Orléans. He sent us to find out when the angelic one will arrive. We have been watching the trial and are very honored to have you fight for us. Is it true that you will lift the siege of Orléans?"

"Good and gentle knights, God will lift the siege with hearts of the men of France. You will, indeed, see us soon. If it were up to me I would be passing under your gates today. Send word to Dunois and the people of Orléans that we shall meet as soon as we have our troops gathered and provisions ready."

The smiles on their faces made the entire process worth it. Joy flooded through me as we disembarked at the king's castle.

The dauphin smiled and greeted me. "There you are, the woman of the hour."

I stood to greet him. "Milord, I am most excited to be of service to my country and my king. How soon can we have men-at-arms ready to march into Orléans?"

"Jehanne, we will need to gather troops—ten to twelve thousand men and arms—perhaps one month. After the Easter holiday this weekend, we will all return to Chinon. Felicitations! You have brought hope to the people of France and to me. Your biggest challenge lies before you, and if you attack the English with as much force or better than you attacked my judges, then we shall be sure of victory." He turned to d'Alençon. "My brother, you will both sit beside me this evening at the banquet since you will be acting as commander of the armies, and Jehanne will be a captain and special advisor under your command."

"Sire, it would be our greatest honor to serve for you and attend the banquet." D'Alençon tilted his head to Charles, his longtime friend. "La Hire will not be too pleased to hear the news of my command."

"La Hire can be a hothead," the dauphin said in a whining tone. "I need someone who will stay cool and knows how to deal with Jehanne. No offense, mademoiselle."

"Merci beaucoup, sire." Words seemed to be caught in my throat. I let his little barb slide by. His assumption about d'Alençon's ability to understand me was more accurate than he knew. "I am most grateful of the position and will honor it well. God is most pleased."

"We have written a letter of intent, warning the Duke of Bedford, and would like to dispatch a herald as soon as possible," d'Alençon said, his voice deepening with the weight of responsibility.

"Whatever you need." Charles turned to leave. "I'll see you tonight. I am most pleased."

"Merci, sire," I sang out.

When the dauphin was out of hearing range I whispered to d'Alençon, "Suddenly I feel overwhelmed. Oh, what did I do?"

"Jehanne, whatever do you mean?" He wrinkled his brow with confusion. "You have what you desired. Isn't this what you wanted?" He tilted his head, drew his brows together and scanned my face for understanding. "I see. . . . Oui, a ride will be good. The responsibility does weigh heavily, especially on shoulders as lovely as yours."

Our horses took us to the ruin of a tiny old church south of town. The smell of earth in the early spring filled the air as the sun sank between the two roofless stone walls of the folly. We sat on one of the horse's blankets and leaned against the cool damp stone facing the sun. "My fair duke, my heart is heavy. I'm afraid we will work together but a year, maybe less." I wanted to hold his hand but resisted.

"Chérie, in that case we will have to make it memorable." He gazed at me with love, his handsome face bathed in the orange glow of the setting sun.

"I'm sorry for suddenly doubting my own mission." My voice filled with emotion.

"Jehanne, I want you to hear this. If we only had a few months, I would not trade this experience for any riches or promises of false safety holed up in a castle somewhere." He took my hand and kissed it. "I feel I was born to do this. I, too, had a dream to fight for the unification of France. That's why I fought in the battle of Broussinere at such a young age. At thirteen the king took me into his household and made me lieutenant general of Alençon."

"My greatest fear is treachery. You saw all those men of Charles's during the examination. Not one I would trust."

"Maybe treachery will happen later, but we are here now. You have a great and authentic love for the people of France, which they can see and feel. You have already made a difference." He shook my hand to make his point. "I am in this from start to finish, no matter how long or short, if God wills it. I promise to be by your side and, together, we are going to evict those Goddons out of Orléans."

I looked to the setting sun and allowed the waning light to bathe my face. "You are right. We are here now. I'll enjoy the moments we have."

We sat together watching the sun disappear below the horizon, taking the light with it. I sensed my angels all around us, in the whispers of the breeze, the waving of the dried grasses, and the soft whinnies of the horses.

"We should go," d'Alençon said quietly. "We have a celebration to attend."

At the dauphin's bidding, I dressed in Marie's quarters with the help, once again, of her chambermaid. I wore a cranberry velvet houpland, a voluminous robe, lined in silk and fastened at my waist with a wide, jeweled girdle. The neckline scooped down, exposing the swell of my smallish breasts. Black silk netting covered my hair, and perched atop my head a matching headpiece, a round box covered in velvet adorned with several pluming feathers. I did not feel this was appropriate given the role I played, but Marie insisted, "My dear, you must wear this attire as it is befitting who you are." She fussed at my girdle. "There, that's better." She paused to assess her work. "Jehanne, you have become one of our most influential court members and you need to appear as such to show the other courtiers how the king feels about you. The better your clothing, the more esteemed you are in the court."

The banquet, held in the grand ballroom of the castle of Poitiers, vibrated with a colorful cacophony of voices and music. The dauphin wished for d'Alençon and me to accompany him and Marie in the grand entrance. D'Alençon gawked with admiration when he saw me dressed so and had to hold my arm so I would not squirm away from such pomp.

The musicians played the royal welcome while we paraded into the golden light of the torch-lit room and through a corridor made by bowing royals who had come from all over France. It was like walking through rows of tall, brilliantly hued flowers. Fabrics of all types, vividly dyed, adorned each royal, cascading from their head to their feet. If every royal man and woman donated the cost of each of their costumes for this evening, we would have more than enough money to outfit our army and feed all of Orléans as well. I could not get used to the opulence. It took miles of expensive thread to make just one of the outfits like the one I wore.

Despite the abundance of food, only a few bites actually made it into my mouth. People from all over our country, the territories loyal to France, wanted to talk with me, ask my advice about God, their duchy's, their mothers-in-law, their husbands, and their wives. They wanted to know how I could hear my voices and how I would save Orléans. Questions, questions, questions. I felt torn. On one hand, I loved inspiring the people. On the other, I craved the quiet peace of solitude and communion with my counsel. My advice to everyone was the same, "Listen to the divine counsel within yourself, cleanse your soul, and appeal to the King of Heaven."

563 YEARS LATER

JUNE 1994

Jane draped her body across an overstuffed chair in the family room of her parents' home feeling relieved at the completion of her plebe year at West Point. It took her a few days to get used to the smaller scale of life in suburbia. She lounged on the sofa, left clothes on the floor of her room, and slept in late to reassert her own autonomy. Backlash from living a life filled with restrictions and monumental expectations. The positive result of all that squeezing and pressure was, like a diamond, she felt honed and sparkly. On the morning of her third day, she decided to return to an ordered routine. She rose early, went for a run on the beach, and cleaned her room. The pendulum had swung and settled in the middle. She found a natural balance.

After breakfast, Mary and Bill sat across from their daughter on the family room sofa, sipping coffee, and listened to Jane relate yet another tale from her freshman year. Story after story had come tumbling out of her since her arrival. The latest tale included exploits of fellow plebes trying to get around the rules in the mess hall when the ringing phone broke the spell of her words.

"Jane, it's Nick for you," her mother said brightening.

The year's passing had softened Jane's grudge against Nick. After all, she was a new woman. She took the call and agreed to go out with him to a party at Brown University that evening. Little flutters in her belly reminded her she still held feelings for him.

Jane squeezed into her favorite jeans, which she had not worn since Christmas break, and peered at her image in the mirror. During her plebe year she had put on nearly ten pounds, which comprised mostly muscle. More than her image had changed in one year, and she wondered what Nick would think.

When the doorbell rang, she calmly sauntered over to the door and opened it. Nick looked amazing. His longer hair curled over his ears and hung over bright, slightly mischievous eyes. He, too, had put on weight. It appeared he had incorporated an aggressive fitness routine. He wore a pale-blue polo shirt over faded denims and sneakers. Exactly what Jane needed. She had not realized how tired she had grown of uniforms, regimented haircuts, and military body language. Nick was a breath of fresh air.

He hugged her warmly. "Wow, Jane, you look awesome," he said letting his gaze rake her form.

"Thanks. You look terrific too," she said and followed Nick to his car. The chemistry between them burned as brightly as ever.

In the car, they exchanged stories about their respective freshman experiences, which could not have varied more. Jane related a snapshot of basic training and life as a cadet, while Nick told her about classes, cafeteria food, and parties.

Jane stared out the windshield at passing cars and worked up the nerve to ask, "So, did you go out with anyone else?"

"Sure. Didn't you?"

She shook her head.

"It's been a year, Jane. Just a few girls. They weren't you, though."

"And that means?" A flash of jealousy ran through her.

"You know. You're the whole package . . . looks, brains, body. You look smokin' hot, by the way. I love your short hair. Makes you look kick-ass." He turned and flashed her a brilliant smile.

The compliment about her short hair won her over and dissipated the flare of jealousy.

When they arrived at Brown University's campus Jane could not help comparing it with West Point. Everything was different—the architecture, the environment, the students who gathered in colorful groups, laughing and goofing around. Relative to the all-gray palette at the academy, the late-spring scene on the hillside of Providence, Rhode Island, was a riot of life. Giddiness replaced the staid and controlled part of her.

The relaxed festive atmosphere of the frat house put Jane instantly at ease. She pulsed to the infectious music, enjoyed an intellectual debate over the origins of life with a couple of physics majors, and allowed the fun part of her to stir. She drank beer from a cold, brown bottle and enjoyed reacquainting herself with Nick.

For every beer Jane drank, Nick drank two.

They flirted, held hands, and pressed their bodies against one another as the crowd thickened. The alcohol warmed her insides. Her bones felt molten and her mind seemed only capable of thinking about Nick. She could not take her eyes off him. Even the sight of his hands aroused her.

"Come with me," Nick whispered in Jane's ear. He wrapped his arm around her waist, his fingers scorching her flesh, and pulled her close. He kissed her and then led her up the stairs.

Jane felt consumed by the heat between them. It did not occur to her to temper her behavior or to consider her options. Lustful feelings drove her. Without really paying attention to where Nick led her they arrived in a dorm room. She did not notice the clothes on the floor, or the posters, or the trash overflowing. The only thought she possessed was concerning Nick's mouth on hers.

They tumbled passionately onto the small bed, exchanging brutish caresses. When Nick began to pull off clothing, his and hers, from far away her mind began to holler feeble warnings at her. It was not until several minutes passed when the message finally got to the forefront of her mind. It came like a wave. Suddenly she felt overwhelmed and fear overpowered desire. At the very same moment Nick was between her legs and thrust hard.

"Oh my God. What are you doing? Wait!" she cried.

"What do you think," he said smirking and thrust again. When he leaned in to kiss her she turned her head to the side and pushed at his chest with her hands. "I'm not ready. I'm not ready. . . . Stop!" Without thinking, she squeezed her legs around his hips, as hard as she could, adrenaline aiding her muscles. She felt grateful for the strength running and physical training at West Point gave her.

"Ow," he said and furrowed his brow in confusion.

When it dawned on her what had actually happened she began to cry. The crying got his attention. She relaxed her grip on him so he could climb off her. "Jane, what's wrong? You wanted this. I don't get it."

In between sobs she said, "I wasn't ready . . . for that."

He gave her an icy stare as he tossed her jeans onto the crumpled bed and bent to put on his own. "Now, how would I know?" His words ran together and he swayed as he talked. All at once, he appeared repulsive to her.

"Guess, I'm driving home," she said sarcastically, thankful that she did not drink any more than she had. She did not want to make a bad night worse by getting in an accident. Loosing her virginity that way was enough. How could life change so quickly?

As they threaded their way to the exit of the frat house people bumped into her drunk and glassy eyed. What seemed like a celebration of life initially, now took on a tone of slovenly decadence. Jane took in the scene. Couples kissed and groped one another in full view of everyone. Chips, pizza boxes, beer cans, and bottles littered every surface. They had almost made it to the door when someone spilled beer on her back.

On the drive home Nick slept, slouched against the passenger door, while Jane attempted to recover her composure. She felt hurt and the sticky discomfort of shame. The memory of the moment Nick surprised her repeatedly slipped unbidden into her mind. And with each mental replay, it seemed as though she fell into a hole. Who was to blame? By the time she turned off Highway 1, the hurt transformed into anger at herself for not keeping control of her behavior, and anger with him for his selfish ignorance of her feelings.

West Point, again by contrast, began to look appealing. Only a few hours before, she felt a dull dread when she thought of returning to the academy. Now, she could hardly wait to dive into the intense physical demands of another summer of military training, this time at Camp Buckner.

———

From her crouched position behind a rock in the forest, Jane could see the enemy illuminated by a narrow ray of sunlight. He huddled low just in front of her. Stealthily she slipped behind him, her footfalls quieted by the pine-needle-covered earth, and squeezed the trigger of her M-16.

"Bang! Gotcha!" she hollered and poked him with the muzzle of her weapon.

This mock battle marked their third day of Cadet Field Training at Camp Buckner. A subtle jubilation underscored every challenge they embarked upon despite their cumulative exhaustion from completing an entire year at West Point. Jane and her squad mates were now officially "yearlings"—sophomores.

Sounds of gunfire reverberated from all directions in the mock battle. From her vantage point, it appeared only a few of the enemy remained. Time slowed. Her senses sharpened. The layout of the entire field fell within her field of vision. She knew just what to do and where to move. A catalytic energy flooded into her body and limbs.

Another opponent on Alpha team appeared behind a tree fifteen feet away. I've got him, she thought, and whispered to one of her Bravo teammates Patrick Ash, "Hey, Ash, to your right. Cover me."

"OK," he mouthed back. "Go!"

She jumped up from the shadowed bunker, somersaulted, and came up on the other side of the enemy. "Ha!" she yelled and jumped toward him. He turned just in time to see the end of her rifle in his face. "Bang. You're dead," she said.

"Aw, shit!" the enemy exclaimed and glared at her for a moment. Sweat dripped down the sides of his face, as he considered his options.

Jane held her position, rifle poised in the air between them. Her eyes locked with his. Jane wondered if he was going to ignore the rules of engagement and flee. After several long moments, he dropped his weapon to the ground and put his arms in the air, but not before he snarled at her.

The enemy consisted of upper classmen, mainly juniors, known as "cows," and seniors, known as "firsties." For many, Cadet Field Training offered their first taste of leadership. Some took it seriously, wanting to train and lead with strength and fairness; others were in it for the ego rush.

Sounds of gunfire continued to rip through the heavy summer air.

A collective throaty cheer rose out over the makeshift battlefield. "Whahoo!"

Her platoon leader's voice bellowed above the din, "Bravo team wins. On my mark line up over here."

"How many kills for each of you?" Jane's squad leader, Cadet Germain, asked sporting his customary smirk. His short blond hair stuck up straight. He was a gregarious firstie, who played fullback on the Army football team. "When I point to you spout off," he said and gestured to each one of his soldiers in turn.

Alex Raphael went first. "One," he said.

"Three," Jack LeClair answered in his usual gravely voice.

"One," Sophia Michaels barked.

"Three," replied Patrick Ash.

"Nice work, cadet," Germain barked, and continued moving down the line.

"Zero."

"One."

Germain pointed to Jane last.

"Four," she declared proudly.

"Nice job, Archer. Remember you are on night watch with Ash tonight—report at 2300."

To the group he ordered, "Great work, everyone. Squad dismissed." He smiled, squinting into the fiery red, late afternoon sun.

"Yeah. Nice job, Jane," Jack LeClair said from behind her and gave her a pat on the shoulder. His deep voice made her heart jump. "You're like the queen of stealth."

"Thanks," she said and fell into step beside him as they made their way toward the even rows of OD-green triangular shaped tents. They walked without talking as music floated to them on the hot afternoon haze from a tent nearby.

As they approached the cluster of their squad's tents, she could sense he wanted to say something to her. She could not help but compare him to Nick. Jack was much better looking, certainly not as loquacious or aggressive as Nick and much more tidy. Even after rolling around in the field Jack appeared neat and together.

"Again, nice work, Archer," he said. He opened his mouth to say something else but thought better of it and turned to leave.

"Thanks . . . you too. Good work," Jane said.

He took one step away, then stopped and pivoted around to face her. He appeared flustered. "Are you with Ash? Are you two—"

"Patrick and me? Dating? No!" Jane said, startled at the sudden display of emotion. She liked seeing him slightly flustered. So, he was human after all. But, she wondered, was Jack too serious for her.

"Oh. Good. OK then. I'll see you later," he smiled, showing bright white teeth, and walked away.

Was it possible that Jack LeClair had a crush on her? Her eyes fixed on his broad shoulders as he walked away. He was built like a warrior—trim, extremely fit, agile, and fast. He gave contrast to Patrick Ash who stood at the same height, roughly six feet tall, but where Jack was trim, Patrick was stocky with short arms. Patrick was a powerhouse, gifted with his Irish father's barrel chest and his Vietnamese mother's facial features.

The friendship between Ash and LeClair ran hot and cold, the cold the result of competition taken too far. When they got along their differences made for success. Patrick's bulldozer approach coupled with Jack's ability to maneuver over or around anything made them a winning team when they chose to be.

Jane crawled into her tent to change from her long-sleeved fatigues to a T-shirt and bumped into her tent mate, Sophia.

"Hey, Jane. Wasn't that fun today?"

"It was awesome," she said. She grabbed a stick of deodorant, lifted her shirt, and swiped at her armpits. "I think LeClair has a crush on me."

Sophia turned her back to Jane and removed her sweat-soaked shirt, still shy.

"I think you're right," she said over her shoulder. "His eyes twinkle when he sees you." After tucking in her t-shirt she unzipped the tent flap and slipped into the late day sun.

Jane changed her clothes in the cramped space thinking how surprised she was at Jack's behavior. She always assumed the guys liked Sophia. With her round blue eyes, full mouth, and long shapely limbs, she attracted men wherever she went. And, true to form, when Jane exited the tent she saw three male cadets gathered around her roommate, vying for her attention like bees buzzing around their queen.

Jane sat on the ground and only half listened to their conversation. Instead she took the time to examine the blisters on her heels. Loose flaps of skin on each heel exposed tender red flesh. She cleaned them up as best she could and applied fresh Band-Aids. Reclining with her back to the canvas tent, she ran her hands through her short hair, tousling it up in an effort to get rid of helmet head. She allowed the sun to warm her tired muscles as it washed the entire camp in orange.

"Archer?" A female cadet called out. She was delivering mail and held several packages in her arms.

"I'm Archer," Jane called out and extended her hand to take the package the cadet pulled from the top. "Thanks."

The package's return address was penned in the familiar angular handwriting of her father. She ripped at the brown paper revealing a hardcover book with the title, *Famous Female Warriors*. "Cool," Jane said out loud and read the yellow sticky note attached.

To our Janey,
Wishing you a year filled with good things. Happy Belated Birthday!
Love, Dad and Mom.

She opened the book at random and leafed threw a few colorful pages. These women were so brave, she thought and wondered if she would be as strong in similar circumstances. A photograph of a bronze statue of a woman astride a horse brandishing a sword caught Jane's attention. The caption of the photo read *"Jeanne d'Arc in Orléans, France, 1429."*

Jane's heart leaped as she turned to the section on Joan of Arc. This young woman, only seventeen years of age, successfully lead men in battle and freed a town in France from a siege. Jane turned the page to see a photograph of a letter Joan had written to members of a town in France. The signature at the bottom of the letter read, *Jehanne.* Something about this woman resonated with Jane. With zeal, she read every word in the three-page section about Joan of Arc twice then closed the book in her lap. Jane noticed her pulse had quickened.

That evening, Jane sat leaning up against the trunk of an oak tree in the forest bordering their camp with her buddy Patrick by her side.

The moon, halfway between new and full, appeared like a creamy, glowing letter D against the deep violet sky. Every now and then, thin ribbons of clouds scuttled across it. The whites of Patrick's dark eyes stood out against his tan skin as he rambled on about missing his grandparents back home in Santa Fe.

"West Point is a slice of heaven compared to the nightmare of being at home in New Mexico with my dysfunctional parents. Ever since I can remember, my life has seemed to be one of extremes. I would go from my grandparent's home, where I stayed during the school week, to the cluttered, rundown chaos of my parents' house. My parents were notorious for not getting me to school on time." He shifted his position on the tree's roots, rested his elbows on his knees, and massaged his fist with the other hand. "My grandparents were my rock. They were the ones who put the papers I got A's on up on their refrigerator and chauffeured me to all my sports. They were the ones who helped me with my admission to the academy. I sure hope genetics skips a generation."

Jane hoped genetics did not skip a generation. She wanted to become a JAG lawyer, her own military version of her father.

Ash talked nonstop for thirty minutes then slipped into a contemplative silence.

Jane felt compassion for this big tough guy who had a soft spot for his grandparents and found it comforting to sit in the quiet with him. She listened to owls calling back and forth and watched light after light inside the tents in the field below blink off.

Jack's image flashed into her mind. She liked him and wondered what the future might bring. Then she imagined how different it would be if she was on "watch" during a real war situation and shivers ran down her spine. The stillness of the forest magnified the tired state of her body. Jane fought to stay awake. Her head bobbed.

Patrick noticed her nodding and said, "You can put your head on my shoulder if you want. Though you really should not be sleeping. Who will keep me awake?"

"I'm sorry. I'll try to stay awake."

"No really. It's OK if you do . . . sleep, that is. I'm kind of a night owl anyway." He tapped her knee.

"How gallant of you, Ash. Is this a come on?" She knew she could be playful with him.

"Archer, don't get me wrong . . . you're cute and everything, but I'm an honorable guy. I feel like you're my sister."

They chatted for a few minutes then grew quiet again. Without the stimulus of talk, Jane found it difficult to keep her eyes open. Her head dropped.

She could sense the enemy creeping through the woods. After only a few minutes, the ground began to vibrate with the pounding of horses' hooves. Distant screams filled her ears, as the ear-splitting sound of canons reverberated off castle walls. Sounds of war moved closer and closer to her.

Jane let out a muffled scream in her sleep. She woke to Patrick shaking her leg and calling her name. "Jane? Jane! Wake up."

"What? Oh no . . . I fell asleep," she apologized, rubbing her eyes.

"I did too. We'll be relieved shortly. It's almost two. . . . I can't wait to go to bed."

Shaking off the disconcerting events of her dream, she checked her watch with her flashlight. They only had ten minutes left.

Two yellow beams of light bounced up and down in the forest. As the lights grew brighter, Jane heard the familiar voices of Jack and Alex, their relief for night watch.

"Don't you two look cozy," Jack teased. Even in her groggy state of mind, she could tell he was jealous.

"How romantic," Alex said, slapping Patrick on the back when he rose from the ground.

The four talked for a few moments and exchanged information. Jane and Patrick made their way through the forest to the open field back toward their tents. Jane never felt more tired in her life, and she pondered how she was going to make it through the next five weeks. Cadet Field Training was more intense than Beast Barracks in terms of physical challenges. A myriad of team building and war training exercises still lay ahead.

"See you tomorrow," Patrick mumbled, clearly as exhausted as Jane.

"OK," Jane said. She climbed into her tent while giving herself a pep talk. Without changing her clothes, she stretched out and fell deeply asleep.

The next five weeks of training at Camp Buckner went by in a blur for Jane. For several of the days she was so exhausted, she hardly remembered anything. The training successfully drove all memories of Nick out of her mind. By the time summer was over Jane had moved on. As she donned her dress uniform for the Camp Illumination Ball, a celebration that marked the end of training that summer, she thought about another man altogether.

"To Camp Buckner," Jack bellowed so his friends could hear him above the din at the ball. All dressed in their India White uniforms, Alex, Patrick, Jane, Sophia, and Tara echoed his sentiments.

"To being yearlings!" Alex added.

Bright, suntanned faces beamed smiles all around the table. "Beat Navy!" They cheered. The entire room was filled with the heady exhilaration born of intense physical challenges endured for six long weeks. They bonded, disagreed, met difficulties head on, and surmounted fears together.

"To friends," Jane offered, her heart swelled with genuine affection for the group.

"Friends!"

They ate, danced, talked, and laughed.

When the party was in full swing, Jack slid up next to Jane. "Come with me?" He asked sweetly and pulled Jane away from their friends and other celebrating cadets.

He led her to the edge of the lake, and following it for some yards they came to a secluded area. He chose a large clean rock for them to sit on so they would not dirty their whites. "Sit next to me?"

"OK." She was pretty sure he wanted this private time with her to ask her out, and enjoyed the fact he was making a little ceremony out of the event. She thought it was about time. At least he was not pushy like Nick.

The sun hovered above the horizon. Jane sat, her hip and thigh touching his, and looked out over the lake. The sky turned from a yellow ginger to a fiery red in a matter of minutes. Thin layers of clouds overhead picked up and reflected the orchestration of colors like a prism onto the water

Looking out over the water, she experienced the relief and the exhilaration of hard work. She felt proud of herself when she remembered how she had met her fear of heights head on with the heart-pounding "Slide for Life." She remembered shaking as she climbed a tower reaching one hundred feet off the ground. When she held onto the hand trolley attached to a cable and slid rapidly down toward the water, she thought her chest would explode. Her plunge into the dark water of the lake seemed to be her baptism into a new self. Every time Jane remembered the moment she let go of the trolley and fell into the water, she felt expanded, empowered, and victorious.

"I'm so glad training is over," she said, trying to make conversation. Her spine tingled with anticipation and the nearness of him. She could feel his depth, and his defenses, and wondered what made him tick. She hoped she could break through the shell that kept him more reserved than the other guys.

"Me too," he said.

The sun slipped slowly toward the lake and hung there, the line of trees black against a blushing pink atmosphere. She turned and gazed at Jack's rapt face. His green eyes sparkled. Without thinking she reached her hand up to his cheek, turned his beautifully chiseled face toward hers and kissed him.

Behind them, the beats of the band pulsed in the evening air. They were awash in color. Jane wrapped her arms around his neck while he kissed her, tentatively at first, then with more passion. His hands on her waist, he pulled her toward him with gentle strength so they sat chest to chest. Jack's kisses were the perfect blend of intensity and tenderness.

"Mmm," he murmured. The deep sound of his voice tickled something inside her. Energy surged between them. Jane felt her body soften and relax. She felt feminine again. Layers of invisible barriers seemed to peel off and float away making her feel slightly unprotected. From deep inside she knew she would be safe with him. He was not like Nick. He listened to her body not just her words. He moved slowly checking with her response before going further. She made herself focus on the bliss of his mouth on hers, the warmth of physical connection, until a twinge of abdominal cramps broke through the moment.

Oh no, she thought, feeling relief and disappointment at the same time. My body is choosing now to start a period. It had been a couple of months since she experienced her menstrual cycle. The same thing had happened during Beast Barracks, only then she had gone nearly three months without flowing.

"Jack," she said, reluctantly pulling away. "I need to get to a bathroom."

"Now? OK. But first, I wanted to ask you if you wanted to spend a couple of days with me once we're out of here. I was thinking we could go horseback riding and hiking."

"Gee, you don't mess around. A couple of days? You know, I'm all right with just dinner and a movie."

"Why should we do what everyone else does? How about it?"

"OK. You have a date." Jane surprised herself with her quick answer.

He smiled. Jane's pulse quickened. He possessed the most radiant smile, for a man, she had ever seen.

As they picked their way back along the shore he grabbed her hand. She realized she needed this relationship and thought he did as well. She did not want to lose the softer side of herself; she reasoned having a boyfriend, like Jack, at West Point would keep her in balance.

ROUEN, FRANCE

FRIDAY, MAY 24, 1431

That morning my guards, priests, and I convened outside in the square of the cemetery of Saint Ouen Abbey. A guard escorted me to one of two platforms on either side of the south door of the church where Maître Erard, doctor of theology, waited. On the other platform, yet another bishop, this one, bishop of Beauvais, and a great number of assessors stood before me. A large crowd had collected and waited, sensing excitement on this spring morning. I drank in great gulps of fresh air and felt overwhelmed with the colors and vibrancy of the landscape. I had not seen this volume of sky in months. Squinting, I cast my eyes heavenward, marveling at the groupings of clouds and hazy sun.

Maître Erard, monk scribe, began sanctimoniously, "Oh noble people and royals of France, behold a true monster." He gestured to me with an open palm. "You dishonor yourselves by trusting this woman, this heretical and superstitious magician." When he finished speaking he lifted both arms in the air, as if invoking God himself. The crowd cheered at his bequest. They were resorting to public humiliation in order to get me to admit guilt, and it was working. It pained me to look into the throng gathered and see condemnation, anger, and hatred on their faces where once there had been joy and acceptance.

After reading and quoting sufficiently he asked me, "Will you revoke all your words and deeds, which are disapproved by the clergy?"

"I defer to God and to our Holy Father the pope."

"By your guilt," he gloated, "you will incriminate your king, Charles VII."

In response to his false accusations, I shouted, "Condemn me if you will, but not the king. I swear to you that my king is a fine and noble Christian!"

"Force her to keep silent!" he shouted to my guards. "The pope is too far away, it's impossible to go to him. You will abjure!" He took a document from Bishop Cauchon's outstretched hand. "You will submit and sign this document now."

The mob began to shout and hurl stones.

"I will sign," I cried, hoping to silence and calm the crowd. I looked at the parchment and could not read one word. I had no way of knowing to what I agreed. I was left with no choice, no other course of action. When I was handed the quill, I wrote an X and put a circle around it, knowing that in my mind I agreed to nothing. Perhaps, since I gave them what they wanted, I will be delivered to the hands of a church prison, I thought hopefully. I would much rather be guarded by nuns than by English soldiers.

"You will submit to women's clothing today!" Erard declared to the cheering, rowdy crowd.

This event contrasted so agonizingly with the other public events of my life. I hoped that I would not be sketched in the history books this way—an emaciated heretic, holding stubbornly to some principal, which was beginning to feel flimsy. Despite the inner turmoil, I held my head high as we made our way back to the castle.

I was crestfallen by the grand degree of misunderstanding of the priests and the crowd. Mostly the crowd. They had no idea how they had been misled by those in power. I wanted to return to my cell to insure my connection with those souls of the future. After my guards clumsily rejoined my chains and left me to myself, I was free to attempt to undo the damage to my reputation.

Archangel Michael's voice sang in my head, *Dearest Jehanne, your reputation is intact. Do not worry over such things. You will be pleased to know there are women in the future who spend as many years training as men. They have the freedom to excel, dress as they choose, marry, and have children.*

Merci, I thought suddenly too tired to keep my eyes open. Reassured, I sunk into my paltry mattress and allowed memories to wash over me. I hungered for the excitement and camaraderie of the past with Jean d'Alençon. Though God had most of me, a portion of my heart would always belong to him. I recalled the early days of our relationship back in Poitiers.

After the conclusion of the trial sessions in Poitiers, we, most of the court, convened in Chinon. Meetings regarding strategy, supplies, and men-at-arms filled our days. D'Alençon and I spent very little time alone; we would not risk sabotaging our mission.

Our first strategy meeting took place in the red room with the other captains. D'Alençon stood at a table with a large map depicting the layout of Orléans and its surrounding environs. He already held himself with the dignity of a war commander. He cleared his throat and spoke, "While I was imprisoned in Crotoy, I shared the small room in the tower with an old wise Scottish commander who fought at the Battle of Agincourt. During that time he shared with me his vast knowledge of warfare and the war habits of the English. From the amount he knew, I discerned that he had had a spy on his payroll." He paused to observe the smiles on the faces of our group and was not disappointed. This news was indeed welcome. "I will go over some of the tendencies of the English and the unique ways the Duke of Bedford prefers to lay siege. In addition, he shared with me their weak points." D'Alençon cracked his knuckles on the table and stopped talking. He squared his jaw, making the muscles along the side of his face pulse, as a shadow passed over his features. "He died two months before I was freed."

"My condolences," I offered. He never shared any of this information with me before, but it helped me understand his faraway looks and the melancholic moods. I imagined it would be challenging for his heart to spend that much time with someone only to have him die.

He continued stoically, "This man spent the entire time in prison scratching diagrams of the battles on the walls and in the dirt on the floor, analyzing strategy and maneuvers. This will surely give us an advantage."

"This is excellent news," Metz said.

I marveled at the amazing ways the divine worked.

"Bonjour, captains and Jehanne." Charles swept into the room with La Trémoille behind him. "I have good news."

We all turned. "Bonjour, sire."

"Pledges of money and supplies are filling our coffers. In addition, royals and men-at-arms are volunteering all over the country. Our army is forming more quickly than we hoped." He puffed with pleasure. "Jehanne, you are to go to Tours to be fitted for armor and whatever else you need for battle, as well as staffing your own military house. We have much to do, men to train, and provisions to be readied."

"Milord, who will accompany me to Tours?" I asked, knowing I would not hear my beloved's name.

"Metz, Poulengy, and Louis will travel with you. D'Alençon, you will remain here," he declared, brushing invisible dirt off his tunic. "Oh, I almost forgot. I received word that two of your brothers will join you there, as well. "

Without saying au revoir he departed the room. His fur-trimmed cloak floated behind as if suspended on a bed of air.

He left me breathless. It was almost too much to take in all at once. My heart tugged in two directions: joy at the idea of my brothers joining me with an entire staff at my disposal, sadness at leaving my dear friend behind. My eyes darted to d'Alençon. His eyes met mine briefly before dropping to the table and map in front of him.

"That is good news," he said, his voice cracking. "We have much to do. Let's break this meeting for now and reconvene in a couple of hours."

In Tours, thirty miles northeast of Chinon, and perched near the Loire, I lodged at the house of Jean Dupuy, a squire of the king's. Monsieur Dupuy's home was made out of stone to resemble a little castle, and it had three floors all decorated nicely. Not lavishly like Chinon, but elegant, by small-town standards. I looked out the window from my room on the third floor, surprised to see the tower of Charlemagne, part of the Basilica of St. Martin rising high above the streets of Tours. I enjoyed the idea of being within its protective shadow.

As I daydreamed and contemplated the incredible façade of the Basilica, Saint Catherine spoke to me. *Jehanne, there is a sword hidden just under the earth inside the church of my name, St. Catherine de Fierbois. Send a rider to fetch it for you and have him look behind the altar. You shall be most pleased with this gift.* Her etheric voice sang melodically in my head.

"Merci," I exclaimed out loud. As quick as I could, I met with Louis and requested he find a man for the job.

Upon the rider's return from the Church, he met up with me near the outer courtyard of the castle in Tours. He broke into a big smile when he saw me, his light hair damp from riding. "Jehanne, I found a sword just where you said it would be. I thought it was useless, covered in rust. However, when the priest wiped it, the rust just fell off," he said, awe in his voice. "She is a beauty. Such fine workmanship, any knight would be proud to fight with such a sword."

I took it from him. "Merci beaucoup." I kissed him on both cheeks and gave him money for his travels. "Thank the good priests of St. Catherine's for me." Upon examination, there appeared five crosses carved along the blade. Ripples of joy made me smile as I traced the carvings with my fingers. I held it out in front of me and sliced at the air. "Magnifique!" A holy sword from Saint Catherine— not only was this a good sign, it would also keep me safe in battle. Merci, Saint Catherine!

When I was left alone I dashed to the church upon the ringing of the bells for midday, eager to spend time with my counsel. My favorite place in any church is the right hand transept, the alcove at the front before the choir. Depending on my mood and how much seclusion I need, I can be out of view of the rest of the parishioners, and still have a view of the altar. On this day I chose to sit as far to the right under the windows as possible.

I knelt, clasped my hands together at my chest, and prayed.

Dearest angels, thank you for blessing me with this much progress on my journey. I ask for continued grace to face the next stage of this mission. Please guide me as to the ways of war and strengthen my behavior and resolve with the men.

The space around me grew warm, my back relaxed, my belly softened, and my heart swelled with compassion for France. I felt the movement of wings all around me.

Dearest daughter of God, we are with you. You stand at the threshold of a victory, both militarily and secularly. You have successfully fanned the flames of hope within the hearts of men and women as word of you travels far and wide. In a month's time, you will feed that hope with a victory in Orléans, deepening the faith of the people of France.

Tell me what I must do next.

Michael's voice vibrated in the air surrounding me. *The time is ripe to act. Have a banner commissioned in white with Jesus in the center flanked by angels. The banner will let your men know where you are in battle and serve to inspire them. We wish for you to practice talking with us all day long, no matter whom you are with. This will enable you to improve your skill at hearing us accurately. We will need to prompt you in the heat of battle so you will be able to hear our guidance wherever you may be, despite any noise happening around you. Agreed?*

Agreed. Merci.

We are ever present with our love for you. The voices continued to fill me with heavenly inspiration. I allowed my shoulders to drop to let in the rejuvenating and replenishing nectar. The murmur of the priest's voice floated to me in a continuous rhythm, echoing through the vast building. My breathing grew even and deep, like sleep. I remained long after the parishioners solemnly filed out.

When I returned to the home of Dupuy, I found my brothers Pierre and Jean waiting for me.

"Brothers, I am so happy to see you!" I squealed with delight and hugged them both at the same time. Tears flowed from all three of us, dampening their ruddy cheeks as I held them tightly. I pulled back and asked, "You haven't come to drown me on Papa's orders, have you?"

They laughed. Pierre placed his large hand on my shoulder. "Non, we have come to join you and fight by your side."

I looked deeply into his copper-colored eyes to see if he was telling the truth. Satisfied, I urged them into chairs near the hearth. "Come sit. Do you need something to eat?"

"Yes, we are famished from riding," Jean answered. The family called him petit-Jean as he looked like a miniature version of our papa, with dark hair, square jaw, and a smaller stocky frame.

I found dried meat, cheese, bread, and wine. We ate, enjoying the fire and each other's company.

"It's been a long time since we sat around a hearth together, eh?" Pierre offered a happy smile, showing his chipped front tooth.

The presence of my brothers helped to fill the hole left by the absence of d'Alençon. "It will be wonderful to have you by my side in battle."

"Maman and Papa are very proud of you. They have become celebrities. Everyone is saying you are the hope of France," Jean said after taking a huge gulp of wine.

"They are not cross with me?"

"At first, when you were in Vaucouleurs and over two months passed, Maman was miffed and stomped around the house. Though she did not tell Papa; we told him you were at our uncle's, lest he mount up and find you to drown you himself. I told him the truth after you left for Chinon with Jean de Metz. He sat in the barn for hours until Maman finally went to him with some wine and sweet talk," Pierre related with excitement. "We are amazed in what you have done already."

"I haven't done anything yet," I said humbly.

The next day my brothers and I had just left the metal smith who would make my suit of armor when we met up with Jean de Metz and Poulengy in the town square. Several men were with them.

"Jehanne," Metz said formally. "These men are assigned by the king to be your military household, your retinue." Pointing to each one he introduced them to me. Jean d'Aulon, a sturdy capable-looking man of middle years, perhaps thirty, was hired as my master of horse and page, a most important role. His job was to take care of the majority of my needs. Louis, whom I already knew, would serve as page. Two heralds, royal messengers, thin weathered-looking young men, Ambleville and Gien completed my secular team. Three chaplains, to my pleasant surprise, had been procured—Brother Pasquerel, an Augustinian friar, dressed head to foot in black robes, compelled to frequent mopping of his broad sweaty brow, Nicolas de Vouthon, a Cistercian monk, and young Mathelin Raoul, my cleric, who appeared, I scarcely think, old enough to have completed his education. "They will be quartered in town with your brothers," Metz added after introductions. To me, under his breath, he added, "To be awarded this many men is tantamount to any high level captain in the king's army. You should feel honored."

I nodded and attempted to appear nonchalant about the whole business.

"Bonjour, messieurs, I am most happy you have joined our cause." I bowed my head in acknowledgment. "We have much work to do for France and the King in Heaven. I trust you are prepared to work hard."

"Oui," they answered. Their ready acceptance of me spoke for the loyal preparation of Metz and Louis, as these men may have felt challenged to be working for a female.

"We will meet later to go over strategy and tasks," I said confidently, trying to make a good first impression. "For now, Metz will take care of finding you food. Adieu and merci." After they ambled across the square out of my sight, I sighed with profound satisfaction and turned to my brothers. "I have one more task this day—to find a silversmith."

"Ma petite soeur. How impressive." Jean tilted his head in disbelief. "What need do you have of a silversmith?"

"It's a surprise; you will find out soon enough. Just lead me in the direction of the smith, and I will see you later." I smirked and wistfully watched a young boy of three years of age run across the square; his chubby cheeks jiggled up and down with his short quick steps. He ran into the knees of his mother who stood gossiping with another village woman. She absentmindedly patted the lad on his head. I wondered how it would feel to have a child love me that way. Perhaps, I mused, after all this battling is done, I will have a family of my own. A light shadow seemed to pass in front of me and my heart faltered. Something told me I would not be a mother in this lifetime.

Jean pointed across the square to a carved wooden sign hanging above a shop with a wrought-iron gate for a door. Shaking off an icy feeling as merely fear, I strode determinedly to the silversmith's gate.

"Bonjour, mademoiselle," the silversmith greeted me. "What can I do for you?"

"Bonjour, monsieur." I cleared my throat. "I am Jehanne la Pucelle."

"I know who you are. We are a small town. It is a great pleasure to meet you," he said with a slight lisp making him seem snake-like as he wiped sweat off his forehead. He had a shrewd, smarmy air, which I did not care for, but I felt he could be trusted with a simple task.

"S'il vous plait, I wish for twelve silver medals to be fashioned for me so that I may give them to my men to wear as protection. I have a specific design in mind: a cross with four even sections like blunt arrow heads, the center would hold the sacred heart of Christ and in each of the four pieces a saint, Archangel Michael, Saint Catherine, Saint Margaret, and Archangel Gabriel." I paused and looked into his gray eyes. "Can you do this within a week's time?"

"For you, mademoiselle." He smiled more honestly. "I can do it, oui."

"Merci beaucoup, monsieur," I sang out over my shoulder and I left, feeling pleased with myself. I used some of the generous allowance Charles gave me to pay for the commission.

From the small courtyard at the back of the Dupuy's home I could hear the crunch of wagon wheels and hooves on the dirt road nearby. The afternoon sun streaked through the clouds as they moved quickly overhead. A rooster crowed and sheep bleated gently from the miniature barnyard next door. I heard the splashing sound of someone emptying a washing basin in the gutter: sounds of everyday life. I longed for the simplicity of peasant chores. The truth was, I felt terrified. The reality and magnitude of what lay ahead of me sank into my consciousness more deeply with each passing day.

Earlier that morning, I had stood for the last fitting of my armor, a beautiful work of art. It was fashioned out a metal giving off a white hue, polished smooth and expertly shaped to fit my body with ease of movement while providing maximum protection. It included a breastplate shaped especially for me, fixed with leather straps over woolen undergarments, and chain mail to protect my skin from the chaffing of the metal. Gauntlets covered my arms and hands while cuisses would shield my legs from blows. I instructed the metal smith to make my helmet without a visor so my men could see my face in battle.

While in full gear, all sixty pounds of it, Metz and I jousted with the lance. He exerted more and more strength behind each thrust so that I would be prepared for the intensity of men who fought for their lives and did not care that I was "the Maid." Many an Englishman would salivate at the chance to fight me and win. So, I worked hard until my muscles threatened mutiny and screamed at me to stop. The warm day, although still spring, gave a hint of what would come as the weather changed from spring to summer and added difficulty to our training. I felt like I was being roasted inside the armor.

Dearest council, I prayed silently from the yard of the Dupuy's humble home, I am terrified. The idea of battle feels overwhelming. Surely this is a crazy plan to put me on the battlefield with men.

Dearest daughter, your fear is only an indicator of places within you that have not yet grown.

Isn't fear a warning?

Sometimes. In this case, it is an indicator that you are growing more spiritually courageous. If you walk a path you know in your heart to be true and you encounter fear, it is showing you that your mind has not yet grown to accommodate your heart. You will grow in faith, knowledge, and ability to match the challenge at hand. This is guaranteed. You see, Jehanne, you have the ability to achieve whatever you wish to achieve, if you feel truly inspired. This is stepping in faith. You walk in your truth despite the fear. That is the moment when you expand into the fullest version of yourself.

I shifted my aching body on the little wooden bench to alleviate some discomfort in my legs. The breeze blew the loose hair from my plaits across my face. Brushing it away I asked, Are you saying that I will become a true soldier, a leader of men, when I stand in front of them with my banner?

Yes, that is exactly what we mean. Sometimes the transition is slow and other times it is swift, depending on the moment and the importance and intensity of the events unfolding.

Waves of divine love swirled around me. I have no choice but to believe your words and your guidance. I feel as though I am walking across a great gully on a very tiny bridge.

We understand and love you for your courage. We hope you understand that we love you even if you could not go another step on this mission. You always have a choice to keep going or stop and take another path.

I don't feel like I have a choice. My right hand began to cramp and throb from having gripped the lance so tightly earlier.

Oh, but you do, Jehanne. Tender mewing sounds of a mother crooning to her child floated on the wind as the clouds covered the sun. I tried to rub the soreness from my arms without succeeding.

Jehanne, you are a brave soul to walk this path. Much is at stake. The enormity of your mission is reflected in the amount of fear you are experiencing. Go ahead and breathe into the fear. Imagine it dissipating. Focus on your body and all of the sounds around you. The more present you are in the moment the less you will feel the fear. We love you and are continually by your side.

Merci, angels in Heaven. I am grateful for your guidance and love. I did as my voices suggested and paid attention to my breathing and the sounds around me. I rode the waves of my breath, in and out. Feelings of comfort began in my chest and spread throughout my limbs, easing the ache in my muscles and dissipating the terror like the tides clear the sands at the beach. I felt washed clean.

"Jehanne?" a male voice called out from inside the house. "Jehanne?"

"I'm out back in the courtyard," I yelled, realizing it was the voice of d'Aulon, my squire. His help over the last few days had been invaluable. Of medium build, broad in the shoulders, slim in the hips, he possessed brown eyes, which often gazed at me openly and quizzically. He had a way of bolstering my spirits and confidence with his calming presence.

"There you are," he said. "I wanted to go over your accounts before we leave for Blois and didn't you want to dictate a letter to the English?" He tucked a stray lock of curly blond hair around his ear and contemplated me with soft eyes. "You look tired. Are you all right?"

"D'Aulon, your attention is appreciated, merci." I forced my legs to support me as I stood and walked with him back into the house. The air grew cool, reminding me that we were still in early spring. "I am sore from training in full armor with Metz today."

He helped me to a chair and poured me a bit of wine. "You should feel better in a few days, as your muscles grow accustomed to the weight of the armor."

"Your wife must miss you."

"She does. We have been married ten years, since I was nineteen." A wistful look spread across his face, and he smiled sweetly at the thought of her. Changing the subject, he said, "I hear you are quite good at the lance, even by a man's standards." He sat in the spindle-backed chair nearest the hearth, leaned toward me and grinned. "Metz boasts about you to any who will listen."

I laughed. "From his lips to God's ears."

That evening, lying in my small bed, I attempted to snuff my feelings for d'Alençon. Despite the fact that my angels condoned my love for him, I felt uncomfortable with it. Shouldn't I be focused only on the task at hand? Will my feelings for him endanger my work in battle? In fact, it seemed the more I focused on closing my heart to him and the more I attempted to squelch my feelings, the more fierce they became.

Night after night, as I lay alone in the home of my host, I'd find my mind climbing the walls, wandering the hallways of my heart, looking for a way out, a way to Jean, my duke. When left alone in the darkened room with only the sounds of the crackling fire, I fantasized about a normal life with him. I imagined what it would be like to sleep lying next to him, curled up in the safety of his arms. I recalled the way he looked at me, his blue eyes turning aquamarine, with love.

Jehanne, allow your heart to open to him. Once your heart is open for anyone, it is open for everyone. The province of the heart can be accessed by anyone. If you are in a state of love for one person, you are in a state of love for all.

My dearest council, you cannot understand how my chest aches; my heart feels confined within the walls of my chest. I can hardly find a comfortable position and must fight the incessant urge to run until I find him.

Try to replace your image of him with the people of France. Send the feelings of love outward to your country.

Pardonne moi, but your solution seems simplistic.

My mind wrestled with my attempts to replace my duke with my people, resisting the substitution. Every part of me wished only for him. I told my angels, I can't do it.

Would you like some help?

Honestly? Not really.

All you need do is ask, they prodded.

I guess I am enjoying being obsessed with love. I am lovesick. This, I cannot believe. I vowed never to act like the foolish girls in the village, silly over a man.

We can help. Your love for him will give you the strength and power you need to inspire all of those other men to great feats of heroism. Love is the weapon of God's warriors. Just ask . . .

I could feel the presence of my angels dancing around me like they were having a good time with this. Little bubbles of joy began to pop inside of me, and I had to cover my mouth so as not to laugh out loud and wake the house. You are not playing fair.

Jehanne, all is fair in love, because it is all love. Every thing on your earth has joy pulsing at its very core.

A picture popped into my mind of d'Alençon knocking at the door of my heart while behind him stood hundreds of people. I knew the vision meant that in order to allow the people of France, and my army, to love me, I needed to allow d'Alençon in first. I wanted to stomp my feet in protest at the unfairness of it all. This love matter did not enter into my thinking ever before. I wanted to get into Orléans and get the job done without concerns of a beloved. My angels seemed to be changing the script on me.

Let me get this straight. You not only want me to save France from the English but you also want me to do so while in love with a man whom I can never marry. Is this correct?

Yes, dearest one. There is more to it than you are seeing now.

I have given my life over to you to do with as you will and now you want my heart to be broken in the process? I am sorry. I don't get it, and it doesn't seem at all fair to me. Tears pooled in my eyes, ran down my cheeks, and dropped onto the bed linens. I have already surrendered everything else to you, I cried silently in the dark, having to sit up so I could breathe. What else do you want?

Your heart, sweet one. That is, the deeper recesses of your heart. Surrender your heart. D'Alençon has managed to stimulate that part of you which is essential to the completion of your mission.

Surely you will take this suffering?

Surrender to it, Jehanne. Let go.

I resisted at first then relaxed. I felt the sensation of lifting and relaxed more as the pain and suffering ended and a deep expanded peace settled through me. I dropped back onto the bed and fell asleep immediately, cocooned in the safety of my own warm heart, dreaming of people welcoming me into their city with love and cheers of joy.

The next morning I awoke feeling refreshed and happy, happier than I had been in a long time. I called d'Aulon in to see me. "Bring a knife with you. We have something important to do."

He looked at me quizzically. "A knife? What need have you with a knife?"

"You'll see." I smirked and winked at him. "Come." I stood before the small spotted looking glass of Madame Dupuy's and watched, resolute, while d'Aulon stood behind me with a knife poised in his hand.

Pulling my hair out of its plaits I spread it around my shoulders.

"Oh no, Jehanne." He shook his head and leaned in close to me. "I will not cut your hair. Give me any other task and I will gladly, happily, comply, but not this. I am not a barber, especially not a woman's barber."

"I want you to cut my hair to the nape of my neck in the fashion of men my age," I insisted.

"No, I can't," he countered firmly, running his other hand through his own blond locks.

"D'Aulon, do you want me to be safe in battle? Do you care for this mission?"

"Of course. You know I do."

"Then cut."

"Are you sure you want to do this?" he hazarded to ask me a third time.

"D'Aulon, this is necessary." I looked up at him from the rickety wooden chair. "Cut!" I demanded.

"You could plait your hair and tuck it into your clothing," he pleaded, his brows coming together, concern shadowing his sweet face.

"Cut, d'Aulon. Cut," I said firmly and thought, do it soon or I shall change my mind.

D'Aulon grimaced each time he brought the knife across the variegated strands of my hair. Eighteen-inch lengths fell to the ground like rushes on a kitchen floor. I gritted my teeth to staunch the emotion as I stared at the new reflection of my visage and noted I resembled a boy with fine features. What will d'Alençon think of my new look? I thought and said out loud, "The less of me that reminds men I am a woman the better."

565 YEARS LATER

JULY 1996, WEST POINT, NY

"Are you ready?" Jack asked as he stepped into Jane's room and closed the door behind him. In two quick strides he crossed the room, grabbed her, and planted a playful kiss on her mouth. When he released her, he said, "I always wanted to kiss a regimental commander. You're the queen of Beast Barracks. How does that feel?"

Jane laughed out loud, grateful for his light mood and the distraction of his handsome face. In the two years they had been together he had softened and grown stronger at the same time and so had she. "I'm a little nervous, to tell you the truth."

She sat on her neatly made bed to tie her shoes and instead of thinking about the speech she was to deliver in a matter of minutes to eleven hundred plebes at Beast Barracks, she thought about Jack. They were now firsties, seniors, and in love. They were not a gushy couple. Theirs was a relationship built first on the deep bonds of a common mission and friendship. Romantic love was the bonus, the sweet surprise, after all their hard work and seriousness of the academy.

"Wow, just look at all those chevrons," he said touching the sleeve of her dress gray uniform hanging in her closet.

"Hey, I earned every one of those," Jane defended. "Your sleeves aren't much different." Jane referred to the fact that he was the regimental operations officer for this detail of Beast Barracks. Both positions were awarded for high academic standings, athletic achievements, and military leadership.

"Here you go," he said handing her sword, scabbard, and red sash to her in a playful ceremonious way.

"We've come a long way," Jane said as she slipped the sword from the scabbard a few inches and studied the blade. This moment felt important to her in some mysterious way. A sensation, like she was falling through time, made her feel dizzy.

"Hey, Jane. Are you OK?"

"What? . . . Oh yeah. Sure." The dizzy feeling passed.

"Go get 'em."

Exhaling a nervous breath, she took her white cap off the shelf of her wardrobe, pushed the gold braid down so it touched the brim, and ran her finger over the pin depicting Pallas Athena's helmet. Goddess of war, Jane thought, be with me.

With Jack by her side, she marched across the macadam, sword swinging against her leg, feeling the pregnant pause—as night turns to day—of predawn. She strode confidently to a spot in front of the American flag, hanging limp on the foggy plain, three hundred yards from the murmuring Hudson River. The spirits of Pershing, MacArthur, Patton, and all of the other illustrious figures of history seemed to swirl around, rise and dip with anticipation. They had stood in this same place, witnessed the same view out of their wizened eyes, and breathed the same mountain and river air. She imagined them standing behind and beside her, their hands on her shoulder blades for support. She felt infused with strength and purpose.

"Attention!" She called out and brought her right hand up to the brim of her hat for a salute. Her voice, crisp and loud, carried across the morning air and landed in the ears of every new cadet.

They moved instantly, as one unit. The bugler played reveille as the sun infused its first warming rays of the day, bleeding light into the inky dark sky. The tiny droplets of water in the fog caught the light and gave the effect of a gossamer curtain hovering above them all. She allowed the notes of the bugle to charge her nervous system in an attempt to quell the butterflies that felt more like a twenty-one gun salute going on in her gut.

When the buglers removed the trumpets from their lips, she called out, "Pa Rade rest!" The entire corps moved again—all eleven hundred and fifty-six cadets and their leaders. The power to move this many people with her voice was intoxicating. She had been very aware of her responsibilities upon marching out onto the plain, but the reality, was weighty, like a female Atlas, her knees almost buckled with the burden.

"Today begins the most challenging portion of Beast Barracks. You will be confronted with your own fears and physical limitations. What you will gain is the strength to break through these limitations, not for yourselves, but for the sake of your platoon."

Jane took a breath and paused in her speech for effect. Sun now reflected off the windows of the barracks behind the cadets, casting dazzling fireballs into the air, as the morning birds' songs added carefree wistfulness. She continued, "You will persevere for your squad mate. You will find courage you did not know you had, and you will find physical strength you did not know you had. Everything you do here has a purpose, from leaving your sink spotless every morning and shining your shoes, to your attention to detail in formation. In the real army if you miss a detail someone could die."

She watched a few cadets here and there wobble and sway slightly. She remembered the feeling of falling asleep while standing in formation when she was in basic training and bent her own knees to insure adequate blood flow. By the end of plebe year, each cadet knew not to lock his or her knees while standing at attention for extended periods of time or risk fainting. She would not be surprised to see one of them keel right over. She hoped they would fall into another cadet instead of the pavement.

She changed the tone of her voice to get the regiment's full attention. "As Douglas MacArthur said in his 84ᵗʰ birthday speech about courage: 'moral courage—the courage of one's convictions—the courage to see a thing through. This is not easy. The world is a constant conspiracy against the brave. It is the age-old struggle of the roar of the crowd on one side and the voice of your conscience on the other.'" She paused, letting MacArthur's words of wisdom sink in. "I say, it's time! Time for you to become leaders. It's time for you to become the epitome of fortitude and valor. As you learn to follow, you learn to lead. Your platoon needs you, the corps needs you, your country needs you. It's time to step up, keep up, and excel!" She took a breath and swept her eyes over the assembled cadets.

"Platoon leaders, address your platoons."

She saluted and released the corps to their platoon leaders who would disseminate the details for the morning, stood watch, and listened. Her body shook, like an aftershock, from the energy of the regiment. The moment, which she knew she would remember for her entire life, felt surreal. Time became rubbery, flexible, and more expanded than normal. She glanced at Jack and her cadre of leaders, all of whom she had known for three years. Now, they were in command, seniors. They were the ones who the plebes would look up to. The realization made Jane shiver more. Leadership felt like stepping into a rowboat, the craft teeters and feels like it will capsize, until one settles in and gets used to the fact that subtle movements yield big effects.

Later that day Jane waited at the post laundry counter for someone to help her, thankful for a couple of minutes to herself. She smiled when she saw one of her favorite people on post come into view behind the counter. Gladys, a fleshy woman whose face seemed to reflect the ancestry of several races, approached Jane with thick open arms.

"Jane!"

"Gladys," Jane said in return and let herself be enveloped in a bear hug. Hugging felt like a nice break from all the saluting. Their peculiar friendship had developed and grown over the last three years. Jane helped Gladys with little problems, and Gladys, besides being a wiz at the sewing machine, worked her magic on a myriad of problems concerning missing clothing or buttons.

"I hate to bother you but I'm missing these items. Can you take a peek and let me know if you have them?" She handed Gladys her laundry slip, tilted her head, and smiled.

"Might take a while. We'll do our best." She tried to smile at Jane but her dark eyes filled with tears, and she began to cry. In between gasps Gladys sputtered, "It's my little brother. He was . . . He was . . . shot and killed. Last week."

"Oh, Gladys. I'm so sorry," Jane said and squeezed Gladys's forearm. It was firm from lots of hard work. "Did they catch the guy? You know, the one who—"

"No," she wailed. "That's the thing. Cops are too busy. Happens all the time in New York City."

"My father's a district attorney in Rhode Island. Maybe I can ask him to check into the matter to expedite your brother's case." Jane hesitated. Am I doing the right thing by getting involved? Deciding it was the right thing to do she said, "Write down your brother's name, the date of the crime, location, and anything else that may be important."

Gladys's face brightened and the tears slowed. "You'd do that?"

"Of course." Jane hugged Gladys; the smell of laundry detergent filled her nose.

As Gladys wrote the pertinent information on the back of a laundry slip her boss hollered, "Hey, Glad-ass, get a move on."

Jane bristled. She resented the way Gladys's boss obviously distorted her name. Couldn't the woman see Gladys was having a hard time?

Gladys handed the laundry tag with the information to Jane and fixed her gaze on Jane's face. "Thank you. I'll check on your white shirts."

"And, I'll take care of this." She waved the laundry tag. "Take heart, Gladys. We'll get this case moving."

Gladys smiled, showing brilliant white teeth; her eyes moist with emotion.

Two weeks of Beast Barracks passed according to the cadre's meticulous plans, each event linked to the next with the entire freshman class standing in formation, only the uniforms changed from Gym Alpha, black army shorts with white T-shirts, to camouflage fatigues, to white over gray dress slacks. Physical training, bayonet training, formation practice, and team sports, all went by in a blur.

She and Jack stole a few hours to relax before launching into the last and most strenuous week of basic training.

"Tomorrow we head to Lake Frederick. Do you remember the summer during our Beast Barracks? Doesn't it seem like eons ago?" Jane asked and rested her head on Jack's shoulder. She gazed out over the Hudson River slipping by. They had driven north toward Newburgh and found a secluded spot to relax in order to recharge and clear their heads. They only had a few hours to spend alone. Both would be busy tending to leadership duties for the next week until Beast was over. They had stripped down to shorts and T-shirts in the car and walked barefoot to their spot, a ten-foot by ten-foot grassy clearing beside the river.

"I loved Beast," Jack crooned and bent his head toward hers. "Almost as much as I love this." He kissed her. She shoved him backward onto the woolen blanket and climbed astride him. Bees buzzed overhead while a robin rustled in the underbrush nearby. The sun on her face made her squint.

"I wish we had more time so we could . . . you know," Jane said as she gently massaged Jack's taut chest from her perch. "I have to prepare for a couple of meetings with some substandard platoon leaders." She let her hand stray to Jack's armpit and wiggled a finger into the hollow.

"Ow!" He pretended to be hurt, grabbed her, and pinned her down onto the blanket. "Bet I know who. Ash, right?"

"You guessed it—Patrick Ash . . . and Wright and Avila. Have you noticed a change in Ash? We used to be such buddies. But over the past two years it seems like we have had some kind of inverse luck going on. With each of my successes he experiences a challenge, and I feel like we slipped further apart this summer. I wonder what's up with him?"

Jack pulled her up to sitting and knit his dark brows together. "He's having some challenges with his parents."

Jane's curiosity was piqued. "Really? Are they OK?"

"His parents aren't like yours. They have issues. I promised him I wouldn't repeat his story."

"You can't tell me?"

"No, really, Jane. Just try to be patient with him. All I can say is that he feels doomed to be a failure like his father."

"Thanks for telling me." Jane said, feeling genuine sadness for her friend who held so much potential. She watched more than one person crash from believing defeating thoughts about themselves.

"Enough about Ash. Where were we?" Jack brushed Jane's hair behind her ear and cupped her head in his hand. "How much time do we have?"

"One hour."

Two hours later Jane found she needed to wrestle her mind back from the memory of the river's edge into the small room back in barracks on post. Patrick sat across from her desk and wore a deep frown.

"Ash, I haven't seen much of you this last year. How have you been?"

He hung his head slightly and brushed his hand over his closely cropped hair. "I know. I've been trying to keep up here. It's not easy for someone like me."

"What are you talking about? You're smart and one of the best soldiers I know."

"Tell that to my professors." He looked defeated. Jane remembered what Jack told her about his parents. She could see that it had gotten to him.

"OK, so I called you here because . . ." She searched for words that would not add to his feelings of failure. "You know I have to talk to all the platoons leaders whose new cadets have more injuries than others. Your platoon is on top—has the most injuries. Can you tell me what's up?" she asked keeping her face as neutral as possible. Their friendship of three years made confronting him a challenge.

At times in the past she found his moods mercurial. But recently he seemed worse. His squad leaders complained that he had been downright mean to some of the plebes and reluctant to help the squad leaders with certain tasks.

When he did not answer her, she said, "You need to pay closer attention to your platoon."

He stared at her. Behind his brown eyes appeared a darkness she had not noticed before. Apparently he did not like to be confronted.

She attempted to keep her face from betraying the nervous feelings bubbling within her. "Patrick?"

"How did you get to be regimental commander anyway?" Resentment oozed off his words.

To keep herself from losing composure, she focused her eyes beyond the side of his head to the grain in the tan door behind him and let her peripheral vision take in the small bland office. "Tomorrow we march to Lake Frederick to begin Warrior Forge. It's imperative you watch closely over your platoon. You know how fast a cadet can drop from dehydration or twist an ankle. You need to be completely squared away." She thrust out her chin and tilted her head in an attempt to appear more confident than she felt.

"Bitch," he whispered. He raised the tone of his voice and said, "Just because you have all those bars on your arm does not make you my superior."

Jane felt electricity shoot up her spine and fought to stay completely still. "Actually, Lieutenant, it does. You're in my command and under my command you will take care of your platoon or you will be removed from this detail." She paused to catch her breath. Her racing heart sucked all the air out of her lungs. "Do you understand?" she said.

He starred back at her, clenched his jaw. She searched his face for traces of their former friendship. When she could not find any softness, she said more loudly with a voice hardly her own, "DO YOU UNDERSTAND?"

He stood and saluted her, "Yes, ma'am."

He refused to give her the respect of her title. There were a number of men who resisted and disrespected women in leadership roles. Apparently Ash was one of them. This was a surprise to Jane. Why was it that a strong female leader was called a bitch? At least it was a slight improvement over being labeled a witch in medieval times.

To his departing back she said, "In the future you will address me as Captain." She paused, but could think of nothing else to say to him. "Dismissed."

She only had ten minutes to collect herself before the next underperforming platoon leader, Wright, was due to sit in the same seat as Patrick Ash. She wished she had Jack with her as he was battalion commander, but he was making sure all of the army vehicles and tactical officers were ready for transporting gear to Lake Frederick. They had agreed to divide and conquer.

Stand in your power. Stay steady and confident. A voice came from somewhere in her head. With the strange voice came a sensation of strength, and she wondered if the pressures of leadership were making her a little crazy.

Oddly enough the strange sensation helped her to have a more successful meeting with Cadet Wright.

When the moment came for her to crawl into bed that night, she marveled at each new ache. Leadership, like a good pair of army boots, needing breaking in. She found her mind racing and overwhelmed with all the details, minor and otherwise, she was responsible for.

The next day, under Jane's command, the entire corps of new cadets and their leadership cadre marched the twelve-mile trek to

Lake Frederick under sunny skies. Temperatures hovered around ninety-five degrees and sunk into the forest adding extra weight to already full rucksacks. But, even with the heat, moods ran high. Voices chanted cadence after cadence, and Jane felt filled with sobering strength. She took leadership seriously and with some measure of humility.

At the edge of the quiet lake, they conducted three days of field training exercises, all to prepare the cadets for the grand finale—Warrior Forge Day. Warrior Forge was a twenty-four-hour long, sixteen-course day, the culminating event at the end of the six weeks of Cadet Basic Training. It was imperative that each platoon and squad leader knew exactly what to do and what to say, that they had consistent commands. What the plebes did not know was just how many hours their sergeants put in to ensure the grueling event went off seamlessly.

Jane wiped sweat from her forehead and squinted into the setting sun at her platoon and squad leaders. "Remember you guys are going to be as tired as these new cadets, and it's your job to hold it together and keep them safe . . . and healthy. Take a minute to remember how much you counted on your squad leader during your Beast. You are these kids' parents, their guardians while they're here. This is why we came to West Point. To guide and protect—it's your duty and your honor. I'm hoping for minimal injuries this year. So, again, starting with Sergeant Ash, pop off and give me the order of events for Warrior Forge Day."

She pointed to Ash and used her most serious instructor facial expression—back teeth pressed together with a furrowed brow. "Ready? Go. Ash!" She said a silent prayer that his attitude would be better today.

"Reveille, MRE breakfast, get gear together for the seventy-five-foot rappel," Ash fired back. "Then check that my squad leaders are squared away with their squads."

Jane let out her breath, relieved he had stepped up and gotten his shit together. His platoon appeared to be working in concert and morale seemed good. The only noticeable change was that he would not look her in the eye, and the once friendly banter was long gone. She had lost a buddy.

Hauling her thoughts back into line, Jane ignored the sweat running down the center of her spine. She ignored her pulsing right shinbone, pretty sure it was shin splints, and took a long swig from her canteen. She listened to her cadre's responses, for the manner in which each one answered. She could tell by their tone, the space between each word, whether or not each was ready. Where there was hesitation there was doubt and a lack of confidence in the task given. It was her job to ferret out these weak spots, get the cadet to face the fear, and hone the resistance until each one of these cadet sergeants felt as confident and polished as a seasoned veteran.

Dawn brought the sounds of gunfire and shouting. A light morning fog hovered over the lake. The men and women were scattered by squads all over the area, up on the mountain, repelling down the cliff-face, stalking through the woods, running through the field, and engaged in mock battles. Jane shouted one order after another and delegated staff to the wounded and dehydrated. She counseled the flagging, tired leaders; though the hardest task of all was to take an overzealous leader and settle him or her down.

During a short break in the battle, while some of the regiment ate their MRE's out of foil pouches, Jane pulled Ash and Wright aside. Jane sent her thoughts skyward as she walked with the cadets to an area out of earshot to others.

"Sergeant Ash, Sergeant Wright, both of you need to ease up on your squad leaders. I'm hearing complaints you are both hazing with too much anger. Leading is not about being mean. Lead by example."

She glanced at each of them. Wright's entire six-foot-four-inch frame was covered in dirt, sweat dripped off his nose, ran down the side of his square jaw, and landed on his broad chest. Formidable was the word she would use to describe him. She found herself thinking that she would want his intensity fighting next to her in a real battle.

She decided to try to channel their energy instead of thwarting it. "Wright. Ash. The new cadets and your squad leaders are not the enemy here. Can you direct your intensity to the opposite team, the enemy? You have great energy; just focus it and watch your tempers. Your duty is to protect your soldiers. Got it?"

They grunted in response, sucking water from their canteens, too eager to return to the battle to give her an argument.

Jane watched the majority of the cadets blossom with confidence and bond as soldiers when they won, and console one another when they lost, and she found herself getting caught up in the excitement and drama of it all.

When the entire regiment marched back onto post from Lake Frederick with the band playing and civilians cheering, Jane finally allowed herself the luxury of feeling exhausted. During the previous twenty-four hours of Warrior Forge Day and the twelve-mile hike back, she held everything together, ignoring her pain and tiredness.

"New Cadets, dismissed," she ordered into the afternoon sun. The cadets scattered, shuffling and limping back to their barracks. Basic training was over.

ROUEN, FRANCE

SATURDAY, MAY 25, 1431

"**B**onjour, Jehanne." Brother Jean Toutmoille bowed several times, his hands clasped together at his round belly.

"Ah, Brother Toutmoille, bonjour." I was surprised at this visit as he was unaccompanied by a priest of higher rank, which was the usual protocol. "To what do I owe the pleasure of your visit?"

He wrung his hands and glanced at my guards, who played at sticks in the corner near the narrow window. "I have come because I feel you were done a terrible wrong. I feel it gets worse each day, and I fear God will punish those of us who have been unkind to you," he spoke in hushed tones so my guards would not be alerted to his near treason to the bishop and the University of Paris.

"Brother, it is not I who judges others but God in Heaven." I smiled at him to let him know I held no grudge. "You need not worry about me. I accept your pledge of apology and understand your position within the hierarchy of the Church Militant."

"Merci, Jehanne. I wish to tell you some of the falsities that have been documented against you," he spoke so low I could barely make out his words.

"I understand most of the claims against me are fabrications and fears of the those in charge."

"Oui, oui, they are afraid of you." He glanced nervously over his shoulder at the guards. "They say that you carried mandrake at your breast as a talisman for wealth and temporal things. They say you will escape from here with the help of the Devil, that's why they contemplate putting you in a cage at times. And, they say that you poured hot wax on the heads of children for an act of divination."

I laughed out loud. "The wax accusation is a new one for me. God in Heaven."

His faced became beet red, and he appeared upset. "I am outraged how they treat you. I believe you are who you say you are. I want you to know this. There are others, but they are afraid to come forward and go against the bishop."

"I am aware of what they say and sadly, my dear Brother, I have no control over their mouths or quills. Take heart and trust that God's grace will cover me no matter what happens."

He took my chained hands in his and said, "May God bless you and keep you in his heart. I will pray for you."

"Merci, Brother. And, I will pray for you."

After he left, I reclined back on my cot and felt hopeful. He said others understood who I truly was. This was good news. All was not lost. Between these men and my friends in the future I felt hopeful my deeds would be understood.

I relaxed. A tiny shimmer of hope glistened within my empty belly. I recalled the first time I was put into a leadership position. It was all about trust then and continued to be about trust here in prison. Recollections from the spring of 1429 floated all around me. I smiled at the ceiling and allowed the reminiscences to seduce me into the always-consoling dream state.

On April 21, 1429, we left Tours, a great caravan of men, horses, and wagons laden with weapons and war machines. Carts loaded with food supplies, and livestock, including oxen and pigs, trekked the muddy and rocky roads slowly from village to village through farmland and vineyard as we headed for Blois to meet up with the remainder of our troops and our commander, d'Alençon. The sky hung low like a wet canopy, and a drizzling rain made the men quiet.

I confidently rode my war courser, a giant black horse with a coat as shiny as the medals in the pocket of my cloak, which I had picked up at the silversmith's the day before. In my right hand, I held the white silk standard, which had been sewn with care by the best seamstress in Tours. Just as my counsel advised, it showed an image of our Lord, Jesus, with radiant angels flanking him, fleur-de-lys, and the words "Jhesus-Maria."

As we rode past waving and cheering patriots of France, fledgling hope gleaming from their eyes at the sight of us, my nerves soared and sank with the varied terrain, rising from excited exuberance and falling into a worried trepidation. Each time I sank low, my counsel spoke kindly and optimistically in my ear, bolstering my spirits. On the afternoon of April 25, we crested a small plateau amidst the verdant greening fields and budding trees, and spotted a series of gray tendrils rising toward thick white clouds—the cooking fires of the remainder of our army. My stomach leaped into my throat with excitement at the proximity of my beloved. A ripple of cheers rolled through the ranks as the men realized we neared our destination.

The acrid smells of the cook fires mixed with the pungent odors of human waste greeted us long before we entered the chaos of camp. The repulsive stench snapped me back into the harsh reality of soldiers and war. Talking in the ranks behind me stopped in anticipation of merging our forces with the thousands of other men who had traveled from provinces far away to defend their country.

"Metz," I called out and leaned over my horse to him. "Have our wagons brought near to those in camp over there." I gestured with my gloved hand to the dozens of wagons already lined up along the edge of the teeming camp. "Then meet me at d'Alencon's tent. I assume it's the largest one there, up front."

"You assume correctly. On your orders, Captain," he hollered loud enough for many others to hear and gave me a wink at the same time. "I'll see you at the commander's tent."

By allowing himself to take orders from me, he essentially gave permission to the other men to do the same, lending authority to my leadership.

I directed my horse and our troops around as much of the mud and waste as I could so he could have firm soil on which to rest his large hooves. He snorted in protest at having to travel this way. I leaned forward in the saddle and patted him lovingly on his sweat-darkened neck. "Good boy," I soothed and to the lieutenants behind me said, "Choose a site upwind of the camp and get the men settled. Be sure," I ordered, "to set up latrine tents for our men. It will help to make camp life more bearable for all."

All around the encampment, men in various states of dress meandered around or sat on stumps sharpening weapons: long lances, swords, billhooks, and the deadly halberd, which looked like a large axe with a spike and was usually wielded by our biggest and strongest men-at-arms. Horses whinnied while vultures swooped in, picked at the debris scattered near the cook tents, and took off again. Women, camp followers, sat on the knees of some of the men or sauntered around seductively flirting, enticing the bored men to passion. I glanced back to see Brother Pasquerel's face redden with embarrassment as we passed one drunken woman with her plump breast exposed. The excitement and anticipation at seeing d'Alençon became overshadowed by my outrage at the disorderly and horrendous state of affairs at this camp. It certainly was not what I had envisioned; even the pigs back in Domrémy lived in cleaner conditions than this sty. A snatch of angry words broke through my critical reverie. My eyes followed the source of the voices and landed on a group of five men assaulting one another, brawling right in the middle of camp. This is not good for morale!

"D'Aulon, follow me. We are going to see Commander d'Alençon before we set up camp," I bellowed, anger rising like a tempest within me.

Upon approaching the commander's tent I hardly waited until my horse came to a stop before I leaped off and stormed toward the striped fabric opening, its fringe flapping with the spring breeze. "D'Alençon?" I called out before lifting the tent's flap and stepping inside.

"Jehanne!" he exclaimed. An expression of warning darkened his fine face.

When I noticed he was not alone I checked myself from launching a verbal assault. He stood with three other men who, by the looks of their field uniforms, appeared to be captains as well. "Bonjour, Captains, Commander."

"La Hire, Rais, Xaintrailles," d'Alençon offered. "I give you the Maid, Jehanne."

"Bonjour," they said. Curious smiles and raised eyebrows told me this first impression would go far.

"Christ's bones. I'll be damned," La Hire blurted out. His bulk, huge arms and chest atop short thick legs, spoke for him as well. This man would be an asset. "We have heard much about you. So, you will be a captain with us, eh? Who knows what Charles was thinking; he must be quite desperate these days. I do hope you have a strong stomach. It is a harsh life, the life of a soldier."

"You'll excuse La Hire, Jehanne," d'Alençon said quickly just as Metz slipped into the tent. D'Alençon nodded to him and continued. "His given name is Étienne de Vignolles but everyone calls him La Hire for his temper."

"I can assure you, Monsieur La Hire, I am quite prepared for whatever my King of Heaven sets before me." I stepped toward him, squared my shoulders, and deepened my voice. "And, he wishes for me to lead an army to Orléans. You should take care with your tongue; there should be no cursing in God's camp."

La Hire raised sandy eyebrows and shot d'Alençon a look of amusement. "Jehanne, may I call you Jehanne?"

Metz smirked and gave me a wink encouraging me to be bold. "Most certainly."

"Jehanne, you do not disappoint." He squared his own shoulders, puffed out his broad chest, and looked me in the eye seriously. "Your fire will most surely be welcome in battle, but you'd be good to watch your own tongue." His gray eyes narrowed with a threat and his face reddened with intensity, causing the scar across his cheek to blanch.

"La Hire, go easy." Rais clapped him on the back to settle him down. I instantly liked his method of combat and ascertained that his success came from watching and calculating action. Even his person appeared formidable but controlled; he was a large man but his size felt tempered by education and manners.

I felt emboldened by his presence. "La Hire, this army has been scraped together under God's grace alone. This is God's army and in God's army there will be no cursing or swearing. Also, my voices tell me there should be no whores following camp as well. This is a sacred mission and must be treated as such. I demand no less!"

All five men erupted at once objecting to my decrees. D'Alençon raised a hand and silence fell.

"Jehanne, surely . . . the men need . . . the prostitutes give the men a way of releasing stress and anxiety before and after battle," d'Alençon said haltingly. I could tell he was having a hard time balancing his personal feelings for me with his role of commander. "Women always follow camp." He shot me a look, pleading with his eyes for me to back down.

"Not anymore; they will not follow this camp, I assure you. Even if I have to throw them out myself." At the sight of him, my heart had leaped. I had to fight with my feelings to stay on course.

"Well, mademoiselle, you may consider that your first task here," Xaintrailles chimed in smirking. With his prominent incisors, deeply set, light hazel eyes, wide forehead, and narrow jaw he reminded me of a wolf. He stood taller than the others, and his body looked as resilient and agile as an animal's.

"Do not call me *mademoiselle*." I tried to calm myself so they would take me seriously. "The dauphin, our future king, appointed me a captain, equal to you. You may address me as Captain, Jehanne, or la Pucelle, the Maid." I paused to let that sink in a little and then continued, "Captains, you would do well not to underestimate me. I have already faced a king and all of his advisors, priests of the highest rank, and other court officials. How do you expect to win a battle with slovenly men of poor moral character? Our soldiers deserve better than this." I took a breath and noticed that they listened to my words, perhaps with an air of condescension, but they listened nonetheless. "One more thing," I added, heat rising in my face, "I bid you enforce the use of latrine tents. The men piss and defecate only as far as their lazy legs take them." I turned, thrust the flap aside to exit the tent and paused. Over my shoulder I added, "Au revior, I will see you all later this afternoon when my chaplain says Mass for the entire camp."

I allowed the flap to fall behind me, my senses assaulted by the foul stench of camp. I shook from the intensity and force of my fellow captains and felt elated at the same time. They were quite a daunting team.

D'Aulon and Louis stood grinning, holding fast to our horses whose tails swooshed constantly at flies. They raised their eyebrows; I was sure they overheard. "Don't look at me like that." I took another glance around camp and shook my head. "We need to get those horses to water. Where's Pasquerel?"

"Here I am, my dear." He appeared from behind the horses. "Our Lord will be most pleased with your desires for these men. A stroke of genius to ban the prostitutes from camp."

"Gather the other chaplains. We have much work to do. Arrange to say Mass to the entire army this afternoon." My hand shook as I reached for my horse's bridle. My heart still wanted to feel d'Alençon's arms around me. Somehow I would reconcile with the idea of loving him from afar.

"Jehanne?" D'Aulon's voice tore me from my thoughts.

"Pardonne moi, d'Aulon," I mumbled and placed my foot in his cupped hands then swung my leg across my tired horse's back.

Louis, d'Aulon, and the other members of our retinue set up camp while I rode with my monks, hardy Brother Pasquerel and soft-spoken Nicolas de Vouthon. They rode behind me, down the uneven rows of men and tents, while I held my banner. Cheers of welcome rang across the field. Some waved excitedly while others simply gazed at me with bewilderment and skepticism, and still, a few seemed to be outright hostile.

"Gentle men of war," I bellowed as the grace of God filled my heart. "I am Jehanne the Maid. The King in Heaven has sent me to guide you to victory." Pausing, I looked around checking the faces of the men I addressed.

"You have been chosen by God to fight this holy fight and to free the good people of Orléans from the English who hold them siege. You are men of God," I yelled while turning my horse so I could proclaim in all directions. "You are soldiers in God's army now!"

Some of the men cheered while others prepared to wait, perhaps, for more evidence from me to lift their pessimistic hearts. "Do you want to win? Do you want to be victorious for God and France?"

A roar of male voices erupted around me. "I bid you put aside your ungodly habits." I pushed my feet into the stirrups. "You must not curse or swear oaths using God's name. You must not see the women who follow camp." The crowd groaned in opposition, but I continued, "You must clear your hearts of any evil thoughts. As soldiers of God you will kneel in front of the chaplains twice each day." Murmurs of descent rolled through the heavy air. Thunder rumbled while rain clouds threatened to let go above my head, but not a drop fell.

"I say again, you are soldiers of the King in Heaven, so you must behave like it and you will be victorious for France." I lifted my banner in the air. "For France and the King of Heaven you will fight, and God will inspire the hearts within your breasts. You will be victorious!"

Cheering and shouts rang in the air. The eyes of the men nearest me flickered with the first flames of hope.

"Brothers." I turned in my saddle and spoke to my smiling chaplains who looked somewhat uncomfortable in the saddle. "Follow me. We are going to talk with the women."

We picked our way to the back of the ranks toward a copse of trees under which clustered three tattered multicolored tents. Half a dozen women bustling around the cook fire halted their chores and watched us approach, mistrust written all over their faces.

"Bonjour, mesdames," I called.

"Bonjour," a few mumbled, unsure of what was coming. I was confident word had traveled to them of my earlier declaration.

"I am Jehanne, and these are my chaplains, Brothers Pasquerel and Vouthon. We have come to ask you to take leave of camp. I am sorry if this distresses you, but you must know it distresses God to see his daughters selling themselves to men." I wanted to be sure I spoke to inspire and not to discourage them.

I could feel the hands of my angels on my shoulders. "Each one of you has been given gifts by God and you do not use them. You are the ones given the greatest joy of the re-creation of our species. Your bodies, therefore, are sacred."

One of the women stepped forward. "How do you suppose we will feed ourselves then? You, who eat at the king's table and wear the rich colors of the wealthy. It's easy for you to judge us." Her dark hair spilled out of the confinement of hairpins in a haphazard way, and her dress hung off one bare shoulder.

"Not at all," I offered. "I was a peasant girl. I believed that I had something to offer France and now here I am doing God's work."

Each one of them looked tired and worn, like they had been through their own private wars, the struggle for survival etched into the lines on their faces and in the dirt under their fingernails.

"If any of you wish to enter the convent, we will be happy to write letters of recommendation for you. There, at least, you will be safe, fed, and clothed," Brother Pasquerel volunteered. "Brother Vouthon and I will be happy to counsel you and hear your confessions."

I added, "The King in Heaven wishes you to know he absolves you all of any sins you feel you have committed." Their faces began to brighten. "It is never too late to change your life, but it does get harder the longer you wait." Many of the women were close to my age but looked older. I felt sad for them. "If any of you have one man who keeps you here, I will bid him to marry you, so that you may be elevated in stature. If your man is married, I bid you take leave and find work that is more worthy of you. Each one of you is special in the eyes of God."

"No one ever tells us these things," a woman with curly red hair spilling down her back, piped up. Her body shook with anger. "Some of us have been abused by men since we were born, including our fathers. How do we change that? How do you expect us to care for ourselves when no one ever has?"

"I cannot answer to the abuse of men," I replied sadly. "But I can say that it is up to the mind of any soul on earth to choose to be happier. Oui, it takes much effort and feels frightening to change, but I am here to tell you it is possible."

We spoke to nearly one hundred women. Some chose to take Brother's offer of the convent while others left to work for relatives. Those who had little prospect, I hired on as cooks for the camp with strict instructions for clothing and restrictions on fraternization with the troops. Of the remaining women, a few married the men they followed and a dozen or so seemed to linger and would not leave or speak with us.

Luckily, subsequent meetings of all of the captains went amicably. The respect for me from the men and captains grew slowly each day like the spring grasses in the fields nearby. I lay night after night, listening to the deepened breathing of the men in my retinue, and awoke each morning eager to do my job.

The day before we were due to leave for Orléans, I woke before dawn and roused my men: my brothers Jean and Pierre, d'Aulon, and my chaplains. Pushing aside the flaps of the tent, I stepped out onto the dew-laden grass. Sounds of the night still hummed in the air while just a hint of light to the east washed everything in a blue-purple glow. I mounted my large black courser and rode to the bagpipers' tent, "Good pipers, rise and begin playing to rouse the men."

We rode, my chaplains, my brothers, and I, to the rise of the only small hill around. One of the pipers dismounted and put his mouth to the blowpipe. From the other side of the field, I could hear the haunting drones of the others, starting off low at first. There were four pipers in all, a benefit of having Scottish allies, stationed around the vast field of men, tents, horses, and wagons piled high with supplies. It all lay before me shrouded in a cool morning mist that hung like a protective blanket over our camp. Trills of the other pipers floated on the morning air, creating a heavenly harmonic. Just as the snake responds to the sounds of the charmer's flute, the sun moved in response to the music of the pipes and began to shoot crimson and orange rockets of light into the sky behind me while over one thousand men emerged from their tents, tumbled off bedrolls, and assembled together as one cohesive group.

The notes and tones of the pipes sent shivers of joy through my body. I called on as many angels as I could to be present in the field with us as the men knelt, in reverence to God, just as I instructed them the day before.

To the sound of the bagpipes we sang. "The day glows red, the day of gladness; the sun of justice gives beams of grace. Present in our guise this day, the King of glory."

The men hesitated at first. Then, with each repetition of the refrain, their voices grew louder and louder. My heart soared as I rode through the men, banner in hand, while they sang, praying they be inspired to great feats of bravery in the days to come. My heart expanded to encircle all who left their lives behind to serve our country. I loved each and every one of them for their courage. Their deep voices and the notes of the bagpipes echoed in the valley off every tree and farmhouse and floated all the way to the heavens above.

We became a unified army that morning as the bleating of the pipes coordinated the beating of all our hearts to the heartbeat of France. This was what I came to do. Profound joy rippled through me. I could feel the fragile faith of France mending and healing with each footfall as I galloped back to the hill where d'Alençon now sat on his horse holding the flag of France. La Hire and the other captains lined up on their horses with him. I pulled up next to d'Alençon, and, side by side, we sang, beacons of leadership and love of our country, with the sun now illuminating the faces of the men.

After the last refrain, d'Alençon and I raised our banners. He held one for France in the air, signifying silence. Taking a breath, I proclaimed as loudly and clearly as I could, "Dearest soldiers of France, God is most pleased with you." I paused to let the squires repeat my words to those in the back of the ranks. "God is with you, and we will be victorious in Orléans." Pausing again, I smiled broadly, joyfully, at my fair duke. "Ready your souls. We will march tomorrow to Orléans. The King in Heaven is most grateful for your service. Whether you live or die, you will be granted your proper reward—eternal life." I hesitated, gathering up as much feeling as I could. "God bless France," I bellowed with a clear voice, echoes magnifying my words a thousandfold, then raised my banner in the air again as a great roar rose from the sea of men in response. The magic of the bagpipes successfully united hundreds of individuals into a nexus of patriotism and faith, one inspired army.

We were ready.

After breakfast, d'Alençon called a meeting of all the captains to go over final strategy for our march on Orléans. We gathered around the commander's table in his tent, d'Alencon, La Hire, Rais, Xaintrailles, Metz, Poulengy, and myself. The energy was high and, overall, we felt optimistic.

"Jehanne, Rais, and La Hire, you will go ahead to Orléans with the supply wagons and a contingent of a few hundred men to meet Dunois, the Bastard of Orléans. I will meet you in a few days time with the remainder of the troops." He cleared his throat and spread out the map of Orléans. "La Hire knows what English and Burgundian troops are positioned where. He has been working with Dunois to lift the siege for the last six months."

"Commander?" I cleared my throat. "May I interrupt for a moment? I have a gift for each of you."

"Certainly," he replied as an inquisitive look lit his face.

"These were made in Tours, for luck and blessings," I said, opening the black velvet drawstring bag and emptying the shiny medals onto the map table. "They are for protection and inspiration and have been blessed by the chaplains. They depict each of my saints and the Sacred Heart of Christ." The medals, shaped like four blunted arrowheads and joined together in the center, showed a saint embossed on each section. I handed a medal and a silver chain to each captain and my fair duke. "Please wear them for me . . . so, I will know you will be watched over," I asked, feeling surprisingly protective of these brave men.

"Merci," La Hire growled and flashed me a lopsided grin. The others mumbled their thanks nodding their heads in gratitude. They passed the medals' chains over their weather-beaten faces and let the silver crosses rest in the folds of the fabric over their hearts.

"May we be victorious for God and France," I said, my heart going out to each of them. "Thank you for believing in me so far. I will not let you down."

It was evening when we approached the east gate of Orléans. Torch lights from the city glowed, amber jewels against the black velvet fabric of the moonless night sky. To our left we could see the golden twinkle of lights from the Church of Saint Aignan. Rumor said Saint Aignan defended the city from the infamous and brutal Attila the Hun. If Saint Aignan could defend against the Huns, I could surely inspire defense against the English and Burgundians.

"Luckily, Dunois, excellent strategist that he is, has created a diversion so that we could approach from this direction," La Hire spoke, his gravely voice optimistic. We had come to a tentative mutual respect for one another after our initial confrontation. I liked his rough confidence, the fact he would righteously do what needed to be done for France. He seemed a great patriot, but would balk if you told him so. *Warrior* would be the best way to describe him. He exuded warrior. From his broken nose down to his short, strong, bowed legs. I could rely on his fearless temperament; nothing would get by him.

In all, there were five gates, five roads into the walled city that enabled crossing of the wide Loire River. The English held siege to every one of them, preventing supplies and men from entering or leaving. While the English soldiers were occupied elsewhere, we slipped in between the Saint Loup gate, to the east, which was a little over a mile outside the walls of the city and the Pont des Tourelles to the south.

A great throng of townspeople, men-at-arms, and nobles with torches ablaze, greeted us as we passed under the imposing teeth of the portcullis of the east gate.

We were expected.

With Rais and Dunois beside me, we paraded on horseback proudly through the pulsating city, the same city that had long occupied my thoughts and the wishes of my angels. When I waved my banner, radiant smiles spread across the tired, gaunt faces of the people. Many threw open windows from the upper stories of buildings along our route and hung out, thin arms flapping, their faces sparkling with hope. Residents spilled out of taverns and inns to welcome us. In all, twenty thousand people inhabited the city, which served as a gateway to the South of France. It seemed as though every one of them greeted us that spring evening.

"Well played, Jehanne," Rais hollered and winked a warm brown eye at me. With a flourish of his hand, he bowed his head in respect. "We might just succeed here in Orléans."

"Merci, Jehanne," Dunois yelled above the din. Torchlight reflected in the pools of his eyes. Dunois was the bastard son of Charles the Duke of Orléans. It was customary to refer to the inheriting male son of a woman outside of a royal marriage as "the bastard;" it was not an insult, but an indication of rank. Though his sandy hair was coiffed in the manner befitting a nobleman, his demeanor held the heaviness of responsibility, and in his face, I saw the weariness of battle and nights spent sleepless with worry. "The people have hope again. We are most thankful for your faith and courage in coming here."

We moved, a giant swath of horses, torches, and rejoicing Frenchmen, through the square, past shops and homes, to the residence of Jacques Boucher, the treasurer general of the Duke of Orléans.

"Jehanne, you will lodge here, with your brothers and the men of your staff. You are in good hands with Jacques." He thumped his good friend on the back. "Take good care of her for us."

"Mademoiselle, it is an honor for me to welcome you to Orléans and my home." Jacques bowed his balding head in my direction and beckoned for us to come inside.

"Jehanne, we will meet tomorrow to discuss plans for assault, yes?" The Bastard swept a bow and leaped back up into the saddle of his gray dappled courser.

"Oui," I replied.

The next morning as the first crimson rays of dawn burst through the darkened sky, I rose, eager to walk the city walls with d'Aulon, to get an understanding of our enemy numbers as they camped just outside the fortified tall gates, close enough in most places to throw a stone and hit a snoozing guard. The morning light washed the stone and plaster walls with an orange glow. Cocks crowed. Cows groaned.

We climbed the narrow stone steps to the top of the west gate. A cool morning breeze carried the moist earth aromas of spring. I pulled the woolen cape around me and leaned against the stone rampart of the curtain wall. The enemy's camp lay just on the other side.

"D'Aulon, there do not seem to be as many English as La Hire and the Bastard let on," I spoke quietly, so my voice would not carry on the light, morning air. "The way they talk, you'd think there were one thousand men at each gate."

"There do seem to be less than I had anticipated." He scratched his blond head and yawned.

"We are going to succeed in lifting the siege, and it is going to be easier than we thought." I paused, watching scenes unfold in my mind. "We will have casualties, and I, myself, may get wounded, but we will be victorious." Joy rippled through me. "I just know it. My biggest challenge is to stay informed of the plans of the captains. Won't it be magnificent to give these good people of Orléans freedom? Our success will stop the Duke of Burgundy's advance on Southern France, as well." A newly found energy and optimism gave me the feeling of buoyancy.

"It would, indeed."

Under Dunois's orders we waited for more reinforcements: archers and men-at-arms. Three days passed, and no word from the English, so I spent time with the people handing out bread, visiting the sick, inspiring encouragement and hope wherever I could. I sent letters, as was customary, via my messenger Gien, to the English, bidding them to give up the siege and return to England.

D'Alençon arrived as d'Aulon predicted, that afternoon, in a flurry of activity. The governor, Raoul de Gaucourt, invited us to dine as guests of honor at his home that evening. For the first time since Chinon, I sat by the side of my dear friend. No longer did he resemble a recovering prisoner of war. Gone were the hollows under his eyes and cheekbones, instead he emanated the robust strength and flawless character of a commander loyal to his king and country. His toned flesh shone and his blue eyes radiated with purpose and conviction.

I could hardly concentrate on the conversations around the room. All I could focus on were the feelings evoked within me by the proximity of his vibrant body. My heart skipped and jumped like a misbehaving puppy throughout the meal.

"Jehanne, I have missed you," he whispered in my ear. "You seemed to have affected the hearts of the people, just as your counsel said you would. It's astounding, really. They call for you wherever we ride. All anyone talks about is *the Maid*."

"Mon beau duke, you know it is God they love, not me." I gazed into his face. His dark hair curled at his collar, and I had to use all of my will power to keep my mind on the business at hand.

"Jehanne, it is you they love. You have stolen their hearts just as you have stolen mine." His blue eyes looked aquamarine in the candlelight and burned with intensity. It felt as if he looked into my soul.

Out of the corner of my eye, I noticed La Hire making his way to us through the multihued crowd.

"Commander, what are our plans now that you are here?" La Hire spoke jovially, rubbing his thick and calloused hands together. "My hands are itchy for battle."

"Soon, La Hire, soon. When Dunois returns." D'Alençon smiled awkwardly, clearly disturbed by the interruption. "We will meet tomorrow morning. Meanwhile, you can reconnoiter the walls of the city to assess the numbers and positions of our enemy."

At the same time, the wife of the governor tapped me on the shoulder wishing to speak with me. "Mademoiselle, Jehanne, may I?" She bobbed, a slight curtsy. "I find I am afraid to hope . . . if it's not too much trouble . . . I was wondering if you could pray for me." Her brown eyes filled up with tears. "It's only that the duke has been imprisoned for so long, and we have lost many. I am terrified to hope. I fear I will die of fright if things don't change soon. You don't know how we live in fear daily. Fear of losing our men, fear of not enough food, fear of arrows flying over the walls . . . It's horrible."

"Madame, I do understand." I took her cold hand in mine. "I grew up as a peasant, living with the fear of Burgundian attacks. You must ask the angels to help you." I turned to face her more fully. "Daily, I ask for courage, help, and inspiration. And daily they comfort me. Trust them. Trust the King in Heaven will lift the siege. It's safe for you to hope, madame."

"Merci," she said as a tear dropped onto her peach taffeta bodice.

Behind her stood others wishing to talk with me. My plate sat abandoned. D'Alençon was also besieged by men seeking his advice. Our moment of intimacy was over. While I felt the pull of him and gentle pangs of regret, comforting the people held precedence over everything.

Wednesday, the day Dunois returned, my voices urgently woke me from a nap, *Jehanne, you must fight against the English now. Rise up and fight. Hurry!*

Leaping off my bed I shook d'Aulon. "Get up d'Aulon, Louis, men of my house!" I yelled. "My counsel told me a battle rages against the English now."

Louis had been instructed to keep a look out for any movement by Dunois. Obviously he failed, missing something. "Alors, how did you not know? Why did you not tell me that our men would fight today."

"Jehanne, I assure you I had no information of which you speak." He quickly pulled together his armor and ran to the door. "I will ready your horse. If what you say is true, we must hurry."

Jacques, his wife, and daughter rushed around helping me buckle the many pieces of my armor. Handing me my battle standard, they said, "May God go with you."

My brothers, Jean and Pierre, rode with d'Aulon, Louis, and me to our first battle.

"Which way? Should we attack English fortifications or Fastolf?" I asked Louis as we tore through the streets.

"There's a skirmish on the side of the Saint Loup Gate," a squire called out to us from the street.

"Merci, monsieur," I called back to him, sun glistening off his scant armor.

Blood pounded in my head and supplied my limbs with adrenaline as I pushed my horse through the streets, dodging people, vendors, and livestock. We exited the east gate and rode the mile or so to the Saint Loup gate. Here I spotted bodies and armor lying on the ground. My heart lost rhythm as my horse jumped over French bodies, littered like misshapen, bloodied rag dolls. Arms and legs twisted in gruesome positions, heads lolled off their bodies. Oh no, they started without me, and now we are being defeated. I must not let this happen. Raising my standard, I bellowed in a voice not quite mine, "Soldiers of France, take heart, the Maid is here. God is with you NOW!"

We are with you, dearest daughter. Be brave and stay with the men. They will win today.

Our men, appearing on the verge of retreat amidst the advancing shouts of the enemy, halted and turned, rallied, and rushed at the bastide. My ears rang with the cacophony of sounds: weapons clanging against shields and armor, men screaming both in agony and in passion, horses neighing in protest. Arrows sprayed through the air in both directions. I pulled out my sword in preparation of attack but found I could only repel assailants away with the steel sides and hilt. I could not bring myself to thrust the sharpened blade into the soft flesh of another human being, though he would be my sworn enemy. Every muscle in my body groaned with determination as our numbers advanced on the bastide of Saint Loup. Sweat soaked the garments under my armor. I continued to ride among the men yelling, "God is with you; fight for France."

I tried to discern which captains were present and wondered who had initiated the attack. Only two captains appeared to be fighting, Xaintrailles and Rais. The others, D'Alençon, La Hire, Metz, and Dunois were nowhere to be seen. My assessment of troops put our numbers at a few hundred and the enemy's at slightly less.

Suddenly the tide turned, the great mass of fighting moved closer and closer to the bastide, the ground appeared to be covered with more English casualties than French.

Within minutes, it seemed, one of our valiant soldiers hollered down from the ramparts within the bastide, "Pour la France!" The sun glinted off his bloodied sword as he thrust it toward the heavens.

A great cheer erupted from the embankment below. More of our men appeared between the crenellations and ramparts at the top of the small tower, grunting in victory, thrusting lances in the air. A quick blast of the English horn signaled retreat and those remaining English who could use their legs fled, defeated.

"Louis, I bid you find a French flag and see that it flies over this gate," I called out over the cheering men. Louis had blood running down the side of his face. "Hurry!" I choked out as emotion flooded through me. Bodies were strewn all over, the wounded smeared with dirt and blood, writhing and moaning in pain, while the dead lay limp and silent. Deep red blood from their bodies turned the earth crimson as it flowed into the soil along the banks of the Loire River. I looked around quickly for my brothers and spotted each of them still alive, disheveled and exhausted but unharmed.

Victory. It was indeed what I had prayed for and dreamed of for many months, but the price seemed too dear. Dearest God in Heaven, this is horrible. The amount of bloodshed is too much, on both sides. Too many precious lives sacrificed for a cause. I cried for my enemy's losses as well. Please see that the souls of all who fought here today are welcomed back into the bosom of Heaven.

Tears flowed freely down my face as I sheathed my clean and bloodless sword and re-clasped the reins. I knew this to be a small battle, and only one of millions throughout history, but nonetheless poignant. Dear God and saints in Heaven I pray now for a new way to settle disputes between countries. This atrocious behavior must come to an end. Please, I beseech you to help us find another way.

I called to my chaplains, who sat on horseback, safe under the protection of a stone archway near the tower. "Please, dear Brothers, can you bless all of the dead?" I asked, still overwhelmed by the massive specter of death. I wondered if I would ever be able to forget the way a man's eyes looked just as he left his body. Like a giant candle snifter, the light disappeared, leaving an empty flesh and bone carcass behind.

"All of the dead? You mean all of our dead?" Pasquerel asked, his round face now pale and set in a grimace.

"Yes, every single body lying here on French soil, whether it be English or French. Each and every soul who fought today deserves to be blessed and ushered into Heaven." I patted my horse's neck, more to calm myself down than him. I continued, "Then I would like you to say a Mass for the soldiers, for our confessions. We must clear our souls of the killing."

To the small army I ordered, "Dear soldiers of France, today the King in Heaven gave us a victory. Give thanks to God and beg His forgiveness for killing your brothers." I paused, allowing them time to pray. The field grew silent except for the low moans of the dying. "This is only the beginning. We will continue to be victorious as long as you keep your souls clean. Pray for all of the souls who gave their lives today and you will set Orléans free."

Out from the right of the gate exploded d'Alençon and Dunois on horseback, with a hundred men-at-arms close behind. La Hire pulled up in the rear. They were in full gallop and poised, ready to attack. Their expressions changed from wary anticipation to shock and surprise.

"Jehanne, what happened here?" d'Alençon shouted at me. He appeared angry and looked formidable in full armor.

"When I came upon the scene, our men were already engaged and ready to retreat . . . But . . . then, they rallied and took the bastide. I have no idea who initiated the sortie. Obviously, it wasn't you. Regardless, we won, d'Alençon! We took this gate back from the Goddons."

He surveyed the area. "By the looks of it . . . the number of French bodies . . . we barely won," his anger continued to flare. "Who ordered this attack?"

"Xaintrailles and Rais were already here when I arrived," I stammered, not wanting him to think I fought without his say.

"Hurray for the Maid," the men suddenly called out. "Hurray for the Maid of Orléans!"

D'Alençon's face softened. "You did this? Inspired these men to victory?"

"She did," d'Aulon said, quick to defend me. "She bid the men to fight for God, and they fought fiercely and won."

I smiled at my commander. He reluctantly smiled back. "This is only the beginning, Commander, we have much more work ahead. We must take back every gate in order to lift the siege," I said humbly just as Xaintrailles swaggered out from the left side of the bastide, covered in blood, a boastful smile amidst a soiled and bloodied face.

"Captain, what happened here?" d'Alençon called to him.

Rais had appeared from the other side of the bastide and answered, "We called an attack, a result of information we received from a spy that this gate only held a small number of men." Rais's voice boomed. "The time was right—"

Xaintrailles interrupted him, "We were just killing the survivors . . . too much of a burden to take captives."

"Not at my command." Rais's face contorted with rage.

D'Alençon and Rais yelled at the same time, "We are not barbarians!"

D'Alençon continued, "We do not slaughter survivors. I am commander of this army. We will attack when I say. Why didn't you come directly to me with your information?" His wrathful voice echoed off the tower walls and flowing river nearby.

A horrible wave of nausea swept through me at the thought of them hacking down the survivors. This was not part of God's plan.

"We felt it wise to act immediately as reinforcements to this gate seemed imminent." Xaintrailles looked completely nonchalant, as if he had no regard for what his commander had just ordered.

"We were right in acting when we did. I sent messengers to everyone." Rais tried to be calm but his face was flushed with battle and the fray between captains.

"Tell me, Commander," Xaintrailles said belligerently, "where are we going to put the captives and how will we feed them? We are under siege. You can announce to the starving people of Orléans that their precious food is going to feed English and Burgundian prisoners of war."

"That is not your decision to make." D'Alençon straightened in the saddle and directed his words at all present. "We will behave in a chivalrous manner, hold to the code of conduct of war. We will not kill survivors. Anyone caught killing survivors will be imprisoned." His fury made his face flush as an incredible force of energy flowed from him.

After we worked at separating the dead and corralling the prisoners, the men of my retinue rode back to town through cheering crowds. I could barely lift my arms to wave in return, such was the ache in my heart. One thought consumed me, get to church and cleanse my mind of the battle. I could still see the eyes of the dead; they seemed to stand beside the living along the streets in Orléans.

Back at the Boucher's, I washed vigorously. Then as soon as I could, with d'Aulon and my men by my side, I strode quickly to church, dropped to my knees, and lifted my eyes to the crucifix.

Please, angels and God in Heaven, forgive me of the deaths of all who fought today. Absolve my men who bravely defended their country. Immediately I felt the warmth and comfort from my counsel. It seemed as though a host of angels descended upon me and the men of my retinue. Bless my men; hold them steady; fortify their minds and bodies, I pleaded silently.

Fille de Dieu, child of God, you are forgiven. You have been asked by God to take on this fight. Lives will be, and must be, lost. It is unfortunate but necessary. Men will continue to fight their brothers for years to come. This is part of the learning, and God is patient with you in the process. One day you will all put down arms and find a new way. However, that day is a long, long way off. War teaches men to value life and one another. God is loving and patient; He does not send a plague because someone has sinned. He does not punish his children. He waits and watches as his children find their way back to a connection with Him, their source.

I clenched my fists, remembering the behavior of Xaintrailles. He entered the heat of battle and became lost in it, lost in the killing. My body cringed with the memory and thought of what they did. I looked around the church to see many people, their heads bowed in prayer. Sunlight filtered through the stained glass and created a dancing array, patterns of light on the large arched columns and the statues of the saints standing watch patiently.

There are men who become caught up in the killing and cannot turn off the brutality. Their souls get lost in the horror of the act and continue to repeat the slaughter. They become disconnected from their conscience and disconnected from their source, God. Ironically, some of these men, their names scrawled in your history annals, have the ability to lead and change the tide of events, return balance to an out-of-balance system. It's the nature of the universe.

I felt as though I was beginning to understand this delicate balance of power. So, if the desire for greed and power begins to threaten the good of the people a shift begins to happen? I asked.

Yes, for the most part. Some day, the people will begin to demand that they have power equal to that of their kings. That's when new governments, of the people, will arise. But, for now, you are here to keep the French crown from being taken over completely by the English crown. The entire church seemed to glow brilliantly and the voice of the priest hummed like the rapid beat of angels' wings.

Tomorrow, you will not fight, because it is Ascension Day. The day after, you will prepare for battle and lead a successful sortie on the Augustinian bastide. On your way there, you will find that no enemy soldiers occupy the bastide anchored on the small island, the Ile-aux-Toiles. They have all retreated to the Augustinian gate where you will defeat them quickly and surely. The day after that, you will attack the great Pont des Tourelles and be victorious. However you will be wounded near your shoulder. Take care and know that the wound will not be fatal.

This is indeed good news. I am grateful for your guidance and inspiration. Please fortify me for battle. I abhor the fighting and cannot bring myself to kill a man. Please, I pray that this change your speak of, that our differences settled by peace and not the sword, happens swiftly. I looked from side to side at my loyal men and my faithful brothers kneeling next to me, their eyes closed in their own contemplative reverie. Please keep them alive; I cannot lose another like Gien.

Remember we have much love for you and all men and women. We are always with you. Call upon us, and we will be at your side.

Their serene presence filled the space around me and wound through me, cleansing my mind and body of the trauma of battle. Fear and revulsion faded, and once again the joy of doing my life's work straightened my spine with purpose. I felt like myself and offered a silent prayer for Xaintrailles.

The news from my counsel renewed my faith and stiffened my resolve. I needed to find a way to get d'Alençon and Dunois to fight before our reinforcements arrived. Twilight greeted us as we walked from church through the square and headed back to our quarters as the smell of roasting fires floated on the evening air.

"Louis, we shall send one more note to the English by fastening it to an arrow and shooting it into the English lines." I sat at the long wooden board in the kitchen of our host with my men of house. "Before I dictate this letter, I need each of you to set up communications with the men of Dunois's house, also d'Alençon, Rais, and Xaintrailles. Tell them you are gathering information. They will do it for me. I must know whenever they get together for war council. It is imperative I attend the next meeting."

"Done!" d'Aulon exclaimed. "I agree and find it outrageous they exclude you. Don't they see you are sent by God and do God's bidding?"

"Thank you for your loyalty—thank you all," I replied. "Now, the letter, Louis."

"Ready."

"Begin with, 'You Englishmen, I am Jehanne the Maid and I have been sent by the King of Heaven to warn you that you have no claim to France. I demand you abandon your forts and return to your own country or I will raise such a war cry against you as shall be remembered forever. This is the third and last time I shall write.'" Sign it 'Jhesus-Maria and Jehanne the Maid.'"

"That's it?" Louis asked.

"Oui, we need to leave the cooks so they may prepare our supper," I said, rising from the bench and crossing the rush-covered floor. "Now affix it to an arrow and have one of our best archers shoot it over to Glasdale at the Tourelles gate."

The next day I received a message from d'Alençon written by his own hand and sealed. Sensing it may contain information that, in the wrong hands, could destroy both our reputations, I sought out my brother Pierre who knew how to read.

We withdrew to my chambers where I unfastened my cloak and draped it across the back of a chair. "Pierre, sit. I have a favor to ask." I walked over, rested my hand on the mantel of the fireplace and stared at the waning fire. "Two or three summers ago, I saw you in the barn with some lass from the village. . . . She had chubby legs."

Flushing crimson he said, "Jehanne, I . . . I'm sorry. I don't know what to say. How is this important now?"

"I held this secret for you. Now I need you to keep a secret for me." I sat on the edge of the bed holding his gaze. "Pierre, I need to ask for your trust."

"Your secret will be safe with me." He furrowed his dark forehead in concern. "What could it possibly be? Are you in danger?"

"No, it's nothing like that." I turned the folded letter over in my hand and traced the crimson seal with my fingers. "Here, will you read this for me? I'm assuming you will understand after you read this."

He took the ivory letter and opened it carefully. Clearing his throat he read:

Dearest beloved Jehanne,

My apologies for communicating with you in this manner; I am hopeful you have a trustworthy friend to read this letter for you. I desperately wanted to get a message to you and felt writing far less of a risk than a personal visit.

We will be holding a war meeting at midday today at the home of the governor, Lord Gaucourt. I request your presence. At this meeting I beseech you to watch your tongue and heed the words of the most experienced captains. It is for your safety I request this of you. While it is incredible the job you have done so far, I am concerned. For your behavior, one could say, is rather impetuous and could be considered dangerous. I am, after all, only concerned with your very life. I realize God, indeed, speaks to you and that you hear His messages clearly. This puts you at a great risk, for I fear many will call you a mystic or a prophet. There will be some who will challenge you and find you a dangerous threat.

Please listen to the strategies of these practiced men-at-arms, for both our sakes. If God truly wants a victory for us, won't He help us regardless of our strategy?

I urge you to burn this after you have read and understand my request.

Your beloved,

Jean d'Alençon

"Dear sister, you should heed his words. I agree with him. Though, I don't understand. . . . Why does he sign it your beloved?" He handed me the letter and gave me Maman's scolding look. "You, indeed, are treading on a dangerous path."

"There are no sordid details, other than a deep fellowship." I snatched the letter out of his hand and flung it into the fire. The edges caught and flared, it curled in upon itself and turned black. Solemnly, I turned my gaze from the fire and looked at my brother's face pulled with worry.

I hardly knew what to feel. I replayed the words in my mind. "Please listen to the strategies of these practiced men. Your behavior is impetuous and dangerous." I railed, shaking my fists in the air. "Does he think I'm an irresponsible child? He claims he cares about me but . . ." I stomped back and forth in the small space. Frustration seeped out of every pore of my body. "Doesn't he see we achieved the first victory in months—a direct result of my actions bidden by my counsel?"

"That's the point of his letter. He does see that you are hearing guidance from Heaven accurately, but he is concerned for your safety, as am I." He grabbed my hand, his brown eyes locked with mine. "Tell me what is going on between the two of you."

"Nothing. Absolutely nothing," I said, looking straight into his prying gaze and pulled my hand out of his. "My angels forbid anything further."

"I should think so!"

"Word of our . . . friendship cannot leave this room, Pierre. You swore secrecy."

"I did. And I honor my word. But you must be very careful," he pleaded, tugging on my arm so that I would turn to look at him. "Promise me you'll be careful—both with him and the words you speak about your angels in Heaven?"

"I can only promise to be true to the King in Heaven; I have better protection than you can imagine."

Chairs scraped from the floor below, my men would be eager to hear that I was, at the very least, invited to war council.

"We must get back downstairs with the others," Pierre replied, sullen.

"I'll be down in a few moments." I took his hand in mine and kissed his rough cheek. "Merci beaucoup, my brother. Do not worry."

The door closed. I listened as Pierre's footsteps descended the narrow winding steps. A faint fragrance of roses wafted by me, reminding me of my bodyguards in Heaven, Saint Catherine in particular.

"Thank you, Saint Catherine," I whispered.

You are most welcome and most loved, I felt her utter in my ear.

I bustled around the room dressing in my best men's clothing complete with the green and gold brocade cape the dauphin had sent to me in Tours. I wanted to look the part for my captains and my commander.

At the governor's house, all the captains sat around the polished oak table in the dining room of the governor's home. There were ten of us in all. Two of Dunois's men, Giresme and Boussac, obviously hardened warriors judging by their scarred hands and confident bearing, joined us for the first time. Nerves strung tight and tempers bubbled beneath the veneer of pleasantries. The room vibrated with suspenseful anticipation: waiting, the worst thing for an army and her leaders.

"Bonjour. Let's begin," d'Alençon announced silencing the discussions. "It has been suggested we wait for more reinforcements from the king before we act against the English." He opened the discussion getting right to the point.

"What do you think, Commander?" I asked as nine pairs of eyes turned to look at me, scrutinizing me, each pair with their own judgment: assumed assessment of my limited knowledge based on the simple fact of my female status.

"I think it would be wise to wait," Dunois interjected. "The townspeople are now well supplied with food and have waited seven months. Surely a few more days will not harm anyone. We do not want to repeat the losses we experienced when Charles de Bourbon tried to intercept Falstof's reinforcements back in February." He glared at me, willing me not to challenge him.

"My heavenly counsel suggests we attack tomorrow," I said, firmly placing my hands flat on the table, my eyes locked with his.

The tension around the room climbed and apprehension swirled in the air. "They say the English have fled off the Ile-aux-Toiles to the bastide at the old Augustinian convent on the far side of the river. Success there will ensure our success at Tourelles since only the bridge separates them."

Passionate male voices erupted. Each man spoke at once, arguing, debating the correct course of action. There were those, like Rais, Xaintrailles, and La Hire who wanted to strike while the memory of our victory still sat in the forefront of our soldiers' minds. Others, Dunios and his men, and d'Alençon, felt reluctant, cautious, only wanting to fight when our numbers far outweighed those of our enemy. Metz and Poulengy appeared divided, though I felt I could sway them to my side. I raised my eyes to the dark beams of the coffered ceiling, pleading for help from the heavens.

"Silence!" d'Alençon roared, rising off his chair. "We shall wait a few days more. Surely a few days will not make a difference." He slammed his fists on the table and swept his gaze around the room daring me, and the others, to challenge him.

Angels, I asked silently. Is it prudent to wait a few days or do we need to attack tomorrow?

Dearest child of God, you must attack tomorrow. The English will be regrouping and are currently in a state of disorganization. It must be tomorrow for you to have the advantage.

"My voices advise attacking tomorrow and no later. The enemy is regrouping from yesterday's losses, not ready to fight. If we catch them tomorrow we will surely gain a victory once more." My voice, strong with resolve and conviction, hung overhead. My sweaty hands left beads of moisture on the polished surface of the table. And in that moment I wondered if I only succeeded in creating an unbreachable gulf between us by challenging his authority in front of his captains. He had to know my commitment to the voices of Heaven held priority. I added, "I have spoken with the people, and they are all willing to fight from within the city walls. Priests, barmaids, and common folk are all willing to fight for their city, manning canons, catapults, and whatever else we need."

This time the others kept silent, their mouths set in firm lines. D'Alençon's eyes dropped to the table contemplating some unseen object on the surface, his mouth set in a neutral line. He did not flinch. His shoulders did not droop nor did he make the least change in his authoritative demeanor. The men watched their commander like a sailor watches the sky, keen for the slightest change in the direction of the wind. Blood pounded in my head. Suddenly everything seemed to be at risk, my mission and my beloved, the only two things that mattered to me. In this moment, the entire welfare of France sat easily on his shoulders.

We waited. Another minute passed and still he did not speak. Several opened their mouths to speak, but thought better of it and did not.

Finally, he lifted his eyes and surveyed the dim room. Firmly and calmly he said, "We will fight tomorrow. Inform your troops we will meet outside the east gate just after daybreak." He pushed back his chair, stood, and walked out of the room as conversation broke out between the captains.

Leaning my back against the spindles of the chair I let out a sigh of relief. He agreed to fight tomorrow, but did he still care for me after I blatantly challenged him in front of his men?

We took the Augustinian bastide just as my counsel predicted. Our men and captains worked together, a unified force, and, after the better part of the day, the English retreated, some through the fields and others fled to the towers across the river.

Citizens of Orléans floated food and supplies across the river so we could remain in the field for the evening to be ready to attack the Tourelles towers before dawn the next morning. I ate sparingly. D'Alençon and d'Aulon ate voraciously. Conversation was minimal.

Later that evening I made my way through the rows of men, their faces reflecting the firelight, to the captains' tent. Song, stories of successful skirmishes, and boisterous laughter floated on the night air with the smoke of the campfires while the captains all gathered to discuss maneuvers for the next morning. Dunois and his men returned to the city to oversee the lay folk who chose to fight within the walls.

I sought out my chaplain as he sat resting on a tree stump to the side of the camp. He had just finished saying the evening Mass for the men.

"Pasquerel, tomorrow, rise very early and stay close to me. Tomorrow we shall do great work and blood may flow from my shoulder." I gestured to my left. The scene had come to me in a vision. My counsel had begun to communicate information during battle to me this way. Showing me flashes of scenes seemed to be more expedient than telling me with words.

"My dear, can you avoid this injury?" He appeared concerned. Haltingly he asked, "Will you die?"

"Oh, non," I laughed. "I have much to do still. As far as I know," I added soberly, shivering slightly in the misty night air as I rose to leave. "I will not die yet. Do pray for me Brother, pray for all of France."

Back at my camp, d'Aulon approached me with the face he wore when he needed to impart bad news to me. "Jehanne, sit down." D'Aulon motioned to a log near our campfire.

Sitting beside him, I knew something was wrong. "Tell me, what is it?" I demanded.

"Again, the captains decided, after you left the meeting, to wait for reinforcements before taking Tourelles. We will not fight tomorrow."

"Au contraire, d'Aulon," I said fiercely. "We will most certainly fight. We will rouse the men early, before dawn. The captains will have no choice but to join us."

He made a doubting face.

"Don't look at me like that, d'Aulon. You know me by now. We must strike because my angels wish it! Bonne nuit." I turned and walked away, sure of what would happen tomorrow with my blood boiling. Why must it be such a battle to get these men to understand the validity of my angelic messages? I gathered the men in my retinue and gave them the news, adding, "Spread the news to only a few, we will begin the sally at dawn. The others will follow—reluctantly—but they will follow, and we will have a victory—one of the best in history! Then get some rest. You will need all your strength tomorrow."

"Jehanne, do you think it wise to go against d'Alençon?" Pierre asked. "Shouldn't you listen to your beloved?" he whispered and smirked with the taunt. The memory of the letter seemed to be fresh in his mind.

"I know what you are thinking. Take heart, Pierre. My advisors in Heaven bid me to fight tomorrow, so I shall. My only concern is how *they* think of me, not with any earthly matter. Will you fight with me tomorrow?"

"You know I will, n'est-ce pas? Sister, do not be angry at my concern."

"It is not you, dear brother, I am angry at." I lowered my voice, sotto voce. "Though I care for him, I am furious he undermines my plans. He must not love me as he claims."

"He is in a complicated position. You must understand," he whispered. Only a few of the fires burned and the cool night air began to cling to my flesh.

"He's the one who needs to understand," I hissed back through clenched teeth.

We woke the men with bagpipes just as daylight began to illuminate the blackened sky. They stumbled up off the ground gaping in surprise to see me in full battle gear astride my loyal armored courser. I held my banner amidst one hundred other men all dressed and ready to fight, weapons in hand, bows at the ready.

"We fight this morning! Rise . . . and fight for God this day. A great victory will be ours!" I hollered as the sun shot rays of light between the towers of the Pont des Tourelles and illuminated the ripples on the water of the Loire.

La Hire was the first captain to ride up and join me. "You are a brazen warrior through and through," he laughed. "I'll serve you Glasdale's head by the end of the day."

"La Hire, welcome." I beamed him a big smile. "No need for his head, I'll settle for shackles. Do you think the other captains will join us?"

No sooner had I gotten the words out of my mouth, when Xaintrailles, Metz, and Poulengy galloped to our side, with Rais not far behind. They had swords drawn and thrust in the air. I could feel the energy rise, like a great tempest brewing—from the captains, men, and horses—all around camp.

Sensing the time was ripe to act, I shoved my banner in the air, signaling the other captains, and together we commanded, "Attack!"

Arrows flew, soaring silently upward. They seemed to hang briefly in midair before their deadly descent. The startled enemy blew horns as my captains and I, leading four hundred men, charged down the embankment, beginning the bloody assault on the towers. Arrows flew through the air in both directions while the men readied the war machines, catapults, and ballistas with their giant forged arrows. The noise became deafening.

Suddenly, from my left, d'Alençon appeared on horseback dressed in full armor, a fierce look darkening his face. He reached out, deftly grabbed my horse's bridle and pulled me out of the chaos.

"Stop! What are you doing?" Lightening flared and crashed between us, but he did not let go. He ignored my pleas and determinedly pulled me back up the embankment and out of the way of the battling men.

"D'Alençon stop," I continued to yell at him, as my body shook with rancor. "I demand you let go!" I attempted to knock his hand away with my armored foot, since I still held my banner in one hand and the reins in the other, but could not manage to both keep my balance and kick at him hard enough to dislodge his hold. I considered jumping off, but didn't because I heard my voices command me not to.

When we traveled far enough into the rolling vineyard nearby and the noise faded, he stopped and turned to me, but would not let go of my horse. I glared at him waiting for an explanation.

Our eyes locked in bitter challenge for one long minute. "You are one stubborn girl," he finally spit out. "I called off battle today because I had a premonition, days ago, you would be wounded here at Les Tourelles. You cannot fight today!" His face filled with emotion.

"God in Heaven, d'Alençon! I already know this. Now let me go!" I tried digging my heels into my horse's sides but he held fast; we went nowhere.

"You are not going back there. If I have to hold you here all day, I will," he bellowed, his face red with passion.

"Then, I will run on foot. My men need me. Let go." Tears of frustration clouded my vision.

"Give me one good reason why I should allow you to ride to your death," he said, trying to provoke reason within me.

"Because I will not die today; the wound will not be serious."

"Are you sure? Your angels told you that you won't die?" His face relaxed with relief.

"*Oui*, I will live. I believe the wound will be at my left shoulder and certainly not fatal." I realized then that his actions had been generated out of his love for me. He received a premonition. He was not yet another reluctant leader but acting out of his care for me. He understood more than I thought. The shield around my heart softened as I allowed this new information to sink in. The soft fluid feeling of love slowly replaced the tense barrier of resolve I erected earlier in the week.

The weight and responsibility I put on myself suddenly seemed too heavy, a weight I thought I carried by myself, alone. I sighed and slumped in the saddle. I understood he carried a good deal of the weight as well.

"Chérie, I felt terrified that you would die today. I still do not feel completely relieved and won't rest until the sun sets and you are still breathing." He shifted in his saddle. "Promise me you will be careful?"

"Mon ami, you must trust. I will be careful but I will still be wounded. I'm not afraid. Well . . . not that much. I feel better knowing that another . . . you, understand me, my work."

His dark eyebrows remained knit together with worry. The mere sight of him took my breath. I let myself admire the strong lines and bones of his face, his hair tousled just so.

"It was torturous, knowing, thinking you would be hurt or worse," he said, pouting. "How could I face the citizens of France without you? They would flay me alive; they love you so. You are already a legend, you know?" He glanced in the direction of the ongoing battle. "So, shall we return to battle . . . evict those Goddons once and for all?"

"Oui, this is what you and I were born to do. We shall meet our destiny together, bravely."

We galloped through the vineyard, across a small neighboring field, around the Augustinian bastide, and plunged headlong back into the ensuing chaos of battle.

The English fought hard. They had, after all, occupied this fortress for seven months. They understood the lay of the land, the flow of the river. They knew the sun would shine into the eyes of their own men by afternoon so they put out tremendous effort all morning. Their archers knew which rampart would give the best angles for the draw of the bow, as well as how far it would fly given the wind over the water.

When I spotted Glasdale peering out of the narrow window on the top floor of the tower only yards away I yelled to him, "Glasdale, yield; yield to the King of Heaven."

"I will not lose to a whore and her churls," he retorted sardonically.

"You have called me whore. I pity your soul and the souls of your men. Today will be your last day in that tower."

"I gave you fair warning, Glasdale," I called back over the din, bile rising in my throat. Rancor gave me a renewed surge of energy.

Around midday, I managed to set the first ladder against the bridge side of the fortress. I held it steady as several of our men climbed up like squirrels on an oak tree. Just as I cheered in success a force propelled me backward. The shock of the impact disoriented me enough so I stumbled over a lifeless body and fell onto my back. Thinking I only sustained a blow, I rolled to the left in the blood-soaked mud and tried to push myself up.

I screamed.

Searing pain shot through my left shoulder. My first thought: it was broken. But as I craned my neck toward my shoulder, I saw it. The arrow from a long bow grazed off my armor and found the soft spot between the plates, managing to go through the expensive chain mail, and lodged itself into my flesh. Exactly where I saw it as a premonition days before, into the area between my shoulder bone and my neck.

"Ahhh!" I screamed as d'Aulon and d'Alençon rushed to my side.

"Get her out of here," hollered d'Alençon.

The faces of the men who lifted me blurred and swam before me. "Careful," was all I could manage through the onslaught of pain as they carried me away from the fighting to a protected area. I didn't think it would hurt as much as it did.

"How deep did it penetrate?" d'Alençon asked as my brothers quickly unbuckled the breastplate of my armor from the arm plates.

"From the looks of it, not too far," my brother Jean replied.

"Let me get it, then." D'Alençon pushed my brother out of the way. "Bandages. Quick! Get olive oil, lard, and bandages. We'll need something to staunch the bleeding when we pull the arrow out."

"I'll pull it out," I said through clenched teeth as I grasped the ash shaft tightly with my gloved right hand.

Angels! Please help me with this.

I prayed fervently and pulled as hard as I could, hoping for an influx of divine love. Excruciating pain shot through me, like someone cut off my arm.

The voices of the attending men seemed to fade while I experienced the sensation of heaviness, falling. Sleep seduced me away from the bustle. I dreamed angels swooped in from all around and doctored my wound. Blissfully, I floated under their care.

When I awoke, I gazed up at white fabric draped over the branch of a tree. A makeshift tent. The pungent smell of olives assaulted my senses, and I remembered. D'Alençon sat by my side. "How long have I been asleep?" I groaned, trying to sit up.

"Don't, Jehanne, you've been wounded. You must lie there and rest." His eyes wide and his voice firm.

"How long have I been asleep? Tell me!"

"Not long; an hour perhaps. Your wound was fairly deep, so you will need a few days to recover," he replied as compassionately as my mother would have.

"I don't have a few days." Wincing with the pain, I forced myself through gritted teeth to sit. My head spun at first, then righted itself. "I must get back to the men . . . now. They need me!"

"Non, they don't," he said more strongly.
"If we have not yet a victory, then they need me. Help me to stand." I felt filled with purpose. "I have an idea."

"Mon Dieu, Jehanne," he said, exasperated with my determination. He helped me to stand with his arm around me, his fingers pressed firmly in at my waist. "All right, tell me your idea, and I will make it happen."

"Non, d'Alencon, the men must see that I am all right." I took a tentative step, but he held me back. "S'il vois plait," I said as sweetly as I could, pouted, and looked up at him. "Help me?"

Without saying a word he walked me to the edge of the fighting. "Men of France," I yelled as loudly as I could. "You will be victorious today!"

The few men who heard me cheered. Their cheers rippled through the fray as they realized I was not harmed fatally. The men of my retinue rushed to tell me of their concern and kissed my cheeks with relief. I felt truly loved at that moment. Upon seeing me, Brother Pasquerel made the sign of the cross and shot a grateful gaze to the skies.

"Here's my idea," I said excitedly. "Gather a contingent of men together to build a barge large enough to hold enough wood to create a huge fire. Then . . . this is the best part . . . we will float the burning barge under the wooden bridge. It must be done quickly. They will be cut off when the bridge collapses, and we will have our victory."

Late that afternoon, with the sun to our left, the men, covered in sweat and dried blood, continued to struggle. The English proved undaunted and held fast to the fortress. I placed myself near enough to Glasdale's tower, under the protective cover of a barricade. In as loud a voice as I could muster, still feeling weakened by the blow, I boomed, "Glasdale, see for yourself, I am still alive. Glasdale, show yourself!"

I watched hawkish English warriors gesture to me over the bulwark. Within moments Glasdale came into view between the ramparts. Cupping his hands around his mouth he cried vehemently down to me, "You must be a witch to survive the arrow from our powerful longbow. Did you call on your lover the Devil?"

Cringing from his insult I fired back, "No, Glasdale, he occupies himself conferring with you. The King in Heaven protected me and healed my wound so that I could see you cast out. You will not win. I warn you, if you do not retreat, you will lose your life."

"For a mere milkmaid, you claim much. Do you profess to be a sorceress, a seer? You are greatly mistaken; it is you who will perish horribly. We will capture you and burn you at the stake," he bellowed with false bravado, as his voice echoed off the walls and hung in the fetid air.

His cruel words wounded and left me shaken.

"Jehanne, you can stop now. The barge is lit and now burns under the bridge," d'Aulon urged, breathless from running to and fro. "You must not listen to him. Come and rest some."

"The men are growing tired; they need encouragement. I can't rest yet." To my soldiers I hollered, "Courage men! The place will soon be ours."

The sun slid further down the horizon, and, still, our men struggled. Neither side seemed to be gaining. The bridge proved slow to catch fire. Dunois sent a message from within the city walls recommending we pull back and retreat for the evening. I ignored it. With loyal and steadfast d'Aulon by my side, I retired to the vineyard nearby to converse with my heavenly counsel. We kneeled, side by side, and faced the sun.

Dearest saints in Heaven, Archangel Michael, what strategy do you recommend? We have gained little ground and the men are exhausted from assaulting all day. I pray for your guidance and that you fortify the men.

Dearest brave one, you are closer to victory than you think. Rest the men. Feed them and give them something to drink. Attack again and you shall have your victory. Have Pasquerel say a blessing while the men eat and plan your offensive at dusk. The enemy will not foresee the assault. They will be caught unaware, relaxing for the evening. You will have your victory. We will be with you.

A gentle spring breeze brushed by me; angels descended and lifted my spirits. I marveled at the diverse nature of God. Vibrant new growth, bright jade and golden, sprang out of dry and seemingly lifeless branches of the grapevines. How strange that life continued to burst forth here while men toiled and sacrificed just a short distance away.

I lifted my face to the sun and tried to absorb as much of the nourishing nectar as I could. Glasdale's words slipped from my memory. Joy in being alive flooded through me. I reached out and squeezed d'Aulon's hand. "Thank you, d'Aulon, for all you have done for me and for France, for God. I am blessed to have a friend and compatriot such as you."

"It is I, Jehanne, who is blessed. You have restored my faith in our country and the saints in Heaven." His tired eyes appeared golden in the afternoon sunlight. "What's next? Do we continue to fight or do we retire for the evening?"

"Both . . . you shall see." Taking one last look around the peaceful landscape I stood, wincing; my shoulder still throbbed. "Let's get the men some food."

We found our commander just outside the skirmish. "D'Alençon, have the men rest briefly and supply them with food and drink. They are tired and need something to sustain them. After, we shall attack at dusk and catch our enemy by surprise."

After the men had their fill of bread, dried meats, and stews, floated to us by the villagers on rafts from the east gate, they were instructed by d'Alençon to prepare for a second rush at the Tourelles fortress.

Earlier, the English had trudged over the smoldering bridge to retire for the evening, leaving the great bastide thinly guarded. Glasdale appeared to have enlisted a number of men with putting out the barge fire we so carefully constructed.

Upon our great cries of attack and surge of men-at-arms down into the trenches and up at the foot of the towers, the English, still in armor, began to run back across the bridge to reclaim their most important foothold.

Sounds of cracking and crashing cut through the twilight. A section of the pont crumbled. Large charred timbers laden with English soldiers plunged into the dark purple waters below. Our men flew to the edge of the river to witness this profound change in luck. Cheers on our side of the river reverberated off the stone towers and mingled with the splashing and screams of men unable to swim in their heavy armor.

I watched, mystified, as man after man plunged into the water. Some tried to steal across on remaining planks precariously perched but lost their footing as they cracked under the weight of so many.

"Storm the towers," d'Alençon bellowed as he ran to the banks of the river with his sword unsheathed. "Archers, bows at the ready!"

They waited for any survivors to crawl up the banks. Just a few managed to survive the chilly water, clamoring ashore, sputtering, only to be greeted by one of our armed soldiers or receiving an arrow in the chest upon standing.

"Jehanne." My brother Pierre ran to me breathless, his teeth reflecting the moonlight as a smile spread across his partly hidden face. "Glasdale is dead. He drowned along with a few hundred of his men."

"I know you want me to be joyous at that news, but I cannot be happy over the death of a human being." I brushed a gnat from my face and took my brother's hand in mine. "Though, I am overjoyed Orléans will now be free."

At that moment, shouts rang out from the tops of the towers. Through the ramparts I could see torches being lit and our flag rising. Not one life sacrificed on our side during the evening's skirmish.

"Jehanne, you did it!" D'Aulon squeezed me hard. Jubilation spread across his face.

"Ooww, my shoulder." I shook the dizzy feeling away and attempted to squeeze him back. "No, d'Aulon, the people's faith accomplished this amazing feat."

Whoops and hollers of celebration rolled through the air. Sounds of the night in May, the frogs' trills and the crickets' chirps, combined with the boisterous joy of the men to create the most magnificent concert. Great cheers erupted from within the city walls.

The next day, we rose, sore and tired. But we needed to be sure the English had completely surrendered. My horse nickered as I approached him; his ears pricked in my direction. With d'Aulon's help I mounted him and rode out to the long line of our soldiers, nearly one thousand that morning, more than double what we had yesterday. We stood in the rolling countryside outside of Orléans, a few hundred on horses with hundreds of archers at the ready. The English stood in line a mirrored version of us, only a few hundred yards away.

I mumbled a continuous prayer for no more bloodshed as we stood, rider facing rider, shield facing shield. "Let's fight, Jehanne," La Hire demanded. "We have the advantage!"

"There will be no fighting today. This will be a bloodless victory." My horse pawed the ground and snorted. "Just wait, La Hire. Have faith."

Suddenly, the English turned their horses and walked away from the siege lines. This was the full retreat I was looking for. I turned to d'Alençon nearest me and smiled. "We did it, Commander!"

Turning my horse to face the men, I rode up and down the ranks and bellowed, "This victory is yours! We rejoice Orléans is freed! Remember to express gratitude to God for this victory."

Cheering sounded all the way to the city walls, as we rode toward the city and crossed over the sparkling river. Men bowed their heads and tried to kiss my hands. My heart exploded with joy at the sight of the happy faces of the townsfolk of Orléans while my body ached like never before and my spirit felt burdened with the souls lost in the skirmishes. In the excitement, no Mass had been said, and I felt the weight of death. I needed a bath and a long visit with my divine messengers. In addition, my wound continued to throb and needed to be redressed.

"D'Aulon, please find Pasquerel and the other priests and order a Mass in the cathedral as soon as possible," I yelled to him over the din of the teeming streets.

"First, I believe we need to get you rest and food." He grabbed at my horse and pushed his way through the crowd.

I sat alone in the wooden barrel, soaking in the warm water, and felt as if no amount of water would wash away the haunting visions of death and the screams of drowning men from the day before.

Angels, please heal the ache in my mind and heart. Please bless all those men who gave their lives yesterday. Help me to heal my nerves and my wound.

Dearest brave daughter of God, it is a magnificent job you have done. Allow God's love to wash over you, cleansing your heart and body. We have lifted the souls you prayed for. Close your eyes and breathe in the peace we are providing for you. Allow yourself to rest completely. Release it all. Let go of the horrors of battle.

565 YEARS LATER

NOVEMBER 1996, WEST POINT, NY

The day blew in with fury, moaning and whistling through the granite ramparts. From her narrow bed, if she turned her head a certain way, Jane could see the November sky. It was six a.m. She felt happy it was Friday. Even though the sky was clear and she hadn't heard a weather report she felt an impending storm coming that would hang around for the weekend. Golden leaves danced and flipped outside her window.

She tore her gaze from the brewing weather, directed it to the ceiling, and contemplated her day. As a firstie, every minute of her day was planned; even her bowels cooperated and moved between morning classes. Her commander and advisor, Captain Cheryl Moss, felt she pulled off the roll of regimental commander of Beast Barracks Basic Training over the summer in grand style and had recommended Jane for another command position for her final year of the academy. Never in her wildest dreams growing up in the little state of Rhode Island did Jane ever think she would be honored with the role of battalion commander for her firstie year at West Point. In her charge were three companies, D-1, E-1, and F-1, consisting of three hundred and fifty cadets, their leaders, and a small staff.

As she dressed for the day and slid her slim arms into her gray jacket, now heavier with the weight of five chevrons on her sleeves, she let her mind review the appointments squeezed into her already tight schedule.

The number of cadets who came to her with problems mounted each week. After over three years spent in the stone fortress beside the Hudson River, she knew the kinds of stresses they were under. Some handled them well, many floundered, and a few took their frustrations out on others. Those who used violence to cope were the cadets she lost sleep over. These were the cadets she tried to picture out in the world and shivered. She would take whining over mean or violent any day.

She prayed the three appointments sandwiched in between lunch and afternoon classes that day were all whiners.

After grabbing a quick bite to eat, she sat at the desk in her small office. Across from her sat a male cow, a junior from company E-1. He looked exhausted. The dark circles around his eyes were typical. "Ma'am. Permission to speak."

"Permission granted," she said in her compassionate mother-like tone. An effective leader uses many tones of voice and many moods depending upon the circumstance. Jane had to admit the mother-like voice was her favorite. Second best was her I'm-going-to-kick-your-sorry-ass voice, because at times cadets just needed a little fire. She tried not to be mean, just firm and passionate. Sometimes she used the what-the-fuck-did-you-do look when someone did something really stupid and got caught. That look always got them talking and spilling details.

"I came to you instead of my company commander because I heard you would know just what to say to me." He took a nervous breath and rubbed his hands together. "I really hate it here . . . the work, the rules, the hours. I'm so tired. I don't think the Army is for me. I should have left three months ago when I had the chance. Now, if I leave I will owe the Army time and money."

"Well, West Point is not for everyone as you know. It's hard. It's grueling. But you have already completed the hardest part. You're over two years into it. Do you want to leave?" She leaned back in her chair and released any expectations of him.

"I'm not sure I can handle a real battle situation." He thought for a moment. "Plus, I'm just tired. Really tired."

"There are other choices besides infantry. How are your grades? Do you want to leave?"

He pondered her questions and she waited.

A full minute ticked by on the large round wall clock.

"My grades are good. But . . ." He paused for another full minute. He shook his shaved head. "No, I'll stay," he said. He pushed his chair back, stood, and saluted her. "Thank you, ma'am."

She saluted him back. Just about every fifth-semester cadet went through the same mental gyrations.

Her next appointment was a female yearling cadet from company D-1. The woman entered her office followed by her company's commander, who happened to be Jane's former roommate and good friend Sophia Michaels. The cadet's body language put her on alert—hunched shoulders, drawn face, clenched fists. Jane's heartbeat kicked up a notch.

"Ma'am." The cadet saluted and sat down.

Sophia saluted out of respect as Jane outranked her and sat next to the young woman. She pressed her pretty mouth together to form a thoughtful line. "This is Cadet Katherine Gage and she wants to report a rape." Sophia said and lifted her doe-shaped blue eyes skyward. As if to say, I can't believe I'm doing this again. The year before, another one of her charges had been raped and beaten. Sophia had taken it hard.

Jane said, "Cadet Gage, do you wish to formally report this rape to your chain of command?"

"Yes, ma'am."

"First, I am sorry this happened to you. Second, you need to know that this process is not simple and may not bring the results you may be looking for. Not many incidents of rape get reported because the chain of command is famous for letting the perpetrator go unpunished and instead questions the integrity of the victim."

Jane shifted position in her chair and folded her hands together on the desk in front of her. "The penalty for cheating on an exam is actually more severe and swift and could result in expulsion from the academy. Rape is different. I must warn you. You may become a bigger target and you may find you will end up leaving the academy. I've seen it happen more than once." Jane eyes met Sophia's. Their unspoken communication was one of pain and frustration that women had to endure this outrageous behavior.

Katherine Gage straightened her spine. "I would like to proceed despite the consequences." Her conviction appeared to give her strength.

Jane asked, "I need to know if you were drinking alcohol and what your sexual habits are?" This was the part of the job Jane hated. She felt humiliated just asking these questions. "These are the circumstances the perpetrator uses against you, so I just want to know up front in order to advise you appropriately."

"No. I don't drink. I've only had one boyfriend since high school." She blushed and looked at her hands in her lap. Tears filled her gray eyes. "I was raped! I did nothing to provoke it, if that's what you are asking."

Jane was about to get out of her chair to hug her when Sophia leaned over and put her arm around Katherine's shaking shoulders.

"I'm sorry," Jane said. She felt sorry for making her cry. Sorry that the situation called for doubt, and sorry men still felt the need to rape women.

Cadet Gage named her perpetrator, a cow from company G-1 whom Jane did not know. They filled out the necessary paperwork then departed.

Jane felt shaken and canceled her last appointment.

"Shit. Shit. Shit," she said out loud. That made fifteen rapes she had heard about through the rumor network, been told in person as a friend, or fielded as a battalion commander that autumn alone. She and her friends estimated that there were on average fifty rapes per year with zero convictions. Why did men rape? She would be sure to ask her father the question next time she was home on leave. Perhaps after prosecuting several rape cases each year he would have some insight.

The next day dawned just as Jane knew it would. Ever since she could remember she possessed the uncanny ability to feel a storm coming ahead of time. She heard the rain before she saw it pelting against her window—loud, fat splats. Great, she thought. She and her cross-country teammates would be running their last meet of the season in the rain that day.

Through most of the previous evening, Katherine Gage's face had hung in her mind. Jane felt powerless around this enemy-rape. She sighed heavily, flicked on her desk lamp to combat the gloom, pulled down Master Tzu's *The Art of War*, and flipped it open at random hoping to find a clue as to how to handle the situation. She read, "Using order to deal with the disorderly, using calm to deal with the clamorous, is mastering the heart."

Jane pondered Tzu's wisdom as she dressed for her cross-country meet and brushed her teeth. Pausing mid-stroke she studied her reflection in the small mirror. Behind her, her room appeared plain, devoid of identity, lacking heart. Every cadet's room looked the same. They weren't allowed posters or knickknacks or decoration of any kind. She hoped Tzu did not mean squelching the heart. Too many leaders, the bad ones, seemed to have a hole where their heart should be.

Racing that day was like running with a full rucksack. The rain and wind hit her drenched body with force. This particular storm seemed to deliver bad news. In front of her a woman from the opposing team moved with the grace and lightness of a deer, in contrast Jane felt sodden and glued to the earth, each step a mighty effort.

She told herself to be the warrior.

Midway through the three-mile race, her feet found the ground and dug in.

In spite of the burdens of her battalion she deftly maneuvered the puddle-dotted trail through the woods. While her mind cycled from footfall to footfall from inhalation to exhalation, her concerns for her battalion became lighter and, like little black balloons, floated away. By the two-mile mark all that remained for Jane was the trail and the rhythm of her stride.

The finish line was a welcome sight despite the fact that she failed to pass the woman in front of her. Jane came in second with one of her worst race times. Shaking off her lackluster performance she immediately jogged back along the course to cheer on her finishing teammates and tried to steady her breathing. Surprisingly, Tara came in right behind her.

"Yah!" Jane yelled and smacked palms with her friend as she walked off the race. "Great time, Tara. Personal best?"

"Oh yah!" Tara's smile cut through the gloom of the day and her dark wavy hair dripped onto her soaked tank top in little rivulets. She blew the rain off her dripping nose and bent over to rest her hands on her thighs to catch her breath, still smiling. They screamed encouragements at their teammates who lunged across the finish line with mud-splattered legs.

"Go Black Knights," they cheered.

After, the team went out for pizza to celebrate their victory and their last meet of the season. In fact, it was Tara and Jane's last cross-country meet of their career at West Point. Jane stayed only long enough to be appropriate as captain and then drove her parents old car back to post to catch up on homework.

The remainder of the stormy day she spent in the library with her longtime buddies, Alex Raphael, who was Patrick Ash's roommate, Sophia Michaels, and Jack.

"Did you hear three cadets got expelled this month?" Alex said as he leaned his nearly shaved head down low, the way people do when gossiping in quiet places.

Jane flashed to the lunchroom back in high school. She could always tell when the rumor mill was spewing gossip. Heads huddled together and voices became soft and conspiratorial. She suppressed a grin. It struck her as funny that a guy as tough and manly and so full of testosterone as Alex would exhibit the same body language as girls when sharing the dirty secrets of others.

"Yah, I heard a cow from company A-4 cheated on an exam, and two women from company I-3 got caught in a lesbian relationship." Sophia said in a half-whisper. "Someone found a journal or something that spelled out details and Command kicked them out. Just like that, they're gone."

"Bummer, I'd like to read that journal," Alex said. "Like back in the eighties when half the corps spied on two girls with a telescope. Wish I was there to see that." He let a mock dreamy look soften his long face.

Sophia punched him hard in the arm. "God, Alex, you are such a pig. Please remind me why we are friends?"

Jack interrupted and said, "Better keep it down guys. Don't we have a military history project to finish?"

Jane could not let the issue drop. "I don't get how being gay can affect their performance on the field. It's grossly unfair and unjust, if you ask me. Out in the real world companies can be sued for discriminating against sexual preference."

Legal studies was her major and, of course, made her father, the lawyer, very proud. Jane's personality strived for justice. It was the lens through which she viewed the world.

"OK, Judge Archer. Enough of your soap box," Jack said, teasing Jane.

Jane scowled playfully. She turned to look at Alex and asked, "How's Ash doing? I haven't seen him in awhile. He used to hang and study with us all last year." Jane was not surprised at his absence and attributed it to his changed behavior during Beast Barracks.

"Don't ask. He's been weird. He's a good roommate though. Keeps up and he's clean."

"Hmm . . ." Jane wondered why Ash's attitude continued to deteriorate and thought it had something to do with the story Jack hinted at over the summer. What ever it was, she hoped he would overcome the issue.

They finished their project a couple of hours after dinner and packed up to leave the library. "Who's up for a beer?" Alex asked. "Benny Havens anyone?"

Jane shot Jack a knowing look and replied, "Naw, I'm tired and need to hit the hay by a reasonable hour tonight." She elbowed Jack.

"I'm done in too," answered Jack.

"Yah, right, LeClair. I know what you have planned," Alex jeered.

Alex headed up to the cadet parking lot for a night out while the other three walked back to the barracks under a clearing night sky. A few remaining clouds scudded across the nearly full moon. The air grew cold.

The rules at West Point frowned upon public displays of affection. Any behavior remotely related to romance was out of the question. As a result, Jack said good night to the ladies and went to his room to drop off his books. He waited ten minutes, then via a circumspect route made his way toward Jane's barracks. Using his military training he shifted into stealth mode. He made sure the hallway was empty, and when the coast was clear, he dodged quickly into her room. As a cadet captain she did not have to share a room with a roommate.

He had barely closed the door when Jane leaped up onto him nearly knocking him over. She wrapped her legs around his waist and kissed him.

He said between kisses, "Soldier, you can ambush me anytime." He carried her over to her small bed and dropped her.

"Hey, that's not playing nice."

He pretended to jump onto her and started unbuttoning her shirt when he thought of something and hesitated.

"Shades?" He asked while turning his head to glance at the window.

Jane had drawn the shades before he arrived.

"Whahoo!" he said and turned toward her; a lascivious smile played upon his lips.

They made love with a fierce passion—half out of love for one another and half out of fear of getting caught. Jane felt the fear made the sex more delicious. Jack was a good lover and knew just how to please her. When he ran his fingers down her spine she became butter in his arms.

Despite the rumor that the chefs put saltpeter (one of the three ingredients in gunpowder—charcoal and sulfur, the other two) in the mash potatoes to keep libidos low, passions in general ran excessively high at West Point. The rigors of intense rules, lots of physical exercise, and the focus on aggressive actions created a hormone-and-testosterone-boosting stew.

Jack had just pulled up his trousers and zipped his fly when they heard a knock at Jane's door. He grabbed his shirt in a lame attempt to cover his bare chest just as the door flew open.

Jane's heart jumped into her throat at the knock. The door opened. When she saw Tara's beaten face her heart sunk. Hastily she grabbed her pants off the floor and ran to her friend.

"Jane?" Tara said and stumbled in the doorway. Her eyes rolled up like she was about to faint. She swayed then caught herself.

Jack closed the door quickly behind her then went to Tara's side. She flinched from his touch at first, then acquiesced and allowed him to escort her over to Jane's tousled bed. Jane blushed at her memory of only a few moments before while her mind raced to conclusions about what happened to her friend. Tara smelled faintly of alcohol. Is she drunk?

"What happened to you?" Jane asked, fearing the answer.

Tears filled her dark eyes. "I was . . ." She swallowed hard and stumbled on the words. "He . . . attacked me."

"Shit! Who?" Jack demanded angrily.

Tara shook her head. Crying, she bawled out, "I can't tell you."

"Tara, You can tell us. . . . It's OK," Jack coaxed and tried to be more patient. He looked outraged and his face turned crimson for the second time in thirty minutes.

"Let's get her cleaned up," Jane said. She grabbed a washcloth, ran it under the water at the sink in her room then began to gingerly wipe Tara's bloody face. Tremors shook her petite frame. The flesh over her left eye and cheek was split and bled heavily. Tara winced in pain. Jane took mental notes and reasoned that the perpetrator was probably right-handed.

"Shh . . . shh," Jane soothed. "You may need stitches." To Jack she said, "Let's get her out of these clothes. She can wear mine to return to her barracks." She stepped away from Tara and dragged Jack with her. Lowering her voice to a whisper so Tara could not hear she said, "I'm going to keep her clothing . . . as evidence. Just in case she changes her mind in the morning. My dad is a stickler for evidence, says you can never have too much."

"Good idea," he said his brow furrowed with worry. Jane felt touched by his level of concern and loved him more for it.

They peeled off Tara's sweater and jeans, careful to avoid the blooming bruises. Jane put the clothes in her empty laundry bag for safekeeping. She tossed a bathrobe over Tara's shoulders and walked her down the hall to the women's bathroom. When Tara stripped out of her undergarments and stepped into the shower, still shaking, Jane took her bra and ripped panties and ran back to her room to stash them in the bag with Tara's other clothing.

Jane said good-bye to Jack and walked Tara back to her barracks. Luckily her roommate was away—home on leave for the night—so Jane slipped into the twin bed opposite Tara's and tried to fall asleep. She was extremely shaken by the event.

Off and on throughout the night, Tara whined and moaned in her sleep. Jane wondered what, if anything, she could do for her dear friend. Twice Tara woke crying out, "No! No!"

Each time Jane jumped out of her bed and rushed to Tara's side to pet her hair and whisper settling words, "You're safe now. You're safe now."

It was a long night.

By the time Jane returned to her room the next morning, the space looked as if a disaster had blown through, which it had. Jane splashed cold water on her face and changed into her running clothes feeling grateful it was Sunday, a lighter day in terms of workload. Sunday was the day she spent catching up on homework and projects.

The air was cold and raw. A layer of pale gray clouds turned the landscape gray. The only notes of color along her route were the occasional tourists dressed in bright colors. By the time she reached towering Battle Monument with the Angel of Fame on top she felt exhausted and beaten. Jane sat on the granite steps to catch her breath and found she needed to blink back tears. The prior evening's events had gotten under her skin. "What's the deal with all this rape?" she whispered into the cold air.

Seagulls floated on the river's air currents and called to one another. There were no other sounds that morning and the eerie quiet made Jane shiver. Craning her neck, she looked at the verdi green angel holding the laurel-leaf crown of victory. It felt refreshing to see a female statue on campus for a change, even though she was an angel. From deep within her heart she could feel it—the urge to fight, to make a difference. But how?

Rouen, France

Sunday, May 26, 1431

They gave me a woman's dress made out of coarse linen and shaved my head. I sat on the edge of my cot, scratching the places the fabric irritated my skin, and waited to be transported to different quarters. Anxiety began to set in after a few hours. My guards taunted me in my new attire. My heart leaped when I heard voices and steps approaching. Perhaps this is the group that will take me to the convent. A small-boned English gentleman entered my cell.

"Good day, milord," Grey said respectfully.

"So, this is she?" The Englishman stepped close to me and stroked my shoulder. "Scrawny, don't you think?"

My heart sank and began to pound out a warning. He pulled up the small worn stool, sat right in front of me with his knees touching mine, and began to slide his hands up my thighs.

My hands and feet, still bound by chains, clenched. "Good sir, kindly remove your hands from me at once." I brushed his hands away with my chained ones.

He said something in English I failed to understand and the guards laughed. This laugh I knew well—one at my expense.

He persisted and again ran his hands up my legs, sliding the flimsy linen fabric over my thighs.

I thwarted his approach with a stronger shove. He batted my chained wrists and held my arms down with one hand as he reached for my breasts with his other. With all my strength, I pulled my hands away from his grip with such force I smashed him in the chin and knocked him off the stool.

"Slut! Devil's whore!" He spit at me. His face reddened and he brandished a fist at me.

"Jehanne, you've done it now. He's pissed!!" Grey bellowed with a guttural laugh.

The lord gathered himself together, stood, and leered at me, his eyes filled with intense hatred. He lunged and landed on me, sending my head into the wall behind. He pinned my shoulders, and yelled, "Grey! Unlock her chains—hands and feet."

"Grey!" I hollered, hoping he would defend me. I had seen a glimpse of compassion from him before. I glared at him, a silent appeal. He looked away.

I kicked into the Englishman's gut with my chained feet and sent him staggering backward. This only succeeded in inflaming his anger and gave him strength. He landed on me again. While he waited for Grey to unlock the chains he took the opportunity to punch me in the face several times. My mind began to slip in and out of my body. Fear pumped through my limbs. My legs kicked fiercely. This was the moment I feared most.

They were on me. Two held me down while the other had his way. From far away I could hear grunting and panting. The men whooped as tears trailed down my face. I did not scream. I would not give them the satisfaction.

When they were done, all three of them stood gloating, making comments I could not discern.

The impulse to retch brought me back into the pain of the present.

Suddenly, I felt the presence of Saint Michael. He dropped into me through the top of my head, thankfully dulling the pain at the same time. I felt my mouth open and heard my voice—though not my voice—boom, "You call yourself civilized men. You do not know what you have done. You cannot even fathom the depth of your mistake! Your violence done today will be retaliated! DO YOU HEAR? Never again will you touch a woman in that way. Never again will you disrespect yourself on the creative force of your kind. You men treat women poorly. If you fear for the health and welfare of your soul, you will heed my words. I am Archangel Michael. Remember my words and me. All actions have consequences that will be wrought upon your heads. Be warned and know we will not forget your crime this day."

My spirit grabbed onto Michael as he removed his presence from my physical body and gratefully I found myself in some other place, like a dream, but real at the same time. Feelings of an all-pervasive love flooded and washed over me. Brilliant light surrounded me and I felt wrapped within a cocoon of warmth and understanding by my council and many others whom I could not discern. With my mind and heart I communicated with them.

Dearest council, please assist me in completing this mission, for my physical body is weary and done in. No longer can I withstand the torture of my guards and the lies of the bishop and his court. Either release my soul through a merciful death or see to it that I am removed from this hell and get to live the remainder of my days in safety somewhere near home to live simply and quietly, have children, and grow old in peace.

Dearest Jehanne, we are most pleased with the job you have done. You will be granted your wish and freed within a matter of days. Now rest for a while with us. Know we love you deeply and are with you and within you.

As if in a dream, the scene shifted, and we sat on the hillside of my home. The river I watched as a child sparkled and flowed below, the sheep grazed peacefully nearby, and birds chirped joyfully. My angels were by my side. We smiled at one another. I took a few deep breaths savoring the scents of the fields and country air. I relaxed and knew everything would be all right. I had done my work and effected the change my soul wished. All was well. A church bell tolled.

I opened my eyes to the sound of the church bells in Rouen tolling the afternoon hour. The horror of the recent event assaulted me again in the aches of my body. My tiny cell was empty. I could see only the sleeve of one guard standing outside of the open door. I heard no voices. Slowly I coaxed my body into an upright position. My head and face throbbed. I winced upon standing and noticed the pile of my men's clothing on the cot next to me. Slowly, I walked the few feet to the latrine. There was a bucket of clean water and a rag. This is odd. Had someone taken mercy on me? I dipped the cloth into the water with a shaking hand, grateful for the refreshing feeling of the water. I began with my face. The entire left side of my face felt swollen. I feebly tried to wash the event away. No matter how hard I scrubbed at the dried blood and bruised tissue, I could not erase the fact I had been cruelly molested. All those years . . . my chastity, gone. Fresh tears flowed as I wiped away the blood and mess on my thighs. My mind began to close. I knew I would never recover from this cruelty.

I can't do this anymore, God. Do you hear me? Not like this.

Once again I donned men's clothing and made my way back to my cot. Trying to ignore the mess, I sunk down on the filthy mattress, and rolled onto my side since I was no longer chained. Curling my knees up to my chest I starred at a smudge on the wall. The smudge shifted and changed. It opened like a window, and I could see the countryside on the outskirts of Orléans. The sun washed the painful memories of my confinement out of my mind and replaced them with the smell of freshly manured earth and feelings of victory.

The morning after we defeated the English, Monday, May 9, 1429, a number of us rode freely out of the city of Orléans. D'Alençon, Metz, Dunois, Rais, and the rest of my retinue pounded down the dirt road, four horses abreast, our cloaks flying out behind us, our horses breathing heavily. Our party consisted of twenty-four men and me. We left the jubilant townsfolk celebrating and already repairing the great pont that we had strategically destroyed by fire. To witness the people of Orléans in joyful celebration filled my heart. I needed no reward or acclaim. The fresh air and wind blowing through my short hair felt heavenly after the stench of battle and the claustrophobic atmosphere of a city under siege.

Wasting no time, we traveled swiftly the ninety miles south to Loches, stopping only for an overnight in Blois. As we made our way through dense pine and oak forests northeast of Loches, I noticed how the feeling of this ride differed from our trip along the Loire, only months ago, to see the dauphin for the first time. I felt nervous then, naïve and vulnerable. Now, I rode side by side with men I'd led into battle and the protection of a victory under our belts. Due to repeated validation of the guidance from my divine counsel, I was now regarded as an equal to these men, someone to consult. They no longer saw me as a mere peasant girl. I was truly a formidable and brave soldier for France.

"It shouldn't be long now," d'Alençon shouted into the wind. We galloped at great speeds, kicking up swirling clouds of dust, so we would arrive before sundown. My horse's dark coat glistened with sweat; his breathing told me he needed to be watered soon.

Entering from the north, after traveling through dense forests, we crossed the dawdling Indre River on a wooden bridge. There, we stopped to allow the horses some water, then headed up the steep cobbled road to the citadel of Loches, one of Charles's favorite castles. We slowed our horses to a walk and sauntered, two by two, as the road inclined rapidly.

"No wonder Charles likes this castle so much," Metz said offhandedly from behind me. "He hides here away from the Burgundians. No Englishman in his right mind would be interested in this far off place, hidden in the woods and sitting on a cliff." He ran his hand through his greasy hair just as I turned to give him a chiding look.

"He's right, oui. This isn't the castle of a king. It's more of a refuge for a nervous recluse," Dunois chimed in. "Jehanne, you'll need to work your magic to make our dauphin into a brave king. Perhaps you need to threaten him, like you did me, with the loss of his crownless head?"

"Shh," I admonished them. "We should be respectful of our would-be king."

Excitement bubbled in my chest as we passed through the tall square stone gate, known as Porte Royal. As we trotted under the guarding structure, I looked up and could see daylight through machicolations, floor openings between the supporting corbels, where men could drop rocks or other materials to deter unwanted guests or invaders. A steel cage, only large enough for one man to sit in, hung in midair in front of the stone retaining wall, just beyond the gate, a warning to any would-be criminals or enemies of the king. The citadel sat on a rocky promontory, approximately sixteen hundred feet above the river. Its keep, a hulking gray stone square tower, came into view as we rounded the ascending road. It seemed to be the largest donjon I'd ever seen, with walls measuring one hundred and twenty-one feet tall.

"Those walls are nine feet thick," d'Alençon said, his face flushed and his hair windblown from riding. Our legs brushed deliciously against each other as our horses took the hairpin turn.

Passing under the stone arch of another gate, we turned left and continued on through a manicured park, filled with flowering trees offering an interesting contrast to the somber walls of the donjon. We passed the odd looking Church of Saint-Ours, with its strange spires, and pulled up outside a smaller building, Logis Royal, the royal castle. The setting sun reflected off its stately rectangular windows. The proximity of the church to the royal quarters lifted my already high spirits. I longed for a lengthy healing visit with my counsel.

After dismounting at the stables and handing the reins to the stable hands, we entered, dusty and tired, through the off-center front door of the diminutive château. The architecture seemed unique here. We were greeted heartily by a few very clean and opulently dressed gentry in the grand hall. I had grown accustomed to the worn and faded attire of the people of Orléans and the somewhat grimy faces of my retinue.

"Bonjour! Bonjour, Jehanne." I recognized Louis, Count of Vendôme, from Chinon, still handsome as ever, with shoulders as broad as an archer's. He extended a leg in a simple bow. "I hear you have accomplished much, madamoiselle."

"Bonjour, Monsieur Vendôme." I smiled in response to his graciousness. "Indeed, we were graced with—"

"C'est bon. There they are . . . Jehanne and my friend d'Alençon." Charles blew into the room gesturing his brocade-adorned arms excitedly in the air. He hugged d'Alençon firmly and kissed both his cheeks.

"Sire." I curtsied.

"I hear I owe much to you. Merci." He smirked, taking my hand and kissing it with a loud smack. "I didn't think it was possible. You have restored my faith." He addressed the remainder of our group. "Merci beaucoup. You shall all be rewarded. We'll celebrate tonight with a great feast."

The weathered faces of both of my brothers appeared awestruck at the sight of the dauphin.

"Sire, may I present my loyal brothers to you . . . Pierre and Jean d'Arc."

They bowed deeply, beaming.

"It is a pleasure to meet Jehanne's brothers. You fought in Orléans with your sister?"

"Oui, sire," they both answered at once, slightly unsure of how to behave in the presence of royalty.

"You must be proud of her," Charles replied, his voice echoing off the dark-beamed ceiling, acting more jovial than I anticipated.

"Pardonne moi, but you all need baths." He wrinkled his thin nose. "Bathe, dress, and return here for a sumptuous feast. Jehanne, I do hope you will return in a woman's gown. Have Louis show you to my wife's quarters. D'Alençon, come with me." He flipped his hand at us, a sign of dismissal, and left the room with his arm around d'Alençon's shoulders. The others ran hurriedly out of the hall. No doubt, they rushed to sample the citadel's great ales and wine, instead of the bathhouse.

"Louis, d'Aulon," I called after them, running to catch up. The others had already exited out the door and raced down the stairs on their way to the cellars near the big tower. "Attends-moi. Wait. I'm going to church before I dress, would either of you like to join me?"

"Non, Jehanne. Merci," d'Aulon replied softly, his eyes looking tired and his body slumping slightly when he walked. "I'd like to take advantage of this time and sleep a little. But, I will come with you if you wish it."

"I will come with you, oui," Louis answered, still full of energy. "Then I will show you to the queen's quarters as Charles bid."

"D'Aulon, go ahead and rest. Will we see you at the feast?"

"Wouldn't miss it!" He waved and lumbered down the drive toward the great tower's lodgings. The darkening sky brought out the king's servants whose jobs were to light all the torches along the avenue. An owl called in the distance. I loved the feeling of space up on this plateau, pleasant fragrances floated to me on the evening's gentle breezes. How different it was here in relation to the close ranks of a city under siege. Here, feelings of freedom and well-being hummed in the air.

Louis and I entered the strangely carved portal of the Church of Saint-Ours. Gargoyles, monkeys, griffins, harpies, mermaids with bearded heads, and other mysterious creatures adorned the carved archway. Inside, candles reflected off the light-hued limestone, creating a warm and inviting atmosphere. Instantly, my body relaxed and a whimsical smile spread across my face. My eyes swept around the strangely inviting church. Typically, churches inspired awe and made one feel a certain reverence for the power of God. This one, however, elicited a sense of love, protection, and unique splendor. Demonstrating this were the two unexpected octagonal arches right in the middle of the central part of the building, as if someone wanted to let out a breath, expanding usual restrictions. The effect felt enchanting. Even though this church was of average size, as churches go, it held the mood of a cozy chapel. I loved it instantly. "Ah, Louis," I whispered. "Cette église est magnifique!"

"Oui," he agreed, somewhat absentmindedly.

Instead of kneeling, we sat up close to the front of the empty nave in chairs. My body ached from being wounded in battle and all the hours spent on horseback. It felt heavenly to sit in a chair in the house of God and lean my back against a firm supportive surface.

Saint Catherine's melodic voice rippled through me. *We are with you, dearest one. Breathe. Let the people's burdens be released from your heart.*

Tears flowed down my face. The simple act of sitting still made me realize how heavy my heart felt from the battles. Grief, for what we did and still had to do, took my breath away.

Jehanne, let the grief go. You don't need to hold it. Imagine taking it out of your chest and handing it to us, your angels in Heaven. No one need hold the pain. Forgive yourself and everyone involved. We are holding the dead and wounded; you don't need to.

I began to sob, great gasps. Louis took my hand and let me cry. I cried for every lost life, every blade's blow, every arrow that found its mark sinking into tender flesh.

So, why do we fight and kill?

Free will . . . and the forgetting.

I released Louis's hand and patted his forearm to reassure him I was all right. The forgetting?

Men forget they have come to Earth only for a short time. Upon death they return to eternity in the form of spirit once again. They feel abandoned and cut off, so they lash out and fight. There will come a day when they remember as you have. You are helping with this. Go now, rest, and enjoy the company of your dauphin and friends.

At the banquet that evening, the king acted more buoyant than normal. I assumed it was due to the progress we made in Orléans. He took a sip of the crimson wine and opened his mouth to speak.

He said, "Jehanne, d'Alençon informed me of your plan to retake the cities along the Loire, so I may safely travel to my coronation in Reims." He grabbed a honey-glazed leg of poultry off his plate and sunk his teeth into it. Since I sat next to him, I could hear him ripping the meat from the bone. Chewing a few bites, he added, loud enough for everyone else's ears, "What do your angels in Heaven think of this plan?"

"Sire, they are in agreement." I let my eyes wash across the nobility, a veritable tapestry of color and fabrics, sitting around tables overflowing with food. More than a few eyebrows rose in surprise at his attention and request for military guidance from a woman. Dressed in women's clothing, I did not feel as confident as I did in my men's hose and doublet. The looks my gown received were not lost on me. The queen, upon her husband's orders, bid me wear a purple brocade kirtle with a high, empire waist. Charles only allowed his most favorite of courtiers to wear purple. It was his fickle and manipulating way of showing who held his favor.

Throughout the feast he asked my advice four more times on matters ranging from battle to which flowers would make the best centerpieces. I answered simply and humbly, trying not to squirm under the heated glares of jealous royals. D'Alençon sat next to the queen. I could not see him unless I leaned back in my chair and craned my neck—a definite faux pas in royal company. I stoically endured this socially challenging meal, which felt like anything but a celebration feast for me.

"Jehanne?" Louis knocked at the door the next morning. "The king bids you rise and join him for a walk," he yelled through the closed door.

I leaped out of the comfortable feather bed, ran to the door, and pulled it open. "Louis, why does the dauphin want to walk with me? Doesn't he see his attention creates animosity toward me?"

"It's his way of controlling his courtiers, and he has nothing better to do than to stir things up." He strode to the window and pulled open the long draperies. A flood of morning light washed onto the walls and reflected off dust particles floating in the air. "Isn't this what you wanted . . . the king's ear?" He pulled a peach taffeta gown from the hulking aged wardrobe and laid it on the bed.

"Oui . . . but . . . not like this. And, I'd much rather wear my men's doublet," I protested, pouting.

"He would not be pleased. For now you must play his game." He smiled, walked to the door, and playfully swept his lithe body into a deep bow. Laughing he added, "It's only for a few days; then we will be off planning war once again. I leave you to dress, mademoiselle."

"It's not funny, Louis," I called after him as he closed the door.

I ignored the taffeta gown and dressed in one of the new man's outfit's made for me as royal gifts.

Upon seeing me dressed in men's clothing, Charles furrowed his brows at first, then smiled and lifted his elbow toward me. I took his arm, which felt thin and weak in comparison to d'Alençon's firm bulk, and he led me along the gravel path between flowering apple trees. He smelled of spice from the Orient.

"Jehanne, do you really think it safe for me to travel to Reims?" he spoke lower today and nervously flinched his shoulder several times. He seemed in an insecure mood. His eyes darted to the small group of courtiers meandering nearby.

"Sire, my divine counsel has assured me you will be protected," I said, trying to make my voice as silvery as possible. I studied him, trying to discern his state of mind, as a breeze lifted the lace collars of his shirt. We walked a few paces in silence, gravel crunching under the hard soles of my boots.

"Can you speak with them now? Will they talk to you in my presence?" He trembled slightly as he spoke.

"Oui. Sire, they speak to me no matter where I am or whom I am with. They tell me we must gather ten thousand men and evict the English out of four strategic towns along the Loire River: Jargeau, Meung, Beaugency, and Patay. Once this is achieved, we will return for you and escort you to Reims." Petals from the flowering trees fluttered to the ground.

"Will you ask your council how long I will live?" he whispered, leaning his head toward mine.

Saint Margaret's no-nonsense voice clipped all around me, loud and clear, *Tell your dauphin he will lead a long life. He fears death because he fears living. You may tell him he will live long enough to see most of the cities, now occupied by the English, return to French hands. Tell him we wish for him to be a more courageous king.*

I had to fight back the urge to laugh out loud at Saint Margaret's remark. "Sire, my counsel advises me that you will lead a long life. Long enough to see the English depart most of the cities they now occupy." I cleared my throat and lied, "They say you are a most courageous king."

"They say . . . I am courageous?" He stopped walking and turned to look at me, his watery blue eyes giving away his little boy need for praise.

I swallowed. "Oui. Oui, sire." I fibbed, hoping I would not blush. "Will you help us gather more men?"

He inhaled, puffed out his chest, and continued walking with me on his arm. "Jehanne, you may have whatever you wish. Ten thousand men, lavish clothing, jewels, perfume from the Orient . . . just name it."

"Sire, I will be happy with the men-at-arms and a couple of good war horses."

"Magnifique! It is done." He patted my hand grasping the crook of his elbow.

Eager to spread the good news, Charles dispatched letters to all of the towns of France announcing our victory and requesting men-at-arms. He felt optimistic that we would be able to gather enough forces within the month to begin the offensive by early June.

Two days later, D'Alençon pulled me aside. A strange look shadowed his handsome face. "Walk with me?"

"Mon plaisir," I said, studying his face for clues to this unfamiliar demeanor. Courtiers and the dauphin's soldiers bustled around the plateau just as low swollen clouds closed off the dynamic view of the valley. Walking at a rapid pace, we appeared to be heading for the outbuildings and curtain wall of the south side of the citadel. A light drizzle of rain drove everyone indoors. It was not until we passed beneath the dense canopy of a copse of deciduous trees that he turned to me and spoke. He said, "I received a letter from my wife. It seems she and my mother wish to meet the famous Maid of Orléans." He paused, watching me intently for my reaction. His face, normally calm, betrayed a look of guilt, worry, and uncertainty.

I inhaled deeply, not knowing how to reply to such news. "Ahh," I managed. The pounding of my heart hammered home the reality of the situation. He was not mine and never would be. I wanted to cry, but willed myself not to. All too suddenly, I felt alone and cast my eyes around for something to lean on. Horses whinnied and a cock crowed in the distance. The rain, more heavy now, made splattering noises on the leaves above our heads.

He spoke first. "We were never . . . our marriage was arranged when I was fifteen. We were never in love. I haven't seen her in nearly six years. She is cool and independent . . . or was. Not the type to fuss over her husband. She fawns over her horses and dogs more than me, preferring to read the writings of Christine de Pisan. She never wanted to marry, wishing instead for the convent, but her father forced her." He captured my hand in his and brought it to his lips. "Mon amour, you are the only one I have ever loved."

"But," I stammered grasping for inner resolve. "I will never be yours or you mine." Pulling my hand away, I said stoically, "I would be pleased to make the journey with you to your family."

When we found ourselves on the road again a few days later I allowed myself to relax into my role of "the Maid," and admire the countryside. The orange poppies seemed more brilliant this year as they bobbed back and forth in the unseen breeze. Fields awash in verdant life as far as the eye could see were interrupted only by the dirt road cutting a tan stripe in the green fabric of the land. Intermittent farmhouses sat watchful of their fields nearby as farmers bent over planting seeds for a new season, little blobs of color against the reddish brown background of the freshly tilled earth.

It felt as though the shroud, which had covered France for so long, had begun to lift, revealing the possibility of joyful living. We still had much work to do to get the dauphin to Reims, but the first and most formidable step had already been successfully taken.

Joy pulsed through everything that morning. I sat easily in the saddle of my favorite horse, held loosely to my reins, and leaned into the ride. The prior evening's rain moistened the road enough to keep the dust to a minimum. We traveled, a smaller group this time, only my retinue and d'Alençon's, two abreast. While the other captains visited surrounding towns to recruit soldiers for our army, we headed west toward Saumur. Stopping only briefly in Chinon for a meal and wine, we followed the Loire along its southern banks until we reached our destination near dusk.

The Castle d'Anjou rose above the small town, a colossal purple shadow of towers and spires, against peaches, pinks, and lavenders of the sky. The sun, only moments before, had slipped below the straight horizon leaving the atmosphere awash with colors and textures. The town seemed fairly clean and untouched by the ravages and pillaging's of war. Two factors contributed to the safety of Saumur: it lay just far enough away from the fray, and its lord, Rene d'Anjou, held a duplicitous alliance with the Duke of Burgundy. Though, current rumors put him in allegiance with France. I hoped our sources were accurate.

My pulse quickened as we all trotted, hooves clacking on the cobblestones, into the courtyard. After dismounting, I bent over in an attempt to stretch my tired legs and flexed my still aching arm. A deep breath did nothing to quell the nervous energy in my chest. How strange to be meeting Jean's mother and wife. The men exchanged comments about the modern accouterments of the stables and outbuildings.

"Ready, Jehanne?" D'Alençon clapped my shoulder in a brotherly way due to the presence of our men, the stable hands, and other castle servants bustling around lighting lanterns. Two plump women, dressed as cooks, with bloodstained aprons, hustled by with protesting chickens tucked under both their arms.

"Those will be tasty later," my brother Pierre laughed. When he felt no one was looking, he shook his sweaty head at me and whispered, "This'll be interesting. . . . You meeting his wife. Are you all right?"

"A little nervous." I nodded and wiped my moist hands on my hose. Following the torches, we paraded through the back hallways of the stately castle toward the main chamber.

"Bonjour, Maman . . . Jeanne," d'Alençon called out to his mother and wife, as his voice, along with the lantern light, bounced off the walls and marble floors.

"Bonjour, Jean," they called out, using his first name, as they hurried along the massive corridor, their shoes clicking on the expensive tile, and their dresses swooshing around their legs.

Embracing him briefly, they kissed both his cheeks. I watched his wife blush slightly at his touch. Both women, slim in frame, dressed demurely compared to the flounce and flourish of the courtiers. They wore simple but elegant bonnets on their heads, instead of lavish velvet and feathers. I shifted my weight and tucked my gloves in the waistband of my tunic, hoping my hands were clean enough. I felt slightly self-conscious and awkward waiting for an introduction.

His mother, adorned in subdued grays and pale lavenders, assessed her son's appearance, smiling her approval. "Mon Dieu, six years . . ." I watched her clench her jaw in an attempt to staunch the flow of tears while his wife, covered in mossy green velvet with a high neckline, appeared ill at ease, as if she were meeting a stranger.

"Maman, Jeanne. I present to you Jehanne d'Arc, the Maid of Orléans." He smiled broadly, and led them to where I stood.

I curtsied in their direction. "Bonjour, mesdames."

"Bonjour, Jehanne." Dame d'Alencon curtsied back. "Enfin, vous voila, at last you are here. We, Jeanne and I, have been waiting to speak with you." She immediately took my arm and led me to a small room adjacent to the large hall. Excitedly she added, "We want to hear all about your adventures. Tell me, what is it like . . . giving men orders?" She smirked, ignoring the others present. Jeanne followed silently along as we made our way across the exquisite carpet to a royal-blue silk upholstered bench in the center of the room.

I inhaled the fragrance of exotic oils and realized that I must smell of horse from riding all day. "Madame, I really should bathe before sitting," I protested, slightly surprised by her exuberant welcome.

"Nonsense, you are perfect. . . . Just as I pictured you. You are legend. You are all we ladies talk about when we gather together. That is, ladies like us . . . ah, shall I say, more independent, learned types," she said, leaning her head toward me and lowering her voice in a conspiratorial manner. She, much to my surprise, looked me over approvingly. "Ah, to wear men's hose and ride free . . .," she added wistfully.

Jeanne sat on a matching chair near us and merely nodded her petite head in agreement at her mother-in-law's words.

"Madame, it is indeed wonderful to ride free and be treated as an equal . . . for the most part." I smoothed my hair and clasped my hands together on my lap, feeling myself relax under their admiration. "Though, it took me awhile to gain the confidence and trust of my captains and men-at-arms."

"Do you really hear the voice of God?" she asked as she absentmindedly fingered the blue and gold tassel of the pillow she reclined against.

"Oui, only God is represented by three angels . . . mostly." I did not want to reveal too much about them, fearing my angels would feel it irreverent.

She corralled me on the lovely bench, asking question after question, for over an hour, until finally d'Alençon entered and interrupted, "Maman, Jehanne's presence is requested at the dinner this evening. Do you think you can spare her from your interrogations long enough to allow her to get ready?"

"Mesdames, I wish to remain dressed in men's clothing, if it does not offend?" I asked, feeling comfortable in their presence.

"Jehanne, here, you may dress however you please," Dame d'Alençon declared, presenting her strong chin and lifting her slight bosom for effect. "We'll have someone show you to your quarters straight away."

"Merci, Maman," d'Alençon replied, raising a brow at me. "You must remember to share Jehanne with others," he scolded her playfully.

"Must I?" she replied, happy to have her son with her and a celebrity by her side. "You shall spend breakfast with me, privately, tomorrow," she decreed, looking at me.

"Maman, Jehanne and I must meet and discuss strategy for our war campaign to come. It is of the utmost importance we formulate an effective plan, this week." He looked serious. "I'm not sure she will have time for woman talk. Surely, you understand the importance of her counsel."

I could hardly believe the turn of events. I thought I would be the third wheel, uncomfortable, out of place. Instead, I was fought over. Dame d'Alençon's attentions only served to increase her son's desire to be with me. I felt for his timid wife who, unfortunately, fell into the role of the outsider.

"I insist. She'll need to eat regardless." She shot her son a firm look, her eyes darkening. "Surely, you can spare an old woman a few moments of your time," she said, lightening the tone of her voice at me.

"Madame, oui, but of course. It would be my pleasure."

"So be it," he said, attempting to sound neutral; I could tell she exasperated him.

I slept well in one of the coveted octagonal tower rooms of the castle and woke to a blue sky dotted with puffy white clouds. Taking in the view in all directions, I gazed thoughtfully at the Loire River as it slipped silently through the flat valley, a blue ribbon winding between varying shades of green. It seemed hard to believe one body of water commanded such attention. Most of our battles would bloody her banks, like many before and, I was sure, many to come. Just how much blood will have to flow into the Loire before the people of France can live in peace? Just how much of man's blood will have to flow in all of the rivers of the world before we will experience peace? It seemed overwhelming and daunting.

Dear one, it's not the amount of blood but the consciousness of man that matters. Man (and woman) lives then dies. Death is part of the process; every man, whether wealthy or poor, must face death. It's his consciousness upon death that makes all the difference. If he holds peace or love in his heart, his death will be easier; if he holds anger or hatred, his death will be fraught with regret, resistance, and discomfort. Blood flows from the body to the earth, ashes to ashes, dust to dust. You will all become part of the earth at the end of your lives. It's up to each man or woman to choose how he will meet that moment.

I stretched my arms overhead and yawned. When you put it that way, my friends in Heaven, it doesn't seem so bad.

Sunlight sparkled off the river, creating glorious patterns of dancing light. *That's because it isn't so bad. We love each and every one of you. Remember this, above all.*

I'll remember.

A knock at the door made me jump. "Jehanne?" d'Alençon called through the closed door. "Hurry, come with me now before my mother commands you to see her."

He sounded insistent, so I padded over to the door in my bare feet and night shift and opened it a crack.

"Hurry, Jehanne," he urged, his brows furrowed over worried eyes.

I had to stifle a giggle; he seemed to be acting lovesick. I liked this side of him—the side that wanted to see me so urgently.

"But . . . I promised to meet her for breakfast." I spoke through the door's crack, giving him my best enigmatic smile. "Wait a moment. . . . I'll dress and we can talk." I closed the door, not giving him the opportunity to respond, and dressed quickly.

When I opened the door, I found him leaning against the opposite wall, arms folded across his chest, and his legs crossed at the ankles. "So, when will we meet to go over strategy? You don't know my mother. She'll have you busy all day."

"She can have breakfast with us, then we can excuse ourselves to talk about war." I tried to placate him and tugged at the hem of my green brocade doublet. He frustrated and amused me at the same time.

"She'll want to come with us . . . be part of the meeting. All so she can tell her royal lady friends she participated in the war plans of the Maid and the king's commander, her son. Oh, I can see her now . . ."

"What do you suggest?" I asked, studying his willful face as I placed my hands on my hips. This mood had turned his blue eyes gray.

"Send her a message that your angels bid you to discuss war immediately. You must cancel your breakfast with her."

"I won't."

"Bonjour, good morning," Louis called, as he sauntered down the hallway toward us, swinging his long arms. "I have a message from Dame d'Alençon. She must cancel breakfast with you, Jehanne. She is not feeling completely well and needs to rest . . . too much activity last night at dinner. She participated in one too many toasts to her son's successes in Orléans."

"Merci, Louis. Tell her I hope she feels better, and that we will do it another day this week." When Louis left, I turned and looked at d'Alençon. A smiled spread across my face. "You're lucky. I wasn't going to use my angels as an excuse to lie."

He smiled smugly. "Guess we can meet now. I'm sorry. I'm just feeling nervous about the Loire campaign. Do you know how important this is? To win back all of the towns along the Loire? I hope your guidance continues to be accurate."

Glancing around the hallway, Louis long gone, I felt satisfied we would not be heard, so I lowered my voice and said, "Was it really war you wanted to discuss?"

He winked. "We'd better get moving. I thought we'd go riding to clear our heads for battle strategy."

"Do you think it wise for us to ride together alone?"

"Most residents of this castle sleep until afternoon. We'll have hours, if we leave now. Our horses stand ready at the stables. You are the virgin, chosen by God, and I am Charles's commander. . . . They would expect this from us . . . to hold meetings."

Jehanne, take this opportunity to spend time with him. You may not encounter much private time in the future.

"Very well." I hoped my saints meant we would be too busy with the affairs of war to spend time alone.

We hurried downstairs, through hallways, and emerged into the cool shadows of the inner courtyard. I had to quicken my pace to keep up with him as we rounded a stone guardhouse and neared the stables.

As he always did, my horse nickered when he saw me, his ears dancing back and forth. He pawed the ground excitedly, knowing we were going riding. When the stable boy helped me to mount, I jumped up and settled in my now nicely worn saddle. Sliding my other foot into the stirrup, I asked, "Mon beau duke, where is it we are riding?"

"Trust me," he said as he squinted into the sunlight. Kicking his horse's side he yelled, "Ha!"

We galloped at full speed, past blooming fields and budding vineyards and, slowing to a trot, entered a profusely flowering apple orchard. Each tree abounded with small pink and white flowers. So thick were the petals, the trees appeared snow covered.

"Alors, c'est beau," I called to him, remembering spring's bounty. Year after year, spring's abundance continued to surprise me. It was as if Mother Nature wanted to make up for the harshness of winter by offering a fragrant bouquet in apology. We walked our horses through the rows of trees and settled upon a small, protected clearing facing the warm sun.

After tethering our horses to a nearby post, Jean spread a plain wool blanket on the ground in front of a boulder and reached for my hand. "Mademoiselle, join me?" He tipped his head down and to the side and lifted his eyebrows.

"Mais oui," I responded playfully, but made sure when I sat on the blanket no part of my body came in contact with his. The scene felt a little too romantic for my liking. Bees hummed busily at the flowers while a hawk screeched overhead.

Sensing my slight discomfort he said, "Be assured my behavior will be gentlemanly. You are safe with me. Don't you know I have fallen more in love with the Maid part of you?" He grabbed at a stick and began to peel the bark. "When I look into your eyes I feel as if I can see all the way to Heaven. When you sit upon your black steed, in armor . . . ah, such a sight. I can hardly explain the feelings you invoke within me . . . like the mighty Athena, goddess of war, herself, has entered into your body and beams out of your eyes."

"Surely, you exaggerate."

"Non, I speak the truth."

We discussed a multitude of battle strategies as we breakfasted on rolls and nuts. Feeling slightly sleepy, I reclined on the blanket, closed my eyes, and slipped into a deep sleep.

In my dream, chaos erupted. I watched as a woman wearing a long crimson cloak clasped by a golden broach scrambled to save her castle. Around her neck she wore a torque, a thick, ropelike, gold necklace, with two knobs in the front; Romans appeared to be kicking her out of her home. She witnessed, horror written all over her face, two Roman guards raped her two teenage daughters. They then dragged her outside to the public square, where they stripped her and began to beat her. The sting of the whip hitting her tender, pale flesh jerked me awake with a start.

"What is it?" d'Alençon asked, searching my face.

"A . . . a vision," I stuttered and pushed myself to sitting, "of a woman, I believe her name is Boudica . . . from Briton . . . centuries ago. The Romans tried to take over her kingdom after her husband died."

"What else? Why are you having a vision of her? What does this mean?" He fired questions at me faster than I could answer.

"Shh!" I scolded. "I'm not sure. Let me close my eyes and see if I can get the rest of it . . . the meaning." I sat up straight, crossed my legs beneath me, and closed my eyes. It did not take long before the scene began to play out in my mind once again.

I watched her and her followers kill hundreds of people in what appeared to be a Roman town in Briton, before she set fire to the entire city. She burned a few more cities like this one and gathered thousands of Celtic men and women to join her in an uprising against the Roman occupation. I saw thousands of people march out of fields and farmhouses, from villages near and far, to join her righteous revolt.

It all seemed to come down to a final battle. Boudica, her voluminous strawberry-blond hair flowing out behind her, rode on a horse-drawn chariot with her daughters by her side. She wove in and out among her warriors, their faces painted for war, yelling inspiring words.

The Romans were vastly outnumbered. Their 10,000 trained soldiers, to her 200,000, organized themselves into a saw-tooth formation. Each man, standing shoulder to shoulder, held a shield close to his body in order to, first, shove attackers away, then, stab them under the rib cage with a shorter knife. It appeared that the long swords, used by Boudica's Celtic warriors, required more space for a swing than was available, thus rendering their use ineffective.

I watched, my own heart pounding as the ground glistened with red rivers of blood from the Celts. Warrior after warrior tumbled lifeless to the ground. Boudica's army began to flee in defeat. In all, she lost 80,000 to the Romans' four hundred.

"Alors," I gasped as the vision ended. I looked around at the teeming, but peaceful, orchard in an attempt to ground myself back into the present.

Jehanne, you know why we showed this event to you.

"I do, oui." I smiled at the cloudless sky then gazed at my beloved. "I now know our battle strategy for the Loire campaign."

For the remainder of the week we, along with both our retinues, sat daily at the Duke of Anjou's prized octagonal banquet table, drawing out battle plans. (Since I could not write, I held the job of approving the drawings.) Even our priests were charged with copying plans onto the creamy scrolls for delivery to all the captains in the French army via only the most trustworthy heralds. In order for us to be ready in less than a month's time, we would need to begin training the troops in the Roman technique immediately. Due to our modern armor we modified the use of the short sword, instructing the men-at-arms to strike into each enemy according to the gaps in his armor. Orders were placed for more pavises, large shields, and short blades, and sent by heralds on horseback to Tours and other cities known for quality work.

"Before we send out the plans, I think we must add ten rows of one hundred archers each, just behind the Roman formation. That is, if we can get enough men." D'Alençon demonstrated with the quill, drawing out the strategy on a scrap piece of paper. "Like this." His feather scrawled over the paper's surface making scratching noises with each stroke. "A long line of archers, from here . . . to here. Gunpowder canons will be placed according to the lay of the land and fortifications of the enemy."

"That's perfect. My voices assure me we'll be successful." I glanced around the large table at our men, so dedicated and full of integrity. I want to achieve this victory for them, for France, more than anything else in the world.

I picked up the pile of parchments in front of me, perhaps a dozen—curled, water stained, or muddy—all from towns and villages suffering under the English sword, requesting my assistance to restore the French flag. Letter after letter came, delivered by the warm hands of tired heralds each day. "I will do everything in my power to restore peaceful living and help to make it safe enough for these farmers and townsfolk to return to their fields without fear of attack, pillage, or rogue Burgundians raping their women," I said passionately, shaking the crinkly pile in the air. "God wills us to help these people."

"We'll certainly do our damnedest," d'Alençon exclaimed, his calm demeanor ruffled for some reason. I assumed it was his way of coping with the awkward presence of all the women in his life gathered together under one roof. Several times each day, both mother and wife paid us a visit, asked what we were up to, and inquired when we would be finished. "You'll know we are finished when we say we are finished," he replied curtly to each of their inquiries. His wife appeared to suffer from his lack of interest and blushed with frustration at her own failed attempts to capture his attention.

"We are ready," I said to the group, several days later. "We will boast decisive wins at all of our battle sites. My angels say the King of Heaven wishes it. We have rested and strategized enough. It's time to move."

"Bon, I agree. We shall leave for Orléans tomorrow to regroup with the other captains and train the men we have recruited." D'Alençon leaned back in his chair and put his boots on the thick table. "Well done. Go now. Relax for the remainder of today; for tomorrow, we journey."

565 YEARS LATER

MONDAY, NOVEMBER 25, 1996
WEST POINT, NY

Jane moves through the forest in the middle of the night following the voice of the moon. Her feet are bare and muddied. Branches tear at her long white nightgown, but she does not notice. She continues onward following the voice as if in a trance. She knows the way and has traveled this path before. It is both familiar and strange.

A deep contentment fills her heart. Her path converges with another, then another, widening. The backs of other women are ahead, each moving at the same steady pace. Trees step aside to allow them to pass. She hears the moon say, "It's time for the reclamation." The blaring alarm clock startled Jane awake. For just a moment she felt disoriented then she remembered.

It had been only two days since Tara showed up in Jane's room bloodied and beaten. It was not just Tara's reluctance to tell Jane what happened+, it was also the phantom look that now shadowed Tara's black-and-blue eyes. Sitting with her made Jane feel unglued and spooked. Somehow, the assailant not only broke through Tara's defenses but Jane's as well. She felt astounded by the attack, like it happened to her, too.

Jane felt the event marred her entire experience at West Point. Everything seemed different now and she hated that fact.

In an attempt to outpace her insidious thoughts, she marched rapidly through the quad. She ducked into the vastness of the mess hall to grab some breakfast and to talk to a few friends. Pieces of the Saturday night mystery needed flushing out.

She sought Alex Raphael and found him at his table razing plebes. "Can I talk to you?"

He gave her a quizzical look and stood. Of all her guy friends, he had the sweetest nature. She felt like she could count on him to be truthful.

"Over here." Jane motioned him away from the tables. "Did you hear about Tara Fiorello?"

He nodded. "Is she OK?"

"To be honest, I'm not sure. She won't tell me anything. Did you see her when you went out to Benny Haven's Saturday night?"

"As a matter of fact, I did see her. Jeremy Cohen was with me." He looked around to see if anyone was listening, "She was with a couple of guys doing shots, but she looked fine to me. Like . . . not too drunk."

"Who was she with?"

"God, Archer, I don't know if I should say. Like, if Tara isn't talking maybe you need to let this lie."

Jane felt her face flame. "Come on, Raphael, spill. If you have information relevant to this case—"

"Shit, man, you're talking like a detective. What case? Who died and appointed you cop? If Tara's not claiming anything—"

Jane was not deterred. "You're covering for someone and you know something." She narrowed her eyes, directing them like lasers at him.

He looked up at the lofty timbered ceiling then down at the floor. He shifted his weight from one leg to the other.

For Jane, the customary din of clanking plates and silverware and the familiar smells of mess-hall food felt comforting. Her stomach growled.

"Alex?" She softened her voice. "What about the cadet's code of honor? A cadet will not lie, cheat, or steal nor tolerate those who do."

He looked her in the eye. "Well, technically, none of those things are in dispute here. It doesn't say anything about a little . . . roughhousing." He laughed.

She did not. "I can't believe you just said that. It's not like you." She lowered her voice, "She wasn't just beaten up. I believe she was raped."

His face betrayed surprise but he said nothing.

She turned to go. "You know where to find me if you change your mind." She took a step and stopped then shot back over her shoulder, "I thought she was your friend too." She turned without waiting for his response and headed toward Jack's table.

She did not think Alex had anything to do with the event. But for him to confide in her, she would need to break through the impenetrable defenses of the suddenly fortified man-code: the pact that kept men from ratting on one another. Somehow she had to convince him he was not selling out his friends.

On her way to Jack's table she saw Jeremy Cohen, the guy Alex had said he was with when he saw Tara, and decided to take a detour to talk with him.

"Hey," she said, reaching up and tapping him on the shoulder. "Got a minute?" She gestured for him to come to her.

He flashed his usual charming smile. "So what's up?" He leaned his six-two frame in close to her in a conspiratorial way.

"I wanted to ask you if you saw Tara on Saturday night when you and Alex went out? You heard she got beat up didn't you?"

His brows furrowed in concern. "Yes, I did hear that. Is she OK?"

"No. That's why I wanted to talk with you. Did you see her?"

He looked pensive for a moment. She was not sure how to read him. "Hmm . . . no. I don't recall seeing her that night."

Lie number one, Jane thought. Jane decided against telling him she had already spoken with Alex and acted nonchalant. "I'm just looking for the truth. . . . You know to help her out."

"You can't handle the truth," he said, a little too loudly, and snorted. "You know, like the movie."

Jane mustered a fake laugh. Suddenly she wanted to run. The males had joined together. All these years she thought she was one of the guys, part of the team, but in a matter of moments the illusion had crumbled. There existed a wall now where once there was trust. This realization stung.

"Thanks, Cohen," she choked out.

"No worries. Tell Tara I hope she feels better."

"Oh, by the way, did you see Ash that night? I haven't seen much of him since last summer."

"Yeah, he was at Benny Haven's. Knocked back a couple of brewskis with us then took off. Don't worry about Ash. He can be a moody SOB. Hey, are you good? Cuz, I gotta go?" He winked at her and turned back to his plebes.

"Yeah. Thanks. See you later."

She walked as calmly as possible through the mess hall, passed the endless rows of tables, forgetting about Jack and her breakfast. By the time she reached the mammoth front doors, emotion washed up and constricted her throat. Instead of screaming, she ran—down Thayer Road—and as she passed Battle Monument she flipped her middle finger at the Angel of Victory. Jane felt anything but victorious. Anger blasted out of every pore of her body. Down the grassy hill and along the paved path, she ran. She did not stop until she reached the river.

Like the ocean, the river never failed to capture and reflect her mood. The cool autumn wind hurtled down from the north and slammed into the point of land where she sat. "Argh," she howled back into the wind and tried to sort the flow of events out in her head.

It was subtle but palpable. The way the guys shouldered together was not lost on her. The only other time she ever felt the sense of not belonging was during Beast Barracks before she bonded with all her friends.

She felt tempted to pray, then realized she would need to double time it back to make class without being late. "Shit!" she yelled at the river.

Jane sat in her military strategy class and only half listened to her professor. Patrick Ash sat across the room from her and up until today had hardly made eye contact with her. She studied him as he took notes and tried to see if his knuckles were bruised or cut, but she was too far away to see anything. Sensing her gaze, he looked up. She faced him without looking away and summoned a half smile. He responded with a slight lift of his chin. The hair on her arms stood up. To break the charged moment she directed her eyes toward their professor.

Pretending she was taking notes, she consulted her list of suspects for the sixth time since yesterday. She wrote, "WHY?" on the paper in front of her. When she dotted the question mark her pencil lead broke off, and she realized how hard she had been pressing down on the point. Shit she mouthed and added a column next to the suspect list. She titled it "Questions" and underlined it with her pencil. Underneath she wrote, "Why do men rape?"

"Archer?" Her professor's voice startled her out of her reverie. She jumped. "So sorry to have interrupted something you're writing! Love letter, Archer? Care to share with the class?"

"No, sir. Sorry, sir"

Across the room Ash smirked and folded his arms across his chest as if to say, serves you right, you nosey bitch. Was he reading her mind? Was he sending psychic warning messages to her? Or was she going just plain crazy?

Thankfully her professor let her off the hook, turned down the lights, and flipped on the projector. The first slide was entitled "The History of the Bomb."

Jane welcomed the dimmed lighting and watched with detachment. Something shifted within her, a minute turn in a cog. There suddenly existed two of her. One part lived and breathed and took notes and wanted to be an effective patriotic cadet and soldier. The other part of her possessed the ability to look through the obvious to see the subtle, pervasive, and unspoken elephant in the room.

Who was she fooling?

Herself. Everyone else.

During trainings, when the cadets cheered, "Ooh. Ahh. I want to kill someone," she cringed inside.

Her professor droned on, "With advancements in the industrial revolution in the mid-nineteenth century, rocket and missile technology took off." He chuckled at his own joke. "No pun intended. The rocket . . ."

Jane blocked out her professor's voice. With all the strategies of war coming into vogue then replaced by more modern and devastating methods for "overcoming one's enemy," Jane never heard any one of her instructors in her four years of taking military history classes address the prevalence of rape in terms of a strategic component. For it had been and still was in parts of the world a successful method of controlling the enemy. It was the threat and fear of rape that often caused the surrender of villages and small towns in history.

As cadets, they were trained in self-defense. They were lectured to about duty, honor, country. They were taught calculated and deadly techniques in combating the enemy, but she could not recall the chain of command ever issuing the order to the men at West Point not to rape. Jane's mind felt pulled in two different directions, like she was on the torturing rack. She knew they did not condone it. But by not addressing the issue head-on it became the elephant in the room—awkward and insidious.

As the slides flashed from one missile to another, one phallic-shaped hunk of deadly metal to the next, doubt and fear began to bleed into her certitude and undermine her confidence.

She thought of Ash's father in Vietnam. Her gut burned with a sudden knowing that Ash was not the only resulting progeny of that war.

It was as if Jane had pressed the hidden button of a secret chamber and a door began to swing open, creaking on its ancient hinges. With a whoosh, the suffering of millions of women in history blew through her. Nausea turned her stomach. She shook in her seat.

It took every ounce of strength and the recruitment of every cell of her body not to jump out of her chair and run for Thayer Gate. Her mind went on hyper alert and adrenaline shot into every muscle. She felt as if she found herself in the enemy's camp by mistake.

She sat still and tried to ride it out. A full-on skirmish was happening inside her body. Blood flooded her limbs. Her ears thrummed. The walls of the room pulsed in rhythm with her pounding heart. She gripped the sides of her desk and held on to her sanity. An earthquake rocked the foundations of her mind. Cracks and fissures threatened the entire structure of her life. A feminine voice whispered, *Breathe.*

Jane surreptitiously glanced around the room to see if anyone else had heard the voice. Her classmates were engrossed in the slides. All appeared normal. So, now she was hearing voices. Who are you? Jane asked in her mind.

You have found your path, my dear friend. Everything is all right. You are fine. See if you can relax.

A picture of the young medieval warrior Joan of Arc, from the book her parents gave her, flashed into her mind. Even though it seemed crazy, Jane felt as though the voice was hers. Suddenly she felt slightly better. Her pulsed slowed and her mind cleared.

When class ended Jane bolted out into the cold sunshine and sucked in several mouthfuls of fresh autumn air. She realized talking to Ash after class was out of the question. Something about him frightened her.

Stay focused on the task at hand. Shake it off, she said to herself. She looked around half expecting things to appear radically different. Under a crystalline cerulean sky, she walked quickly toward the cadet laundry building to meet her friend Gladys.

Everything looked the same as before but there was an inchoate difference. Jane could not put a finger on it. The world's edges appeared crisper. The jagged stone of the buildings cut into the atmosphere at sharper angles than she remembered.

With each heel strike to the pavement Jane began to feel more and more like herself and by the time she reached her destination, cadet laundry, she almost forgot the entire episode in class.

Almost.

"Hi, Gladys," Jane said to get her attention. "Can I talk to you? It will only be a minute."

Gladys beamed every time she saw Jane. Her obvious joy at seeing Jane transformed her brown chubby face into a countenance of cherubic sweetness. Their friendship had grown even closer ever since Jane's father had lit a fire under the feet of the NYPD to find and arrest the person who shot her brother. Her family had found peace because of Jane. "Sure, just a minute." She spoke a few words to her supervisor, who nodded, and joined Jane outside and out of earshot of everyone else.

Gladys hugged Jane. "Uh oh, you look worried. What's up?"

"Gladys, I need your help. Something bad happened to a friend of mine over the weekend." Jane hesitated. "She was attacked, and I wanted to know if you could keep an eye out for clothing with blood on it." She clarified. "Men's clothing . . . ripped or bloody. I'm looking for someone. I know this is a lot to ask."

"OK, girl, I can tell this one has you all wrapped up. We get thousands of articles of clothing in here from all the cadets and officers and frankly I don't look. Nasty stuff. I'll do my best, though. Can't promise anything." She patted her friend on the shoulder. "The world can be a cruel place. But . . . if you focus on the right things it can be beautiful too. My brother's death taught me this."

"Here's a list of people to help narrow things down. Though, if you see anything else will you hold them for me?"

"Sure. Not for long though. People complain, you know."

"Yes, I know," Jane said hoping she was doing the right thing.

As she walked back to her barracks, Jane realized if she wanted to get anywhere with her investigation she would need to change her strategy. She needed to get tougher, stronger, and smarter. Even if Tara's attack was not the shot heard round the world, Jane felt it initiated a battle for her. It was her tipping point. This battle against female sexual violence would need to be fought using weapons of a different sort.

Maybe it was time to ask for help from the voice.

Jane marched back to her barracks her mind swimming, fighting to stay above pounding thoughts. Whom could she trust? Was there anything she could do to repair the break? This new solidarity between her male friends set her on edge and made her feel even more determined to get to the bottom of the whole thing. Then there was the nasty sense one of her friends caused significant harm to another human being and on top of it the others were engaged in the cover up.

She neglected to salute the plebes who passed her in the quad chanting "Good afternoon, ma'am," and left a trail of cadets in mid-salute waiting for her response. They'll get over it, she thought as she stomped up the stairs and stormed into her room.

The dismantling of her belief that she was one of the guys, that if she did everything they did, she would be the same, rocked her to her core. She literally felt a ripping in her chest.

She threw her things onto her desk, kicked off her shoes, peeled off her jacket, and sat on the edge of her bed. After over three years of life at West Point, she felt just plain weird. The way forward did not look clear. This was not about challenge. God knew how she continually challenged herself physically, mentally, and emotionally. This dilemma, this shift, she did not even have words for. If someone had issued an order or given her a task, she would set her mind to achieve the objective. But this uncertain and uneven ground put Jane into a state of perpetual vertigo and unease.

She jumped up and began pacing. When she considered just how much time and energy she put into being one of the guys her shapely knees nearly buckled. Her sense of identity blurred. She unbuttoned her gray shirt, stepped out of her gray woolen slacks, and stood in front of the small mirror over her sink. She took in her reflection. Short brown hair, round golden-brown eyes, cute figure. Her breasts were squished into her sports bra, minimizing her curves. Just about every woman at West Point, all fifteen percent, went to great lengths to prove they were just as good as the males at everything.

She paced from the window to the door and back. She felt like a caged tiger.

Frustrated she threw herself onto her bed and sat with her bare back against the cool wall and closed her eyes. OK, Jane. Let's get it together.

She considered why Tara's attack had dug so far beneath her skin and set off such a chain of unnerving experiences for her. "What am I supposed to do with this?" Jane asked out loud directing her gaze to the heavens.

Jane. The voice was at once faraway and deep within and the same image of Joan of Arc popped into her mind's eye.

Yes? Jane thought. She had not expected an answer.

You know me as Joan of Arc, but you can call me Jehanne. I am here if you want my help.

Jane wondered if she was losing her mind. She decided to play along. OK. Shoot. Can you tell me what's going on? She asked in her mind.

You are a very brave woman and you have achieved so much already.

Jane's breathing slowed as a feeling of calm wrapped around her.

Women have come far since my time, but there are still attitudes that need to change.

Rape, Jane thought.

You have the power to make a difference. I'm here to encourage you, to tell you to trust your feelings of inspiration.

To be honest, Jehanne, my country's military women continue to have no voice, no power when rape happens. I'm wondering how and if we can change this. Suddenly Jane felt self-conscious. It felt odd to talk to a nonphysical being.

One step at a time, Jane. I will guide you, if you wish it. Jehanne's words sprang from another world but also flowed from a spring bubbling out of the deepest caverns of Jane's own inner landscape. Jehanne's silvery intonations struck a cord within Jane's heart. She could sense this was her path. It certainly explained her preoccupation with Tara's attack. I don't want to be known as a feminist. That would not go over well here and certainly kill my career.

We are not talking about female against male. This is a human rights issue.

Wow. She was right. She let Jehanne's words sink in. They rang true. Her body thrummed with the challenge. In a strange way everything felt in order.

Can I think about it?

Yes. I am here for you always—just ask.

OK. Thanks. Jane did not know the proper etiquette for ending a conversation with the beyond so she saluted for lack of a better idea.

Jehanne laughed as her presence faded.

"Strange," Jane said aloud. "I can't believe I'm speaking with spirits." But the fact was she felt clearer and calmer. She knew just what to do.

ROUEN, FRANCE

MONDAY, MAY 27, 1431

Every muscle in my body ached, my face throbbed, and my resolve to stay strong waned. Events of the previous day haunted me. My stomach felt tied up in a permanent knot. I would not recover from this assault on my body and my spirit. My angels hovered close by and continued to remind me that my time of freedom would come soon enough.

Next to the heavy wood plank door, the only exit in the room, one of my guards, William Talbot, had fallen asleep in the wooden chair he had precariously leaned against (balanced on two legs) the grime-covered walls. His mouth hung open, his face dirty and unshaved. From where I lay, I could see crumbs from his most recent meal on his surcoat, stale bread and crumbly cheese. John Grey did not speak to me nor had he looked me in the face since yesterday. His remorse would haunt him to his death, just as his actions would haunt me. This I was sure of.

I knew I would not live to witness the aging of my body; my hands would not become bony; my face would not see a wrinkle. The realization of my fate became more evident with the passing of each day. I would not make my twentieth birthday.

It was the thoughts of others and how I could best serve my country and God that buoyed my heart. This was the only way to get through the suffering, the endless days of confinement. As I had grown so accustomed, I called upon the comfort of my memories and slipped far away from the misery.

On Wednesday, June 29, 1429, after our army won back all of the towns along the Loire River, we reconvened in Gien and picked up our precious cargo, the dauphin. We traveled as a huge entourage of men-at-arms, horses, and weapons, from town to town behind enemy lines toward eastward toward Reims. Successfully, we had taken pivotal towns on either side of Orléans and held possession of all the strategic river-crossing sites, pushing the Duke of Burgundy and his troops back northward. So great were our numbers, we kicked up clouds of dust forty feet into the air. People from all over filled the streets of the towns we visited, their faces painted with the colors of Charles's royal house, waving flags with France's colors. They waved, threw flowers, blew kisses, or marched along with us.

We arrived in Reims, unharmed and without resistance, on Saturday, July 16, to the cheers of thousands. "Noel, noel!" they cried, equating this great occasion with that of Christmas.

Inside the massive cathedral, where most of the kings of France had been consecrated, gathered the majority of noblemen and women who dared to travel through hostile territory. The dauphin's own wife and mother-in-law had elected to stay behind. Every bishop, except Pierre Cauchon, supporter of the Duke of Burgundy, stood as witnesses to this momentous occasion, dressed in their fur-trimmed crimson robes, their headpieces denoting positions of rank within the church.

Jean d'Alençon, my beau duke, bedecked in a navy-blue surcoat made of the finest velvet and brocade embroidered with gold fleurs-de-lys, stood in front of the dauphin, who kneeled on a red velvet cushion. Jean rested his hand on the Charles's shoulder while he murmured the blessings for knighthood. The dauphin needed to be knighted before he could be crowned king. Ceremoniously, Jean tapped Charles on either shoulder with the famous blade of Clovis to the cheers of the crowd.

The archbishop of Reims, his most formal crimson robes flowing from his corpulent belly, anointed Charles's bare head (using the substance from the sacred Sainte Ampoule of holy oil, believed to be the same oil used to anoint Clovis in the fifth century) before he placed the jeweled golden crown upon his head. Dunois and d'Alençon draped the royal robes on Charles's shoulders. Our new king turned to the crowd and lifted his golden staff in the air. The crowd called out, "Noel, noel," as trumpet blasts and shouts shook the great walls of the church.

After each noble "peer" and ecclesiastical "peer" greeted him as King of France, it was my turn to approach him on his royal throne. Dressed in my armor, I clattered up the steps and across the red carpet. Tears of relief and joy streamed down my face as I dropped to my knees and bowed my head to my new king's feet. Lifting my head, I gazed into his sparkling exultant eyes and said passionately, "Noble King, God's desire has indeed come to pass. You are now truly the King of France."

"Rise, Jehanne d'Arc. Your country is most grateful for your service, your faith in God, and your bravery in battle." His voice boomed more confident than ever before. The crowd cheered even louder.

After the ceremony, I rode on horseback, with the king's entourage, through the jubilant streets filled with crowds cheering for the new king and equally loud for me. "The Maid, the Maid," enthusiastic citizens shouted in waves. There seemed to be a unity of the people, a unique patriotism France had perhaps never experienced before. The challenges against the English and the threat that Philip of Burgundy, one of our own, would jeopardize the very existence of our country drew everyone together. It was a powerful, poignant moment for us all.

A sudden wave of melancholy sobered my thoughts and my heart weighed heavy. Turning to the archbishop, who rode next to me, I said, "When I die I should wish to be buried here among these good and devout people."

221

"Dear girl, what would make you think of death on the occasion of your greatest success?" he drawled, his deep voice cutting through the noise of the crowd.

"I have done what my King in Heaven wished me to do. I wish that God would allow me to return to my home, my sister, and my brothers before I come to the end of my work."

Ten days after the coronation, at the castle in Château Thierry, halfway between Reims and Paris, d'Alençon and I met with our new king. He sat confidently, his leg swung over the arm of an ornate upholstered chair. It seemed he avoided my gaze, however, as I looked upon him from my seat next to d'Alençon. The king's advisor La Trémoille stood staunchly at his side.

"Sire." D'Alençon took a breath, wanting to phrase our ideas in the gentlest of ways. "It would be wise to take advantage of the élan we presently hold and attack Paris as soon as possible."

"Dear and gentle King," I interjected. "The same voices that guided you to your crown believe that if we attack Paris now and bring you into the city, the entire war will be over. The people of Paris will see your strength, and the English will flee all of the remaining towns they now occupy."

"As it so happens," La Trémoille said and shot a look at the king, who continued to avoid eye contact with me, "we have entered into a temporary peace treaty with Philip the Good of Burgundy." His face appeared pale and drawn and his small dark eyes, floating above tremendous dark circles, narrowed. He pressed his thin lips together. "We've been negotiating for weeks."

"With all due respect, sire." D'Alençon ran a nervous hand through his dark locks. "Burgundy is only buying time in order to reinforce the city with men and canons."

"My voices say the Duke of Burgundy holds no intention for peace; he's manipulating you." I grabbed hold of the side of the carved chair on which I sat, allowing the feel of the wood to calm my escalating nerves.

The king flinched, his eyes widened. "My dear, no one is capable of manipulating me. I am older and wiser than the two of you, and I, not you, have been chosen by God to be king. King I shall be and will not be talked down to by either of you."

"Jehanne, I would be careful how and of what you speak. The bishops of the University of Paris are investigating all of the recent events that you instigated." La Trémoille took great pleasure in placing this palpable wedge between my king and me.

"Instigated?" I questioned, incredulous of this accusation made against me.

"You mean, the battles she won for you, sire?" d'Alençon spit out, in an attempt to stand up for me.

My rapid heartbeat and shallow breath signaled a shift within my king. Instantly, I knew I would spend the remainder of my days dodging the harmful daggers of treachery. My heart squeezed closed as I placed both feet firmly on the stone in an effort to steady myself. La Trémoille's treacherous jealousy scared me right to my bones. We would need to placate them both in order to preserve our lives.

"You may have our forces ready to fight the first week of September when the truce ends, but not a moment sooner. If Burgundy doesn't sign another treaty for prolonged peace, we will launch on Paris and I will enter the city," Charles declared as he shoved back his chair and stood.

We continued to sit in silence for a few moments, attempting to digest the turn of events, the sudden change in the king's mood. I looked at d'Alençon with wide pooling eyes. He glanced at me, tightened his jaw, and shook his head in response. We were stunned, paralyzed. Slowly we rose from our fine seats and left the room.

"Let's go outside where we can walk and discuss what just happened without being overheard," he spoke through gritted teeth. I could feel him seethe, his anger growing with each long stride. My own temper began to boil. I clenched and unclenched my fists in order to move the uncomfortable mounting energy surging through my body.

"That ungrateful connard," he said as we stepped into a garden of lilies bordering the castle. Other courtiers milled around, shaking hand fans in the heat, uninterested in us.

I paced back and forth under the late-July sun. "We've lost Paris because of this delay. Even if we fight in September, the Duke of Bedford will have enough time to completely rebuild and fortify his army in Paris."

"We have no choice. As angry as it makes me, we must wait and watch out for that snake of a man, La Trémoille."

I wrung my hands with worry. "Jean, I fear my time is coming to an end. I can't see a way out of this for me. What about the people?" Sweat ran down my back as I peeled off my heavy doublet. My gauze blouse allowed the light breeze to cool my body.

"Nonsense, chérie, your angels will protect you as they have done already."

"Suddenly, I'm not sure. I must converse with my divine counsel. Give me leave so I may sit in church."

The air felt ten degrees cooler in the chapel than outside. I sat in a small chair to the back of the empty building and hung my head. Angels in Heaven, I implore you. I am not good at this political intrigue and maneuvering. What is it I must do? As always, calm began to replace my panic and worry.

Dear one, we are with you. Remain strong. Try not to succumb to their fear. Fear will cause you to make choices that may not be in your best interest. Fear causes you to doubt and lose faith. It is best for you to remain as calm as possible. Keep your mind clear. Ask for guidance and listen to our responses. We will guide you. All you need do is listen. We will always be here for you . . . no matter what happens.

Merci, merci. I closed my eyes and allowed the fear to drain out of my body; slowly my shivering heart began to open and warm again.

That evening at banquet, the king treated us as if nothing happened. He bid us sit next to him just as he had at numerous banquets in the past. "I'd like to honor Jehanne la Pucelle, the

Maid, by asking her what she would like as reward for helping to save the crown. Whatever you ask I will grant it. Even if it makes the kingdom poor, I will grant your request," he bellowed to the entire hall.

His announcement caught me by surprise, and I did not know how to respond to this request. Was he sincere or was he intending to trick me? "Sire, it is most kind of you. My greatest reward is God's favor. However, O gentle King, if out of your compassion you will speak the word, I pray you lift the taxes of my village, Domrémy, poor and hard pressed by the stresses of war."

"Is that your only request? Nothing but that?"

"Oui. It is all. I have no other desire, sire." I felt the color rise in my face.

"But that is nothing. . . . Not nearly enough. Ask . . . don't be afraid."

"Indeed, gentle King, press me no further. There is nothing I need."

My king paused and looked around the room, smaller than most banquet rooms, in an attempt to comprehend my unselfishness. "She has won a kingdom and crowned its king. All she asks and all she will take is this small grace for others, not a care for her. It is fitting. Her actions are in proportion to one who holds in her heart riches beyond those any king could provide. Try as I would, I could not give more."

He picked up his golden goblet of wine and swung it in my direction. "I shall grant your request. It is decreed that from today forward, Domrémy, birth village of Jehanne d'Arc, Deliverer of France, known as the Maid of Orléans, is freed from all taxation . . . forever."

"Merci, sire," I replied, picking up my own goblet, truly grateful and not a little confused. "To the King of France," I cried in my best voice.

True to our word, we waited most of the month of August as our troops sat idle. On August 28, we marched our men toward the city of Saint Denis, just north of Paris. The city was named after the first bishop of Paris in the third century. Legend told how he walked, carrying his own head, cut off by a Gaelic sword, for two miles and continued to deliver a sermon.

D'Alençon, our stewards, captains, and I stayed at the royal abbey adjacent to the majestic Basilica of Saint Denis. It served as the final resting place of many kings and queens of France, housing marble tombs under its numerous stained glass windows.

The next morning my fair duke knocked at my door. "Jehanne, open up. I must speak with you straight away."

Curious and fully dressed, I opened the door to him. "Bonjour, Jean. What disturbs you this morning?"

"I have an uncomfortable feeling about all this." He looked earnest as he closed the door behind him and crossed the room in a few long strides. Standing next to the window arrayed with burgundy velvet draperies, a shadow passed over his face. "Please come away with me after the battle?" He grabbed hold of both my hands and implored me with his eyes. "I will have the king annul my marriage and you can be my wife. We shall live in a small chateau, somewhere far away from all of this. . . . We can go further south, where the winters are mild."

"Mon ami." I kissed both his cheeks. "There is nothing I'd like better than to be your wife, but . . . so many lives are dependent upon me. We have pulled many men out of the fields to fight. This will be a scant winter with the reduction in crops resulting from a smaller labor force all summer long. I must not disappoint the people." I thought, he loves me enough to be his wife. I could see the disappointment in his eyes, but I could not possibly leave court now. I continued, "What about my reputation with the people as 'the virgin Maid'? The people would be disheartened to hear that I've pulled you away from your wife, and then I will no longer be the Maid of Orléans. What about my honor with God? Our people need the hope of our example through this coming winter, to comfort them when their bellies are growling with hunger."

During the remainder of my days, I relived this moment over and over again. If I had only known what horror my future actually held I would have gladly given in to his request.

"Chérie, you care too much. Do you think our king considers the bellies of his people? Non, I assure you he only cares about his own back and crown, however uneasily it sits upon his thin head." He swept me into his arms. "S'il vous plait," he whispered in my hair. "I can't lose you."

"You can never lose me." I reassured him by tenderly stroking his cheek. Looking into the blue depths of his eyes, I held his strong face between my small hands. "Oh, I do love you . . . more than any man," I said and pulled away from him. "Maybe in the springtime we can reconsider your plan?" I spoke the words but they rang hollow in my ears. I knew it would not be so.

"Oui, I will wait," he vowed.

I spent numerous hours in prayer and silence under the huge stained glass windows of the Basilica while we waited for our king to arrive. Because my angels gave me warning of a challenging time to come, I found myself trying to become as still inside my mind as I could. I would need to think clearly and calmly in the days to come. My beloved's offer of marriage continued to haunt me. I loved him dearly but felt my love and concern for the people took up more territory within the space of my heart. My angels reassured me that infinite love would be mine if I took care of the people first. I trusted their advice and found their guidance sang in my soul.

Meandering between the tombs, I ran my fingers along the smooth white marble effigies of kings long gone. There prevailed a sense of impermanence. Our lives, so brief, so swift. We have but only a short time to make a difference, to make a small black mark on the voluminous pages of history.

By the time our king arrived and we were given the go ahead for battle, I was ready.

On Tuesday, September 8, we woke to a gauzy white sky. All of our armor-clad captains mounted our horses, lined up side by side, and faced our soldiers. Many of the faces were familiar now, eliciting memories of their valor and strength in past skirmishes. My captains, more like brothers, each exhibited their prebattle habits of fussing with armor or re-buckling their saddles, idiosyncrasies that gave me comfort. Every one of them appeared confident of victory. It was a couple of hours past noon before we were ready to attack.

"Soldiers of France and of God, pray for the surrender of the English. Fight valiantly and bravely knowing that the King in Heaven is with you. Our own king waits for our signal so that he may enter Paris and end this long war once and for all," I shouted to the men. "With me!" I hollered, shoved my banner in the air, and kicked my horse's flanks, giving the signal to begin battle. We rode toward the siege lines of the English, north of the Saint Honoré gate.

Screams and shouts filled the air. Clouds of dust filled the sunless sky. Arrows rained down upon the enemy and showered in equal number at us. Men-at-arms with lances, short swords, and long swords, fought hard, hand to hand. The ground vibrated with the deafening blasts of gunpowder canons. The battle waged on longer than all anticipated. When night fell, some of the captains wanted to break and regroup until morning.

"We must continue," I cried out over the din. "We are too close to stop now." Running on foot across the darkened field, just outside the walls of the city lit only with flaming torches, through the battling men, I yelled, "Fight in earnest, men. Victory will be ours! Take heart!" Suddenly, I felt a blow to my left leg. Ignoring it, I tried to walk and crumpled to the slick, blood-covered ground. Men sprawled dead or dying all around me. Sounds of screaming, metal clashing against metal, floated to me from the darkness. Running my hand down my leg to just above my knee, I bumped into the cold metallic end of an arrow lodged in my thigh. The leather vanes signaled to me this was no ordinary arrow. It was made of iron and shot out of a powerful crossbow. The tip of the arrow pierced the edge of my leg armor.

"Mon Dieu," I cried, grabbing the sides of my leg. Xaintrailles scooped me up and carried me to cover, along the sides of the battle lines. La Hire and d'Aulon set up a barrier of large shields so we could assess the damage. Like the arrow to my shoulder, it did not penetrate too deeply. D'Aulon, catching me by surprise, yanked hard at the bolt, removing it quickly.

I screamed for a full minute. Scalding pain shot from my leg up into my spine, causing my head to spin. Everything went black for a moment, but I did not pass out this time, willing myself to stay strong. My own warm blood ran freely down my leg and dripped onto the sodden ground. Angels? Please take away this pain, I pleaded, and immediately, I felt their comfort.

We are with you, dear one. Take heart.

"Jehanne, are you hurt?" I heard d'Alençon's voice somewhere behind me.

"Oui, it is not serious." I looked at my captains. "Get out there and fight! Stop fussing over me."

"Non, the men are tired. We will call the battle for now. Tomorrow we will return to win," d'Alençon said firmly. "Give the order to fall back."

The next morning, just as our troops gathered to resume attack, we received a message from our king. "On behalf of King Charles VII," the herald read of the parchment from the back of his gray-speckled mare. "He hereby orders the battle of Paris abandoned and wishes to see Commander Jean d'Alençon, and Jehanne the Maid, immediately."

We rode side by side, in silent anger, northward, back to Saint Denis. I attempted to keep my head clear so that I could hear advice from my heavenly counsel. However, the pain from my leg wound and my fury at the curious behavior of the king, proved too overwhelming.

"I have decided to disband the army," Charles announced coolly when we approached him. He sat alone at the large oak table in the gathering room of the royal quarters and lifted a sweet roll off a china plate. La Trémoille, oddly enough, was absent. Two stone-faced guards stood by the carved door. He waved his hand at us indicating for us to take a seat at the table with him.

"Sire, you want to disband the army? Now? Today?" I seethed, unable to control my temper. "You must be as crazy as your father was. We sit on the edge of victory."

He dropped the sweet roll back onto the plate with a clatter. "Jehanne, I assure you I am quite sane. I am saving you from a loss. You were wounded yesterday. I can't afford to have you die and I can hardly afford to pay all of these soldiers. I am sending them all home as of today!"

"Sire, I urge you to reconsider this decision." D'Alençon's voice shook somewhat; however, his anger was more contained than mine. "We would be victorious if we fought today. We made much headway and would have breeched the walls. The people of Paris would have changed allegiances if we were successful. They love Jehanne. If she entered the city with you, we would have it all."

Charles leaned forward to make his point. "Of all people, you two understand the difficult position I'm in. I have the people of France to consider, the views of the archbishop and his church, and my chamberlain, Trémoille, who keeps track of the kingdom's finances. The archbishop and La Trémoille feel you have become much too popular with the people. You know how uneasy the crown sits when his commanders garner too much favor." He chased an unseen object around the surface of the table with his jeweled finger. "I also have Philip of Burgundy to contend with. My desire is to strike a treaty of peace—one that will hold. This is delicate business . . . trying to reunite a country threatened by schism."

"Sire, I am all for peace . . . more than you know. Each time I witness a blade or arrow plunging into a man's flesh . . . it causes me great pain." I winced and rubbed my sore leg just remembering yesterday's bloody battle. "I would much prefer not to fight. But, the Duke of Burgundy is not to be trusted, and he does not care about a united France. My angels say you will have it all."

Lowering his voice the king replied, "You must understand how I am squeezed, caught between all of these greedy, unscrupulous men in positions of great power. I will deny every word of this if you repeat any of it elsewhere." He looked around to make sure no one was near and continued, "They are frightened of you and wish to see you brought down. They will do anything. The archbishop is threatening the validity of my crown, saying a heretic witch used magic to get me to Reims. He is prepared to declare to the public that your voices have abandoned you. This is the best way I could think of, disbanding the existing army, to protect both our skins."

"Sire, there must be another way," d'Alençon pleaded. His hands, folded together on the table, appeared bright red, he squeezed them so tightly.

"There is not. One more thing you must know. La Trémoille threatens to spread rumors that you two are having a love affair and that the Maid is no longer a virgin." He pushed the tiny plate away with a shove. "Do you see? I am protecting us all by doing this."

"I— Of course I'm a virgin! Are you sure La Trémoille is loyal to only you?"

Jehanne, hold your tongue, speak softly, and allow all of these events to play out. In a strange way, he is doing the best that he can.

"It would not be the first time he played both sides. This is why, Jehanne, you will return to Gien with me, and d'Alençon, you are free to return to your wife. We must do all we can to protect the gains we have made."

My pulse raced, my head throbbed. I never anticipated the king would separate us. I froze, unable to comprehend this abrupt change.

"The two of you are forbidden to gather troops or fight together," he added, watching for our reactions. Brushing crumbs from his crimson velvet doublet, he added, "We leave for Gien tomorrow."

"Sire, I don't think . . ." I stuttered and glanced at d'Alençon, who repeatedly clenched the muscles in his jaw.

"Tell all of the other captains they are free to return to their homes. You are dismissed." He waved his hand in the air.

When we did not move he yelled, "Now!"

"Sire, you are making a big mistake," d'Alençon warned as he rose slowly from his chair and bowed.

I followed behind him, limping, struggling to keep up with his long strides. He turned to me, his eyes glassy and cold with anger. "We'll need to ride back to our men and give them orders of dismissal."

My comrades, upon returning to Saint Denis, stomped into a pub to drink their feelings away, and then we joined the king for our trip to Gien, which felt somber. Conversation barely existed as each man tried to reconcile the failure of Paris with the king's new plans for a limited army. He would let most of the army go after we arrived safely in our own territory. My brother Jean departed immediately from Saint Denis for Domrémy upon receiving word my sister lay dying. D'Alençon rode up ahead. The threat of a rumor about us kept me from his side. I dared not even look at him for fear that others would feed the erroneous rumors.

The day we arrived at the castle in Gien and the king was safely escorted inside, most of my comrades, and my beloved, rode away on horseback. Unbearable grief made my heart feel like a stone. I didn't know which felt worse—my heart or my leg. I ached to the bone. Only Pierre and d'Aulon remained. The other men in my service were also dismissed by the king. Louis, my chaplains, and my heralds all traveled home. Not only did I miss my beloved friend and worry when I would see him, if ever, again, I missed my men and fellow captains. I felt adrift, lost, and lonely.

Over the next three months I spent time at court and led small skirmishes on the behalf of my king and La Trémoille. La Trémoille used me to run from town to town, battling men who had wronged him in the past. When I was not fighting his battles, he had me residing at his beautiful river-front castle in Sully-sur-Loire, whose curtain wall actually abutted the river's edge on two sides. Vast lawns and gardens wound from the river to the small drawbridge protecting the property. During the course of my stay I learned he possessed a number of enemies and understood why he wanted me residing in his castle. This strategy served two purposes at the same time. My now legendary presence kept would-be attackers at bay, and since our king stayed in Chinon or Loches, he would not have the benefit of my advice. It was no secret how La Trémoille and I held differing opinions concerning every facet of Charles's reign, from war strategies to public policies.

Just after Christmas, Charles declared my family nobility, giving us titles, our own crest of arms, and money befitting a comtesse. This enabled me to gather troops and raise money on my own, allowing me to assist those towns whose letters I received requesting aid in some way. Their needs varied from relief from a siege to simple requests for prayers.

I continued to converse with my heavenly counsel, who always advised me to keep peace with my king and La Trémoille, however hard that seemed. Their comforting presence helped me to remain calm and focused upon the task at hand.

Finally, in April of 1430, while staying at Lagny and launching unsuccessful skirmishes, I decided it was safe to see d'Alençon. When at La Trémoille's in Sully sur Loire, I felt terrified and imagined he had spies everywhere within the riverfront estate. The last thing I wanted was for him to spread rumors about my loss of maidenhood, so I dared not communicate with d'Alençon. For over a month, La Trémoille seemed to have lost interest in me and paid little attention to me. Rumors, too numerous to count, about towns struggling under the hand of Philip of Burgundy and rogue mercenaries, reached my ears daily. Citizens wrote me letters begging for my help. My heart could scarcely bear the weight of the suffering of the people. Each and every citizen of France felt like a dear friend to me. Several times each week, I asked the advice of my council, inquiring whether or not it would be wise to raise an army and fight. Their advice was to wait. By April, when I could stand it no longer, I dropped to my knees in the chapel of Sully sur Loire and prayed in earnest.

Dearest Jehanne, we understand your distress over remaining within the walls of La Trémoille's castle. However, we suggest you wait a while longer.

Archangel Michael, dearest Catherine and Margaret, you can't imagine how awful it is for me to remain here when there are those suffering in fear and under the forces of the Duke of Burgundy. Charles, our king, does nothing for his subjects. I don't understand why everything seems like a struggle now.

You, dearest one, believed your own negative thoughts and those of others. That's all.

"What do you mean?" I shouted out loud, frustrated.

How did it feel before Chinon? Did you feel like you had to struggle, or did you feel like you were guided and taken on a journey? Notice what happened to your feelings about your actions before the coronation, and compare them with how you felt after.

It feels like a struggle now, uncomfortable. But, I must do something to help the people.

If you recommence battling, you will be captured.

Where will I be captured? I put my hand to my chest to stop the sudden thudding of my heart. When a vision of someone pulling me from my horse began to run through my mind. I squeezed my eyes shut in an effort to stop it.

We cannot say, as events have not played out yet to provide details, but we see that you will be captured before St. John's Day in June.

Well, I will do what I can until then. I must help those who are in danger. I pray you will protect me.

We always protect you; know your soul is ever safe, especially when you act on the behalf of others. Know that if you are captured you will live on in legend. It will be safe to meet with d'Alençon at the end of this month. As always, know there is much love for you.

Merci, my friends.

Acting out of pain, I took this opportunity, against the advice of my angels, to raise a small army and decided to venture to Lagny in order to thwart forward movement of the Duke of Burgundy.

While in Lagny, d'Aulon, my loyal brother Pierre, and I, along with a small army of men, some of dubious character, captured a nefarious Anglo-Burgundian mercenary and known criminal, Franquet d'Arras, responsible for causing much trouble, attacking and pillaging small businesses, as well as harassing the citizens of the town. With his capture, his men quickly fled the walls of the city.

The next day I left d'Aulon and Pierre and rode northward to Crépy-en-Valois to meet my beloved in secret. He told me of a château in the hills, far away from those who would betray our relationship. I rode most of the day and arrived at the bridge he referenced in his last letter with a pictorial diagram, so I would understand. My heart leaped for joy upon seeing him, dressed in a heavy charcoal-gray traveler's cloak, astride his gray speckled courser. Seven months had passed since we were together. He looked much the same. My hands began to shake while my poor heart, which had ached continually during the past few months, came to life and swelled in my chest.

We embraced in the deepening emerald shadows as the sun sank below the small mountain to our west. The sky blushed, washing the rolling countryside in a rosy glow and, together with a gurgling stream, provided us with sweet ambiance. Lights from the town nearby twinkled in the cool night air. I savored his warmth and his arms around my shoulders.

"Jehanne, mon amour," he whispered, his breath hot on my cold ears.

I buried my face into his chest and cried. Tears ran in rivers down my face and my chest heaved with sobs. I did not realize how hard it had been, holding it all together: the political intrigue of La Trémoille and the archbishop, the insidious nature of court life, the fear of betrayal around every corner, and the mystifying behavior of my king.

"Come," he said, grabbing the reins of our horses. We walked down a small lane, following the terrain of the stream, to a quaint cottage. By now it was night, and under a crescent moon and starry sky, the cottage sat nestled beneath a copse of pine trees, against the side of a hill. Golden light spilled onto the graveled path, creating glowing patterns on the scrubby grass. It looked inviting and cozy— just what I needed. "The inn belongs to folks who will not know who you are. You can relax and rest," he said. "Are you hungry?"

"Famished," I replied, feeling lighter than I had in months. I realized just how much I missed him. He had a way of making me feel safe, understood, and cherished all at the same time.

"You look too thin." He pinched me playfully, bowed his head under the low lintel and escorted me into the tiny pub adjacent the inn. To the older, fleshy serving wench he said, "Two ales."

We sat opposite each other at one of only three worn, wooden tables and peered into each other's eyes. His loving look drank me in. "I missed you terribly," he breathed.

"Surely your wife must have kept you company." I untied my woolen cloak and spread it on the bench next to me.

"It's not the same and you know it," he defended, narrowing his thick dark brows. He didn't take his eyes off mine.

The wench plunked dripping tankards of ale down on the table with a thud. "Food?" She asked coolly.

"Oui," he answered. "Whatever you have this evening will be fine."

"That's good, since we only serve one meal here," she added sarcastically, wiping the ale off her hands with her worn, but clean, apron.

When she was out of earshot, I added, "At least you had someone's arms to hold you; comfort you."

"Need I remind you, I offered you marriage last fall and you refused," he argued.

"True," I said flatly, and took a long draught of ale. The cool liquid soothed my parched throat and served to warm my empty belly. I smiled sweetly at him. "Truce?"

"Truce," he said, his eyes softening.

After a bland but filling meal we found our way along a narrow cobblestoned walkway to the small room at the back of the stone building. Only one bed, slightly larger than the one my sister and I had shared, sat squarely in the center of the clean space. D'Alençon removed his boots and proceeded to peel off outer layers of clothing, tossing them onto the room's only wooden chair. Suddenly, I felt concerned. "Jean, you are going to honor my virginity aren't you?"

"Chérie, of course, oui." He brushed my hair off my forehead and helped me with my cloak. "I understand the gravity of such a mistake."

Even with his promise I felt uncomfortable and fiddled with the ties of my doublet. "I've never been alone with a man like this. Maybe this was not such a good idea."

He wrapped his arms around me. "Shh, you are quite safe with me. I promise. Haven't I always treated you with respect? Surely, there is no other man alive who cherishes his beloved more than I."

"Perhaps I should accept your request of marriage now?" I asked shyly.

"Jehanne, sit." He led me to the edge of the bed and sat next to me. Holding my hand between both of his, he said, "My wife is with child, due in the middle of the summer." He looked into my eyes waiting for my response.

I did not answer him immediately. His announcement caught me completely by surprise. My shoulders dropped and my world seemed to shrink. The tumblers of my future shifted and clanked noiselessly into a different configuration. Just like that, dreams I had for my life changed. It felt as though someone put a fist into my abdomen. My breath left my body. I realized then just how much I counted on being with him someday. "We can't be married then. It would be cruel to leave your wife with a child." I panicked. "The king can't annul your marriage. Alors, mon Dieu." I pulled my hand out of his and jumped up. "I mustn't stay here with you. This is all wrong."

Tears stung the corners of my eyes, pooled, and ran down my face. I looked around the room, searching for somewhere to go, but there was nowhere. I racked my mind for a safe place to go and came up with nothing. I had no home. No one sat waiting with a light for me. The man of my future suddenly disappeared. He was the husband of another with a babe on the way. I slumped to the cold stone floor and sobbed. He tried to comfort me but I pushed him away.

"Jehanne, it will be all right." He held out his hand and pleaded. "We can still be together."

"Like this . . . having to sneak around. If you think I will be your mistress for the rest of my life, you are mistaken. I don't care how much you love me. You ruined this. We could have had it all. Now we have nothing. Nothing!" I screamed at him, anger and sadness weaving together a mighty tempest within my breast. I tried to stand, to get up and run out of the room, but my muscles wouldn't move. My fury and grief drained me to the bone.

"God, what do you want of me?" I screamed to the beamed ceiling and continued to sob into my hands on the floor.

D'Alençon lay on the floor next to me and held me gently from behind. I no longer had the strength to push him away. "Shh, shh . . . chérie. Everything will be fine. God loves you more than anyone I know."

"This is love? Then . . . why does he torture me with success and take it away? He gives me love and takes it away. . . . I don't understand. What am I supposed to do now?" I spoke in gasps, trying to catch my breath.

He pulled his cloak off the chair and, making a pillow out of it, placed it under my head.

I woke the next morning to daylight streaming through the small window. Morning doves called to one another, soft mournful songs. We had fallen asleep on the hard stone floor and remained there, fully clothed, all night long. I did not want to move. Life would feel different now without the dream of my beloved. When I looked to my own future, all I could see was my narrowly avoiding death at every turn. One wrong move and I would be imprisoned, possibly murdered by the church, my own countrymen, and my enemies. My pride kept me from compromising my beliefs.

"D'Alençon." I nudged him awake. "I'm going to leave and go home to Domrémy to see my family." I remembered the warning of my divine counsel, about my capture before St. John's Day on June 24.

"I will ride with you," he said, stretching his arms overhead and yawning. "It's the least I can do, to make sure you arrive there safely."

"Oui, I accept your offer," I said, resigning myself to a seemingly colorless, danger-fraught future. My entire body felt weighed down, lethargic. I didn't even want to pray to my angels to feel better. I wanted to give up and go home.

"You know I will love you forever; you are in my blood. My heart is broken too, chérie," he pleaded as we walked out the door, down the gravel path toward our steeds.

I ignored his pledge of love, closed my heart to him, and mounted my horse as a few drops of rain began to splatter in the puddles on the dirt road.

We traveled with the spring rains beating down on us, southeast, over one hundred miles of rutted, muddy roads, and arrived in Domrémy three days later, our horses steaming beneath our sodden shivering bodies. The convivial cheers and broad smiles of my old friends and fellow villagers, in combination with the open arms of my parents, served to thaw our throbbing limbs and lift our sagging spirits.

"Jeanette, we are most grateful for your bravery and the good fortune of paying no taxes," numerous townsfolk repeated over and over again, calling me by my childhood name, little breaks of sunshine in a cloudy sky.

They seemed truly happy to see me and threw d'Alençon and me a humble banquet. We enjoyed the lack of pretense and contrast (from royal banquets) of genuine care the villagers showed us. I loved the simplicity and familiarity of home but it no longer felt like *my* home; I felt out of place. Gone was the little girl, Jeannette. No longer sure of who or what I was, one thing seemed certain, I did not fit there, either.

My parents, looking sad over my sister's death during the winter, rejoiced at the homecoming of their famous youngest daughter. My heart lightened with their joy and the simple fact that I had helped the town immensely by removing the heavy burden of the king's taxes.

"Jeannette, we are proud of you. What amazing feats you have accomplished," my father said. He rambled, retelling stories of my battles, which had traveled from town to town. My mother hugged me repeatedly, reassuring herself that I was home alive.

We left after two days, knowing we had a long ride ahead of us, back to Gien to see the king. Upon my bidding, d'Alençon treated me as a sister. I could no longer bear his proclamations of love and devotion. We had no future together; thoughts of anything else would be not only futile but torturous.

Conversation between us was minimal. Except for logistical discussions—where to stop for meals, which roads would be the safest and quickest—we rode in a pained silence. It was May; spring shone her splendor once again, but I hardly noticed. I did not notice the myriad scents and smells of the moist earth, nor the rows of greenery lining the dark soil, resembling the pattern a giant comb would make if drawn across the land, or the delicate buds of the flowering fruit trees. I did not notice the tired, weathered faces of the farmers after a long day in the fields or their merry greetings as we rode past. Instead, I decided to focus on containing my feelings, hardening my too-soft heart. I resolved to do my best to protect and help the people neglected by the French king. It seemed I had nothing left to lose, or so I thought then.

We parted coolly after we arrived in Gien. "Au revoir, Jean. May God bless you and keep you and your family safe." I kissed both his cheeks, trying not to remember how wonderful his arms felt around my shoulders, how his throaty voice made my blood flow faster, and how his deep love gave me courage.

"Au revoir, Jehanne." He hugged me hard. Pulling away, he whispered, "I will always love you. I know you love me, too, despite your behavior. Maybe someday . . ."

"Hush. . . . It will not be." I turned away from him, from his brilliant blue eyes awash with sadness, and walked toward the river. It felt as though my heart had split in two pieces, one part stayed with him and the other remained with me. Only now it belonged to France. I cried no tears for fear that if I started, I would not stop. My tears, if allowed to flow, would fill this lazy river to overflowing and wash away the fragrant fields below. I resisted the urge to slump to the grassy bank and let the new growth of spring cover me, dissolving my flesh and bones. I wished for the vines of the nearby ivy to grow thick all over my body, to choke out all feeling, all desire, all love. Fighting the tidal waves of self-pity, I imagined closing the door to romantic love and walked back toward the château, my spine straight and my head held high.

There waited several messages from towns requesting my help, as well as a letter from the city Compiègne, specifically its defender Guillaume de Flavy. They wished for my attendance at a reception. Also invited were my friends: Louis, Count of Vendôme; Jean Poton de Xaintrailles; and Regnault de Chartres, archbishop of Reims. Happily, I accepted the city's invitation. Another truce, centering on the safety of strategically important Compiègne, had ended on April 17. The populace chose not to align with Burgundy and wished to have us present within their cities' walls as a statement of alliance with the king.

Before I left for Compiègne, I begged the king's permission to have my previous chaplain, Pasquerel, travel with me again. To my joy, he acquiesced. I sent messages to d'Aulon and Pierre with orders to take all the men, our meager three or four hundred, and meet me outside of Compiègne in a week. Soliciting a few more men from Gien, I rode excitedly toward my destination with a new mount, a powerfully strong, dapple-gray courser, and dressed in my finest gold cloak, a gift from my king. I had not forgotten the warnings of my divine counsel regarding my capture. I decided to meet my fate head on.

565 Years Later

Tuesday, November 26, 1996
West Point, NY

Jane walks through the darkened forest barefoot, following the path illumined by the moon with a sense of urgency. She runs through a shallow river and up a muddy bank where she loses her footing. On all fours she clamors up the bank, stands, and begins running. A wolf joins her on her left side and a stag on her right, like bodyguards. Together they run like the wind barely touching the ground. Up ahead, Jane sees a clearing in the woods where a central fire blazes. Jane's alarm jolted her awake. Just that dream again, she thought as she took a deep breath, attempting to settle her racing nervous system. What is going on with me? Strange dreams, talking to spirits—might I have too much stress in my life?

Once her heart settled down she knew she was fine. Jane remembered reading in the history books how Joan of Arc acted upon guidance from her angels, and she was regarded as one of the most amazing warriors of all time. Jane decided she was going to trust the information coming to her no matter the form it took.

Jane brushed her teeth and dressed for classes. It felt clear to her that her first step included making another attempt to talk to Tara.

Jane moved from class to class, ate lunch in the mess hall, and met with cadets on her staff with the efficiency of the best Army officers. Around four o'clock, she threw on her Army sweats and headed over to Tara's barracks.

Outside Tara's room she knocked twice on the door and walked in, as she always did, without waiting for a response. She opened the door just in time to see Alex Raphael sitting next to Tara on her bed. He was handing Tara her watch. They both flinched when they saw Jane.

"Hey," they both said at once.

Jane decided to play it cool. "Fancy meeting you here, Raphael."

"Just checking on our friend," he said.

"How are you?" Jane asked as she sat down on Tara's other side.

Out of the corner of her eye, Jane caught Tara slide her watch under her thigh. "I'm feeling better. The bruises hurt less even though they look worse." It looked as though Tara wore heavy eye makeup. Each eyelid was puffed up and dark purple with a yellow swath stretching toward her temples.

Jane sucked air threw her teeth. It hurt her just to look at Tara's face.

An awkward silence built between the three of them. She had to bite back words and wrestled with her mind not to question him outright. He appeared more upset than guilty.

Just let this moment play out, Jehanne said in Jane's head.

Jane thought the advice was perfect. She smiled to herself, feeling like she had her own private consultant.

"I'm going to take off," Alex said and rose to leave. "I'll let you two catch up."

"Thanks for coming, Alex," Tara said.

"Sure. Later."

"Later, Alex," Jane said. When he closed the door behind him Jane turned to her friend and asked, "So, really, how are you?"

"Good. I went to classes today. It felt weird. I don't like people looking at me with pity. I'm so happy we leave for Thanksgiving break tomorrow," Tara said. She massaged her jaw with her fingers. "Jaw still hurts."

"Jeez, Tara . . ."

"Don't!"

"So you are not going to tell me? Still?"

"Jane you know nothing good will come of it if I tell. I don't want to mess up the rest of our senior year. If I tell you, then you will be involved, and in your position as battalion commander you will be compelled to report it. I don't want to compromise your ranking. I want to put this behind me. The fastest way to heal is for me to keep my mouth shut. By the time I return from break I should be back to myself. "

Before Tara could stop her, Jane grabbed the watch from beneath Tara's leg. "So, why did Raphael have your watch?" She held the leather band and dangled it in front of her face.

Tara attempted to snatch it back from her friend, but Jane's reflexes were quicker.

Jane studied the object. "Nice watch."

"Come on, Jane." Tara held out her hand.

"There is blood on the band, Tara! Who's is it? If it's your attacker's this can be used as evidence you know."

"Jane, I want you to stop. Please? I'm pleading with you to let it go. I want the whole event behind me."

They starred at one another. When Tara's bloodshot eyes filled with tears Jane said, "OK. I'm sorry. It's just that I want your attacker punished. What if he does it again?"

Tara did not answer. Suddenly she appeared small and fragile to Jane.

"All right. For you, I'll let it go," Jane lied.

She left Tara resting on her bed and jogged over to cadet laundry as the sun sank behind the Cadet Chapel to check in with Gladys.

"Is Gladys still working?" she asked the woman behind the desk.

Without answering Jane, the woman turned toward the workroom and yelled with a deep southern drawl, "Glad-ass."

Gladys grinned upon seeing Jane. "I have something for you," she said lowering her voice. "But I can't give it to you here." She checked the clock on the wall over the desk. "Can you meet me in the parking lot near the Cadet Chapel in thirty minutes, at five thirty— I mean 1730?"

Jane's stomach flipped in anticipation. "OK. That's great."

While she walked up Mills Road she spent a few minutes nervously contemplating her position. Did she really want to know who committed the attack? Just where would all this lead? She decided to check in with Jehanne and stepped off the road and into a copse of trees.

Twilight lent a cobalt-bluish cast to the buildings and shadows. The absence of sun amplified noises and faraway voices as the air grew cooler.

"Jehanne?" Jane whispered and waited. About twenty seconds passed. A breezed ruffled the hair at her neck. She cast a wary look around and thought hard, I want to know if I am on the right track. Should I go through with gathering evidence?

Yes, Jane. I am with you. Gathering evidence will help with your mission. It will aid you on your quest for truth. You may want to be careful where you go afterward. I suggest going straight back to your room when you leave here. Just ask and I will be with you.

Thanks, Jane thought, thinking how lucky she was to have the guidance. Just as Jane made it to the top of the hill she saw Gladys pull up in an older model Toyota. Jane got in the car.

When they parked near the chapel, Gladys reached into the backseat. She grabbed a laundry sack and handed it to Jane. "This may be what you are looking for."

Suddenly Jane felt bad. "Gladys, I'm sorry. I've put your job at risk."

"Nonsense. After what you did for me. The way I see it I owe you a few more favors."

When Gladys's car pulled away Jane sat on a bench in the clearing near the chapel to think. She placed the laundry bag on the ground between her feet.

Jane you need to leave that place. Go back to your barracks.

Jane ignored Jehanne's advice thinking she knew better and that she was perfectly safe there near the chapel. She felt captivated by the moonlight. It was a beautiful autumn evening, and the rising moon cast long slats of light through the trees. She thought about Jack and how much he loved her. She thought about her more-than-promising military career. Maybe she should let all this go? Why risk everything? After all, even Tara wanted to put the whole thing behind them.

Men raped. Fact. She decided she would not look in the sack and instead return it to Gladys in the morning. Just as she bent over to grab the bag from the ground, she heard a sound behind her. She jumped up and turned her body to face the sound in one swift move.

"Oh, it's you. You startled me for a moment," Jane said relaxing her vigilant mind in the presence of someone she trusted and smiled.

She opened her mouth. "What—" But the words caught in the back of her throat. Her body picked up mixed signals. A surprising dose of adrenaline coursed through her limbs. Just in case she needed a quick escape, she surveyed her surroundings.

"Do you have a minute?" Ash asked. He took three steps closer to her and stopped about six feet away.

"Sure. What's up?" she asked trying to sound non-pulsed.

"I wanted to talk to you about all this Tara nonsense."

"Oh?" She did not like the fact that he used the word 'nonsense.'

"Why are you noising around so much? You know if you push her, the whole thing will only end her career."

"Really, Ash?" She said with a sudden surge of confidence. The fear she felt only moments before became consumed by mounting anger. "So who are you protecting?"

"I don't think you want to know the answer to that question, or your career will be . . . let's say . . . less than—"

"Are you threatening my career? Because I just want to get this straight."

He did not respond verbally and instead took a step forward. "Come on . . . Jane. We're friends."

"Correction, Ash. We were friends until you called me a bitch last summer. What's up with you anyway?" She stepped away from the bench and tilted her head. She really did want to know the answer to her own question. Deep down she still cared about him. He had so much potential. He was one of the smartest cadets she knew. He had a physical adroitness, which would make him a great field officer. And, up until this year, she admired his integrity and ability to be a team player.

He took another step forward. A faint scent of alcohol floated to her on the evening breeze.

"Have you been drinking?" she asked and stole a glance at the laundry sack laying partially hidden under the bench.

"You are little miss busybody, aren't you?" He reached out and shoved her shoulder with two of his fingers. "Maybe it's time for you to mind your own business."

The three-quarter moon slid from behind clouds and cast a bluish light on his face. His lips pressed firm making the muscles along his jawline bulge, and his tawny eyebrows drew together creating a deep crease on his forehead. In the moonlight he appeared out of character, almost sinister.

"It was you. You did it . . . hurt Tara. How could you?"

In a flash his right fist appeared in the air. Moonlight glinted off his West Point class ring. Without even thinking Jane lifted her left arm, blocked the punch, and reflexively struck him in the gut with her right hand. He grabbed her extended arm and pulled her around so she was pinned, her back against his chest. He squeezed her with such force she could barely breathe.

"You're going to let this go. Right?" He hissed in her ear.

She could feel his powerful chest heaving with the mighty strength of a cornered animal.

Be careful with him.

There was no way that she was going to give in to him. Time slowed down and gave her a moment to think about her next move. She considered whether or not he would chase her down and really harm her if she got away. Another option was to fight him. Even though she had her fair share of combat and martial arts training, she knew he would surely win. The last and most distasteful option was to concede to his demands. But then what? She could just lie and tell him she would let it go and walk away, but something inside of her could not do it. She did not want to play the threatened, beaten woman.

"I don't want to hurt you," he said. But his words and actions failed to align, for as soon as he spoke he increased the pressured of his arms encircling her.

It felt as though he had the ability to crush her. Her rib cage felt compressed, on the edge of breaking. She had to fight for breath. "I will not shrivel or shrink just because you threaten me."

She began a quick prayer in her head. Jehanne, I will not back down to him. Can you help?

I am with you. Your actions are in alignment with what is truth. You are stronger than you believe.

A blast of energy drove Jane to move. She lifted one foot and kicked back into his shinbone as hard as she could and with both thumbs dug similarly into the soft flesh just above his elbows.

"Bitch," he growled and released his hold long enough for her to slide down the front of his body, out of his grasp, to a squat and leap away from him. She heard him grunt behind her, then felt her body jerk backward. An image of a brown grizzly bear playing with its quarry flashed into her mind. He caught the back of her sweatshirt, spun her around, and punched her in the face.

She fell to the ground and lay facing him as he took a step closer, towering over her. She swung her right leg up, brought her knee toward her own shoulder and violently thrust her heel into his groin.

He doubled over, his face contorted in pain, giving her time to push her hands into the ground and propel her other foot upward for a strike square in his face. As her heel made contact with his nose she heard it crunch.

He staggered backward and dropped to his knees.

Jane leaped up and began to run. She zigzagged through the trees, across the macadam in front of the Cadet Chapel and headed for the long narrow stairs that lead down behind the mess hall. She took two steps at a time listening for his footsteps behind her.

Oh, God. Please don't let him follow me, she prayed.

She leaped off the last step and sprinted as fast as she could toward Jack's barracks, passing only a few cadets who took very little notice of her. To them she appeared like any other cadet running through the quad in sweats. As she reached Jack's door and flung it open, a sob escaped her mouth.

Jack jumped up from his chair knocking it over and assumed a fighting stance until he realized it was Jane. "Jesus Christ, Jane! What the hell happened to you?"

She stumbled over and sat down on his perfectly made bed with its wool blanket and military corners. Tears of frustration and fear ran down her face mingling with blood on her left cheek where Ash's class ring had split her flesh. She put her head in her hands still panting from her escape and cried.

"You're scaring me, Jane. What happened?" He sat next to her and pulled her to him.

Jane knew exactly how Tara felt. As she sat there reeling from the attack, she wondered how much she should tell Jack. For the first time, she felt confused, caught in between the lines of the cadet honor code, the behavior actually expected from cadets, and a basic moral obligation to stand up to unjust violence.

She let Jack hold her until her tears ran out. As she dabbed at her nose with a tissue she remembered the laundry sack. "Oh shit!" she said and jumped up. She grabbed Jack's hand and pulled him up. "You have to come with me right now."

"What? You're gonna need stitches before we go anywhere."

Jane touched her cheek with her fingers and winced. "Stitches have to wait. We need to go now."

"You come crashing in here . . . bleeding and crying, and now you want me to follow you?"

"I'll explain everything. Just come with me now. We don't have a minute to lose."

"It's a good thing I love you so much," Jack said and stood.

As they retraced Jane's frantic path from only fifteen minutes before, Jane told Jack about her talk with Tara, her conversations with their buddies, and her deductions about Tara's attacker. She spoke in hushed tones while her eyes raked over every cadet they passed, hoping not to run into Ash. Her skin prickled with watchfulness. Every shadowy corner sent her pulse racing even though Jack walked right by her side.

"Jane, you do realize that you will open a huge can of worms if you go any further with this. Why are you compromising yourself?"

"I'm not compromising myself, I am just trying to do what's right. . . . Being a good leader. Isn't our class motto 'With Pride We Defend'?"

"I'm not sure I get it, but I know you and trust your judgment."

She recounted the events with Gladys, the laundry bag, and finally the altercation with Ash as they mounted the last few steps on the side of the Cadet Chapel. "The only thing I'm not sure of was how long Ash stood behind me, and whether or not he saw me with Gladys," she said.

"Jeez, you broke his nose?" He laughed bitterly. "That's my girl. Good thing you did it or I would have to. Ash better not be up there or—"

"Wait," Jane whispered when they reached the top. She pulled on Jack's arm to stop him from moving out into the open then held her breath as they surveyed the area.

No sign of Ash. All was quiet.

"OK, let's go," Jane whispered. Her heart thumped in her chest as she approached the clearing with the bench. Her body shuddered remembering the fight and how afraid she felt when Ash stood over her. She shook the memory off and let her eyes adjust to the shadows.

"Where did you leave it?" Jack asked.

"There it is," Jane said. It lay just as Jane left it, crumpled under the stone bench. She bent down to retrieve the evidence that could potentially change lives.

ROUEN, FRANCE

TUESDAY, MAY 28, 1431

On Tuesday, May 28, Bishop Cauchon and several of the judges entered my cell and grew furious upon seeing that I wore men's clothing once again. I did not care. Ready for the end. I was ready for death.

"Did you not abjure and promise not to resume this clothing?" the bishop demanded, dumbstruck at this change in events.

I ignored his question and said, "I would rather die than be in irons! I will be good and do as the Church wills if I am allowed to go to Mass, and am taken out of irons and put into a gracious prison with a woman for a cell companion."

"What injury has befallen you that your face is swollen?" the bishop asked, his lips glistening with fat from his breakfast.

Birds chirped cheerfully outside the window, creatures of absolute freedom. I envied them and wished I could grow wings and fly away.

"I know not of what you speak." I was unwilling to divulge the loss of my virginity.

"Do you continue to claim that your voices are Saint Catherine and Saint Margaret?"

"Yes. They speak to me because God wishes it."

"On the scaffold in the cemetery, you did admit before us, your judges, and before many others, that you untruthfully boasted your voices to be Saint Catherine and Saint Margaret."

"I only denied them out of fear of the fire. I would rather do die than endure further suffering in this prison. I have done nothing against God, in spite of all they have made me revoke. I had no idea the content of the document I signed. I did not intend to revoke anything except according to God's advice. If you wish, I will resume a woman's dress; for the rest, I can do no more."

"We have no choice but to find you guilty of all the crimes you are accused. May God be with you." Cauchon's angry voice made the priests in tow, his most staunch allies, shake.

When my inquisitors left my prison room, I sunk back into the mattress, now stiff in places with my dried blood. Everything smelled rancid; my skin crawled. My remaining memories were painful ones, yet they needed telling. My desire was to disclose it all to the future. Lay it all out for more open-minded folks to discern the truth of what happened to me on this journey of faith. And, as always, it was a relief to look back at the past. I began to realize I could have made other choices. My pride and my doubt wrote the remaining cosmic script and changed the fate of my last days. Had I been gentler on myself and my beloved I would have had all that I wanted.

I allowed my mind to replay the events of only one year ago.

May of 1430 was unseasonably warm. Just as the hot sun stirs the wasps from their nests, the lengthening spring days stimulated the heated quest for power within the higher echelon of Charles's court. Uncomfortable with anyone else's fame and popularity, those who held the king's ear connived and conspired to shift the status quo in their favor, regardless of its effects. Too soon they found I would not play their fearful game. I would not concede or join in the greedy scramble for wealth or position. Had I allowed myself to put up with the ploys, and fluff the fragile egos of court, I may have lived to tell a different story. But then, would my story be of any interest? I think not. I followed the path of my heart with determination, grit, and integrity. The people know who acts on their behalf and who does not. I leave the ultimate judgment to them and to the King in Heaven.

On May 13, I reached Compiègne, where I was greeted heartily by her townsfolk with a reception. Upon my entrance I caught the disdainful eye of Archbishop Regnault de Chartres, adorned in his fur-trimmed, crimson holy robes. He nodded his mitered head toward me and current hostess, Mary le Boucher, wife of the procurer of the king.

During the reception, I noticed the archbishop across the hall engaged in a heated dialogue with the governor, Guillaume de Flavy. Unfortunately for me, there always existed a certain tension between the archbishop and me. The truth was that he could not comprehend that a woman could claim favor with God, and he was not alone in this viewpoint. He had humored me in the past because the king favored me. Now that my king grew fickle and his interest in me waned, I would need to watch this man and be wary of his actions. He wielded a good deal of power.

Flavy's fiery response to whatever the archbishop had said reddened his already ruddy complexion. Flavy's large belly appeared odd, distended, over legs that were too thin, a typical physique of the wealthy, subsisting on an ample diet of too rich food. At one point they both turned to look at me. I pretended not to notice. I could almost hear the archbishop weaving a web of deception against me. Flavy shook his head several times in an attempt to refuse whatever it was the archbishop proposed. It was then the archbishop produced a folded parchment and handed it to Flavy. With my breath held I watched furtively, moving amidst the guests, my fists clenched at my sides. Flavy crumpled the paper angrily and dropped his arms to his sides, a position of resignation. Perhaps the message listed a series of war crimes and confirmed rumors of his liaison with the mercenary, Franquet d'Arras, whom I had captured in Lagny. I felt for Flavy, understanding the perilous journey from being in favor to the discomforting position of being out of favor.

After the reception, my men and I traveled to Pont-l'Évêque to defend the small city against an attack by the Burgundians. Upon our return to Compiègne several days later, we found that the city had unfortunately come under siege by John the Duke of Luxembourg, the Duke of Burgundy's most capable captain.

"I fear we don't have enough men to lift this siege," Louis, the Count of Vendôme exclaimed, lines wrinkling his fair brow. We reined in our horses and paused in the neighboring village assessing the numbers of our enemy.

"Never fear!" I answered. "We have enough men. I must go and help the good citizens of Compiègne."

The Burgundian soldiers would allow only Louis and me into the city to see what had transpired during the short time we were away. My angels told me this city would be the location of my capture, so I measured each of my movements carefully and decided to stop briefly at the Church of Saint James to pray. I still held out hope that events could unfold favorably, that perhaps the tide could change, and I could once again lift the siege of a town under the strong arm of the Burgundians.

While I stood, leaning against a pillar in the crowded church, I received a clear vision of my capture. In the vision I was roughly pulled from my horse. I asked my angelic guides, Please tell me my fate here in this town.

Dearest daughter, we are with you. As difficult as this is for you to hear, your capture is part of God's plan for you and the path you have now chosen. We will be with you giving you strength and courage.

I gazed around the crowded cathedral and knew I would stop at nothing to help these people even if it meant my capture. Please insure that my time in prison is short without the threat of torture.

We will do all we can for you. Know that this moment is of great consequence for the future. Your love of the people will be returned to you one hundredfold. Trust, dear child. Go forth in faith, with love.

I sighed, resigned to the idea of capture. If it be God's will, I will succumb to my destiny.

Later that day, just beyond the walls of the city, we engaged in the battle I most dreaded, as there was no other choice for me. Twice, we drove the enemy from their positions, but the third time the overwhelming influx of reinforcements dominated our small group made up of the few mercenaries I could afford with the allowance given by Charles meant for the running of my household. Had my other captains and superb commander Jean d'Alençon been with me we may have been victorious.

Sensing defeat, we began to withdraw toward Compiègne, rushing to the makeshift bridge Guillaume de Flavy had made for us across the Oise River, flowing more like a stream that day. I waited for my men to get to safety. Some retreated to the fields toward Picardy. Others fought heatedly at the foot of the bridge leading to the outer gates of the curtain wall. Without warning the heavy gate began to close before we all made it to safety, cutting off our retreat. I cried, "Halt! Halt! Don't close the gate!"

In disbelief, I fought, attempting to hold off the attackers as long as I could so more of my men could make it through to the town. Flavy must have given the orders to close the gate prematurely, leaving me exposed. My chest constricted. This was it. The moment my angels spoke of. I had been betrayed. My capture felt imminent. Cold breath blew at me from behind. The ground shifted and rumbled beneath me, my horse reared.

"Surrender to me and tender faith," an angry English archer aimed his bow at me and yelled up to me from the ground below, his face flushed with battle.

"I have sworn faith to another higher than you and I shall keep my oath!" I yelled back over the din of clashing swords. I attempted to turn my horse and run but could not. Burgundian and English

257

soldiers surrounded me. One English soldier held fast to my horse's bit, preventing me from controlling my mount. All movement slowed down and all sound evaporated: I saw men's mouths open in a battle cry and swords meeting but heard nothing. I looked around and knew. Seeing no way out of the situation, it seemed I watched the events from the side as an observer.

I watched an archer on my left, filled with vengeance, grab hold of my gold doublet and pull me violently from the left side of my horse. I watched my men rush in an attempt to free me. I watched the tide turn, victory now written on the faces of my enemy, and loss on the faces of my men. My horse reared in protest, pawing the air with his hooves, vigorously fighting for me to no avail. The sudden force of the ground hitting my shoulder forced the air out of my lungs and sent a jolt through my entire body. My armor slammed into every body part, rattling my senses and wrenching my neck. Strong hands gripped at my fist, still holding fast to my banner, and began peeling my fingers off the staff. I held on as tightly as I could as unseen hands tore my inspiration from my fist. I watched my banner sail through the air and land in the mud several yards away. Horses and fighting men trampled the white silk cloth and drove it to the bottom of the turbid river.

Sound returned to normal when the archer aggressively flipped me over and shoved my face in the mud. "Surrender!" he bellowed amidst the frantic din. My men fought fiercely for me. However, the reinforcements of the Burgundians proved overpowering. Swords clashed, arrows flew, and men fell all around me, dead in the shallow mired waters. Anguish gripped at me. Black hooves approached at a gallop down the embankment and stopped within inches of my face. Tall boots dismounted and strode toward me spraying mud. "I am Lionel of Wandomme. On the behalf of John, Duke of Luxembourg, I demand you surrender faith!" he bellowed, shouting over the commotion.

Resentment, anger, and fear all began to boil within me. "I will never surrender to any who represent the vile English!" I spat out, tasting blood on my tongue.

"We have no care for your words. You are the Devil's whore!" He shoved the archer hard with his boot. "Roll her over so I can see her face! You can say anything you like; the fact is, we have you," he laughed. "Good citizens of Compiègne and royal soldiers hear this," he barked. Cupping his hand around his mouth he puffed out his chest to take in a large draft of air. "We have your 'maid'! Let's see how victorious you'll be now!" Shouts and grunts intensified all around us. To his archer he ordered, "Tie her good and get her out of here! Quick!"

"Captain, we have her steward, Jean d'Aulon, and her brother," called out another man from the opposite bank. His clothing told me he was a Frenchman turned mercenary for the English.

"Good, take them to our camp at Margny. We'll hold her there until the Duke of Luxembourg arrives. Send for the Good Duke of Burgundy! Tell him of our joyous news—that we captured the Maid herself. Make haste!"

I bristled. It upset me greatly that my brother and dear steward fell to the enemy as well. I voiced a silent prayer as I was manhandled into the field and away from the fray: Please angels watch over any of my men who have been captured and help the dear people of Compiègne to make it through this siege, which I failed to lift.

The tent of the Duke of Luxembourg sat on the far side of the camp under the protection of a small forest of oak and pine trees. The smell of mildew assaulted my nose. Inside sat two thin cots with batting for warmth, a table with maps curled at the edges, and a small wooden stool next to a pair of well-worn leather boots. I waited inside alone and took the opportunity to scan my surroundings for a weapon of some sort. Not so much as a small knife. They thought to remove anything that could be used as a method of self-defense. Two guards stood vigilant at the opening of the tent, and I could see a shadow of a guard on at least one other side. I sat on the cot with my hands bound in front of me, vacillating between fear for myself and concern for my men. My throbbing shoulder reminded me of my failure.

Dearest Jehanne, it is now most important that you become a warrior inside. Watch your speech; harness your tongue. Be ever careful of what you speak. By this we do not mean surrender spirit. On the contrary, we mean for you to be courageous on your inner planes. The battle still rages, but your task has changed. We will fortify you and lift you up. In some ways this portion of your journey is more important. This victory will appear as unseen; unrecognized for the time being. But, the history books will record your inner valor well.

I feel as if I did something wrong. This cannot be my journey. I don't like this—being a prisoner. Tears began to flow. Please! I appealed to my voices for understanding. Why does this hurt so much in my chest? The pain is excruciating!

Child of God, the pain you feel is not just yours. You have always been able to feel the pain and suffering of others. Mankind is ready to make a shift. Humanity needs to shift for the greater good of all. Unfortunately, it takes a big event to get into the hearts of men and to widen limited thinking. Your time as a prisoner is of utmost importance to those of faith. It is this part of your journey that will go down in the history books as extraordinary. You have the opportunity to impact a great number of souls. Have faith. Trust in yourself and your ability to withstand this great challenge.

Warmth spread throughout my body and settled my turbulent mind. The tent became filled with magnificent angels, overflowing with love and brilliant light. They held me, soothed my frayed nerves.

You are an infinite being, Jehanne, there is more to you than your flesh and bones. You are a vast spirit capable of incredible feats. All men have this capacity.

If all men have this ability why do they act so small with violence, resentment, jealousy, and hatred?

It is those negative behaviors, limiting beliefs, and attitudes that block the flow of the infinite. One has to surrender, become humble to the greater self. The greater self is the self of the universe. This can be accessed by all men if they lay down their resentful armor. This is what you must do now. Lay aside your sword, leave your shield behind, and step into the protection of God and the infinite.

Philip, the Duke of Burgundy, swaggered into the tent with two of his men, his vassals John, the Duke of Luxembourg, and Lionel de Wandomme, my capturer. I recognized Lionel by his boots. His clothing, dirty and disheveled from battle, made an interesting contrast to the clean opulence of the other two. Philip, also called Philip the Good, held his narrow chin aloft, the mark of extreme confidence. His pasty skin accentuated dark piercing eyes. Though he smiled, his eyes told me a different story. He had the eyes of a man who continuously plotted, connived, and always got his way. His shoulders sat upon his chest in such a manner as to say "you'll not challenge me."

Where Philip the Good appeared cultured and educated, John, the Duke of Luxembourg resembled a burly field-worker up on his luck. Philip dressed himself in darker, austere fabrics, which offered an interesting contrast to the deep purple velvet doublet of John. Even their builds gave contrast to one another. Philip stood almost a head taller than his stocky, more muscular, vassal. Their celebratory manner disturbed me, as it was at my expense.

"Bonjour, mademoiselle, Jehanne the Maid, I am Philip, Duke of Burgundy." He bowed slightly. "You are smaller than I thought."

"Sire." I lowered my head slightly. "What do you intend to do with me now that you have me captive?"

"I heard you were direct." Taking two steps closer he reached out and grabbed the hair on the top of my head and forced it back so he could scrutinize my face. "I never saw a witch before. You don't look like a witch to me, just a scrawny girl in men's armor." He thrust my head back a second time and let go. "What happened? Did you lose your powers?" His hand came out of nowhere and cuffed me hard on my left ear. "Answer me, girl!"

"There is no equal to the power of God. You insult me? You, who have betrayed your own country for money and power!" I cried out with such force, the smug smiles on the faces of his men were replaced by looks of surprise. I disliked him instantly. His face, maybe once considered attractive, wore the ugliness of one who rarely consults his heart. "Your English allies, sire, will lose power within seven years!" I exclaimed fiercely. "France will rise again and be united!"

"Is that a curse?"

"No, an accurate statement of what is to come at the hand of God in Heaven." I slammed my hand on the armor plate covering my leg to make the point. "God's favor is with the loyal French."

A few moments passed in silence. He stood firm with the strength of character befitting a king. I thought briefly of my own weak-willed Charles, bendable by threats and manipulated by fears. I understood then how men of weak convictions could be swayed to the side of this confident leader.

"Jehanne, I have only allied with the English to further the cause of France."

"Pardonne moi, sire. You allied with the English to further your own cause and your own purse."

Ignoring my comment, he touched his thick golden necklace from which hung a pendant of, what looked like, a droopy sheep. I noticed John wore a similar necklace. Philip then lowered his voice and said, "Your king, the king you have been pledging your loyalty to, does not regard you with the respect you deserve. He doesn't see what an asset you are. The people love you, respond to you, are inspired by you, and your men-at-arms will follow you anywhere."

I hardly knew what to say. He spoke the truth. My own king no longer welcomed my ideas and showed his support through minimal troops and provisions.

"I have a proposal for you. Hear me out before you respond. I would like to offer you a very esteemed position as a knight in my Order of the Golden Fleece. Back in January, on the occasion of my new wife, I formed this order for the purposes of honoring the Holy Mother, the Church, and preserving the chivalric code." His fearlessness and obvious ease with power felt refreshing and caught me off guard. "Become one of my captains. I will give you whatever funds and men you need. Jehanne, together we could unite France, and you will be given one of these." He lifted the golden sheep off his chest and gestured to John's matching necklace. "What say you?"

"Sire, what you don't understand is that my loyalty lies only with God in Heaven," I replied calmly. I did not expect this.

"S'il vous plait, by all means take counsel with your God in regard to this matter. You have some time to think about my proposal. Until then you will be sequestered by John of Luxembourg here." He clapped John on the shoulder and said, "Keep a close eye on her—two guards at all times—do you hear?"

"While I appreciate your—" I attempted to refuse his offer.

"No need to rush into anything! Take your time." He bowed slightly. "Au revoir, mademoiselle," he said and swept out of the tent with his men at his side. Outside I overheard him say, "John, if she does not consent to join us we will exact a hefty ransom from King Charles. I do believe God is on our side now!" Their shadows faded on the tent wall.

I shivered. The shrewd duke left me contemplating my options. Perhaps there could be a way I could save France and myself at the same time.

The next day, we were taken northeast to the fortress at Clairoix. Four of us—Pierre, Jean D'Aulon, Jean's brother, and I—traveled with our horses tethered to four other guards, our hands tied behind our backs.

As we passed under the angry teeth of the portcullis gate to the fortress of Clairoix, the Burgundian crowd cheered upon seeing me captive by the English. I wanted to slump forward and sleep off this nightmare, but my armor kept me from tumbling, holding me up straight. I looked braver than I felt. My stomach growled, but I did not want to eat.

From Clairoix, we traveled to the castle of Beaulieu, one of Luxembourg's holdings. Inside we walked through the stone halls and down a wide sweeping stone staircase into a gathering room with a fireplace on one end, boasting a large ivory and limestone mantle. Roughly, I was shoved onto a wooden bench in the hall lined with tapestries and gossiping courtiers. In their rich clothing, silk brocades and velvets, they assessed me ruthlessly. I wanted to yell, "Judge ye not, lest ye be judged." But did not. They stared and whispered to one another and laughed at my expense.

Sitting in a large mahogany chair, the back piece shaped as an upright triangle, sat John, the Duke of Luxembourg, richly dressed in a red damask jacket tied tightly at the waist, puffing out at the arms. He wore matching stockings over sturdy muscular legs and sat leaning on one elbow nonchalantly. He stiffened when he saw me enter the room, and a smirk spread across his ruddy face.

Thankfully my anger came up. My energy returned as I stood in front of this egotistical lord. My spine straightened, my shoulders squared. "Let me look at the woman who wants to be a man and claims she talks to God and God talks to her. Jehanne, you don't fool me, but you've managed to fool all your French friends. In some ways this ruse worked for you . . . up until now, that is. We will see what happens to your king and your country, your comrades, and your loyal soldiers now. They will crumble like babies and cower back home to their fields now that they don't have your witch's tricks to lead them," he spat out. Standing, he sauntered over to me and leered in my face. His breath smelled of wine.

"Oh what folly. Let's just see how you feel in a few weeks' time. Let's see how much your precious king will pay for you. Archbishop de Chartres is proclaiming to everyone that your capture is your own fault, that you ignored Charles's orders, and that your angels in Heaven have abandoned you."

I seethed, stung by the archbishop's betrayal. I wanted to leap up from my seat and declare my truth. Instead I bit my lip.

"Take her away. Put her in the room in the tower and put her in women's clothing. I will have none of this men's clothing. She is to wear women's clothing in my castle."

I opened my mouth, itching to share my own opinions but my angels stopped me. *Jehanne, say nothing in response. Trust us, your guides in Heaven, and say nothing. Do not anger this man. Nor do you want to feed his righteous fire.*

I closed my mouth, turned, and proudly walked out of the pompous man's presence.

Two male guards led me gruffly to the back of the castle and up the narrow stone stairs to the tower room. Shaped like a half moon, the chamber held a small, graying wood table, a decrepit wooden chair, and a pine plank bed with a thin mattress. Wide plank floorboards creaked and groaned with our weight.

"We'll be back," the bearded guard barked, "with clothing." They closed the bulky timber door behind me, the wrought-iron hinges squeaking noisily. When I heard the click of the latch settling the door in place, I walked over to the small window set in the rough stone wall and took in the limited view of the land and earth beyond. Dense foliage rippled with a stiff wind. Sounds of hooves and wheels crunching on the gravel drive alerted me to the comings and goings of Luxembourg's small court. This tower must be located nearest the gate, I mused, wondering if there would be any opportunity for my escape or a rescue.

The click of the door's latch alerted me to the return of my guards. The bearded one brought in a board of food—broth, bread, and white cheese—and dropped it with a thud onto the old table. The thin one tossed a bundle of clothing onto the bed, turned abruptly, and they both departed without a word. I pulled a chair to the table, held my hand over the small bowl of broth and felt the moist steam seep into my palms and fingers. Cupping the bowl in my shaking hands, I brought the liquid to my lips and drank. It helped to settle me a little. I did not realize how hungry I was. As I nibbled on the little chunks of cheese I felt an odd sense of safety. My fear of capture seemed worse than the reality.

After eating my fill, I leaned my elbows on the cracked table and rested my chin in my hands. The table rocked on the uneven stone floor. Calling upon my angelic helpers, I closed my eyes. The air smelled dusty and stale. Soon, the familiar, soothing feelings washed over me. My breath deepened and my belly relaxed. I felt lit from within.

My beloved angelic friends, I'm grateful you have followed me into this prison.

We are with you everywhere. See if you can remain positive while you are captive, answer their questions as straightforwardly as you can without divulging too much. Be simple, humble, quiet. Have faith, and we will see you through and bring you freedom.

The wind whistled through the irregular panes of glass.

We are proud of all you have done. For now, we urge you to listen to your own positive thoughts, heed our guidance, and allow yourself time to heal and be quiet. We are with you always.

A rap at the door startled me out of my reverie.

"Jehanne?" The sound of my brother Pierre's voice startled me. He pushed open the door and stepped through accompanied by d'Aulon.

"Ah, bon!" I jumped out of my chair, sending it tumbling to the ground. "How happy I am to see you . . . and without chains." I kissed them both and offered them the only remaining seats in the room.

They sat at right angles to me and rested their forearms on the rickety table. Both wore concerned looks on their unshaven faces. Their presence here and unshakable loyalty gave me courage.

"How are they treating you?" I questioned, hugging and kissing both men. Their capture, as well as my own, weighed on my shoulders.

"Fine. Our lodgings are sparse, but clean. We ate already. The guards said we are allowed thirty minutes each day to meet and visit with you," Pierre offered. "Dear sister, we are concerned for you."

"You see how I am kept here, away from everyone. What do you think they will do with me?"

D'Aulon spoke first. "Usually with prisoners of war, they request a ransom from the family or royal crown. In your case, a large sum was requested from King Charles. He has not sent word yet as to his intentions." Noting the troubled look on my face he continued, "I'm sure he will pay it as long as he can pry La Trémoille's fingers off the purse strings of the royal treasury."

Pierre huffed, "Well, it doesn't look good then, if the whole business is left to La Trémoille." His brown eyes narrowed. "That man has done nothing but try to sabotage you since the beginning."

"I agree." I was not as hopeful as d'Aulon. My brother's observations seemed more accurate.

"You have a point," d'Aulon interjected, always the diplomat.

I lowered my voice and leaned into the center of the table. "What of a rescue? Surely our captains are more than capable of breaking me out of this short tower."

"The king forbade anyone from gathering men together. He doesn't want to compromise the peace treaty he's negotiating with Burgundy. I know . . . before you say anything—"

Angrily I interrupted, "Burgundy holds me captive and fears not the repercussions from our king. If only our king were stronger . . ."

Pierre slapped his hand on the table. "Sister, the archbishop of Reims is muddling your chances of rescue as well, sending letters all over France telling the people and the other high-ranking bishops of the University of Paris that you have been forsaken by your divine counsel, and that you acted for your own benefit in all your deeds."

D'Aulon gave Pierre a look, entreating him to keep quiet, then spoke to me in a conciliatory manner. "Charles is like a man on the torturous stretching machine. La Trémoille and Burgundy each hold one of his legs while the archbishop holds his arm. You, Jehanne, must know, you hold his heart." D'Aulon tilted his wavy blond head in my direction. "But, without arms or legs, a king has nothing."

"That's all very poetic, d'Aulon. What then, are we to do?" I leaned back in my chair. "My angels tell me to wait patiently. . . . This, I have a hard time doing."

"I agree with your angels," d'Aulon said plainly. "Wait. Simply wait. It's out of our hands. Meanwhile, try not to inflame Luxembourg or his men. Unlike Burgundy, with his steely self-control, Luxembourg is more volatile and inconsistent."

A fortnight passed and we heard no word from our king. Saddened that he sent no ransom or troops to rescue me, and because there existed little for me to do, I allowed myself to be consumed with worry. My angels told me to be steady and wait. Waiting is the one thing that makes me pace the floor and pull at my hair. Anger and resentment against my king mounted with each passing day, as boredom ate away at me. My complaining and worrying mind grew strong in this confined cell, though I lived with a strange sense of safety, plenty to eat, a roof over my head, and a bed to sleep in. From my earliest days, I always occupied myself with physical tasks, countless menial chores, which needed to be done for the well-being of my family. As a result of this unaccustomed idleness, I began to experience bad thoughts. I harbored thoughts of resentment, despair, and even hatred for the English and my king, who appeared to have forgotten me. I reviewed every movement of my life, every decision, wondering where I went wrong. I berated myself for not accepting my beloved d'Alençon's offer of marriage last year. Every word I ever spoke to my king was replayed in my mind. If only . . .

"D'Aulon, I am forsaken by my king and my God," I said during one of our thirty-minute visits.

"I can't speak for God, but I can tell you our king is weak politically and chooses not to exert himself." D'Aulon's vehemence surprised me. He too, must have been falling prey to the insidious boredom of waiting. "You gave him his crown! He regained status and stature thanks to you and his army, but it appears he feels no loyalty to you, or to God, for that matter."

I stomped my boot hard on the wood floor. "If the king does not pay the ransom soon, I will be sold to the English, who are very superstitious. They will try me as a witch and heretic, or worse, stuff me in a bag and throw me in a river." How could the king sit by in his royal bath, eating richly, while I'm imprisoned? "It's an outrage, I tell you. How can he . . . be so selfish? What shall I do?"

Seeing he had roused my ire, d'Aulon settled himself down by heaving a great breath. "Do nothing, my friend. Keep yourself safe." He crossed his arms in front of his chest. "We have no choice." He paused and looked at me with sad brown eyes. "I have other news for you . . . d'Alençon's wife miscarried her baby." He watched me for my reaction, knowing of some relationship between d'Alençon and me.

My heart skipped a beat at the awful news. Several thoughts at once passed through my mind. Was d'Alençon sad at the loss of his unborn child? Poor Jeanne. She seemed fragile. Would she be all right? And a more selfish thought—we could have been together after all. I blushed at my own feelings and turned away from d'Aulon so as not to give my thoughts away. I decided not to say anything in regard to the baby and changed the subject.

"My voices tell me to stay put; that we will be free soon. I trust them, but I feel a compulsion to be out of this prison now!" Suddenly, I wanted to leap onto a horse and ride until I found my beloved. I paced back and forth in the small room causing the floor to creak with my agitated steps, racking my brain for a solution, a way out.

"Jehanne, I think you should heed your voices."

I stopped pacing and bounced up and down on the noisiest board. Kneeling on the floor, I tried to pry up the loose plank. It shifted and moved with applied pressure. "D'Aulon, this timber is rotted and loose. If I lift it, I may be able to slip through down to the room below and escape."

"Jehanne, if you do escape where will you go?"

"I will steal a horse and ride back into our territory." Excitement lifted my mood as the idea of freedom pulsed through my body. "When my guard sleeps tonight I will pull up these planks and slip through."

"Pierre and I are not well guarded so we can slip out and meet you near the gate." He looked as hopeful as I felt. "Here, let me help you to loosen the boards now. Quietly . . ."

I woke, my head throbbing and my ears ringing. Blinking in the darkened room, I tried to see. The smell of mildew and dirt assailed my nostrils and my shoulder ached. Then I remembered my failed attempt to escape. The porter caught me just as I slipped into the corridor off the tower and hit me on the head with the hilt of his short sword. He tied my arms tightly behind my back and half dragged me to this underground room. It felt suffocating down here. Little air traveled down this far. I tried not to panic.

Angels, what have I done now?

Jehanne, you believed your own fearful thoughts and acted out of fear instead of calm knowing. Are you beginning to understand what happens when you do this?

Oui, but I can't seem to get the bad thoughts to go away. I shifted my position from lying on the dirt floor to sitting. The simple movement proved challenging with my hands bound behind my back.

You don't need them to go away. You only need to replace them with positive thoughts.

With all due respect, my dearest angels, you can't possibly understand the challenges we have in our bodies and minds. There are so many things of which to be afraid.

Dearest daughter . . . all the more reason to get control of your mind.

I fell asleep with their voices sweetly floating around me, comforting me. When I woke in the abysmal darkness, I had no idea the time or day.

After what seemed like hours, the door finally opened. The hulking shape of a guard filled the dim light of the opening behind him, and I gasped with relief as fresh air rushed into the hovel.

"We are bringing you to see Philip of Burgundy." He reached down and lifted me up off the floor roughly. My legs tingled from lying in one position for too long and threatened to give out on me as the guard half dragged me up the uneven wooden stairs into the sunlight. "I'm sure he has plans for the likes of you. First, you must change back into the clothing you came in."

They took me in a heavily guarded carriage to the palace in Noyon. Philip of Burgundy's strategy—allowing me to experience some of prison life—almost worked. I considered accepting his offer of becoming one of his decorated knights in the Order of the Golden Fleece. While sitting in the carriage, riding through the fragrant countryside, with the sounds of summer humming from all over, I decided to get control of my mind. I settled my breathing down, calmed my racing mind, and tried to think of positive thoughts. God loves me. My freedom will be soon. I always do the right thing. By the time we arrived at the gothic palace in Noyon, I felt deep satisfaction and some relief from no longer feeling afraid. I knew the correct course of action.

Escorted by two stern-faced guards dressed in the duke's livery—the blazoned argent, two crimson jagged staffs in the shape of an X—upon their surcoats, we stepped ceremoniously into the large hall.

"Bonjour, Jehanne la Pucelle," the duke's voice rang out and echoed in the cavernous space. Tapestries of brilliantly dyed yarns hung off the lofty walls. "Come closer and meet my wife, Isabelle."

"Sire . . . Duchess." I bowed and waited for him to continue. I had little to say to the man who held me, and most of France, captive.

"You look pale. Prison life doesn't suit you, mon chérie." The duke smiled and looked at his wife. "Well, here she is in the flesh." To me he said, "My wife has been wanting to meet you. It seems you are well loved by the women of both countries." He laughed, thinking that the fact women loved me was because they did not possess the intellect to deduce truth from fiction.

I burned inside knowing what his laugh meant, and I was not alone in this sentiment as his wife scowled at him as well.

Ignoring us both he began to speak with a sweeping gesture of his dark-robed arm. The golden-fleece pendant, hanging around his sinewy neck, glittered in the afternoon sunlight streaming through the tall windows. "Jehanne, my offer of making you a knight in the Order of the Golden Fleece still stands. You've had plenty of time to think about this outstanding opportunity before you. I needn't remind you that your king has sent neither ransom nor letter on your behalf, and has left you to our devices. You have two choices: Join me and become more of a legend. You will receive money, clothing, and a small castle somewhere. Or, do not join me and be sold to the English."

"I heartily decline your offer," I said with conviction, standing straighter than I had in weeks. A part of me hoped I would not regret this decision.

He frowned. "I will give you one more chance. You will be moved to Beaurevoir Castle, the home of John of Luxembourg. We will hold you there until such time as I decide what else to do with you, or, you change your mind."

"Sire, I can assure you I will not change my mind," I replied sternly.

"You must know that the English would like nothing more than to see you tried under the provisions of the Inquisition as a heretic, and they will cheer when you burn at the stake." His narrow face darkened as he attempted to control his raised voice.

Our eyes locked, his milky brown ones smoldered. I held my ground and said nothing in reply. He fully expected me to join forces with him, and when I did not, he appeared shaken, angry, and bewildered. "Take her away. Have her moved to Beaurevoir within the week." His eyes settled on me once again. "You will change your mind. Until later, au revoir."

Philip of Burgundy kept his word and had me transported immediately to Beaurevoir Castle to the north.

Mercilessly, two guards held a firm grip on each of my arms, nearly dragged me up a sweeping marble staircase, and shoved me into an ornately adorned bedroom in my new prison, the castle at Beaurevoir. My brother and d'Aulon were not allowed to accompany me to this castle prison. I felt utterly alone and forgotten. My belly tightened then relaxed when I realized I was brought to the quarters of Dame Luxembourg, the well-known powerful aunt of John of Luxembourg. Two women, one older and one younger, greeted me dressed head to toe in courtly finery, from their uncomfortable-looking shoes to their powdered faces. It seemed ghastly to paint one's face in that manner. It made them look surreal, cold, and inhuman. Though when I looked into their eyes, they appeared kind.

"As you bid, madame . . . the prisoner. John says to tell you, be sure she does not escape or it will be on your head," the taller guard barked.

"I know my responsibilities perfectly well. You are dismissed," she ordered coldly and turned to me.

"Ah, finalement, Jehanne la Pucelle. Let me look at you," she said and walked around me in a circle, with a flourish born from many years in court. "I heard much about you. Is it all true?"

"Madame, I know not what you have heard," I offered tentatively, unsure of her personal agenda. After much time at court, I finally realized that my answer to any number of questions should depend upon the questioner's position and state of mind. Too many times, I spoke candidly before ascertaining what was at stake. I decided to play it safe and not divulge too much.

"You are cautious. All the better." She led me to an upholstered couch. "Please sit. While you are under my supervision you will live like a civilized lady. Despite the fact that you will be quartered in the tower, I have seen to it that your accommodations will be comfortable. I intend to hear all about every one of your adventures." She brushed a wayward gray ringlet around her ear. The white powder caked in the wrinkles on her forehead and around her mouth, making the tiny lines appear deeper. "Oh, my manners. This is Lady Jeanne of

273

Bethune, John's wife, and I am Madame Jeanne of Luxembourg, John's aunt. He has all of this because of me." She swept her arms around her and a proud smile parted her dry lips.

"Would you like to bathe?" Lady Jeanne of Bethune asked haltingly. She also had powder covering what would be considered a pretty face. She looked at me with welcoming hazel eyes.

"Oui, merci," I answered, beginning to realize that I was in the presence of two kind admirers. They were curious about me and wanted to ask more but hesitated. The younger Jeanne bit her lip and looked to the older for direction.

They lead me to a bath, a smaller room off the larger chamber. A large wooden tub sat beneath a bank of leaded-glass windows. The younger handed me soap and linen, curtsied, and left the room. I peeled off my clothing and climbed into the luxurious bath. Letting the lukewarm water sink into my skin, I attempted to wash away the humiliation and the sadness I felt from being imprisoned without benefit of my brother and dear friend. Life here, I mused, would not be too different from life at La Trémoille's castle. Thoughts of my brother Pierre and d'Aulon pulled at my heart. Their daily visits at Beaulieu and their support over the last year gave me courage. I hoped they were allowed to ride safely home. God, please protect them for me.

I wondered how long it would be before I would see them again. I missed all my men, especially d'Alençon. God, why have you pulled those I love away from me? Taking a breath, I sunk beneath the water. I liked the quiet. When my lungs protested, I surfaced with a gasp and let the warm liquid trickle down off of my forehead into my eyes. Tears slipped out from underneath my lashes and dripped silently into the water.

The door opened, startling me, and the two Jeannes entered with sheepish expressions on their faces. "Jehanne, we are sorry to bother you," Lady Jeanne offered. "John wanted us to see you naked and check your body. . . . You see, he thinks you may be a relative of Melusine." She wrung her hands. "I told him he was crazy, that

Melusine was a character in a fairy tale, but he has a superstitious side and thinks you may be half serpent. Since it is Saturday and Melusine's tail becomes visible on Saturdays, he bid us to check you for a serpent's tail."

"Ha, Ha!" I laughed and silently thanked my angels for providing me such entertainment. "This is the best and most humorous rumor about me I have heard yet." With an arm across my breasts and the other hand covering my pubic area, I stood in the tub and turned around so the ladies could see my thin, but nevertheless, human legs. "What do you think? Feel free to touch me to see if I have any scales."

"We are so sorry to insult you." Dame Jeanne looked taken aback over my reaction.

"Non, madame, I am not upset at you. Smile. I am grateful you came to me with such a story. I was feeling sorry for myself, and you lifted my spirits." I sat back down in the tub, sloshing water over onto the floor. "It is a shame that when women show any strength of character men feel they need to label us as witches or in league with the Devil. What they don't know . . ."

"You speak the truth," the older Jeanne said lowering her voice and taking two steps closer. "For years, I felt the need to hide my intelligence from my husband and sons. Now that I am older, I don't care what they think. I speak my mind, and it feels good. The lords of Luxembourg have always been paranoid about strong women who seem to have too much 'good luck.' It's that folk tale about Melusine."

"As women, I feel we have to trade our true words, thoughts, and feelings for security," Lady Jeanne whispered, gesturing to the closed door, indicating the presence of a male guard just outside.

"Sadly, it is true for many women at court and in the countryside as well. Though my father did welcome the ideas and insights of my mother. In addition, I found that when I put on men's clothing, my words held more meaning in the world of men, and I felt the security of which you speak," I whispered back.

"We should leave now. John is waiting for a report as to your condition." The younger of the two women bowed her head respectfully. "Merci," she whispered and departed, following the older woman.

After bathing, I dressed in clean women's clothing. I decided to wear it for only as long as it took to launder my men's clothing. Tall, taciturn guards escorted me to my room several stories up in the tower of the castle keep.

The two ladies followed behind and entered the room with armloads of women's clothing and linens. "Merci, mesdames." I allowed their kindness, their tenderness, and answered their noninvasive questions as plainly as I could.

After the door closed with a click, I took the time to survey my new surroundings. A mahogany bed larger and more ornately carved than the one I used at La Trémoille's castle, and covered in a royal blue damask, down-filled quilt, took up most of the space. The room also housed a carved wardrobe and a small writing desk with a comfortable chair.

A moat beneath the castle sparkled in the morning sunlight. In the distance, the trees cast dark shadows on the rolling green hillside. I had to admit this part of the country was beautiful. There was an easiness to the land, a little more green than the Lorraine or Loire River valleys, more shade, more trees, steeper hills, deeper shadows, and strange scents. It felt cooler, for a summer day. I thought of my family in Domrémy and I longed for home. I imagined standing in my papa's garden or looking into the eyes of my family's sheep.

After only a few days, I became friends with the two Jeannes as well as Lady Jeanne's daughter from a prior marriage, Jeanne de Bar. The youngest Jeanne was a cute girl, with auburn curls and a fair face, only a few years younger than I. Each day, my guard, Haimond de Macy, a tall, burly knight of John's, would escort me to Dame Luxembourg's quarters. There, we would talk and exchange stories for hours, breaking only for tea and meals. I related the tales of battle and scant information about my divine counsel, preferring to keep those experiences sacred. She saw fit to share her vast knowledge of courtly ways, laws, and regulations. When I was not with either of the Jeannes, my guard, Haimond, would frequently visit and talk with me. Some days, like most guards he questioned and bated me, and frequently tried to touch my breasts. On such occasions, I would slap his hand away and discontinue conversation with him.

When the summer nights turned cool in late August, Dame Jeanne's conversations took on a more urgent tone. She felt ill a good deal of the time but continued her tutelage. "Jehanne, I want to share with you my knowledge of ecclesiastical court proceedings," she said from the numerous pillows on her massive bed.

"Madame, surely this can wait until you are feeling better." I sat on the bed next to her reclining figure and clasped her bony, cold hands in mine. "This can't be that important."

"Mon chérie, this can not wait. I'm not sure how much time I have left. I'm old, in my sixties. I would like to be of service to you in some way. Fate has a strange sense of humor, bringing me a saintly friend such as you, at the end of my life. I could have used your camaraderie and bold strength years ago." She coughed into an embroidered handkerchief.

I rubbed her hands between mine to comfort her when she settled back into the pillows.

"First, my dear, neither Philip of Burgundy nor my nephew John has received any ransom from Charles. By the way, did you know I was Charles's godmother in 1403? Anyway, that man is making a huge mistake in not remaining loyal to you. The men closest to him have regained his ear now that you are here." She paused and looked at me with the love of a grandmother. "I believe when I pass on, you will be sold to the English. I have threatened to pull all of my money away from John if he does anything harmful to you while I am still alive."

Feeling appreciation for her patronage and respect for her courage and wisdom, I kissed her hand. "Merci, I know you have gone to great lengths on my behalf. The King in Heaven is most grateful to you. But, hush, you have much time left here." I hoped she would live longer than she thought, for my sake and for hers.

"It is of increasing importance that I remain in the good graces of the Almighty as my days draw to a close. I wish to share with you what the questioners in the University of Paris may ask you, if you should be sold. You will be tried under the Inquisition system.

The inquisitorial trial generally favors itself. They will get you to perjure and incriminate yourself. In addition you will not have the right to ask questions of the court."

"Dame, I have been questioned before by bishops and other high-ranking politicians." I attempted to end the discussion due to my own increased feelings of discomfort.

Jehanne, listen to her wise advice. She shares information of vital importance to you.

"This will be different. You, most likely, may be tried by the English. They are out to discredit you and their superstitious nature will have them on the defensive against a woman as influential as you. Do you realize, you have the entire world wondering about your powers?" She spoke intensely, screwing up her face to get her point across. "You must understand that to accept you as a powerful, but normal woman, would challenge their very existence and every belief they hold about the order of the world we live in. They will fight to undermine you and your claims as vehemently and vigorously as possible. Oh, my dear . . ."

"Dame, I understand your concerns and agree with you. However, you must remember that I rode on horseback into battle as a captain at arms. I've been wounded and lived. God will surely protect me in court against a bunch of pompous, overeducated men." I patted her leg and smoothed the bedcovers around her. "You should not worry about me, but I will listen. Go ahead and teach me what you know."

For the next couple of weeks we met daily, going over piles of transcripts she secretly obtained from other trials. I never asked how she obtained them, and she never divulged her informant. My angels gave me advice and taught me more techniques on how to remain calm and confident. I prayed for the life and soul of Dame Jeanne every spare moment. Not only did she prove to be one of my most loyal friends, she mentored me in the most astonishing ways. She seemed to be an angel on earth, keeping me safe and intervening on my behalf whenever and wherever she was able. Her love inspired me to stay focused and restored my resolve to hold to my truths.

On the morning of September 18, I woke with a start. I threw on clothing and ran with Haimond to Dame Jeanne's room. Her physician was at her side. Her chest heaved up and down as she fought for breath. Her dull eyes grew bright when she saw me, and she reached out a shaking hand.

"Shh, do not speak. Save your strength," I urged, clasping her hand. She looked ashen, and I could feel and see the presence of angels all around her. Beautiful diaphanous wings billowed around her, coaxing her spirit to release from her body. Feelings of love rippled the air as time seemed to separate and dissolve. I knew. This was her time. I tried to hold back the flow of tears but could not. They spilled onto the lace coverlet near our hands.

"Be strong for France," she urged, barely a whisper, and closed her eyes for the last time. I felt the gentlest of breezes brush against my face as her glorious spirit slipped from her body and drifted upward.

"Haimond, get her out of here," John demanded from his vantage point nearest the window where he stood waiting for his aunt's death. To me he hissed, "I have no idea what she saw in you."

Through my tears I glared at him, and replied curtly, "Non, sire, you wouldn't." As I was led out, I made brief eye contact with Lady Jeanne, who dabbed at her own red and swollen eyes. She, too, knew it was the end of our friendship as well as the death of her beloved aunt-in-law.

The next day rumors came to me that one of the heads of the University of Paris, a bishop, Pierre Cauchon of Rouen, negotiated a deal with John of Luxembourg. Dame Luxembourg had not even been entombed yet. After only one day, word of my sale to the English spread quickly. Apparently John and Philip exacted a great sum, 10,000 crowns, for me.

Haimond, acting against John's orders, brought me news daily. "Jehanne, many of your soldiers and townsfolk all over France are protesting the way your king has treated you. They march, barefooted, yelling and cursing the king. Masses are being said on your behalf. Your captains are rumored to be plotting for a rescue."

"Haimond, that is good news." I sat looking out over the valley far below. "What other news have you?"

"Compiègne is under siege again. This is Philip's attempt to squelch any thoughts any Burgundians have of turning loyal to France. He's threatening to massacre any who have sided with France in the past."

"Non, surely Charles is raising an army to retaliate?"

"My sources say he is not and will not try to lift the siege," he said and walked toward the door. "I should get back outside, in case John comes to check on you."

He left me pacing. Between my grief at the loss of yet another dear friend and my concern for my friends in Compiègne, my mind plunged headlong into worrying. My emotions flowed in and around me like a tremendous storm. The pain in my heart became unbearable. Action and movement seemed my only way through the burning angst. I must do something. Dear angels in Heaven there must be a way for me to get out of this prison and help my friends.

Dearest one, please do nothing. The siege will lift and the people will be spared. All will be well. They tried to console me, but I felt not a bit relieved. My thoughts left me panicked and shaken. I could not bear the pain in my heart or the anxiety in my mind. I thrashed about searching for a course of action, obsessing about escaping.

As I knotted end upon end of the linens in my room together to form a rope my angels pleaded. *Don't do it, Jehanne. All will be well.*

I didn't listen. Something snapped in my mind. I felt consumed with anguish for Compiègne, and thought, irrationally, if I climbed out the window and down the makeshift rope, I could get in touch with my captains, maybe find d'Alençon. They would free Compiègne, and I would avoid the trial for heresy.

Dressed in the outfit I was captured in, I climbed out the window. The seventy-foot drop made my head spin momentarily. Slowly, I let myself down, hand over hand, until the whole business came loose, and I fell to the ground below.

Rough hands pulled at me as I woke. My entire body felt crushed, and I screamed with excruciating pain as I was carried over the strong shoulders of a guard back up to my room and tossed onto my bed. Upon John's orders a physician looked me over. "Nothing broken. She is lucky. She'll be sore for weeks, though, by the looks of her."

"Good. I want no harm to come to her. She is too valuable. I'm tripling the guards. Board that window." John's grating voice jarred my bruised body.

While I lay recuperating, I overheard the guards speak of my friend the Count of Vendôme and how he raised an army to help the people of Compiègne. The siege lifted shortly thereafter, around the same day I was moved to the town of Arras, further north, one of many stops on my way to Rouen for trial.

My stay in Arras dragged on longer than we anticipated due to an early snowstorm. Snow did not typically fall this early in the season—mid-November. My captors acted bothered and frustrated at having to delay our departure. I believe my presence, and the hearty reception by the people of Arras on my behalf, made them uneasy. They assumed I possessed powers to harm them as a witch would and attributed the storm to my fictitious powers. Did they think I held power over nature herself?

On our way out of the busy town we passed by a small lake. I gazed out the carriage window, where I sat chained by my hands and feet, in awe. During the tempest, snow fell on trees whose leaves had not yet fallen, I believe them to be beech and a few pines, outlining the small lake. All around the lake, the snow-laden trees bowed into the water and became frozen there. The now slick surface of the water held fast to the branches of the younger trees. The spectacular scene on this bright sunny morning gave a lift to my senses. The caravan stopped to marvel at this wonder. I gasped. Mother Nature knew exactly how I felt.

By the time we entered Rouen, snow fell gently but thickly from a silver sky. My tattered gold silk cape, an extravagant gift from my king at a time when I held his favor, offered little protection against the biting cold. Tiny snowflakes swirled on the wind, seeming like they would never land, cloaking the town in a white shroud, and blew into the carriage in drifts. I noticed nature often delivered the biggest snowstorms with the tiniest flakes. Each lacy flake, fragile, yet when massed with others of its kind could halt armies and kill without reservation.

When we rumbled across the drawbridge and pulled into the inner courtyard of Bouvreuil, the Earl of Warwick's castle, in Rouen, a thick layer of fresh snow covered the roads, roofs, and the tops of every exposed surface, including the heads and shoulders of the men who rode as guards beside my carriage. My blood chilled. For some reason, this snowfall reminded me of the ash-covered ground in my hometown of Domrémy, after the Burgundians had burned our church.

My biggest battle lay ahead. This time, I was at the mercy of an enemy more powerful and frightening than snow or armies—human fear.

565 YEARS LATER

NOVEMBER 28, 1996, KINGSTON, RI

Jane Archer slept deeper than she had in months. A familiar blue haze filled her bedroom in Rhode Island. Upon waking she smiled and snuggled deeper into her soft bed. It was eight thirty a.m. Anytime she slept past six, she experienced mixed feelings of guilt and pleasure. The stimulating aroma of turkey roasting reminded her it was Thanksgiving Day.

Home.

Her mother put the huge bird in the oven at the crack of dawn so they could gather around the dining table by two o'clock. She had done the same thing every year since Jane could remember. The continuity of her mother's traditions gave Jane a sense of firm ground, sturdy roots.

A feeling of security lay in the softness of the furnishings, and all the love that was put into her parents' home and her bedroom over the years. She marveled at the irony of feeling greater safety here than in the angles, the stone, and the guns of the fortress that was West Point and giggled out loud. She spread her arms and legs wide on her queen-size bed, relishing the space, like da Vinci's Vitruvian Man. I am Vitruvian Woman, she thought.

She soaked it all in. In great gulps, she let her body take in the unseen nourishment. A ray of sunlight streamed into the room through a crystal her mother had hung in the window years ago and cast rainbows onto the overstuffed chair in the corner.

On the chair sat the laundry bag. Her smile turned into a thoughtful line. She planned on opening it with her father later that day after the turkey dinner. The thought of opening the bag sent Jane's pulse racing. She wanted to be wrong about Ash.

Jane touched the stitches on her cheek. The skin felt swollen and still hurt. She wondered how Ash was and if she really had broken his nose. Tuesday night, after they had retrieved the bag, Jack took her to get stitches at Keller Army Community Hospital on post. The doctor made twelve tiny stitches for the one-inch gash on her face in order to reduce the scarring.

"Scar tissue is stronger than skin," the doctor said in an Indian accent in an effort to boost her mood.

At the time Jane wondered how that statement applied to her situation. To her, it seemed more metaphorically true. When shit happens we get stronger.

Jehanne had warned her. In the future, she would heed her messages. She would always have the scar on her cheek to remind her to trust her inner voice.

The rumble of low timbered voices through her bedroom floor reminded her that Jack had come home with her and had slept in her father's home office, the room directly below hers. This was the first Thanksgiving Jack spent with the family, though they met the summer after yearling year.

She closed her eyes and leaned back against the bank of pillows behind her and cast her eyes toward the ceiling. Jehanne, how do I know your voice isn't that of my inner saboteur? Sorry, I'm doubting again, but it's strange. Are you my soul?

Dearest Jane, I am of the same essence as your soul, connected and separate at the same time. You know I am of the truest part of your soul when what I communicate to you rings true. If you hear a voice that makes you feel fear, rest assured it is not mine. Our advice will always be for the greater good, and we, all your guides in the spirit realm, will only call you to action when it is for the sake of truth and righteousness. Do you understand?

Yes, what you are telling me makes sense. For example, I don't need you to tell me that my getting involved with the battle . . . no, that's not the right word. What is it that I am doing?

A mission?

Yes, that's it.

You are part of an initiation for change: the beginning of the end of a great injustice done to women. Your soul chose to assist in the start of the process. There is no rush. You merely need to drop the pebble in the pond and allow the ripples to move outward and grow larger and larger. You will not walk this path alone nor should you. There will be many to help you. Trust your inner knowing and as always I will help you, guide you, and protect you.

Jane knew Jehanne's words were true, from the marrow of her bones to the goose flesh on her arms. All of this was meant to be. She went to West Point to do just this—protect women. Her heart swelled. She opened her eyes to see flashes of rainbow light glistening in the air.

Thank you, Jehanne. I welcome your help. But first I need to convince the two men downstairs of the importance of my . . . mission.

You are most welcome. We love you.

Jane rose from her bed and fought a dizzy spell. She still experienced a dull headache from the fight and the bruise on her right buttock cried out as she walked down the stairs. She hugged her mother good morning.

"Oh, I hate seeing your face like that. Be sure to get some ice on it." She turned and resumed unloading the dishwasher. "Your sister is still in bed and I suspect will remain there until noon. Can you help with this?"

Bill sauntered into the kitchen and refilled his coffee mug. "Mary, do you mind handling that as I want to talk to our Janey."

Mary nodded her head.

"Dad, you and Jack aren't going to ambush me, are you?" Jane said pouring herself a cup.

"Now, would I do that?" he laughed.

In Bill's home office Jack lounged in one corner of the worn leather sofa. The sun streamed through the oversized windows making the temperature feel five degrees warmer than the rest of the house. Jane leaned over Jack, gave him a kiss, and sat down next to him.

"OK, you two look like coconspirators. What have you been cooking up in here?" Jane said looking from one to the other.

Bill answered first, "Jack's been filling me in on some of the details of this last week, and frankly, Janey, I don't like this. I can't see how you can stick your neck out and not be adversely affected. You've only got six months to go before graduation. Why on earth would you jeopardize that?"

"My thoughts exactly, Bill," Jack replied.

"Dad, did you know there are, on average, fifty rapes per year at West Point? And, do you know how many cadets get punished for raping?" She paused for effect and narrowed her eyes. "None. Cadets get expelled for lying but get no punishment for rape. How sick is that? I thought, of all people, you would understand. You prosecute these cases every day."

"Honey, sexual assault cases in the regular world are different than in the military. What you don't know is that you have fewer rights as a member of the military. As an officer, you are subject to the UCMJ, the Uniform Code of Military Justice. Under that code if a case is going to disrupt the morale and cohesiveness of a unit the case will not be filed. I did a little research myself over the years. Only fifteen percent of rape cases get reported and of those a miniscule number of perpetrators are convicted. All of your victims will be dragged through the mud, their reputations ruined. And you will be a victim of the same. Your career will be on the chopping block."

She turned to Jack. "Do you agree with my father?"

Jack ran his hand over the top of his short dark hair and looked Jane in the eye. "He's right. It is such a big issue. And . . . it upset me to see you bleeding the other night."

Jane tore her eyes from his and studied the designs in the oriental carpet in front of her father's mahogany desk. She felt disappointed in her men. "I know there is a way. Your resistance only makes me want to fight this more. Dad, what would you say to me if I was raped?"

Bill scratched the stubble on his chin and looked up at the ceiling. His eyes filled. "That is the point. I want to keep you out of harms way. If you embark on this journey you will become a target. Those who got away with it up until now will suddenly have a vested interest in keeping you quiet. You don't get it, Janey, I've watched women's lives crumble after they've been assaulted. It does something to them."

"That is exactly the point, to save women that anguish. Dad, I'm sorry you are afraid, but it's my life."

"Well, I'm not going to stand by and watch you throw it away," he said, stood, and began to leave the room.

To his departing back Jane said, "That means you don't trust my judgment."

He turned. They stared at one another for a moment. She waited for her father to say something like, "I don't like it, but I support you and will give you the help you need anyway." But he said nothing and continued out the door.

"It doesn't matter. I don't need your help or your approval," she called after him.

The atmosphere around the Thanksgiving dinner table felt thick with unsaid words and brooding emotions. The afternoon brought with it dark storm clouds blotting out the sun. Gloom descended on everyone present despite the copious feast Mary prepared.

Jane dropped her fork onto her dessert plate displaying the remnants of pie and vanilla ice cream. "Let's go for a drive and a walk on the beach before it gets darker," Jane said to Jack.

"Sounds good to me," Jack said.

Mary cleared her throat. "Before you go. I have something to say." She placed both hands on the table. "Jane, I want you to know that I am with you. I think what you wish to accomplish is both admirable and needed. You have my support." She glared at Bill then Jack.

Neither responded. Jack stared at his empty plate, and Bill glared back at his wife.

Jane stood. "Thanks, Mom. Your support means a lot to me," she said with very little expression, still disappointed in her father. She tapped Jack on the arm. "Let's go."

Jane tossed the laundry sack in the backseat of the car and drove down empty streets to the beach. Neither spoke. She contemplated all that happened over the last few days and wondered how she could have handled things differently.

The laundry bag had taken on a life of its own; a heavy weight surrounded it like an anchor. It lay in the backseat patiently waiting for her to open it. It held the power to destroy a friendship and a life, if the perpetrator were prosecuted. She pondered throwing it in the ocean and being done with the whole thing.

She maneuvered the car into the deserted Scarborough Beach parking lot and parked as close to the beach as she could. Wind shook the car.

"You have been feeling like a stranger lately," Jack said.

"What do you expect? I got beat up. You've been the sullen one"

"No. It's been since Tara." He shifted in his seat and looked at her. "That whole thing shook me up too. Don't get me wrong. It was terrible seeing her like that. But you . . . I don't know."

Jane thought for a moment. She knew he was right. She was different. But, she felt more like herself than ever. She did not shift into someone new; she merely allowed what lay under the surface to have life. Maybe he only loved what he wanted to see, not who she was down deep.

"Hmm." She reached into the backseat, grasped the laundry bag, and rested it in her lap. "I'm still me. Maybe it's just that there are many sides to me. Guess you don't like this particular side." It felt like he was slipping away. Her heart clenched.

"It's not that."

"No?" She wanted to change the subject. The conversation felt dangerously close to a break up. "Let's get this over with," she said and loosened the drawstring of the bag. She looked inside, and noticed three articles of clothing. Each had a photocopy of a laundry tag attached. "These look like civilian clothes. If they belong to cadets their name should be stamped inside or on the tag." Intense flutters in her belly almost kept her from looking at the names on the tags.

She held up a pair of men's white briefs pinched between her thumb and forefinger. They had blood and other stains on the waistband. "Ew! The tag says 'WHITE, CM.' She repeated the name again, "White, CM?" Then it hit her. "Oh my God. Carl White."

"Who's Carl White?"

"One of the female cadets in my battalion reported a rape at the end of last week. She named him as the perpetrator."

"God, Jane. Really? You didn't tell me that."

"I'm not supposed to. It's confidential battalion information."

Thinking the revelation was a stroke of luck for Katherine Gage, she dropped the underwear back into the bag and pulled out a pale blue oxford shirt. She turned it around, being careful not to touch too much of the fabric. It had blood on one cuff and spattered on the front. "The tag reads, 'Captain L. Vincent.' A captain? I don't know who that is."

Jack rubbed his head with both hands. "Sure you do. He's a military history professor. Didn't you have him plebe year?"

"Right. We called him 'Vacant-Eye Vincent.' I hated that guy. He was such an asshole. Why is his shirt in here and why does it have blood all over it?"

"Maybe he cut himself shaving? At least there's nothing for Patrick Ash. Maybe you were wrong."

"No, Jack. There's one more," she said. She reached in with pincerlike fingers and pulled out a royal blue polo shirt with blood smeared on the chest, the placket, and buttons. She sagged in the car seat. "The tag reads, 'ASH, PA.'" She gazed at Jack then slipped the shirt back into the bag. "Shit. I really hate that I was right."

"Jane, I have to hand it to you, you solved it. You now have evidence that can royally fuck over our friend. Are you happy?" He sounded angry with her.

His anger made her blood simmer.

They sat in silence and watched the waves crash. The beach, the water, and the sky all blended together. Even the buildings and tarmac appeared like a giant artist coated it all in a drab gray wash. The information about Ash sat uneasy with Jane. His behavior, the evidence, and the circumstances all pointed to his being guilty, but something felt off. She decided she would try to call Tara when they got back to the house. Perhaps, in the face of this evidence, Tara would tell her story.

Meanwhile, she felt her relationship with Jack was becoming yet another casualty. "Let's walk?" she asked in her sweetest voice and reached for Jack's hand.

He pulled it away but said, "OK."

Cold wind pummeled them as they made their way along the shore. Despite its force, the breeze felt refreshing. Jane let herself be carried away by the noise of the surf and the wind. The sounds were so loud they drowned out all thoughts from her head. Wind struck each cresting wave and created dancing water sprites.

They walked in the sand until the gray became inky dark. There was no sunset. Light simply left the sky. Their drive back, like the afternoon, was dulled, devoid of talking or touching.

When they pulled into her parent's driveway Jack said, "I can't lose you. It was hard enough when I lost my father almost four years ago." His green eyes turned brighter with tears.

Jane finally understood and took his hand. He squeezed hers back.

Jane stared at the bright wash of light on the closed garage doors in front of the car and remembered the day during yearling year when he had shared the story of his father's sudden death. His father had suffered a heart attack only a few months before Jack reported to West Point for Beast Barracks. At the time, Jack's sobs broke Jane's heart and bonded her to him at the same time. "You won't lose me.

Jack, pursuing this cause is the right thing to do. Don't ask me how, but I just know." She stroked his cheek with her hand. "And, I have you to protect me."

"God, Jane, I don't know. Ash is formidable. What if he comes at you again and I'm not there? You may not be so lucky next time. And there are a lot more guys out there who will not like what you are doing."

"So, we will be careful. Also, I'm not sure about Ash. Something tells me I need to try again with Tara to get the whole story."

Jack turned to face her. "Promise me you'll be careful."

"I promise."

Jack kissed her and hugged her over the center console of the car. He pulled away smiling. "Maybe there is a way you can achieve your goals without putting yourself on the line. I'm sure your father can help us figure something out."

"That's my guy," Jane said and covered his face with loud playful smooches.

Jack put his mouth to Jane's ear and whispered, "I love you."

"I love you too," Jane said and buried her face in his warm neck.

The next morning while Jack and Bill slipped out to play a round of golf, Jane sat in her father's leather chair in his office and contemplated her options. A deep sense of unrest and feelings of a grave miscarriage of justice roiled around inside her. She thought about the laundry bag, Ash, Captain Vincent. All those rapes.

She heard Jehanne's voice say, *Jane you know what to do.*

She grabbed a yellow legal pad from the top drawer and began to list all of the women she knew had been raped over the last three and a half years. She wrote and wrote. When she exhausted her memory, she went back and counted the names. Seventy-three. "Holy shit." She said out loud, figuring there would be even more she did not know about.

Yes, someone needed to do something about this insidious problem.

From the very recesses of her being she knew it was up to her, but how? Jane leaned back in her father's chair and took in her surroundings. A bank of walnut bookcases filled with law books and journals stretched along one wall of her father's home office. Stained glass tiffany lamps rested on mahogany end tables and flanked the leather sofa. The room felt warm and cozy especially during the middle of the day when the sun flooded through the large windows.

That's when it hit her. The answers, some of them anyway, lay right in front of her. She jumped up and grabbed two books, one on civil procedures and one on criminal law, off the shelves. With notepad in hand she curled up on the leather sofa and began to read. Her self-imposed law career had begun.

She read rules on evidence. She discovered rape was considered a felony, a crime in which a person is caused harm. To be found guilty of a crime the plaintiff needed to present proof beyond a reasonable doubt. This could pose a problem with rape cases where the victim's moral actions fell into the debate.

She read about class action suits and civil rights, and learned that the plaintiffs in civil cases only needed to provide a preponderance of evidence. She was about to dive into a book about the court systems when her father and Jack returned from their golf game, their faces flushed with fresh air and exercise.

Bill walked over to Jane, pushed aside the pile of law books, and sat next to her on the sofa. "Jack and I have been talking. He told me you intend to move ahead with this no matter what. Is this true?"

"Yup. I've been studying all day." She indicated the pile of books and notes littered around her.

"Impressive. I don't love this but, you have my support. This way I can keep a closer eye on you. Jack promised me he would look out for you too."

Jack winked at Jane.

"Thank you, Daddy," she said and kissed him on the cheek.

Dinner of leftover turkey sandwiches with Jack, her parents, and sister became a mini law lecture, as her father shared with them the legal pros and cons over criminal versus civil cases and how best to make an impact on the military system.

"Jane, you don't have to rush anything. Do your homework and gather as much evidence and information as possible. If you're careful you can launch this whole thing and keep yourself and your career out of harms way." Bill looked at his daughter with pride. "Call me anytime, OK?"

Jane nodded. The way she figured, she had three battles to address. The current mystery of Tara and Ash, the greater problem of rape at West Point and the military, and the world culture of rape as a strategy of war.

After dinner, for her first step, Jane decided to call Tara.

Tara's mother answered and told her she was out. Jane said she would just see her back at West Point. She hung the phone up, partly relieved that she did not have to tell her friend about Ash in that moment. Instead she dialed Sophia's home number. They chatted a few minutes about their respective Thanksgivings.

"I have some good news," Jane said. "I found some evidence that might just support Katherine Gage's claim against Carl White."

"That's great! Jeez, Jane," Sophia said half laughing into the phone. "You never cease to surprise me."

"Well, Sophia. I'm about to surprise you again." Jane smiled and switched the phone from her right ear to her left. She looked at the notes on the desk, her plan of action. "I have a plan and I need your help. Aren't you sick of the way sexual assaults are handled at West Point?"

"You know the answer to that question. What do you have in mind?"

"Just listen."

ROUEN, FRANCE

WEDNESDAY, MAY 29, 1431

Though a state of calm resignation had set in, I woke feeling the remotest hope of spring. Birds chirped outside my window and every now and then the smell of spring earth wafted to me. I spent very little time awake that day and found I barely had the strength to keep my eyelids open or move aching, numb limbs. The past now came to me in smaller recollections of random carefree childhood days, feeding the sheep, lounging on the hillside, winters around the fire in our cozy home.

"Jehanne. Jehanne, wake up." A male voice startled me back from my reverie.

I opened my eyes to see Jean Massieu, a Dominican monk and assessor, standing over me. "I have brought you something." He reached out his hand and dropped a ring into my palm. "Your ring. I thought you might like it back since your fate will be decided by tomorrow. The Earl of Warwick is demanding an end to these proceedings."

My heart leaped. I slipped the ring onto my bony finger. Could it be true? Maybe I will be sent to a convent after all, I thought and remembered the day my father gave me the ring. He had just returned from a trip east to Toul to trade some of our special wool for barrels of wine.

"Jeannette, I have something for you," he said and handed me a tiny package wrapped in burlap and tied with twine. The package appeared small in his large calloused hands. "A late birthday gift. I can hardly believe my littlest one is now sixteen years old."

This was a first, a gift from my father. Carefully I untied the twine and unfolded the fabric. "Oh my," I gasped. Lying inside was a ring. I picked it up and twirled it through my fingers looking at the markings on the side. It had the words "Jhesus Maria" and three crosses all carved around the outside. "Oh, Papa, I love it!"

He added, "The merchant said it belonged to a Templar Knight. See, it has the equal cross pieces like the Templar cross. Do you like it? It fits with the rumors in my family about our relation to Godfroi de Bouillon, the first Templar Knight. Legend boasts he is a relative of Christ," my father's sonorous voice boomed around the room.

"How can that be?" my sister and mother exclaimed together. They shared a practical skepticism of legends in general.

Ignoring their comments my father continued, "His noble lineage can be traced back to Charlemagne and to the Merovingian kings." He, too, was a practical man, but believed in the power of a man's heritage and bloodline.

If the legend proved true, it seemed possible that there could be several hundred relatives descended from Christ all over France. Nobles were notorious for siring children in and out of wedlock. The legend would certainly explain the presence of angels conversing with me. I pushed the ring comfortably onto the pointer finger on my right hand. Massieu shaking me brought my attention back to my cell. "Jehanne, did you hear me!" His inflamed face only inches from my own. "I said you have one more chance to recant your claims and don women's clothing. If you do not renounce your voices and change your clothing you will be found against the Church and punished with the pyre."

"You know my answer. Again, I will not speak against my most loyal friends and God's messengers. God is my earthly and heavenly judge. I need no other. Also, I will not relinquish the safety of men's clothing." Even though I had promised the bishop the previous day that I would wear women's clothes, I felt strongly that if I had been dressed in men's attire when the abusive English lord visited I would not have been raped.

"So be it," he said, turned, and stormed out of the tower room.

The dire nature of my situation sunk in deeper still. My body used sleep to cope with the nightmare that had become my life. I closed my eyes and wished with all my heart to be somewhere else, for the whole business to be over.

Go ahead and rest, Jehanne. You are safe, Saint Catherine said softly in my ear. I swam in her rose-petal scent, feeling freedom.

Little did I know that Bishop Cauchon at that very moment was overriding all of the information gathered, and without waiting for the verdict from the University of Paris, single-handedly determined my fate.

565 YEARS LATER

DECEMBER 1996-MARCH 1997
WEST POINT, NY

"What happened to your face," Tara asked.

"It's a long story, I'll tell you later, OK?"

"Did Jack do that?" Tara reached her hand out toward Jane's face then pulled it back. "Now I understand how you felt when you saw me. It's awful."

"No, Jack didn't do this," Jane said, contemplating the best way to approach Tara. She looked out the dirty window of the Chinese restaurant in Highland Falls, just outside of West Point's southern gate. It was a dreary day, their first day of classes after break. A cold drizzle sent folks scurrying to and from their cars.

Tara offered. "I'm feeling much better. The swelling is gone on my face. I can finally see normally."

"You look better," Jane said. She cast her eyes around the empty restaurant with its red paper lanterns, feeling dread about the news she intended to share with her good friend. She decided to plough forward despite her discomfort. Tara needed to know. "Tara, I'm not sure how to tell you this, but . . . I have some evidence, from cadet laundry, implicating Patrick Ash in your attack."

Tara gasped and said, "Jane! Patrick isn't the one who hurt me, how can you have evidence? I thought you were going to drop this."

"Yes, well, I had already set wheels in motion. So, what do you mean Patrick isn't the one? Are you sure?"

"Don't you think I'd know? Jane, it's a good thing we are such good friends."

"But he threatened me to drop all this. He's the one who attacked me." Jane pointed to her swollen cheek. She felt baffled.

"He did that?"

"Why would he threaten me if he is innocent?" An alternative possibility just began to dawn on Jane. "OK, so he's protecting someone. Who is it?"

"Me," Tara admitted. "He was protecting me."

"What do you mean? Why would he need to protect you if you got beat up and—"

"Because I was drunk. I feel really ashamed about this. If I tell you will you let it all go? Promise? Cadet's honor?"

"Tara, I'm not sure I can promise. You were really hurt. Someone is to blame for that. Tell me the truth and we'll see, all right?"

"You've broken me down. I think you missed your calling and instead of law the military should use you to interrogate terrorists." She laughed awkwardly and pushed her lo mein noodles around on her plate. "OK, so I was at Benny Havens Pub and ran into Ash. We had a few drinks. You know how sexy and charming he can be. Well, we decided to leave and grabbed a ride from his friend Captain Vincent." Her voice got thin when she said his name.

Jane's mind raced. "Did you say Captain Vincent? Vacant-eyed Vincent with the alien neck?" That explained the other shirt she had in the laundry bag back in her room. Ash would not be prosecuted but Vincent could.

"Yes, he's such a creep. Jane, I was really stupid. I feel awful. I can hardly tell you."

Jane watched Tara's eyes fill. Nether spoke for a few minutes.

Tara pushed her plate toward the center of the table and leaned on her elbows. "So, Vincent drove, and I sat on Ash's lap, because his car is just a two-seater. We were all pretty drunk. We started kissing—Ash and I—and that's when Captain Creepy asked if he could watch. This is awful, Jane." She paused and shook her head. "I can't . . ."

"Tara, I don't judge you."

"I know." Her voice sounded shaky. "He drove us to the lower fields and had a key to the field house. He watches Ash and me—you know. By then I'm feeling really bad I did something that kinky. Ash leaves to go to the bathroom and suddenly this guy is all over me. I kicked him and fought but couldn't . . . All the time, I'm thinking, where did Ash go? By the time Ash got back, it had happened, he . . . he . . ."

"Raped you? Damn."

"Yeah, Ash grabbed him and punched him hard in the stomach and kidneys. He pretty much leveled the guy. Then he picked me up and carried me back to the car. He took the captain's car and dropped me off on Thayer Road near your barracks. He told me to go see you."

Jane was stunned. "I'm so sorry, Tara." Her brain attempted to make sense of the new information. Ash did not rape Tara. He did, however, make a few bad choices when he punched Jane in the face, and she did not feel ready to let him off the hook so soon.

"This is a huge mess. All because of me," Tara sobbed.

Jane agreed—this was a mess. She weighed the new information and reasoned there would be no charges brought against either man. The way the system worked at West Point, Tara's own testimony would sully her reputation in the eyes of the chain of command. They would have a field day with her drinking and sexual behavior, claim she asked for what she got, and Vincent would be exonerated. Thankfully the Tara/Patrick piece only played a small part in her master plan. This hiccup would be easily rectified.

"You're right, Tara. The best course of action is none. I don't want to see your future compromised by that . . . jerk." She made a mental note to return the other articles of clothing from the laundry bag to Gladys; it had already been almost a week, and she didn't want to get Gladys in trouble.

The door to the restaurant opened. Sophia walked the short distance to their table and sat down. Cold and damp clung to her uniform. "What am I missing?"

Jane shot a look at Tara who said, "Oh, not much."

While Sophia knew Tara was harmed, she did not know the details. Jane was true to her word and told no one of the events.

"So, Jane, tell us the plan," Sophia said as she leaned forward in her seat, her pretty eyes wide.

"Before I do that," Jane said, and reached into her satchel. "Here. This is for Katherine Gage." She put a small plastic grocery bag on the table. "Cadet White's nasty briefs."

A serious look crossed Sophia's face. "Thanks. This will be a big help."

Jane pulled out her notebook and said, "Tara, your attack signified a tipping point for me. You are only one of . . . too many women who have been sexually assaulted in some way. So, I've decided to do something about this problem. Sophia's in it with me. We wanted to see if you wanted to join our little secret group and launch a plan."

"Depends on what you have in mind. I can't testify." Tara blushed, still embarrassed.

"What am I missing?" Sophia asked and frowned at Tara. "Shit. That explains your bruises and the rumors." She placed her hand on Tara's arm. "I'm sorry."

Jane continued, "Tara, you won't have to. My plan is bigger than a single case. I've done a little research, legal and otherwise, and I think I've come up with a good plan." She paused and gave her friends a serious look. "Are you both sure you are up for this?"

They nodded.

"First, all of this must be orchestrated to come off immediately after graduation. We have not come this far to jeopardize the last few months of our cadet lives. My intention is to take this to the top."

"The commandant of cadets?" Tara asked, biting her lip.

"No. The Department of Defense and the Pentagon." Jane widened her eyes, shimmied in the plastic chair, and laughed awkwardly.

"Oh my God. No way," Tara said. "That is outrageous. Are you sure, Jane?"

Sophia put her hand on Tara's arm, "This is totally doable. Jane told me some of her ideas on the phone. I think it could work."

"Sexual assault is not only pervasive here at West Point but everywhere in the military and the world for that matter. My dad has this legal database on his computer. I found lots of very interesting information. With more and more women showing up in military units all over the world the problem is growing. My plan is to gather together all the women who have been victims and get them to petition for a class action suit and more. I'm going to get the addresses of all the female graduates and draft a letter asking them to come forward. Of course, all of their information will be confidential. All of this must take place under the strictest secrecy; that is, until we are ready to launch the whole thing after graduation in May. I'm willing to put myself on the line to see women get some sort of protection. After all, we are not living in medieval ages, are we?"

"Yeah, but it sure seems that way sometimes," Sophia said.

"My dream is to bring attention to this problem in the most professional way possible. We can't be seen as whiny babies. We also need to increase awareness, maybe seek some reputable press. I'm hoping we can make permanent changes to our military laws, the Uniform Code—"

Just then the door opened and a male firstie walked through. Jane did not know him personally. The three of them froze and tried to act nonchalant.

"Hi," he said. He checked out each one of them as he walked to the register to pick up an order to go. While he waited he leaned his back against the counter and folded his arms across his chest. "You girls look like you're up to no good."

Jane cringed with his demeaning manner and decided to ignore him. They made small talk until he sauntered out through the door and down the sidewalk.

"He's an asshole. That was close," Tara said in a near whisper.

"Yes, we need to be careful, take precautions," Jane said. "I intend to keep my notes with me at all times." She patted her satchel. "Maybe we need to come up with a code name."

"Right. And we need to find a better location to have meetings," Sophia offered.

They doled out tasks, made plans for the next meeting, and left the Chinese restaurant charged with purpose and conviction. Jack would want to know his friend was innocent—apart from the beating he gave Jane. As she walked quickly back to barracks in the drizzling rain, avoiding puddles, she thought about Tara and wished that she could find a way to catch Captain Vincent. Jane's intuition told her Tara was not his only victim. Though, by the time she reached Jack's barracks she realized her time would be best spent on the bigger fish. If Jehanne could inspire men during the medieval times to great deeds so could Jane in 1997.

———

Winter passed cold and dark, though Jane and her friends barely noticed. They drafted letters, conducted interviews, and spent hours on research all for the cause of keeping women safe.

"Have you read the book, *The Reclamation*?" a female cadet asked Jane as she crossed over the gothic bridge toward Taylor Hall on an unseasonably warm day in late March. The phrase, The Reclamation, was the secret code name Jane had come up with for getting the word out. It was time for women to take back—reclaim—the power lost as a result of sexual threats and assault.

The sun shone behind her head making it hard for Jane to read her face. Making a visor out of her hand Jane stepped to the side in order to obtain a clear view of the cadet's eyes. She looked for signs of trustworthiness.

This type of thing had happened several times each week since January when Jane, Sophia, and Tara launched their e-mail campaign and began their quest. Jane's nerves twanged. Concern she would be found out dominated most waking moments.

Jehanne's voice whispered her approval, *She is worthy.*

Jane relaxed and dropped her hand. "As a matter of fact, I have read that book, and I have plenty to say about it." She handed the woman a plain white business card. In black ink, simple lettering read, THERECLAMATION@mail.com. If you e-mail me I will be happy to share my opinions with you.

The woman thanked her with a faint smile on her lips and departed. It had been four months since Jane, Tara, and Sophia came up with their code name and the business card idea. With the help of insiders in the Cadet Affairs and Association of Graduates offices, they had been given addresses of all the female graduates since the first class of female graduates in 1980. As a result they had collected the stories and testimonies of hundreds of women. Unfortunately only a dozen would join the class action suit she and her father had set up with a team of outside lawyers.

Jane felt exhausted. In late February, she had experienced a moment of weakness. Her love for West Point and her naïve optimism sent her to the superintendent's office to appeal to his sense of honor in protecting the women in his command.

"Sir, we need your help," Jane said and held up the ream of return e-mails she printed to demonstrate the far-reaching episodes of sexual assault on campus. "With the greatest respect for the chain of command, I request, on the behalf of the women here at West Point, that you consider the predominance of sexual assault and what may be done to change the social and moral order, so that fifteen percent of your cadets feel safer and supported."

"Cadet Archer," he said in a patronizing tone.

He leaned back in his chair and flashed her a warning look. Her spine bristled. Even before he finished his sentence Jane knew she would get nowhere with him. "You are training to be leaders, officers in the Army." He consulted the file on his desk. "Cadet Archer, you have an excellent record. I suggest you focus on your studies so your can graduate in good standing with honors. Let this little matter go. OK?"

Jane nodded. "Yes sir." In her mind she repeated, "little matter." He called rape a little matter.

He smiled and closed her folder. "Dismissed."

The meeting only served to fuel her conviction. She spent more hours than ever researching and e-mailing, and because she went to the supe, she needed to be even more clandestine with her moves. On top of their covert campaign she still had all of her responsibilities as a cadet and a commander. The stress began to take a toll on her.

After saying good-bye to the cadet who had asked her about *The Reclamation*, she leaned against the stone railing on the bridge and pulled out a tissue, blowing her nose for the umpteenth time that day. No matter how many vitamin C tablets she chewed she could not shake the cold she'd had for the last two weeks.

Over the top of her tissue she spotted Jack and Patrick walking toward her on the bridge. Her heart leaped as it always did when she saw her boyfriend's handsome face. Jack flashed her a big smile. He said, "Patrick wants to talk with you. Do you have time?"

"Sure. I have a meeting in ten minutes upstairs." She gestured toward the Administration Building.

"I have to run. You two play nice now," Jack said and left her alone on the bridge with Ash.

"See you later," Jane said. Patrick's face appeared soft and welcoming. She could see why Tara found him attractive. It took Jane a couple of months to get used to the idea he and Tara were dating. They had spoken little over the last few months, and Jane continued to feel on edge in his presence. Though she heard he had cleaned up his act and was working hard at being a better platoon leader. Even though he was innocent of raping Tara, he remained in her mind, a loose cannon.

"I never officially apologized to you. I'm really sorry for hitting you." His words were accompanied with a sincere look of regret.

"It's OK. I'm sorry too for—" Jane remembered hitting him in the face with the heel of her shoe and felt only a little bad.

He raised his hand to stop her from talking. "No need. I want to tell you how much I admire what you are all doing. What I witnessed with Tara . . ." He shook his head. "It was horrible. It changed me. No woman should have to endure that kind of humiliation. If you need anything you can count on me."

Jane felt truly surprised by Patrick's words. "Wow" was all she could muster as a response.

"I want you guys to be really careful OK. While I think you are doing the right thing, I am concerned for your safety."

"Thanks."

"You take care now," Patrick said with a smile and continued across the bridge in the opposite direction.

Tears flooded her eyes momentarily. He had caught her off guard. Patrick's support made her realize how on edge she had been feeling. She felt proud of him. He had come a long way since the previous summer, and she was happy she did not have to count his friendship as a casualty. By the time she reached the open door to her advisor's office, Jane had regained her composure.

Jane paused at the threshold of the door when she realized her advisor, Captain Moss, was on the phone.

Captain Moss gestured with one honey-colored hand to Jane to come in and sit in the chair in front of her desk. In her other hand she held the phone. She had been Jane's advisor since yearling year.

Jane sat down. While she waited her eyes gently scanned the captain's extremely neat desk. Only a few items lay on its surface, a blank white pad and pen, a lamp, the phone, and one item that sent Jane's pulse racing—her plain white business card. While she struggled to maintain her composure and steady her breathing, Jane contemplated running out of the building. She considered lying. Thoughts of court martial and expulsion from the academy ran through her mind. It seemed like an eternity before Captain Cheryl Moss hung up the phone.

Jane saluted her, "Ma'am."

Captain Moss smiled and saluted back. "Hello, Jane. Before we begin, would you mind closing the door?"

Jane stood on shaking legs and moved toward the door. I could still get away, she thought then she heard Jehanne's voice. *Relax, Jane. Everything will turn out fine.* She closed the door and returned to her seat with trepidation pounding through every muscle of her body.

"Good. How are you?" Captain Moss asked. Her face appeared neutral but Jane had noticed a shadow dulling her normally radiant onyx eyes the last few months.

"Fine. I'm good," Jane said stiffly.

"I wanted to talk to you about something rather important. You know I served in the Gulf War, right?"

"Yes."

"Well, I recently got together with a friend of mine, another woman, who served with me. She informed me of a secret movement. A group of military women who are covertly working as activists around the sexual assault issue. Do you know anything about this?"

Jane's heart pounded so hard she thought Captain Moss could see her shirt pulsing. She could not speak and merely shrugged her shoulders in a noncommittal way.

Sensing Jane's discomfort she offered, "That's too bad, because I think it is amazingly brave, genius."

Jane could hardly believe what she was hearing. She blinked away threatening tears for the second time that morning. They locked eyes. Captain Moss's face was soft and open.

"Ma'am. You think it's brave?" Jane relaxed her posture somewhat feeling Captain Moss was being honest. She glanced absentmindedly around the small office considering her next words.

"Yes. I want in on the project."

"You do?"

"My sources tell me it's you, Cadet Archer. That you are the one heading this operation."

Jane flushed. "Your sources are correct," she conceded.

"I don't have to tell you we are speaking within the strictest confidence here."

"Of course."

Captain Moss's face grew serious, her dark brows knit together. "I was raped . . . twice. Once overseas, and once right here, on post. My peace of mind is shattered. I don't mind telling you, I'm ready to give all this up. The military, that is. I'm planning on resigning my commission in May, and I'd like to go out with a bang."

"I'm sorry," Jane said.

"I've had a great career. Graduated from here in 1984, served thirteen years," she said. "Here's what I have in mind. I am going to press charges against my rapist, Captain Vincent. Be sure you warn your friends about him. First-class creep. I have DNA evidence and even a witness. I want his balls," she said vehemently. "One of my own colleagues . . ."

Jane's pulse quickened when Captain Moss mentioned Captain Vincent. Shit, she thought. We have to get this guy. Jane wondered if she should tell her advisor about Tara and Captain Vincent.

Captain Moss continued, "Also, I have been working on a draft for a petition to the UN Security Council. There needs to be a resolution to address the predominance of rape and sexual assault as a crime of war. I have piles of research about victims from the Vietnam War, Gulf War, Bosnia, Rwanda, you name it. This is a human rights issue, Jane. Rape has been and will continue to be a crime against an entire segment of our population. That is, unless we stop it."

"I agree," Jane said. The more Captain Moss spoke the more excited Jane became. "Will you join our class action suit against the Secretary of Defense William Cohen? We're also suing former Secretary of Defense James Perry, as he only left office this January, for mishandling of a number of cases. Did you know one woman was raped by a fellow soldier and became pregnant? Her command would not let her go to a base hospital. She had to leave her unit and miscarried on the way home."

"Just awful. You have been busy. Yes, by all means, count me in."

They spent the remainder of the hour talking about strategy and launch times. Her level of conviction and sense of purpose felt renewed and recharged. Even the symptoms of her cold seemed better.

Jane skipped down the first few stairs when she felt the back of her neck tighten. Something felt out of place. Though it was a warmish March day, cold seeped out of the walls and slid icy fingers down her spine. She forced herself to focus on the hem of her gray slacks.

Suddenly Jane's vision shifted. Her slacks morphed into a natural fiber cloth, heavy linen. Soft-soled leather boots covered slightly smaller feet. The feel of cold stone through the thin leather sent a paralyzing chill through her legs and the fine blond hairs on her arms stood alert. Right before her eyes the square stairwell transformed into antiquated rounded castle walls. She put a hand on her chest and let out an audible gasp.

She heard shuffling footfalls echoing in her head while her heart beat out a more rapid rhythm with each downward step. She grabbed hold of the handrail to steady herself; she was in two locations at once, a palimpsest of sorts. Impressions of a time long gone bled through into this time: split, in mind and spirit. I'm feeling another time, Jane thought.

Some unseen hand tethered her to a dark, fearful scene. Death hovered quietly by her side, waiting. Her chest constricted as she gasped for air. The scent of burning wood stung her nostrils.

Somehow she had parted the delicate fabric of time. French voices swam in her head. Movement was all around her, hands pulled at her. Tired, hungry, and discouraged she wanted to slump down, give up. Far off noises of a gathered crowd made her ears ring. Jane could feel Jehanne crying out. Oh, dearest God, help me!

Forcing her weakened legs to move, Jane tore herself away from the horror and let the curtain fall. With each step, history faded and the present stairway felt more solid under her patent leather shoes. She slid her shaking hand down the metal rail, allowing the cool steel to ground and steady her nerves. The disconcerting vision departed by the time she reached a small landing, though the threat of death lingered. Somehow, it slipped through time and stayed with her. "Go back," Jane whispered into the empty stairwell. Jehanne's high-pitched feminine voice hung in the air like ashes caught on an upward breeze. As she pivoted and ran down the last flight, tears stung at the corners of her eyes and panic rose from her chest and squeezed through her tightened throat.

Oh no!

Reaching the bottom, she punched the door's horizontal handle downward, stepped into the fresh air, and let out her breath. Everything appeared normal. She glanced down at her shoes and felt only slightly relieved. A shimmer of the shadow remained with her as she strode across the macadam toward her barracks.

The mere two-hundred-yard distance seemed to have lengthened since she walked this path two days ago. The quick tap-tap-tap of her footfalls echoed off the stone facades surrounding her on all sides. She tried to outpace it but, like her actual shadow, it remained affixed to her heels. Entering her barracks, she took the stairs two at a time to the third floor. The panic feeling lingered. Then it hit her. Jehanne was going to die.

A torrent of emotion welled up from Jane's abdomen and, stifling a gasp of grief, she ran down the hall and into her room. A surprising amount of sadness ripped at her heart, her chest felt like it was splitting in two pieces. She's going to die. They're going to burn her alive and there is nothing I can do from here.

Oh, Jehanne, what can I do?

Dearest Jane, do not weep for me. I am grateful for you to have born witness to my suffering. But, I am as eternal as the night sky, as are you. I will live forever in your heart, in your brave deeds. Rest. Sleep. All will be well.

Jane lay on her bed without taking off her jacket and closed her eyes in an attempt to rid her mind of the vision of Jehanne's death. More than ever Jane felt happy she pursued justice for women. Jehanne's voice and presence settled her down. Jane let her exhaustion catch up with her and fell deeply asleep.

ROUEN, FRANCE

OLD MARKET, THURSDAY, MAY 30, 1431

" Tell me the news Brother," I asked the young monk known as Brother Jean Toutmouille. Small beads of sweat dotted his partially shaved pink head. By the way he squeezed his smooth chubby hands, and the way his entire face drooped, I sensed the news would not be good. I felt nervous and picked at the scabs on my wrists. For months iron manacles had chaffed at my skin and caused perpetual, angry sores.

"Jehanne, before I relay the news, I must tell you." He leaned down and whispered in my ear, "I believe you are sent by God, and that God and God alone is and has been your only inspiration. It causes me tremendous pain to see you treated thusly. I bow to your courage and chastity. You, indeed, are the bravest woman I ever encountered." The last word "encountered" left his mouth as a gasp. He ran out of breath, he spoke so quickly. Straightening upright, he wiped a tear trailing down his ruddy, round face with the brown sleeve of his robe.

"Merci," I whispered back, as tears filled my own eyes. "God will surely reward your soul. He waits for you with open arms in his Kingdom in Heaven."

"It is with great heaviness of heart I have come to take you to. . . . The judges have ordained that you will be burned at the Old Market, today." What I did not know then was that the judges had not decreed my sentence. It was the sole hasty and ruthless decision of Bishop Cauchon that demanded my death.

"Et alors! Burned? They used me, cruelly. This is my worst fear to be consumed by fire! I'd rather be beheaded seven times than burned at the stake." A shudder ran through my thin body, and I pleaded with my eyes for the good Brother to do something.

"Come, we must see the bishop. He's waiting for you now, downstairs." The brother pulled me to standing and led me down the circular tower steps. Twice I slumped to the cold stone, dizzy with fear, and twice he gently pulled me up. Chains at my hands and feet restricted my movement. I could hear the raspy voice of Bishop Cauchon waiting for me on the ground floor. I wished God would take me now so I would not have to be subjected to the pyre. *Please God!* I pleaded silently.

"Bishop, my death marks your soul," I said, glaring at his red face upon reaching the landing. His steel blue, bloodshot eyes opened wide with anxiety. Waves of fear almost knocked me off my feet. I could feel my mind slipping sideways—fear turning into a certain giddiness. This bishop, this man of God, was responsible for my death sentence. I looked at him now in his holy robes, and saw only a small man standing behind the fur-trimmed shield of God. Were it not for the robes he would be the same as you or me.

His mouth worked nervously before he spoke. "Jehanne, be realistic, you die because you held not to what you promised and have returned to your first evil-doing by wearing men's clothing." His lipless mouth formed into a cruel sneer.

"If you had put me in the prisons of the court of the English, or the convent to be guarded by nuns, instead of this military prison . . . I appeal against you to God." I wanted to spit in his face for clearly overstepping his bounds and sentencing me unfairly. It should have been the job of the secular judges to decide my punishment.

Jehanne, be still! We are with you. If you allow it, you will be filled with divine grace to strengthen you for your death. Remember, you are a beloved daughter of God! You are all equally naked before the eyes of God, stripped of clothing, riches, and stature. My voices from Heaven reassured me. Calm began to spread throughout my entire body, settling down the fear, softening the harsh reality of my impending death. My body expanded as my soul began coaxing me upward.

Not yet, Jehanne. Soon . . .

The bishop and two devoted brothers led me outside to the cobblestoned street where a cart sat waiting. The bishop climbed up to sit next to the driver while the good brothers lifted me, and my chains, onto the back. The brothers climbed up and sat on either side of me on the weathered wooden seat. At that moment, a heavenly spring wind blew through the castle's courtyard, and I remembered what it felt like to be free.

As the wheels of the cart crunched over the well-worn stones, I filled my lungs with gulps of fresh air and my strength returned. Sun streamed between the buildings, creating deep shadows and stripes of honey-colored light on the rutted road. Soldiers, dressed in the colors of England, lined the streets. Drinking in the all-but-forgotten sunlight as it fell on my face and shaved head reminded me of the joyful days of independence, fighting for my king, on horseback. It had been a year since I rode freely welcomed by the cheering crowds in every town in France. The presence of my heavenly counsel floated gently around me and lifted my spirits, nourished, and invigorated me.

Welcoming the familiar surge of courage I took a breath to speak, thinking this my last chance to get a private word with the bishop. My voice rang loud and clear in the spring air, "Bishop, no matter how high you build the pyre, no matter how hot the flames rage, you will not be able to consume the joy within me." I lifted my chin proudly and continued, "You see it is the joy of following the path where God and I converge—my own heart. Do you understand that there is no earthly power strong enough? Whether it be the advancing army of my enemies, the unjust treatment of my guards, a trial by sixty bishops or one thousand men, or a witch's stake, you can't touch my joy and my love for the people of France."

The cart lurched over debris in the road, sending us all wobbling. My short speech weakened me but I had more to say. I took a breath and with great effort continued, "Hope has returned. It is in the air now and no one can obliterate it, no one can wipe it away." The wind helped to carry my words, strong and full of conviction, to the ear of the bishop. "You may try. In the process you will only make yourself and others miserable, as you have done already."

His face turned crimson and he clenched his fists but he did not speak, so I persisted, "You don't have to take my word. As a child of God yourself, you will one day understand what you have put me through. Your name will live on, but not in the way you think, and you will die in fear."

Jehanne, look around you and notice how spring has brought everything back to life.

Tearing my attention away from the bishop I took in the scene around me. The air sparkled, crisp, electric, and smelled like our fields back home after a lightening storm. Spring showed herself in full glory, blossoming trees dotted the courtyards we passed while bright pink hyacinth and red geraniums danced with the breeze in the window boxes of the split-beam, Tudor-style buildings leading up to the square. The brilliant, clear blue canopy overhead reminded me how vast we were.

However, as we approached the square, my serenity and strength dissipated with each turn of the wheels. Sounds of a large crowd rumbled in my ears and my stomach lurched when we came into view of the platform holding the stake to which they would tie me. The square teemed with a thousand people, soldiers, priests, royals, and common folk, even children. Murmurs rippled through the crowd as they caught sight of our procession. Men-at-arms walked alongside the cart, their hands poised on the hilts of their sheathed swords.

I can't believe it will all end like this. . . . My death at nineteen years of age.

Jeannette, come, the wind beckoned, sounding like my mother's voice calling me by my childhood name.

The scaffold groaned when Pierre Cauchon stepped up to publicly announce my sentence. "We declare you, Jehanne d'Arc guilty of numerous crimes of idolatry, invocation of devils, and other heretical acts. Therefore, after admitting your errors, it is evident that you have returned to those same crimes. Wherefore we declare you a relapsed heretic."

Surprisingly, a deep serenity settled around me and helped me to realize there was something I needed to do. "Wait!" I yelled, "I have something to say."

"Proceed," Brother Martin, one of the few who quietly supported me during the trial, said quickly. He did not want me to die without having my say to the crowd.

"First, I call upon the blessed Trinity, all the saints in Paradise, God, Jesus, and Maria. I thank you for your love and blessings. I call upon you all in Heaven to forgive all those who have harmed me, treated me harshly or unjustly. I hereby pardon all of you English, royal dukes, bishops, and clergy." I paused to catch my breath. I could barely stand and the crowd swam before my eyes. I willed myself to stay steady and finish. The crowd now silenced by my forgiveness. "Please pray for me as my soul ascends beyond this suffering to Paradise." Again, I had to pause. "I forgive you all! Do you hear me? I forgive you all and ask that God in Heaven forgive your misjudgments and the harm you caused me! May God bless France, her new king, and all of you! Know this, all of you, friends and enemies, you men of my time and you men of the future, until the end of the world, know that the voices I heard came from Heaven. With this last proclamation, my mission is accomplished."

Many in the crowd began to weep; others jeered and hissed. I continued, "I beg each priest here to say a Mass for me, to remember me! Brother, please bring me the cross from the church and hold it in front of my eyes until I die?" I beseeched him as humbly as I could.

"Absolutely," he answered and hurried to the nearby Church of Saint-Sauveur to fulfill my wish.

The executioner wound the chains that bound me, all these months, around my body and looped them around my wrists. He threaded the long links through a metal ring attached to the stake above my head and finally wrapped the last portion around my neck. He pulled my arms up over my head with my wrists chained together, then hooked the whole ghastly concoction through the rings, so that, if I tried to lower my arms, I would choke myself to death.

He lit the torch and touched it to the pile of branches and sticks in three places. Three fires leaped, instantly creating a semicircle of flame at my bare feet. "Dear Jesus!" I yelled. Brother Ismbart returned with the cross and lifted it before me. "Thank you, dearest Brother! I am most grateful. Please remember me."

Out of the crowd, a lit torch sailed, end over end, through the air, struck my left shoulder, and dropped to the kindling, igniting yet another set of flames.

I held my gaze as steady as I could at the cross as the flames leaped, licking at my feet and legs. The pain in my wrists and shoulder was excruciating. The pain in my heart worsened by the smoke filling my lungs. But, I finally understood everything. Thankfully, the flames from the pyre at my feet grew tall enough to obscure my view of the cheering crowd. The blue sky turned gray with smoke. I felt a deep and profound peace settle over me as I slipped inward.

I floated back to my earliest memories as a little girl chasing butterflies in the tall grass on a hillside overlooking the Meuse valley. I hoped to catch the yellow butterfly. I believed that it was an angel and I wished to have it with me always. My older brother Pierre crouched on all fours pretending to be a wild cat stalking me. This was one of my favorite games. He pounced on me and tickled me as I giggled with joy. I was four years old then and he was ten. My father would give Pierre a short break from his many daily tasks. Every now and then Pierre would spend those precious minutes with me. We loved each other so. Neither one of us realized that those moments of simplicity would slip away. Beautiful moments are to be cherished at their hour. Just as the brilliance of a new day dawning does not last long, so too are simple moments of joy. I am thankful for those comforting memories.

Suddenly, I crashed back into the fire. Biting pain shot up my legs, into my back, settling into my heart with a new fierceness. The movement of the fire caused the stake to shift, sending more pain through my entire body. I could not feel my feet or legs any longer. The heat and smoke seared my lungs. "Please remember me," I squeaked out.

My lips continued to move in prayer. Saint Michael, Saints Catherine and Margaret, dear God please allow me to be reborn in the arms of God. Take my mind back to a pleasant memory and away from this ghastly horror of my imminent death.

Jehanne, notice the colors and vibrancy of spring. All things have their time and all things are reborn. Feel the hope you have given the people of the future.

I snapped back into the fire as it consumed me. The cheers from the crowd lessened, replaced with wailing. Perhaps I did have an impact on this crowd after all. "Jesus! Jesus!" I cried with my last breath.

Surrender, dearest one! You have succeeded magnificently! Feel oneness with the flame. Can you feel the hope from the future? Can you see how many souls you have influenced with your devotion and love for humanity?

A wave of bliss washed over me. I understood. More waves flowed through my body, no longer mine, no longer flesh and blood but only vibrating energy in the form of a body. Love and bliss flowed into the top of my head and filled me from the inside. This feeling, coupled with the intense energy of the flames, blended together and began to swirl. My entire being became a magnificent vortex of love and joy spiraling upward.

I slipped out of my charred body and with an "Ahh" drifted upward. I understood then it would take many more years, and many other people, to plant the seeds for this change in consciousness. My heart now free from the restrictions of suffering in physical form, expanded, and I felt soft and full. I soared on the spiral of love, rising into the wondrous, all encompassing light.

Radiance around me grew and pulsed everywhere. The pain, the grief, and the suffering, all dropped away. I was free to be pure love once again—one with all. Connected. The deliciousness of the peace enveloped me, healed me. At once, I was welcomed home by my inspiring guides: Archangel Michael, Saint Catherine, and Saint Margaret. They flowed to me, and we connected in a complete embrace. Heart to heart we spoke. I overflowed with gratitude and they did as well.

566 YEARS LATER

May 24-30, 1997

Jane rose before dawn on graduation day, donned shorts and a T-shirt, laced up her running shoes, and ran her fingers through her short hair. She grabbed a neatly folded sweatshirt, gray with faded black letters spelling ARMY, from her bureau and walked quickly out of her barracks. She saluted the guard, jogged through the quad, ran under the huge teeth of the portcullis gate, and wound her way along the streets of West Point for her last run as a cadet. The castle-like architecture never failed to invoke a feeling of living in another time. Ashen stonework of the buildings and fortress walls appeared to glow a deep blue-purple as a sliver of light peeled the night sky away from the horizon. The stillness of this time of the morning added balance to Jane's hectic life. She would miss this.

Graduation came with feelings of joy and sadness. When Jane considered how much she had grown she felt proud of herself. Hooking a right onto Thayer Road, she ran toward the south gate, past post housing and the golden lit windows of other early risers, and turned right onto Mills Road. As she cruised up the hill she could hear the low murmurs of the bubbling stream to her right. She wanted to commit it all to memory.

At the top of the hill the Cadet Chapel sat regally silent. She padded up to the large carved doors and turned the black handle to see if it was open. It gave easily, and she stepped into the hushed empty interior. The ever-burning candle dedicated to prisoners of war gave a reddish glow to the entire space. Moving swiftly but quietly she made her way toward the front and sat a few rows back. The softness of the bench's scarlet cushion felt nice under her thighs. Folding her hands in front of her she prayed. Instead of closing her eyes she directed her gaze at the carved relief of Archangel Michael. This statue was the primary focal point in the front of the cathedral and hung over the altar.

"Hi, Jehanne," she whispered. "Thanks for helping me get to this day. I graduate today."

As always, you are welcome.

"We launch our offensive this week. I sure hope it all works. Many women have put their careers on the line. Will you help protect them?"

We, me and others, like Archangel Michael, will be with you and your team through the whole thing. You have indeed dropped the pebble in the pond and have begun a most profound rippling of events. Your mission will make a difference for many women and men.

"Thanks again," Jane said and bowed her head toward the Archangel Michael stone relief. Then she ran back to her barracks to change for the graduation parade and ceremony.

Under a clear blue sky, at 10:20 a.m. Jane sat shoulder to shoulder, all in dress grays over whites, with her fellow classmates on the field of Michie Stadium. The president of the United States, William Clinton, stepped up to the podium and spoke. He encouraged everyone to seek to shape history, to make steps toward global peace. He spoke of the growing effect of NATO and his hopes for the future. He said the graduates must act when their values are at stake and their mission should be for peace at all times. They must prevent the widespread slaughter of any country and strive to make the world a more secure place.

Jane felt like he directed his speech at her specifically, and it served to give her more conviction for her mission. She could hardly believe she made it safely to that day and pondered the distance she had traveled since high school graduation. Relief flooded through her and mingled with a humble pride. She did not allow herself to think too far into the future because she was not sure what it would look like. She spent hours over the last few months wondering what the consequences for her actions would be. Would she be sent to some godforsaken country as retribution? Would they kick her out of the military and make her pay back her entire West Point education, which could amount to hundreds of thousands of dollars? Or would she be allowed to pursue her dream and report, as planned, this fall to Judge Advocate General School in Charlottesville, Virginia to begin her JAG career?

Shoving all thoughts aside she focused on President Clinton's words and scanned the crowd for familiar faces. There were so many. Nostalgia swooped in with armloads of memories. She experienced countless challenges and just as many successes. If there was one thing Jane learned from attending West Point it was that each challenge came accompanied by a solution. And each time she faced a challenge with courage, the challenge turned into a personal victory. As her eyes wandered around the stadium, they landed on Captain Leonard Vincent. He appeared to be chatting up an attractive civilian by his side. Revulsion washed through her body and made her shiver. Nothing seemed to lie behind his narrow, black-hole-like eyes, making him appear inhuman. His too long neck and developing paunch strained at the starched fabric of his uniform and added to the effect of his coming off as more animal than human. Just you wait, Vincent, Jane thought to herself. You will get what's coming to you when Cheryl Moss sues your ass in criminal court in a few days. It was this detail of the plan that gave Jane the most satisfaction. Captain Moss went ballistic when she heard Vincent raped a fellow cadet. Jane was hard-pressed to find anyone who could match Moss's retaliatory venom and this pleased her immensely. Justice would be served on Tara's behalf after all.

Finally, the moment all cadets dreamed of: Their First Captain, Dan Hart, announced heartily, "Class Dismissed!" Every graduating cadet tossed his cap into the sky with its cotton-candy clouds. A thunderous cheer filled Michie Stadium, and true to tradition, waiting children rushed onto the field to snap up a cadet's cap as a souvenir.

Jane received her second lieutenant bars, cleared her belongings out of her barracks in record time, jumped in her parents' car, and headed back to Rhode Island for a long awaited leave of nearly two months. She had said her good-byes at the banquet the night before and had plans to see her best friends and Jack in less than a week.

On the ride home, her parents gushed congratulatory comments. Her mother, Mary, said, "Mostly, Janey, we are so happy you made it to graduation. We felt you were playing with fire. Don't get us wrong; we admire your courage, but as your parents we are relieved you are out of there," Turning around from the front seat she gave Jane's knee a squeeze. "JAG School should be more civilized."

Jane smirked and shook her head thinking, it's still the military. She loved her mother for caring and gathered from her comments that her father did not relay all the parts of the reclamation campaign. He had been a tremendous source of information and helped her to interface with the law firm in D.C. She was so grateful to him. She leaned forward and patted him on the shoulder. "Dad, thanks for all your help the last few months."

When she awoke in her bed in Rhode Island on Wednesday, May 27, flutters of apprehension upset her belly. Doubting questions plagued her. Were they doing the right thing by stirring up all kinds of attention around sexual assault? Still in her pajamas, Jane sat in the chair in her father's office, munching on rye toast. Lying on the desk were two fat manila envelopes. Each held copies of nearly two hundred letters from graduates, former cadets, and cadets at West Point, detailing various episodes of assault. There were letters laying out the events themselves and the devastating effects the events had on these women's lives. Many told of the humiliation felt at the hands of fellow cadets in the chain of command. Tales of coercion, ending military careers, post-traumatic stress problems, and resulting physical ailments filled those envelopes addressed to the commandant of cadets and the superintendent of cadets, the top command at West Point.

Attached to the testimonials Jane affixed a letter she and her team drafted to beseech the men in charge at West Point to consider implementing and enforcing changes to the nonexistent policies around sexual assault. In the letter Jane mentioned the other steps her coalition planned to take, the civil suit against the Department of Defense, the criminal suit against Captain Vincent, the petition to the UN Security Council, and at the bottom lay her signature. This was the first time she used her new title, Jane Archer, 2nd Lieutenant, US Army.

Brilliant sunlight bounced off the hood of Jane's car as she drove, deep in thought, to the town's post office. At that very moment, their team of Washington, DC lawyers would be filing the civil action suit, made up of plaintiffs from every branch in the military, in Virginia Federal Court. She gripped the steering wheel tighter to steady her shaking hands. Along the way, she noticed mothers walking babies in strollers, children playing in a school yard, two men in business suits talking near a coffee shop. These everyday moments felt mocking to her. This course of action triggered a deeper fear than walking on a thin steel beam over the lake at Camp Buckner. At a stoplight she glanced at the envelopes sitting on the empty seat next to her. Suddenly she longed for a simple life, wearing blue jeans everyday, settling down in a suburban home. She did not have to go through with sending the letters. Technically her name was not on either lawsuit because she was not an actual victim. Captain Moss had issued her letter of intent to resign her commission and on that same day would be filing her own criminal suit in the state of New York against Vincent.

The car behind Jane's honked, startling her out of her reverie. She drove through the light, put on her turn signal, and pulled over into a shopping mall to think. Maybe I have done enough. She had her diploma and the privilege of attending JAG school in less than two months. Why would she risk it all? After all, maybe she could do more good as a JAG lawyer later on.

The familiar grounding iterations of Jehanne's voice floated around her. *Jane you know what you need to do for your path. Try imagining your future without sending the letters and then imagine your future sending the letters. Notice how each path feels different.*

Jane closed her eyes and imagined the two different courses of action. She actually felt the difference. The imagined path when she did not send the letters felt dull and empty, while the other path felt uplifting and clear. "Damn, Jehanne." Jane hit the steering wheel with her palm. "I know it's right to send these. I just feel frightened. You know they instill fear of these military leaders in us as cadets. Those men seem so untouchable, powerful, godlike to us. They could ruin my life."

They are just as human and just as fallible. Yes, undoubtedly you are taking a risk—but one that will be well rewarded. As always it is your choice.

Jane closed her eyes and slowed her breathing. She listened to the birds chirping through the open car window. The pungent scent of salty sea air brought back happy memories of her childhood at the shore. After a few minutes the fear subsided, her mind cleared. She put the car in drive and pulled back onto the road in the direction of the post office. Thanks, Jehanne, she thought.

Three days later, Jane pulled into the small retreat center just outside of Greenwich, Connecticut.

"You'll be in the rear conference room," the receptionist said and handed Jane registration and release forms to sign. As she filled in the section indicating that day's date—May 30, 1997, she realized it was the exact anniversary of Jehanne's death. How fitting, she thought, and made her way to the designated room. She spotted Tara, Sophia, and five other women who had helped to put the plan in motion, including a radiant Cheryl Moss milling around.

"Are you ready to walk on fire?" Sophia asked as they hugged.

"As ready as I'll ever be," Jane replied and greeted the others heartily.

"Everyone, may I have your attention," a large-boned, middle-aged woman announced. "My name is Anna, and I will be your "fire master" for the evening. Please follow me outside," she said indicating the door. She wore her brunette hair long and tied back with a colorful scarf. "Please form a circle around the logs."

The present gender mix made Jane smile. There were twenty-five women and nine men. When the crowd settled around the six-foot tower of stacked logs, Anna prepared to light the fire. "People have been fire walking for thousands of years as a way to bond warriors—teams, now-a-days—and gain courage. As I light the fire I would like each of you to consider your intention for coming." She touched a flaming twig to the logs in several locations. The kindling caught quickly. As Jane contemplated her intention, the flames spread and in a short period of time the entire pyre was ablaze. The sudden heat made several folks within the circle take steps backward away from the warmth.

Jane could not imagine the fate of her friend and mentor-in-spirit, Jehanne, being burned at the stake. She imagined the flames toasting her own feet and shuddered.

"By the time the sun has set and the moon rises the coals will be ready for raking out and the walking will commence. For now let's go back inside and prepare our minds and bodies for this journey."

On their way inside Jane whispered to Sophia and Tara, "Did you know Joan of Arc was burned at the stake on this very day,"—she paused and did the math in her head: 1997 minus 1431—"exactly five hundred and sixty-six years ago."

"That is so cool," Tara said.

They spent an hour and a half in the cozy, carpeted room bonding as a group, sharing intentions as the sun slipped lower and lower. When the outside light waned and deep shadows filled the space, Anna lit candles and led them through breathing exercises and a guided visualization. She instructed the eager participants to imagine a place of great beauty where they would feel deeply relaxed. She had them visualize finding courage they never knew they had, power they had only imagined.

Jane had never felt so peaceful in a room of some near strangers before.

When Anna's assistants informed her the coals were ready, the group filed out into the dark evening to the site. Clouds partially covered the nearly full moon and a breeze jangled the leaves on the trees all around them. A sensation of déjà vu pushed the experience in the direction of the mystical. The scene felt reminiscent of her recurrent dream from last fall. Jane and her friends gasped when they saw the bed of coals, raked out in the shape of a twenty-foot-long glowing carpet, like her mother's red oriental runner in the front hall, only with flames dancing along the edges.

Cheryl whispered in Jane's ear, "How on earth are we going to do this without getting scorched?"

"I have no idea," Jane offered. She thought Cheryl looked more relaxed and the sparkle had returned to her dark eyes.

"By the way, I feel better than I have in years. Received my honorable discharge this week and filed suit against Vincent. We go to trial in a month," Cheryl said.

"Captain Moss," Tara said. "I want to thank you for all you're doing."

"Please call me Cheryl. I think we are beyond formalities at this point," Cheryl said and reached out to hug Tara, who hugged her back, her eyes filled with tears.

"Don't you worry," Cheryl said. "We're going to fry his ass."

A smile brightened Jane's face as she watched Cheryl and Tara together.

Anna's voice cut through the chatter. "Everyone line up in a circle around the embers and hold hands," Anna instructed. When the circle was formed she continued, "When you feel like it's your time to go, simply step to this end and feel your own internal power. It will feel like a surge of energy inside you." She indicated by walking to the top of the rectangle of fire. "And, walk like this." She sauntered the twenty feet across the smoldering coals, smiling at the crowd on both sides. When she got to the end she did a victory jig and displayed the soles of her feet. "See," she said, "no burns."

The crowd cheered.

Anna rejoined the circle. "If you wish, you may go in pairs."

Several minutes passed before anyone worked up the nerve, then a thirty-something woman stepped up and ran across the coals. She laughed and hooted as her feet landed safely on cool damp grass.

Jane felt the surge of energy rise up to her heart from her belly. She released the hands on either side of her and stepped to the top of the coals. "For Jehanne . . . Joan of Arc," she announced to the circle, feeling Jehanne by her side. Without hesitation, she stepped onto the cinders and moved quickly. The heat from the flames at the edges could be felt on her legs more than the warmth from the coals touching her feet. With each footstep, joy built within her. When she reached the end she simply walked back to her place within the circle, smiling more broadly than she had in years.

After everyone had a turn, Jane, Tara, and Sophia decided to join hands and venture across together. Thunder rumbled in the distance and the wind picked up. Before walking they cried out in a unified voice, "For the women." They ran giggling; kicking up sparks, along the entire length.

Others paired off and did the same.

Spirits ran higher and higher as each soul ran over the coals while thunder boomed closer. A flash of lightening illuminated the air all around. The first drops of rain made the simmering coals sizzle and sent diaphanous smoky shapes into the night sky. It was not until the rain began to come down in earnest that the group flocked back inside.

All, except Jane. She knew Jack would be waiting for her inside, as they had planned to begin their vacation together that evening before they reported to their new bases in Virginia. He would be at Fort Lee and she at Charlottesville for JAG school, only one hundred miles would separate them. The distance was not ideal but definitely doable. Instead, she decided to stay near the fire for a few minutes with the hope of making a connection with Jehanne.

Rouen, Old Market, France

May 30, 1431
Later That Day

We, my angels and I, watched as the executioner dowsed the flames with buckets of water. We watched as Bishop Cauchon, and others, checked my body to be sure I was indeed dead. This seemed to be typical protocol when burning a witch. They needed to verify that after execution I was human, a woman, and actually dead. Satisfied, they rebuilt the pyre, and lit it once again to fully consume my remaining flesh. We watched as the flames reached high into the blackened sky and ash began to fly around the town square.

From my vantage point I could see the incredible beauty of my joy, my inspiration, and my love for the divine, floating all over France and the world. I could see into the future as a young woman named Jane Archer ran across a long row of burning embers. Curious, I went to be with her. It filled me with joy to see women miraculously conquering fire. I waited until she sat by herself in the rain.

Jane, I am very proud of you. You and your friends have helped to initiate the return of the Heroine; for she lives in everyone who exhibits courage and acts on the behalf of others.

Jehanne, I did this workshop for you. I wanted to turn fire into a positive thing. It was so awful what they did to you. I could feel your pain and wanted to help.

Dearest Jane, let the rain bring you my joys as well. The short moments in prison and in the flames could not destroy the good I accomplished. My soul is intact, healed.

I waited and watched as Jane let the rain deliver my entire story to her. She turned her face to the falling rain and smiled. Thank you for letting me experience your journey. I will do my best to make a difference here.

You already have. Now I must go. I will be around and within you always. I left her and returned to Rouen where I could see the ashes from my body lifted by the wind and carried all over the city. They landed on fields, rooftops, and the heads of the spectators who lifted their hands to catch the ash raining down upon them.

The fire, instead of obliterating my existence, freed the energy of what was Jehanne d'Arc. When nothing remained of my body, and the flames died down, the executioner, once again, checked the space I once occupied, and found, amidst the ashes, my heart. It would not be consumed. With a shovel, he scooped up the ashes and my heart and threw them, unceremoniously, into the Seine River. My heart disappeared into the blue-green depths, as the ashes swirled around and became absorbed by the water. Nothing could please me more than to become part of the water that fed the plants and nourished the animals that would be consumed by my countrymen. My love would live on in the soil and the bodies of men, and my heart would forever be within a river, flowing through France.

AUTHOR'S NOTE

While Jehanne d'Arc is based upon the historical figure known as Joan of Arc, I took the liberty of inferring the conversations and spiritual teachings that may have passed between Jehanne and her angels.

Typically in France during the 15ᵗʰ century people addressed one another according to forenames but since there were numerous men in her life named "Jean" (d'Alençon, d'Arc, d'Metz, Dunois (Jean d'Orléans), d'Aulon, Xaintrailles (Jean Poton) and the chaplan Pasquerel), I used their surname or last name (or their place of origin) to discern one man from another.

The fact that King Charles VII found the need to separate Jehanne and Jean d'Alençon inspired the unrequited love theme. The relationship seemed a natural and organic result of their shared experiences. I included d'Alençon in the Orléans scenes because it helped to establish how Jehanne and d'Alençon shaped a trusting relationship and I wanted them to be together as much as possible before Paris.

In May 1429, my resources cite the dauphin in two different places. One source had the dauphin residing in Tours and another at Loches. I selected Loches for its location and scenery. I took advantage of the freedom of fiction to put d'Alençon there as well.

I selected the castle of Anjou instead of the town of St. Laurent as the location for the meeting between Jehanne and d'Alençon's mother and wife. It is a charming castle and it explains how René d'Anjou changed his loyalty to Jehanne and King Charles VII.

For the West Point portion of the novel I drew upon my own brief experience in 1980 as a West Point cadet. The stairwell scene was loosely based upon an actual event during my stay at West Point. Those moments in the stairwell were the catalyst for the entire novel.

In the Camp Buckner scene I changed the accommodations for the cadets from steel sided buildings to camp tents simply because I remembered what a striking scene the tents posed when I was at Lake Frederick.

All the characters in the modern day section are purely fictional.

ACKNOWLEDGMENTS

My gratitude is extended to all those who have researched and translated trial transcripts of Joan of Arc. Here is a brief list of my favorite references:

Pernoud, Regine. *Joan of Arc, by Herself and Her Witnesses*, Lanham, MD, Scarborough House, 1994.

Nash-Marshall, Siobhan, *Joan of Arc, a Spiritual Biography*, New York, NY, The Crossroad Publishing Company, 1999.

Newman, Paul B., *Daily Life in the Middle Ages*, Jefferson, NC, Mcfarland & Company, Inc., 2001.

Pernoud, Regine, *Joan of Arc: Her Story*, New York, NY, St. Martin's Press, 1998.

On-line trial transcript credit is given to: The Saint Joan of Arc Center--stjoan@stjoan-center.com.

My deepest gratitude goes to: Lisa Tener, writing muse, for inspiring me to write this story; Stuart Horwitz, the book whisperer, for his exceptional coaching; Heather Grant Murray for her remarkable copyediting; my son Matthew Howley, for his unparalleled imagination and creative cover design; my husband, Guruatma S. Khalsa, and my sons, Matthew and Mitchell, for their loving support and tireless encouragement; my parents, Robert and Barbara Pezzini, for passing on the love of literature and listening to all my dreams; David Howley, for his steadfastness; readers and friends, Pamela McIntyre, Cathy Corcoran, Christine Alexandria, Scott Schreibstein Bill Hinchey, David Pezzini, Robert G. Pezzini, Sat Bir Khalsa, Gurudharma Khalsa, the rest of my family, my teachers, all my students and everyone else who encouraged me along the way. Special thanks to the USMA at West Point for making an indelible impression on my life, however brief my stay. My deepest gratitude goes to Archangel Michael and my own angelic team—their infinite love keeps me going.